To HUNT A HOLY MAN

MICHAEL FLETCHER

Black Rose Writing | Texas

The author grants the final approval for this literary material.

First printing

This is a work of fiction. Names, characters, businesses, places, events, and incidents are either the products of the author's imagination or used in a fictitious manner. Any resemblance to actual persons, living or dead, or actual events is purely coincidental.

ISBN: 978-1-68513-236-1
PUBLISHED BY BLACK ROSE WRITING
www.blackrosewriting.com

Printed in the United States of America
Suggested Retail Price (SRP) $23.95

To Hunt a Holy Man is printed in Book Antiqua

*As a planet-friendly publisher, Black Rose Writing does its best to eliminate unnecessary waste to reduce paper usage and energy costs, while never compromising the reading experience. As a result, the final word count vs. page count may not meet common expectations.

- Gloria Tibi Domine -

To my departed son, J. Max. He was a kind-hearted man whose spirit helped me endure life's hardest lesson. To my generous wife, Khun Janya, who is a never-ending source of inspiration and the touchstone for my stories about Thailand. Without her, there would be no stories for me to tell.

Thank you to my colleagues and friends, Karen Pechilis and Ron Felber of Drew University, and Jennifer Herdt and Fredrick Simmons at the Divinity School of Yale University.

I owe a personal debt of gratitude to my lifelong friend, Scott Douglass, a Vietnam War veteran and wise man who knows the truth about so many things.

TO
HUNT
A
HOLY
MAN

[signature]

10/23

PART I: HUNTER

CHAPTER 1

The door-gunner grabbed the fire extinguisher and jumped out of the helicopter as the first skid hit the landing pad. He ran down the starboard side of the aircraft and pushed open the engine cowling, peering into the guts of the UH-1 Huey. They had taken a few rounds inbound to the airbase – no major drama – but the pilot felt he was losing power and there was radio chatter about smoke. The gunner was looking for fire. There wasn't any. Lucky day. Thumbs up.

The sole passenger on the priority mission, 1st Lieutenant Frank X. Coltrane, slid back the port-side cargo door and stepped out. He made his way forward, ducking his tall frame until he cleared the rotor zone. *Back home*, he thought, and then added, *Shit!* as he reached for his Camels. He lit a stick and sucked in deep. The sweet tobacco mixed with hot JetA-fuel exhaust and the acrid smoke from smoldering garbage mounds just outside the perimeter.

Tracking down AWOL soldiers was Coltrane's specialty and he suspected that his talents were being summoned by his commanding officer, Lt. Colonel Earnest Hargraves, as he sauntered towards the Old Man's office just off the flight line. Coltrane was planning an R&R trip to Bangkok in two weeks, and *hope like hell that whatever Hargraves comes up with, it's not going to fuck that up.*

1

*　　*　　*　　*　　*

He could hear the thud of heavy jungle boots on the half-inch plywood floor as the colonel made his way to the door. "Hey Cole, get your lanky ass in here!" barked Hargraves as he yanked open his office door. Coltrane followed him in, and the Old Man clapped him on the back with the greeting he hated.

The light-bird colonel came from old-money Congregationalist stock up in Boston, but he desperately wanted to be "one of the guys" and made awkward attempts to fit in. With the noncoms and the junior officers, he trotted out a throaty good-old-boy drawl to put a more manly resonance to his New England twang. But Coltrane had Hargraves nailed for the imposter and fawner he was.

They made it over to a large desk in the middle of the colonel's inner office and took up their positions: Hargraves in a Naugahyde executive chair and Coltrane on an olive-drab, folding metal stool. Coltrane's eyes shot between the exit door at his 9 o'clock and the metal table behind Hargraves' desk which had a squat coffee pot, three dirty plastic spoons in a cup of milky water, and a near-empty can of Folgers ground coffee – the remnants of his wife's most recent CARE package. Coltrane smelt the aroma from the freshly brewed pot and swallowed hard. He could have used a good cup. He wasn't offered any.

"Evidently, we got some renegade loner, a peace-nik priest – a Catholic chaplain from the 25th out in Tay Ninh," began Hargraves, straightening his spine. "He's decided that this man's Army wasn't cuttin' it. Nope."

He shot a quick look at Coltrane and tossed the confidential report from the US Embassy in Bangkok across his desk. It slid on top of the Plexiglas sheet that covered a flattened 1970 calendar and a single, faded Polaroid picture of the colonel's last vacation trip to Maine – wife, two small girls in dresses, wicker picnic basket, checkered blanket, and a one-man kayak painted sky-blue with white enamel lettering. It landed in Cole's lap.

He didn't have time to crack it open before the Old Man launched again. "Seems he walked into our Embassy in Bangkok, said he's had enough, and then sashayed out the damn door. Just like that."

Hargraves took a sip of coffee to wet his throat and lowered his voice a few decibels in case God was listening to what he had to say next, "I don't want some wise-ass chaplain – and a *Catholic* chaplain at that – to make fuckin' monkeys out of us."

Tugging on his lapel with the silver oak leaf cluster he added, "This guy's an officer. Not your run-of-the-mill AWOL grunt flunky. You get me?"

Hargraves stood from behind his desk, the sudden animation stoking his boiler. His volume control was back to ten. Cole peered at him over his Ray-Bans which had slid down his sweaty nose.

"Hell, Coltrane, you know the drill. Nobody's gonna get away with this kind of fuckin' stunt while I'm runnin' the show here. Give me the middle finger and then skedaddle off to Thailand." He fumbled around for more words to pile on but paused, drawing in the breath that was going to exhale the finale.

But it was puny. "No fuckin' way... That ain't gonna happen." He reached for his cup and took another sip.

Hargraves turned his stare away from the specks floating on the coffee's surface and looked at Cole, the crimson draining from his varicose cheeks. "Understand me?" he asked again. But his question was not an order to a subordinate. He was seeking Cole's validation of his short rant, endorsing his self-important role in this little patch of the US Army's vast Vietnam enterprise.

Cole was not offering any relief. He knew better than to jump in with a quick affirmation when the steam was venting from the Old Man. He let it ride.

Like many untested officers who hid behind their rank, Hargraves had an unearned verbal swagger and liked to rub your face in his indignant version of the moral high ground. *Man, he can beat this shit to death. Just gimme the fuckin' orders, you asshole*, thought Cole. But he checked those thoughts at his lips and waited. He knew there wasn't much Hargraves would add past the forced expletives.

Cole sneaked a look at his Casio watch. It was 15:05. Only a couple more hours until happy hour at the Officers Club and he could then sit down with his Scottish girlfriend from Glenlivet, Scotland. He liked meeting her there. He liked her because she was nice and neat, and three fingers would do the job. But best of all, she was uncomplicated.

The Old Man sat back down. *OK, here it comes*, thought Cole. He was right.

"I want you on the next C-130 to Bangkok tomorrow morning. I want you to get this bastard priest and bring him back. He can't have dropped off the face of God's green earth just like that."

The colonel paused and looked at Cole across his desk, his arms outstretched with small clenched fists at the end of each. He squared their eyes, "Don't let me down, young man."

Cole mechanically rose from his stool and gave a snappy salute, and then a quick about-face. He was halfway to the door when he heard the familiar refrain repeated, "Don't let me down!"

"I won't come back empty-handed, sir. You know you can count on me," he said, trying to stifle the contempt he held for his light colonel boss.

"Yeah, I know. That's why I picked you for this job. Now get your ass in gear and get goin'!" Sticking out his jaw as far forward as it would go, he added, "I wanna see you back here with that priest, and I mean pronto!"

Cole pushed open the door and stood in the jam with the embassy file tucked under his left arm. The screen door hit him on the back as he lit up a smoke and flicked the match into a red butt-can full of brown, fetid water. A mosquito took flight from the can and he made a feeble attempt to swipe at it.

"Yeah, 'I mean pronto'," he mumbled sarcastically with the cigarette dangling from his mouth. At least he was going to Bangkok – *but my R&R is definitely fucked.*

He ground his teeth, biting into the unwelcome assignment from Hargraves. *If you got such a hard-on for this guy, why don't you go get 'em your fuckin' self?* He then added, unintentionally out loud, "You gutless jackass."

"What was that?!" bellowed Hargraves as he came around his desk and headed for the door.

"Nothing, sir. Just commenting on the weather and what a good day it is to start the hunt for this son-of-a-bitch."

The Old Man came to a halt and stood there scratching the crown of his bald head, causing a scab that covered a small scrape to slough off and slide down his oily neck and into the back of his shirt collar.

"R-i-i-i-ght," he said in an unconvinced acknowledgment. Having to have the last word, and struggling to act chummy he added, "Well... Good huntin'!"

"Smart-ass bastard," Hargraves mumbled as he returned to his desk and plunked back down in his Naugahyde chair. "You'd better not come back empty-handed, alright."

He flicked a fly off his now-cold cup of coffee and shouted to his orderly, a pimple-faced PFC from Las Vegas, "Perkins, get your ass in here!"

CHAPTER 2

Cole decided to kill the time before happy hour by chasing down Gus Digman, a high school buddy from his hometown of Truth or Consequences, New Mexico. He took the shortcut across the tarmac, infested with UH-1 Hueys being combed over by their crew chiefs. He knew several of those guys from the missions they flew on together, and they exchanged nods.

The Jim Croce look-alike from the 3rd of the 5th AirCav, named Peacock, gave Cole a grin and the finger. Cole returned the respect. They had been in the soup together on more than one occasion, and the pair recently chased tail in Saigon last March after they joined up on Cole's last arrest: nabbing a wiry Black cook from the 101st who had tried to go native with twin-sister bar girls. Cole got his man. Peacock got some stick time on the way back. And Cookie got a few lumps on his head for his amorous misadventure.

·   ·   ·   ·   ·

Many of the crew chiefs knew Cole as an even-handed man. But others knew him as a mean and ruthless piece of work who would hump through 100 klicks of hell to capture a wayward soul. *"He's kind of a dark angel... he'll just swoop out of the sky without a sound and nab his prey... and then they're totally fucked.*

Next stop: the slammer at Long Binh!" they would all testify, sitting around piles of crushed beer cans and conjuring up images of his legendary feats.

And Coltrane enjoyed the freedom engendered by this bad-ass reputation – a reputation clinched when one of his prisoners "jumped out" of a chopper at 10,000 feet. Seems that there was some altercation in the back of the Huey and this guy decided to fly. The only other witness that day was the door-gunner, and his version lined up with Cole's. The jumper had evidently played "hide the weenie" with some nine-year-old girl from up-country. The chief investigator later told Cole outside the hearing room, "Nobody will care about that dude nor his fucked-up story." And that was the end of that.

And yet Cole had no problems with following orders, provided that those orders aligned with his war-wrought sense of justice. He believed in the Army as an institution, and all that it stood for: its history, its wars and battles, and its great men. Cole was proud of what it brought to his life, from being a dirt-poor, trailer-park reject in New Mexico to a decorated first lieutenant in a highly respected division, and prospects for further advancement on the horizon.

He saw no problem with the war being mired down. *It was only a matter of time before the tide would turn,* he told himself. *Never admit defeat.* Incompetent leadership aside, life was good. He just couldn't abide those *bastards* who, by their cowardice, had dishonored their oath and *left their brothers in the shit to pick up the slack. Straight-up betrayal.* Unforgivable.

Now where the hell was that jackass Digman? he wondered.

·   ·   ·   ·   ·

Buck Sergeant Angus Digman was not only the class clown in his Truth or Consequences High School, he was also the town's best scrounge. He had the knack for getting his hands on discarded crapola here-and-there and then turning it into fast cash. Gus once found two junked Amana freezers along the side of Highway 187, just north of Las Palomas, fixed these up and sold them at the Sunday swap meet in Las Cruces. He cleared $76 worth of beans and beer money on that deal.

And now he was quite the guy in his unit's little patch on the Tan Son Nhut Air Base. He even made an impression with the Old Man. He knew how to nudge Hargraves' ego in just the right way so the boys could get some decent perks: steaks at the mess hall, on-time mail calls, and colder beer – the major priorities of the every-day grunt.

Gus also had a special talent for ferreting out snakes that inhabited the unit's bunkers: bamboo vipers, banded kraits, pit vipers, king cobras, you name it. Gus would go into the bunkers and come out with a snake, every time. Never failed. He knew how to handle them, and better still, he knew how to kill them. Gus' technique was to grab the snake by the tail and then crack it like a bullwhip, snapping the head clean off. The problem with this technique was that you would now have a snapped-off snake head zipping across the bunkers with its mouth agape, fangs and venom glands intact. If you got hit by that thing, you were going down.

The grunts stood around like morons and laughed their asses off every time Gus did this. But the Old Man kept his distance, safely peering out from his screened-in office windows. Maybe that was why Gus had his way with him. Gus was crazy. But living in Truth or Consequences your whole life would probably have given you a good start in that direction.

•   •   •   •   •

Cole spotted Digman from behind. Nobody could mistake that big, bulbous head that seemed a size-and-a-half too big for his body. The kids at school called him a mutant and taunted him, saying, "Your mom must have been pickin' up trash out at Alamogordo when they lit off that A-bomb they dropped on the Japs. Those x-rays she got fucked you up royally, man!"

One thing was for certain, finding a GI hat that would fit his monstrous head was a job no Army quartermaster was yet able to do, and Digman always got away with being "uncovered" while outside. He eventually came up with a proper bush hat and the local tailor must have used a watermelon for the model. It was huge, but it fitted him perfectly. Around its brim hung five rusty grenade pins that Gus kept as souvenirs from his few times in the bush. On the front he had stitched a small New Mexico flag, "Land of Enchantment," and on the back, an embroidered patch of the Harley-Davidson "Willie G" skull, both now yellowed by months of furious sweat.

Gus was fed up with spending his tour "in the rear with the gear," being a "rear-echelon motherfucker" – an ignoble REMF, the tag pinned by infantry grunts on their wannabe counterparts back at the base. He managed to break up the monotony with an occasional foray up-country on resupply missions, but it was not the manly, balls-to-the-wall action he had signed up for back home.

Like many gung-ho REMFs, he itched for the chance to make his mark during the last two months before going back to The World. Back to his Land of Enchantment. Back to the 1960 FL Duo-Glide Harley his uncle was keeping for him under a parachute in his body shop. Gus dreamed of fixing up the old girl and taking her out on Interstate 25 when he got back, cruising up north to Albuquerque, and on to Denver and Cheyenne to catch the Frontier's Day Rodeo next July. Truth be told, that was Cole's dream, but Gus laid claim to a piece of it. To being the loyal sidekick.

"Hey, Gus! What's up, dude?"

Caught from behind, Gus pivoted his bulky frame. "Well, fuck me! If it ain't Francis Xavier Coltrane, his damn self!" He rose and gave Cole the brothers' handshake and a quick clench.

"Cole, my man! What's goin' on, dude? Was just thinkin' about your tired ass the other day and wonderin' where in the hell you've been – and here you are. Big as life..."

"And twice as ugly" would have been Cole's worn-out, routine comeback but today he was not in the mood. The meeting with Hargraves saw to that.

"Shit, you know... hangin' around... flyin' here-and-there. Busting the balls of bad guys. Same ol', same ol'. You know..." was all he could come up with.

"Yeah, I get it," Gus threw in. He nodded for a few beats without speaking and then cocked his head towards his old friend. "Hargraves is always blowing smoke up everyone's ass about what a go-getter you are, and how you always come back with a scalp. Shit, man, you need to get a lodgepole to hang all them scalps."

Gus lingered to grin at the image forming in his mind, and then added with a clear note of envy, "Fuck me, dude, you're really something else..."

Cole didn't take compliments well, even from his best friend. He kicked some loose gravel around with the toe of his right boot. "Yeah. You know. Just doin' my job, dude."

"Yeah," affirmed Gus with a mock serious look. Then mimicking Cole he added, "'Just doing my job.' Fuck you!"

They both cracked up, releasing the tension with a laugh that only best friends could pull off.

"So, where you headed now? Wanna grab a beer?" asked Gus.

"Nah, I got a date at the OC, so I'm gonna scoot over there now. Besides, I gotta get up early tomorrow and catch a flight to Bangkok. Got to track down some fucking priest who's gone AWOL."

"No shit!" Skipping over the part about the AWOL priest, Gus said, "Just think that by tomorrow night, you'll be hitting the bar scene there and landing some sweet Thai poontang for the evening. Ye-e-e-s-s indeedie!" Gus gestured performing a hand-job on himself as he rolled his eyes up into his huge gourd, sharklike, and stuck his stubby tongue out from the corner of his mouth.

Cole brought him back to the ground, "No, man. This is gonna be all business – and not monkey business, you stupid asshole."

"Well, good luck with that. And you say this guy's a priest?" He tilted his head towards Cole who was lighting up a smoke, finishing his first pack of the day.

"Yeah, a priest."

Gus looked out over the flight line and folded his burly arms across his chest. Cole had taken his fourth puff from the cigarette before Gus spoke again. "You know, that reminds me..."

Gus trailed off as his big brain took him back to Truth or Consequences. "Come on, I'll walk with you over to the Club. I got something to tell ya. Lemme grab my lid."

Gus disappeared into his tent and came back with his XXX-size boonie hat. "OK, man. Let's beat feet," he said.

•　　•　　•　　•　　•

"Dude," opened Gus. "I got my hands on a letter from the DA's Office in Sierra County – you know they look after T or C, right?"

"Yeah, I know." Cole flicked the butt into the gravel. "So, what did it say?"

"Well, the letter was sent to the Old Man, and that PFC clerk was 'spose to file it – you know, what's his name?"

"Perkins, his name's Perkins. And?"

Unfazed, Gus went on, "Well, Perkins and I get along real good – I help him get girls and weed – and he can't stand that asshole Hargraves. So Perkins takes the letter and passes it to me to read. Perkins was lookin' for you but you were out, who-knows-the-fuck where, and –"

Cole cut him short, "For fuck's sake, dude, just get on with it!"

"So, the letter was from that beaner cop back in T or C, Contreras – the cop that was looking after the case, right?" Cole turned his head away from Gus and back towards the direction they were heading.

"Well, Contreras tells the Old Man that you and I – mostly you – are still considered… uh, 'persons of interest' in the death of that priest they found washed up on the Rio Grande, and that Hargraves should keep an eye on you."

Cole reached for another Camel and lit it in stride. The cover of the matchbook was from the "Minefield Bar – Come in and Get Legless" the bi-line went. He took a look at Gus, who was walking along with his eyes cast down and the brim of his bush hat pushed back.

Gus was starting to regret that he mentioned Contreras and the dead priest. *That whole mess should not have been mentioned*, he thought, because it was about to be relived by both of them.

CHAPTER 3

The two serious crimes in Truth or Consequences were being investigated by Sheriff Detective, Luis Contreras – "Pepe" as he was known outside the Mexican community. For a small town like T or C, the chances of having two sensational cases at the same time were slim-to-none. And Contreras knew that the chance that these were unrelated was zero. He was a seasoned cop, tough as javelina jerky. But he had to connect the dots and so far he had nothing.

•   •   •   •   •

Staff Sergeant Frank Coltrane had just arrived back home from his first tour in Vietnam when he learned about his kid sister, Abilene. On her way home from her high school freshman-class orientation, she was raped and then knocked unconscious by an assailant just a week before Cole's Greyhound rolled in from Albuquerque.

She had suffered major trauma to the head – her skull crushed by the only factual evidence in the case: a muddy, discarded brown brick with fragments of her blood and hair embedded in it. She was comatose, but at least she was still alive thanks to her quick transfer to the County Hospital in Las Cruces where they had the proper life-support facilities.

Both his grandmother and his best friend, Gus, knew that Cole was on his way back to Truth or Consequences, via Travis Air Force Base in California and Albuquerque, and he would be home by the end of the week. But nobody dared to write to him and say anything about Abilene, or to call his unit in Vietnam and let him know what had happened. Cole would just have to find out when he got home – when he stepped off the bus and saw Gus' long face. His grandmother stayed home. She did not have the strength for that encounter. She knew Cole loved his kid sister above all things in T or C. Above all things in the whole lousy state.

●   ●   ●   ●   ●

And when he found out, he came unhinged. Fistfights erupted down at the Giddy Up Cafe, where he would pick on strangers who were merely passing through town, trying to enjoy some good Tex-Mex and a few beers. People only had to look at him with the side-eye and it was on. Gus, still a civilian then, did what he could to run interference for Cole, smoothing things over with the manager and buying his victims a beer or two.

A week later, the Sheriff was called out to the Oasis Inn, south of town on the I-25 connector, because some trucker had made a few off-hand comments about the "stupid, lousy war" and Cole wanted a piece of him for the insult. He had followed the trucker out of the bar, and when the guy went to his rig to get his log sheets, Cole hid out in a small stucco alcove near the man's room. He was about to sucker punch the trucker in the face when he was caught mid-swing by Gus' big, meaty arm.

"No!" shouted Gus. "That's not the way, my man. They'll put you in the hoosegow and that will be the end of you. I don't care how many fancy fuckin' ribbons you got pinned to your chest."

The terrified trucker was spared from getting his face reorganized and ran for his room, dropping his key twice before he rushed inside and bolted the door. Gus, although equally stewed, managed to pull Cole back across the parking lot and shove him into his uncle's body shop tow truck before the cops arrived. They took off like scalded dogs.

Cole was silent for a long time, then reached for his smokes, popped one into his mouth and pushed in the white knob on the cigarette lighter, sticking out from the bottom of the truck's rusty dash.

Gus saw the Oasis growing smaller in the rearview mirror, and with the adrenalin draining from him, he said, "Man, that was some freaky shit back there!"

"Yeah," affirmed Cole, having difficulty lighting the end of his Camel with the meandering red, glowing circle. "Freaky shit, like Long Ranger freaky shit. Me Long Ranger. You Tonto."

Gus gave him a one-up smile. "Dumb shit, it's *Lone* Ranger, not *Long* Ranger. You dumb fucker!" They both laughed like jackasses as the Ford F250 wrecker barreled north, up I-25.

Cruising into town, they saw a Highway Patrol car with flashing red lights race by in the opposite direction, headed south. "Maybe a wreck," offered Gus. "Yeah, maybe an 18-wheeler just shit his pants," replied Cole. More jackass laughing could be heard, whooping out of the open windows as they drove past the T or C Dairy Queen.

One of the local high school cheerleaders spied the duo through the truck's cracked windshield, turned a perplexed face to her letterman boyfriend and said, "Hey, isn't that Abilene's big brother and that idiot Gus? Now what in the heck are they laughing about?"

. . . . .

Over the days that passed, Cole's initial rage ebbed and flowed, much like the black bellows that worked up-and-down within the glass canister next to Abilene's bed in Las Cruces. He would drive down there and sit for hours at her bedside, watching her future fade, before drifting back up to T or C where the booze helped him shed that darkness like a burnt snakeskin.

The community was generally supportive of Cole, given his veteran's status and more so because he was a Viet Vet in a part of the country where such a thing still meant something honorable to the local folks. Even the cops were reluctant to do much more than to calm him down and send him home after his violent episodes. Coming back from the war and discovering that your kid sister's life had been destroyed before she could get started made everyone cut him miles of slack.

But enough was enough. Cole was finally hauled in one night for kicking down the front door of Our Lady of Perpetual Help. Gus wasn't with him – so he had no one to stop him from doing *such a dumb-shit thing*. And when he sobered up in the can the next morning, he couldn't explain to Contreras what made him do it. He could only mumble a refrain which he kept repeating, "Fucking priest." Lucky for Cole, the Church was not interested in pressing charges and he walked out of the Sheriff's Office that morning, scot-free.

On his way out, Contreras thought he heard Cole adding, "He'll get his," but he wasn't quite sure because Cole was clenching a fresh smoke between his dehydrated lips. He needed a drink.

●   ●   ●   ●   ●

Father McGowan was his local parish priest, and Pepe felt kicked in the guts when two local fishermen found the priest's body washed up on the banks of the Rio Grande, about a mile downstream from the commercial district of town. It was not clear at first whether he had simply slipped, fell into the river and drowned, or was it foul play. The clues were confusing. Father McGowan could not swim, and there were no contusions or bruises on the body – no wounds of any kind. But he had a half-gallon of brown river water in his lungs.

Pepe thought, *This river flows all the way down from its cold headwaters, high in the mountains in southern Colorado… it surely wanted no part in the killing of a priest. What the hell happened here?* Worse, the death of Father McGowan came close on the heels of the rape of Abilene Coltrane – the priest had disappeared and then reappeared, dead, on the banks of the Rio Grande barely two weeks after the horrific attack had shattered Abilene's life.

Some rumors circulated in town which alleged that the priest was "overly friendly" with the high school kids. But nobody in town had come forward to corroborate any of this loose gossip. At 75, Father McGowan was long overdue for retirement, and the very thought that the septuagenarian would have tracked down a high school freshman, somehow mustered an erection, raped her, and then bashed in her head was so far out of kilter with reality, Pepe's architecture for the case came crashing down every time he tried to tinker around with such an improbable scheme.

Maybe there's just a simple explanation, he thought. *Maybe some young punk killed the priest to cover up a confession… something like a theft… or maybe it was a homo misstep… and the perp wanted to seal off forever their embarrassment and getting kicked out of this tight-ass community.* But the detective's notepad Pepe carried in his shirt pocket contained mostly blank pages despite the many hours of sit-down dinners, eating his way through mounds of carnitas and enchiladas. Apart from the brick, he had no hard evidence. He was stuck. Father McGowan could have died from an accidental slip; Abilene could not ID her assailant and the prospects for her coming out of the coma were not looking good.

•   •   •   •   •

All the dots led to Cole. Contreras thought the obvious thing: *Cole comes back to town and kills the priest... he probably heard the rumors about Fr. McGowan being sweet on youngsters, put two and two together, and drowned the holy man who he thinks attacked his sister.* As misguided as this was, it certainly was a motive to kill the priest.

Add the fact that Father McGowan disappeared exactly five days after Cole arrived back in T or C – after the fights at the Giddy Up, after the Oasis Inn, and after the door-bashing madness at Our Lady's. So the timing was right. And for years, the local churches held community picnics at the town's riverside park and everyone, including Coltrane, would have known that Fr. McGowan couldn't swim. *Maybe he just shoved him in... made it look like an accident.*

But these explanations seemed much too simple for Pepe. *Both Cole and Gus were tricky bastards – too tricky for some simple scheme like this.*

Two more troubling pieces remained for Pepe. The first was that Cole was heading off to Travis Air Force Base and then back to Vietnam for his second tour in five days' time. The other problem was that Cole's troublesome sidekick, Gus, had enlisted in the Army and was due to go for basic training the following week at Fort Polk, Louisiana. He had signed up for a three-year stint and made a "buddy deal" with the recruiter, getting assigned to the 16th MPs Special Investigations Unit, headquartered at Tan Son Nhut Airbase, Vietnam – the same outfit as Cole's. *Sure, that shit makes perfect sense*, he thought. *Those two are as thick as fleas.*

Sheriff Detective Luis Contreras assured himself that he did due diligence with the witnesses he questioned, including Cole's grandmother – a strong-willed reverberation of the Old Southwest who was broken-in-two by her grandson's decision to return to Vietnam for the second tour. Pepe also questioned folks at the bars and restaurants within the county who may have had run-ins with Cole, or heard him mention anything about the priest or the church. He also spent long hours with the parish congregation and McGowan's replacement, a young Jesuit priest from Trinidad, Colorado, Fr. Felipe Azul. But he was grabbing at straws.

Pepe had placed Cole and his sidekick, Gus, in the hot seat at the Sheriff's Office and grilled them on several occasions. But each time he came up with goose eggs. Nothing more could be gleaned from the uncooperative duo, and Pepe knew that the well was drying up, even for a circumstantial case.

He found some consolation in the thought that, although *these two misfits* were going off to Vietnam, Cole on his second tour and Gus as a newbie, he had them "captured" should the cases break. They wouldn't be going anywhere he could not reach in and get them. And besides, while Army recruiters were notorious liars, Gus got his wish. After AIT, he would be on his way to Vietnam to join Cole's unit. *So better still*, thought Contreras, *two jerks in one basket. Maybe those fools just might get themselves killed over there, and that wouldn't hurt the prospects for a safer and more peaceful T or C. That would be a real bonus.*

Leaving these two persons-of-interest on ice suited Sheriff Detective Luis Contreras down to the ground. Besides, he still had the other half of his major problem to work on: finding the connection between the death of Fr. McGowan and the monster that raped and then nearly killed 13-year-old Abilene Coltrane.

He was not going to leave any stone unturned before he found that guilty dog. But he needed more time.

•　•　•　•　•

The Sunday after Cole left for Vietnam – and the Sunday before Gus was to leave for basic training at Ft. Polk – Pepe went to visit Father Azul at Our Lady's. It was a half an hour before mass. He told the Jesuit priest that he would need a miracle to crack these two cases, to bring justice to the victims – and to the perpetrators. Fr. Filipe smiled and said softly as he was placing his vestments over his street clothes in preparation for the service, "Yes, my son. I know. You work hard, but you must pray harder."

Pepe needed a miracle, alright. And he prayed for one during mass that day – and every Sunday that followed.

CHAPTER 4

"Yeah, well, thanks for the dope on that letter from Contreras. That fucker will never give up. It's been damn near a year now and he still thinks I'm mixed up with the death of that sick bastard priest."

"No shit, I hear that," said Gus, giving his huge noggin a couple of nods. "He's on the wrong track. That trail's gone cold, dude. And nobody seems to give a shit about that nasty ol' priest anyways, right?"

"Yeah, I wish that he'd spend half as much time tracking down the fucking monster who did that number on my kid sister. Left her for dead. I wish I could get my hands on that son-of-a-bitch. I'd put a full clip through his skull."

Cole sucked in deep, and then let out a breath so long that the residual smoke floating around at the bottom of his lungs since morning escaped at the very end of it. "Shit man, this is where I get off," pointing to the wooden planks and bamboo railing that formed the entrance to the Officers Club.

"Alright then, my man. Take care and let me know how your hunting goes in Thailand." Gus was not about to jinx Cole's hunt by saying something stupid like, "Don't let us down," even if that was a choice opportunity for both of them to mock *that asshole* Hargraves.

So Gus just said, "Cool, now give me some skin."

. . . . .

Gus split back down the road for his digs, and Cole made for his usual chair at the far-left end of the bar. He told Nguyen, the bartender – *and likely VC spy* – to tell his girlfriend that he's here and would she care to join him. Nguyen gave him a grin, flashing his craggy yellow teeth, and turned to reach for Cole's private stash of Glenlivet he kept at the bar.

"Make her nice and neat, Charley." Nguyen grinned again, winked at Cole's VC reference and poured, by sight, a double-shot of the whiskey in a heavy, leaded glass. Cole put it to his mouth and gave her a kiss. He figured he would have time for two or three more before he would need to stagger off to his room and get some sleep.

He glanced around the bar and saw the same old crowd. They would pour in here at the magic hour, drink the same old drinks and tell the same old war stories. Any new story usually dealt with someone they knew getting wasted, followed by a few seconds of silence as they gazed into their drinks until someone started to talk about baseball scores or some other mundane dribble.

He ordered up another shot and pulled a Camel from the wrinkled pack that was stuck in the bottom of his pants side pocket. On the seats to his right, facing the bar, were two warrant officer pilots. From the insignia on their fatigues Cole could see that they were part of a helicopter transport outfit whose main job was to shuttle gear and grunts, wherever they needed to go. He overheard their conversation not by choice but by the sheer volume of the WO3, the more senior of the two. Cole placed his accent as West Texas, not too far from his own stomping grounds in southern New Mexico.

The guy was loud and full of himself and usually this would be enough reason for Cole to get up and move, but for some reason he took a shine to him. Maybe it was *this guy's dumbass laugh* that Cole needed to hear, just as much as he needed his Scottish girlfriend's company. So he sat and listened to the tale being told. Charley was also soaking up the story as he stood behind the bar, wiping a dry beer mug. The WO3 was recounting his trips over the past couple of days to a PsyOps outfit in Phouc Ninh, north of the Cambodian "Parrot's Beak." He was ferrying in supplies for those guys who were doing radio propaganda as part of the most recent "hearts-and-minds" campaign.

He told the WO1 sitting on the stool next to him, "These guys at the base were s'posed to be blastin' the airways with all kinds of pro-government propaganda the Embassy in Saigon sends up every week. Recorded reels of this stuff. That's the kind of shit we've been shuttlin' up to these guys."

He stopped for a moment, took two big gulps of Pabst Blue Ribbon and noted with pleasure that Cole was listening in. He went on, "So these guys from the 411th have been droppin' bags full of AM radios into the local villes, just so the dinks could pick up the radio propaganda bullshit the PsyOps boys were supposed to be dishin' out."

"But it seems that..." he took another swallow of PBR and cracked a wide, spreading grin, "...instead of that recorded government bullshit, those PsyOps dudes have been blastin' the airways along the Cambode border with the Stones and them other hippie-freak bands!"

Screwing up a concocted frown the WO3 added, "I would have much preferred Buck or Merle – but the Stones kick ass, just fine!"

"Fuck yes!" said the Wobbly 1, approving the minor subterfuge. Taking his own swig of beer he reached for his air mic and shouted, completely out-of-tune, "I can't get no..." to which the good old boy from West Texas chimed in with a booming, "Sa-tis-fact-shun!"

They both finished the refrain with cartoon-like sounds on air guitars, imitating Keith Richards' classic intro riff to that battle hymn, polished off with long gulps from their beers in complete enjoyment of their own performances.

The WO3 went on with a pidgin English vignette, "Yeah, I can imagine some scrawny gook dude having dinner with his sexy little wife, and he turns to her over a bowl of fish-heads and rice, and asks, 'Hey mama-san, what da fuck is *sadis-fak-shun?*' To which she says, 'Me no know, papa-san... but me like dat fuckin' *gee-tah* too much'!"

To this suggestion both pilots burst out laughing, and even Cole managed to crack a quick grin. At least it was not a story about death – about hair, teeth and eyeballs being pasted into the trees.

From the stage at the back of the room, a four-piece band from the Philippines had just finished their rendition of Christie's "Yellow River." This number was followed by a half-dozen Creedence Clearwater tunes, topped off with their version of "Born on the Bayou." They weren't bad, and with each drink they sounded better. But by the time Cole was having his last sip, Creedence was done for the night and the Filipina lead singer started in on "Feelings" to end their set.

"Peelings, nutin' more dan peelings..."

OK, that was it. He flipped a few bills for Charley's tip, gave him a shot with a finger-and-thumb pistol to which Nguyen feigned a hit to the heart. *Charley's a piss-poor actor... probably a commie fruitcake to boot. Dumb little fucker. But who cares,* thought Cole as he plied his way across the empty dance floor, out the door and down the wooden plank steps, and headed off in the general direction of his bunk.

CHAPTER 5

His nightstand stood next to his bunk in the Military Police officers' barracks and was made from cheap fiberboard covered with peeling, brown veneer. It was missing all its knobs, but held his basic toiletries, like a well-worn bar of yellow Dial soap, a small can of Mennen pit stick, a tube of Pepsodent toothpaste he paid one of the local cleaner gals to pick up for him downtown, and a frayed toothbrush for his grill.

Tucked in the back of the top drawer, Cole kept a small, dog-eared copy of *Catholic Prayers* with its red-leather cover and gold-embossed lettering. It was a relic that his Grandmother Elenora had given him on the day he left for Fort Ord, California, and it was the only thing he owned from his past that he wanted to hang on to. Not so much out of sentimentality – it was more a sense of duty.

His grandmother died after he returned to Vietnam for a second run. Perhaps that decision killed the old lady, and perhaps he kept the book as a way to honor her. He truly loved that woman, but Cole knew his eyes were in the front of his head for good reason. He was not a creature designed to look back. Still, that red book was there. Unexplained. A thin thread back to the good times before his teenage dark-streak, and the crazy and dangerous world that followed.

•   •   •   •   •

Cole was a hard-ass as a kid. But his grandmother had a knack for knocking sense into the boy and fought him with every fiber to produce a good, God-fearing Catholic boy. Elenora pushed her version of the Inspired Word on him from the very first day she placed him in his cradle, smack-dab in the middle of her double-wide's living room. She even insisted that he be named after her favorite saint, Francis Xavier. It was a name that Cole hated because it sounded "too sissy." He thought of himself as "Jesse" – and then "Max" – in elementary school, but he stopped fighting about it when he grew older and understood that people were not actually defined by their names.

Brenda Coltrane had no thoughts whatsoever about naming her unwanted child. On the very same day she ran away with Buster Ironheels, a brutally handsome rodeo star and wild bull rider from the Chiricahua Apache Nation, she told the boy's grandmother, "Just go ahead and pick any ol' name you want."

And her indifference grew with each passing year, and the visits to the Desert Star Trailer Park became scarce events. She and Ironheels only dropped by when passing through from Tucson or El Paso, always looking for a handout from Elenora. Like a place to stay for the night, or a free meal. Usually both.

Her visits ended altogether on a blistering hot July day. Cole had just got out of juvy for the third time when Brenda stopped by Elenora's tidy trailer and dropped off baby Abilene, a child named after the Kansas town where the pair had hunkered down for a year of seasonal work. Their best rodeo days were over for them, but at least the girl was given a name.

And Abilene was their parting gift to the old lady, seeing that both Brenda Coltrane and her ex-rodeo-star boyfriend, Buster Ironheels, were killed about 11 months later. Their Dodge pickup had slammed into the rear of a slow-moving wheat combine that was following the July harvest north on Kansas 81.

Cole's grandmother got the newspaper obituary in the mail from a cousin who lived in Glasco, about a month after the pair were buried in the rich topsoil of Cloud County. Elenora didn't have the money for the bus trip to the Kansas cemetery, but that suited Cole just fine. There was no way he was going to get on that bus, money or not.

The boy's blood father was also from the rodeo, and the likely suspect was part of a gang of bronc riders who passed through town, the summer before he was born. But "who exactly" was only narrowed down to a shortlist of two men. Their names were once scribbled on a napkin by the boy's runaway mother, sitting alone at the trailer's bright-pink, Formica kitchen table.

Elenora's best efforts finally could not reach down inside of him and correct Cole's inbred contrary nature, and the wayward boy had constant run-ins with the cops, going to "juvy" three times before he was fifteen. His best friend, Gus Digman, knew Cole was a tough customer, but he was always trying to get his goat. Sometimes it worked. Most often, not. In high school, Cole knocked out two of Gus' front teeth because Digman didn't know when to shut up and stop playing the fool – and using Cole's full name in front of the cheerleaders sent Gus' teeth flying out of his mouth like bloody Chicklets.

Nobody got away with getting under Cole's skin, except his kid sister Abilene, and his high school girlfriend, Imelda Murietta. She was a honey-sweet Mexican beauty who was his Rosa in Marty Robbins' "El Paso". When he drove his big-block Ford Ranchero over to her folk's place and picked her up in the evenings, he often imagined her stooping to kiss him goodbye, just like the final passionate verse in that emblematic song of the Southwest.

The vast badlands of southern New Mexico always put them in the mood, and they would park along the Rio Grande and play games with their bodies, buck naked in the middle of a thousand square miles of wide-open space, under a dome of a million, bright midnight stars with the smell of crisp sage in the cool night air.

But all of that passion disappeared. Cole could not ultimately resist the lure of danger, the smell of cordite and the feel of heavy bullets, and he was pulled into the Army, enticed by its manly allure, flag-waving slogans, and a highly decorated recruiting officer who once paid a visit to his high school. He bit into that bait. And the price he paid for his love of the Army was high. His girlfriend-turned-wife, Imelda, left him during his first tour and went to live with her parents in Las Cruces. She could not compete with his love affair with the Queen of Battle. His first great lesson about women was that they could be insanely jealous of a man's devotion to his work – sometimes more so than his wandering attention to other women.

His wedding ring, which he had kept on his dog tags after the divorce, was gladly sold at a pawn shop in Da Nang. He took that money and blew it all in one night, buying drinks for everyone at the bar, and spending the evening with two of that city's busiest girls.

·　·　·　·　·

Cole flopped onto his bunk and mulled over the day's events and tried to picture the face of his prey. This holy man. It was all old hat to him, but the notion of hunting a priest gave it a new and enjoyable twist. Still, he wondered what kind of quarry the padre would be, and whether this was going to be an easy hunt? He cinched up the notion of a quick kill, thinking, *Probably a push over. Choir boy type. Probably some holy-roller fag.*

One thing's for sure, the less this fucker knows about me on his trail, the better. And whoever he is, he's not gonna put a dent in my 100% recovery and conviction record. Cole was counting on keeping that record right where it was. Good for his promotion to captain, even if that were to follow quickly on the heels of his recent field commission.

He thought about the priest's picture in the dossier that Hargraves gave him this afternoon, but it contained just a stock Army photo of his runaway prey. He knew that these photos were next to useless. Cole wanted to know what this guy's face actually looked like, and what kind of eyes were sunk into a skull that would make someone go off the rails like that. Were they beady snake eyes or were they big and shifty? Whatever they were, Cole was sure that Captain Mordechai Goodcut's eyes were *no damn good* and would ultimately betray the cowardice of someone who chose to go AWOL. He always saw it in the eyes of the men he captured. They all had that same, weak and lousy quality that he despised.

But never mind, he would have time to get a jump on things at the American Embassy in Bangkok tomorrow. The C-130 flight out was at 06:30 so he had to get some shuteye and make sure he was at the flight line an hour before.

His Scottish girlfriend was singing a Highlands tune when he finally closed his eyes. He loved her more than he did his wife – almost as much as he loved his departed grandmother.

●　　●　　●　　●　　●

Cole had just dozed off when he heard the knock on his door. Somebody was slowly working the knob. He instinctively reached for his .45, hanging in its holster on the bedframe. But before he could bring it fully around, Gus walked into the room. He was carrying a small brown envelope.

"Jesus, man! I could have shot your sorry ass! Fuck me!" He rubbed his forehead and eyes downwards with the palm of his left hand and ended with a scratch at the stubble on his chin, trying to focus in on Gus and the thing he was holding.

"Were you sleepin', man?"

"No, dude. I was chokin' my chicken – what the hell does it look like, you asshole?"

Gus half-grinned and approached Cole who was propped up on his left elbow. "Dude, I've got something I want you to keep for me. It's a note, in this here envelope."

"So, what the hell is that? Get out of here – and take your fuckin' love letter with you! I need to get some sleep." Cole looked askance at Gus.

Gus managed a full grin, but it quickly dropped off is face. "No man, somethin' serious. I want you to hang on to this. In case something happens to me, I want –"

Cole jumped in, "Nothing's going to happen to you, you big faggot. Now get the hell out of here and let me sleep!"

"No, man, listen to me. You gotta do this for me, dude. We go way back, you and me. You know. And I've been havin' these feelings, these dreams, like I'm not going to make it back to T or C. Like I'm not goin' back at all. I'm gonna get it over here. I can feel it, and it ain't the beer or the weed talking."

Gus took another step forward and laid the envelope by Cole's left arm. He added, "If I do get killed over here, promise me you'll open this then."

Cole propped himself up on both elbows and stared at the envelope and then at Gus, and he reached across with his right hand and tossed the letter at Gus. "You're full of shit man, now get out of here – and take this fucking letter with you! I'm not interested in runnin' around the place, carryin' your stupid-ass will… or whatever the hell you got there."

Gus stooped down in slow motion, picked the letter up from the worn wooden floor and replaced it on the bed. "You got to do this for me, man. I never asked you for nothin' before, so do this one thing."

Cole could see that this was going to drag on into the night because Gus, like himself, was a *stubborn son-of-a-bitch*. So he told Gus, "OK, OK. Leave it here. Now, would you please get the fuck out of here and leave me alone! My flight leaves in another four hours." He gave his pillow a good punch, and then rolled over.

Gus stood there for a while, looking at Cole, now with his back turned to him. He took off his huge hat and held it in his left hand and just stood there, looking at Cole.

"Well," mumbled Cole, "What in the hell are you waiting for? Beat it!"

"Swear that you will do this, Cole."

"Alright! Alright already!"

Gus moved backwards a few steps towards the door, passed out sideways and disappeared.

Satisfied that Gus had finally left, Cole rolled over on his back. He stared at the spotted gecko lizards chasing bugs on the ceiling. He couldn't help thinking about the fact that his newest target was a Catholic priest. The very notion added a degree of relish to the hunt. He hated priests. He hated religion. He stopped just short of saying that he hated God, but he was inching in that direction.

His last thoughts of that night were of his kid sister, lying in bed in the Las Cruces hospital, comatose. *Could she dream?* Was she dreaming about their trip to the Sangre de Cristo Mountains in southern Colorado when she was ten and caught her first rainbow trout? Or was it a continuous nightmare about what happened to her just before her skull was crushed. *Where was God then?* he wondered, carefully avoiding any semblance of prayer.

You know, maybe I do hate you after all...

PART II: HOLY MAN

CHAPTER 6

Father Mordechai Goodcut grasped the prayer stole that was coiled in the breast pocket of his jungle-fatigue jacket. He yanked it out with a blood-encrusted hand, kissed the embroidered cross and draped the purple cloth over the back of his neck. The ends fell with precise symmetry across his chest in a maneuver he perfected during his year-long slog in the bush. He blew out a long breath through parched lips, but it was not a sigh. It was merely hot air escaping, and the prayer that proceeded from his mouth was without solemnity. It was only a reflex. A bad habit.

He looked into the young, placid face and its incongruous smile and prayed, instead, that the still-warm PFC with the blood-filled ears could not hear his rambling thoughts. He reached for the dog tags: Wordsworth, Joseph, 483-63-7705, Methodist, AB+. Father Goodcut closed his eyes to pray and imagined the boy ambling away on his journey home, looking back over his shoulder and forgiving him *for being part of such a fucked-up mess. "Don't worry, father,"* he heard the boy say. *"This life was my treasure to forfeit, not yours."*

Mordechai nodded in agreement and began his absolution with words that sounded more pagan than Catholic, *"Yes, you will be remembered and spoken of with honor around the campfires back home."*

Father Goodcut cradled PFC Wordsworth's head in his lap and, using the blood from the man's shot-away left ear, made the sign of the cross on the soldier's forehead and uttered the mechanical last words, "Through this holy anointing may the Lord in his love and mercy help you with the grace... May the Lord who frees you..." His mind flickered back home where his performances at hospital bedsides were staid occasions, where nodding faces gathered around the dying and the words of the final sacrament landed softly on sterile bedding. Even violent car wrecks were somehow more measured affairs, where time slowed down and firemen doffed their helmets. All would stand in silence as Fr. Goodcut's prayers filled the crevices of twisted metal, the words washing over icy streets littered with shattered glass. And amidst all of this, God was still good.

But at this LZ, reality was savagely different. Here the world spun around in a chaotic circus. Shouting men crouched and sprayed 5.56mm bullets into the treeline that marked their tenuous perimeter. Soldiers moved swiftly, darting in between oblique and shredding tail rotors. The deep, concussive blasts of incoming mortars provided the bass counterpoint to the soprano wailings of the mortally wounded, laid out in neat rows in Father Goodcut's patch of the chaos.

He sat there in the mud with rivulets of blood flowing under his legs and smelled the full-on panic all around him. His mind dissipated along with the whirling purple and yellow smoke that marked the LZ. He struggled to finish the simple prayer he had said so many times before, but finally blurted out, "May the Lord who frees you from sin, save you and raise you up."

Mordechai stroked the hair of the dead PFC whose eyes were as vacant and soulless as his own. His beloved Christian world was falling apart. The holy object of Mordechai's adoration had split the scene, and God had repossessed the good priest's soul as He left. Father Goodcut was "losing his shit" – and he wanted out.

• • • • •

Three days later, and two weeks before he was due for his R&R in Bangkok, an exhausted Captain Goodcut braced against a bamboo fence in a village that Delta Company, 3rd Bn, was sweeping. He took a deep drag on a Pall Mall that one of the men had passed to him, and the uninvited jingle popped into his head, "*Outstanding... and they are mild.*" He held out the cigarette at arm's length and admired its taper. *Real-deal smokes, for real-deal men,* he thought. *But such bullshit.* He flicked the butt into a ditch in front of him.

He stared blankly at the string of displaced locals, shuffling along the dusty, red laterite road that snaked its way from the limestone karst mountains in the west, to the rice paddy at his feet. A group of haggard women with bawling children gathered under a nearby copse of broadleaf trees and squatted there with their fellow villagers. He watched as they wolfed down scraps of food they had snatched from their homes as they fled their villages and took to the road.

In the midst of the crying and the dust, there came a tug at the end of his shirtsleeve, just below his elbow. It was where he rolled up his fatigues to keep the malaria mosquitos away from the sweet, white crook of his inner arm they constantly sucked at. Regretting the hasty toss of the cigarette, he ignored the tug. His eyes swept the ditch for a telltale puff of rising white smoke. *OK, there you are...* But before he could go and fetch it, the tugging on his shirtsleeve resumed. Stronger. It wouldn't quit.

"OK! Aright! What the hell?!" he snapped. The charitable priest was already in the red zone from operational orders that would direct the battalion through two more villages that afternoon – and the VC resistance was heavy. *More dead boys. For sure.*

He turned and saw a petite Vietnamese woman, perhaps 20 – or maybe she was 50. It was impossible to tell because she was craggy from the war, stripped of any clues that would reveal her true age. Her eye orbits were sunken, teeth yellow and cracked, yet her hair was as black as boot-shine, save for a narrow white streak that ran down her left forelock.

She looked up at him, but not at his face. She was staring at his chest. He reached for his gold chain and Virgin Mary amulet and tucked them back in.

Without words, she slowly lifted her sun-bleached, green-and-red checkered scarf up to his face and began uncovering the thing she had been cradling. At first, he thought it was something she was trying to peddle, like a small stone statue… *or some other useless shit… They're always trying this kind of crap with me.*

He started to pull away from her, but she then removed the scarf completely and exposed the object she carried. Mordechai paused. He lingered, doubting his senses. He couldn't make out exactly what he was looking at – but then, slowly, it started to come into focus. It was a baby monkey, a baby monkey from the forest. It had a tiny face. Yet it had no fur. It had no paws. Its skin had an almost-human texture, but its entire body was black-and-blue as if it were bruised all over. And it was breathing in rapid and short, raspy breaths. *But this is not a monkey.* Mordechai's scalp flexed back and the hair on top of his skull stood up. It was a monkey-like creature – *but this is human. This is a human baby!*

In all his time in the bush, Father Mordechai Goodcut had never seen such a wretched thing. Not dead Marine jarheads, not dead Army grunts. He didn't know how old the child was. Five months? A year? He may have said something like, "Sweet Jesus!" And if he didn't, he should have.

Whatever the woman may have had in mind for the baby, that didn't matter. With one arm he grabbed the woman and her child and they beelined it to the LZ where the medics were dug in, doing their best with the wounded. Scrambling along, Mordechai couldn't keep his eyes off the miserable creature. He knew it was a human being. But just barely.

Mordechai caught one of the medics by the arm as he was trotting back from a stretcher run to a departing chopper. The medic spotted the captain's bars and then eyeballed the woman. She froze for an instant but then squatted at their feet. Mordechai bent at the waist, hands on his knees.

The medic squinted, wiped the sweat from his crow's feet and stared at Goodcut, then at the woman and child, and then back to Goodcut's pasty, white face. Without saying a word, he bent down and took the baby from the woman's grasp and laid it down gently on a gray plastic tarp that minutes before was the final earthly stop for SP4 Andrew Dunbar, rifleman, 25th Infantry, now bound for Concordia, Kansas.

The medic removed the checkered scarf and Father Mordechai Goodcut could now see that this woman's treasure was an emaciated baby girl. She laid there, arms outstretched on the gray plastic *like Christ taken from the cross,* he thought. Her last raspy breath was her death rattle. "Sweet Jesus, indeed!" Goodcut gasped out loud.

Without trumpets or heavenly fanfare he sank down on his knees and crossed himself. And, as he clasped his hands to pray, he saw in his mind's eye, small eruptions of blood flowing from the tiny, dirt-brown palms of this dead child. Her body was sending the priest a sign to mark, with immense sweetness, the grace that was flooding over him. It was a stone-cold epiphany.

And he lifted his hands above his head to pray in thanks for the pure redemptive power of this moment. For Father Mordechai Goodcut understood with intense clarity that this death was a sacrifice, and it was being offered to shock his hardened heart and to call him back to the land of the living – back from the mayhem that prowled the jungle. "Amen and Amen" he prayed, again. And again.

Father Mordechai Goodcut was a spent bullet. He had emptied himself. His calling to the priesthood had been crushed under the heel of the God of War. The artifacts of his former Christian world fell away in shambles, then and there, on that dusty laterite road.

He knew that he no longer belonged in The World of Hurt – and now his grateful tears flowed without stopping.

CHAPTER 7

During his first nights back at Division HQ, Goodcut found pleasure in the company of Mr. Jack Daniels, and the two of them joined forces during their nightly raids to the PussyCat. It was the precise place on God's green earth where Mordechai would finally satisfy his stunted compulsion to enjoy life's physical pleasures. To resurrect his rise to manhood. It was a craving he had once kept throttled – and it was now howling.

And the mesmerizing, soft brown skin under the white *áo dài* dresses of the local talent brought the beleaguered Mordechai back to life. The enlisted men all agreed that the girls, the sex, and the booze were just what the padre needed. They all got him loud and clear. Five-by-five. They knew he had shot his wad doing hard time in the bush, and no one was now going to give him *some useless crap about getting back to his priestly gig*. That priest had packed up and left, and without remorse or a second thought, Father Mordechai Goodcut made his move.

• • • • •

Mordechai dragged a bamboo stool back from the bar at the PussyCat Club, and pulled out a $10 bill from his pocket, tossed it on the bar and shouted to the bartender, "Cold beer, big one." He sat facing the bar, but in the mirror behind the wall of booze bottles behind the bar he could see customers milling about, mostly other GIs and a few local girls. His stool afforded him a good view of the elevated dance floor where two local beauties were gyrating their hips to the saxophone music honking out from the jukebox.

He was a regular there and the folks at the club knew his routine. They also knew that he was a captain and a priest, but none of that made any difference to them. They had no idea what it meant for a man of his background to be drinking and whoring around. And even if they did, they could never fathom the distance he had placed between his calling as a priest and the gratification they were offering him. Their only concern was that he showed up with the green stuff, and he did not get himself wasted on the way back to the base. It was all good for them when the dollars and drinks flowed, and dresses were pulled up over slim waists. And Mordechai was only too happy to play his part.

He had come to know one girl he liked best. He called her Eve, and she was truly the first woman for his Adam, now emerging from the priestly cloister. She had once given him her real name, but he could never remember it nor pronounce it correctly. And Eve seemed a good fit for her. She had no thoughts of her own about the name Mordechai gave her, one way or another. In truth, she had few thoughts beyond the job at hand. This delicious beauty had long, straight black hair that was parted in the middle, and she would tuck it behind both ears with a giggle when she climbed on him. It was enough for Mordechai to mark her.

She was from Hue and her English was far better than the others. Goodcut had the ridiculous notion that she actually cared for him – at least she had a fairly convincing way of showing interest in him that the other girls couldn't muster. She was shamelessly stunning and talented, and before her career was cut short by an 81mm mortar barrage two years later, she would listen to the outpourings of many GIs, perhaps none as obscure and floundering as the confession she received from Mordechai on this night – his last night in Vietnam before escaping to Bangkok on R&R.

. . . . .

Mordechai had started his night pretty much as usual. A couple of Pabst Blue Ribbon beers to loosen up, and then a few shots of Jack to bring it to a boil. Within an hour he was feeling good, losing the blues that had dogged him every day since leaving the bush. The same old ragtag group was making noises in their usual spots in the club, music was flowing and sounds of laughter were erupting from the corners of the main bar area when the girls, on cue, made their way into the club from the back.

Sometime after the third shot of whisky, Mordechai felt a small hand reach around from behind him at the bar and fondle his balls. It was her signature greeting. He lifted up his right elbow and Eve ducked under it and hugged him around the ribs. Even before he could turn to see her, he could smell the perfumed soap that lingered on her skin. He inhaled it deeply. It was wonderful. In competition with the jukebox, she exclaimed loudly, "Mor-dee-kai!"

She had on a bright white dress and, drawing her closer and kissing her ear, he could smell the Jean Naté perfume that some GI must have bought for her at the PX. To Mordechai, she looked saintly. She glowed. And he fumbled for the words to say so but needed a few more drinks before he could scare up much more than, "Hi Eve. Don't you look pretty tonight."

She beamed back at Goodcut. Perhaps the poor girl really did care for him. The bar girls had an uncanny ability to pick out the most lost and troubled souls and then gravitate towards them, avoiding the horny, groping cowboys who were a dime-a-dozen and too quick on the trigger. Perhaps the girls felt a sense of kindred spirit with the losers. They could see the suffering in the eyes of these GIs and they knew very well what it meant. They knew more about that kind of suffering than any of the girls back home would ever know.

"Here, Eve, let me buy you a drink. Have you had your dinner?"

"No, me OK. But whisky sour good. And you need buy me one. Me no want trouble." She took a sideways glance in the mirror to look for Papa-san, but he was glaring at another girl, one of Eve's friends, sitting on a Black GIs lap. He was gesturing to her to get the man to drink, and to drink quickly.

"Right, right." Mordechai reached for another $10 and plunked it on the bar. "Whisky sour for the young lady."

Turning to Eve he asked, "So how *have* you been? What's new?" He took a sip from his drink and peered down at her. He was lousy at small talk. Mordechai Goodcut was lousy at any talk with women, and only the whisky got him to a state of conversation where he felt in control, where the right words would flow out of his mouth, and he wouldn't need to study each before speaking – like a dull farmer, deciding which apple to pick from the tree and in what order he should pick them.

"Me? OK. I got some money save. Gonna see mother soon. She live in Hue. Me need bus."

Mordechai nodded in understanding and approval. The music seemed to bump up a notch in volume, so he popped off the bar stool and grabbed both of their drinks and they made it over to a table at the corner of the bar, farthest away from the music, the clinking glasses and spurts of laughter.

The PussyCat Club had a pink and white neon sign outside. It was the cartoon version of the Pink Panther from the movie, and the glass-tube figure had a top hat that he would lift off-and-on his head with alternating pulses of the neon. The bright-pink light from the sign came directly through the blue and red, glass window panels of the Club, and it lit up their table with colorful patterns. Mordechai looked upon this with a foggy sense of appreciation – to find something that soothing and somehow reminiscent of church windows, *in a joint like this, of all the fuckin' places.*

Eve looked even more beautiful in this light, but she hadn't noticed the lights nor their effect. She had probably been in the same seat, at the same table, under the same lights a hundred times before.

"Listen, Eve," Goodcut began. "I need to tell you something."

Her eyebrows shot up, and she disarmed him with a smile. "OK, you tell me."

Goodcut shouted across the floor to the bartender to bring him another couple of drinks, "A whisky double and another whisky sour."

He was already feeling the effects of the first several drinks and was getting in the mood. The liquid courage was helping. Tonight he would probably skip smoking the joint or two that Eve usually carried. But he was definitely going to tag this beauty who sat across the table. It would be a crime to manhood everywhere not to.

"Listen Eve," he repeated. She took a little sip of the sour. "I've got something I need to say. I need to get this off my chest."

The bartender brought over their two drinks on a flat service tray. Goodcut flipped a wrinkled 20 on the tray as the bartender set the drinks down. The man gave a furtive glance at Eve, but she did not return his look. Instead, she stared at Goodcut. She hoped what he was going to say would be about her. About her prospects for leaving her rathole existence.

But the only thing she would hear that evening was about him. That he was about to leave. *Sure. Sure.* It's always about them, she knew it. Why would this be different? She had no idea about the stuff he was jabbering on about. But if it made him feel better, and if he left a big green note under the pillow in the morning, that is all that really mattered to her. Bus money.

Goodcut went on, "You see Eve. We are bad men. We are sinful men. We come to your country. Many people die." He paused and took a sip. Eve did not move.

"We are supposed to be good men. To believe in God. But I think God has left Vietnam." His eyes trailed off, as did his dying voice and he mumbled, "Anyway, I know he has left *me*."

"Why he leave you? No, I no believe. I know you good man, Mor-dee-kai. You no kill no body."

The lift offered by Eve may have been heartfelt, but it provided no relief in reducing Mordechai's guilt which was reaching a crest since the drinks had kicked in. "No, Eve, it's same-same. I bad man just like others." He took another sip.

Eve had finished talking for the rest of the session, she didn't want to say anything more. She didn't finish her first drink, nor even start on the second.

"So, I hope that God, if he ever does come back, forgives me. And I'm sorry if I have offended him. Maybe that's why he left. I don't know. But I hope that I will do no more bad things when I leave here."

"You leave here?" Eve came back into the conversation.

"Yes, I leave, dear. But not tonight. Not tonight." And with that he stood and pushed away from the table and tried to steady himself.

He righted his head and looked at the light in the hallway upstairs, and said to her, "Come on, honey, let's go upstairs and say our prayers."

"OK. No problem. We go upstairs." And she added with a wide grin now that the conversation was back in her territory, "Go upstairs and boom-boom!"

His confession was at an end, and now the well-stewed Mordechai could only meekly answer, "Sure. Boom-boom."

And with that, Eve once again placed herself under his right wing and helped him mount the stairs to the rooms at the top. His favorite room, with the light-blue wall paint and a mirror on the ceiling, was locked from the inside and he started to give the door a kick. But Eve pulled him back and led him by the hand to the room directly across the hall. Mordechai turned and gazed at Eve for a moment, and then nodded an OK.

He thought it would be funny to scoop her up with both arms and take her into the room, bridal style. She may have seen that move in a Western movie since she squealed with glee as he clumsily moved to pick her up, right himself and then rush into the room and throw her on the bed.

All was going well, until he tried to get past the doorway with his "bride" and he knocked her head on the door post. "Aiye-e-e!" She shouted. "What you fuckin' do, Mor-dee-kai?! You stupid number fucking ten GI! Me hit my head. Oh, it hurt too much!"

Mordechai tried his best to console her, kissing her time-and-time again on her forehead. He was truly sorry, but the absurdity of what just happened descended on him and he started to laugh. Eve, angered by his insensitivity, tried to push him away. But he held her close and repeated his apology until she yielded – and then smiled. She kissed him back.

They both stood, and Mordechai locked the door while Eve pulled her dress over her head. She undid her bra and slid out of her panties and was under the top sheet in one continuous and graceful move. Mordechai turned away from the locked door and looked at this beauty staring back at him. He was ready. He had been ready since climbing up the stairs from the bar.

Mordechai tried to mimic her in the removal of his clothes, now twice their normal weight from the outpouring of sweat in anticipation of the act he was about to perform. The unraveled priest was not yet an expert, but he was now well-past the fumbling novice. These two weeks in paradise had taught him well. He undid his shirt, then his trousers. He got one leg out of his underwear and then did the one-legged underwear dance as he tried to get the other leg out. He hopped around the room to the amazement of Eve who sat up on her elbows, her small breasts appearing just over the top of the bedsheet. "You OK, Mor-dee-kai?" she asked.

"Yeah, OK," as he finally flung them off the end of his right foot. They went sailing across the room and landed on top of a purple table lamp with a gaudy, yellow lampshade depicting water buffalos. The 25-watt bulb underneath was doing its best to light up the room, but now, with Mordechai's underwear blocking out half the light, the room grew dark.

Mordechai stumbled into the bed and embraced Eve. Without a moment's hesitations she asked, "How you like it tonight, Mor-dee-kai?" She asked as if taking an order for cooking some eggs. "You want *mis-jun-hairy* style, or like last night? Like doggie."

"It's missionary, *mis-shun-air-ee*," he repeated the four syllables with emphasis, as best as the whisky would allow him to do. "But OK, OK, like doggie OK."

She turned on her stomach and drew in her knees, propping herself on her forearms. And as Mordechai approached her from behind, she reached for an apple from the nightstand and took her first bite. She kept nibbling at it until they were both done, and neither said a word – not even "goodnight."

He would stay with Eve that last night, all night, holding her in a goodbye embrace. His flight to Bangkok was at 16:00 the next day, so he reckoned he would be OK.

•   •   •   •   •

Father Mordechai Goodcut's explosive rebirth as a man's man occurred on the second floor of a whorehouse above a bar in

Vietnam, with empty whisky bottles on the table and panties rolled down and tossed on the floor in the shape of silken figure-eights. The outward signs of his former vocation were abandoned in a wooden footlocker. Like a casket. He shed his blood-stained prayer stole, his clerical collar, and a photo of his investiture as a priest that was folded down the middle – as if the crease itself depicted his divided nature. Good man. Bad man. Sinner. Saint. Christian. Buddhist.

By the time the four Allison turboprops on the C-130 screamed down the runway, Father Goodcut's priestly vows had been extinguished. But Mordechai Goodcut, the holy man, remained a steadfast seeker of God's face, and in his heart-of-hearts he hoped he would soon find that elusive visage.

He bowed his head and prayed, *Please, Jesus, let me keep it together. Let me walk the path, but not tread too far away. Not too far. No matter what happens next, let me remain tethered to you. Please, dear Jesus, guide my steps* – steps which Mordechai feared might lead him away from his *Holy Best Friend.*

CHAPTER 8

The Thais rarely concerned themselves with zoning laws, and jumbled combinations of businesses were found everywhere along the streets and alleyways of Bangkok: duck restaurants next to stores selling bags of cement; next to Pepsi distributors with ceiling-high stacks of empty bottle-crates, and their dilapidated delivery trucks, double-parked and blocking traffic outside; next to greasy engine-repair shops that pitched discarded motor oil into street gutters, running by the ubiquitous street vendors who sold peeled papayas, diced mangos and pineapples on ice.

Nobody seemed troubled by this mismatched backdrop or much of anything else as Mordechai sat, slurping down his second bowl of fish-ball noodles in a grimy shophouse restaurant, wedged in between a barber shop on one side and a post office on the other. It was a dish he enjoyed many times over the past several days and, although he was on a tight budget, he indulged himself with a second bowl. Seconds were necessary to tide him over since he was now eating only one meal each day. He knew that Buddhist monks only ate one meal, at noon, and he wanted to see if he had the necessary discipline and stamina for what was coming.

For holy man Mordechai Goodcut was teetering on a spiritual fulcrum, balancing the tattered remnants of his

Christian self with the other instantiations of God on earth. Although he was no longer a priest, he still loved his Mary, Joseph, and all the saints. Above all, he loved the Sacred Heart of Jesus. And yet he knew that the Eastern religions had found their versions of the revealed truth long ago. And now, here he sat in the very epicenter of Buddhism in Southeast Asia. Thailand. Mordechai knew it was providential.

He had come to know a lot about Thai temples, temple life and Buddhism, and he was intrigued to learn that the famous temple of *Wat Bowonniwet* had allowed several foreigners to join its community: four as novices and three as ordained monks. He visited them often, his curious mind asking many questions of the foreign monks, probing them to find out everything he could about the rituals and liturgy of Thai *Theravada* Buddhism.

He was struck by the similarities between the "bells and smells" of the high Catholic Church and the Buddhist practices he observed: the kneeling, the bowing, the candles, the heavy floral incense, the proliferation of statuary depicting holy figures, and the way the Thai monks prayed, not in Thai, but in the ancient Pali-Sanskrit language – not unlike the Latin Catholic mass he attended as a child.

Goodcut knew that, philosophically, the religions had significant gaps – reincarnation, for example, was not a subject you would hear coming from the pulpit during the Easter Morning homily. But he was making strong connections, and his monk friends at the temple – the foreigners and their Thai brethren – were drawn in by the curious spectacle of an animated Mordechai, extolling the links he had "discovered."

They were amused by his energy and arm-waving antics which took over when his language failed. They felt warmed by his presence. To the man, they liked Mordechai – his *nee-sai dee*, his good and honest spirit.

In Goodcut's mind, the allure to walk the Buddhist path grew. It was his insatiable curiosity that drew him in. Time and place aligned, and the chance meeting with the foreign monks was clearly auspicious. It was irresistible. Compelling. He stood at the threshold of a second calling and set his mind for the great journey ahead – his transformation into a truth seeker under a saffron robe.

Goodcut made quick work of his second bowl of noodles.

·　·　·　·　·

He pulled a few sheets of toilet paper from the plastic decanter on the folding table to wipe his mouth and then tipped the toothpick jar to select a sharp, thin one. He stared out into the busy streets where pink and yellow taxis, pedestrians, and brightly painted *tuk-tuks* were vying for the same small slab of concrete road.

He had an appointment that afternoon with a liaison officer at the US Embassy, an Air Force 2nd Lt named Richard Clarke who was posted to the State Department by the Military Advisory Command in Thailand. Mordechai had something important to say to him, and as he stared at the traffic and picked his teeth, he imagined how his life was about to take a drastic turn.

God knows, he assured himself.

CHAPTER 9

Mordechai sat with his back against the cool brick walls of the bunker-like room in the Embassy basement, staring at the spartan clock, its second hand sweeping the numbers around its face. He didn't have long to wait before Clarke came down the hallway with a coke in one hand, and a doughnut and a yellow writing pad in the other. He had a wide, goofy grin that said "hayseed" when Mordechai stood and shook his hand. They both sat down.

"So, what can we do you for?" asked Clarke in that twisted GI parlance which was supposed to be edgy and funny. Taking a bite into his strawberry-glazed doughnut, he added, "I'm Lt. Clarke from MACThai, and I've been assigned here to assist our GIs when they're passing through the 'City of Angels'." He paused and checked Mordechai's reaction to his introduction. There wasn't any.

He went on, "As you may know, we're here to help guys who've run out of dough, or have been in scrapes with the locals, or..." Clarke then flipped over his right hand, palm up and flexed his fingertips. He gave Goodcut a wink "...dealing with local cops who have cases against our boys. You know, that sort of thing."

He paused again and looked at Mordechai for a second time, sizing him up. He figured him for a noncom, maybe a Staff

Sargent or Sargent First Class who had been robbed by a local hooker – he had seen that sad, detached look in a GIs eyes before. And yet there was something different about this guy. Goodcut's face had an odd, steely resolution. It was a hardcore countenance and Clarke was growing unnerved.

"Well," started Mordechai in a slow and measured voice, "I'm Mordechai Goodcut, Captain Mordechai Goodcut, and I'm a chaplain with the 25th Infantry in Tay Ninh Province, Vietnam."

Clarke raised himself slightly from the slouch he had taken in his office chair and took his right foot off the round trash basket next to his desk. He had this guy pegged wrong. He thought for a second about standing and giving his superior officer a salute, but the awkwardness of doing such a maneuver overrode the call for military protocol – and besides, Captain Goodcut was wearing shorts, flip-flops and a vividly painted yellow dashiki. *No*, he checked his thoughts. *Let's just get on with it. What's this guy's problem, anyway?*

"And what can we do for you, Captain?" Adjusting his voice, Clarke asked the question again – the untwisted version this time.

Mordechai rose slowly from his chair and stood at the edge of Clarke's desk, looked at him from his hairline to his chin, and said, "I've come to give you my ID card and dog tags."

Clarke put his doughnut down, looked across his desk at Mordechai and said, "I'm sorry. Come again. I thought you said –"

"That's right," interrupted Goodcut, "my ID card and my dog tags." Goodcut reached into his back pocket and pulled out his wrinkled cowskin wallet. He tugged his green US Army photo ID out and laid the dirty and dog-eared card gently on Clarke's desk. He then reached for the chain around his neck that held his dog tags, and using both hands, slowly and purposely lifted it over his head – as if he were lifting the host for the priestly blessing at mass. Goodcut coiled the beaded metal chain around the index and middle fingers of his left hand and laid it gently in a symmetrical pile next to his ID card.

"There," he said in a flat tone, admiring the relics of his former life laid out and on display on Clarke's desk, now an altar.

"I was supposed to be back in 'Nam two weeks ago. But, you see, I'm not going back. I'm resigning. I'm going to be staying here in Thailand now. I'm going to become a Buddhist monk," he added with a satisfied smile.

And with his head tilted down and peering over his wire-rimmed glasses, he conjured up an afterthought. "You know, I've seen too much with these eyes." He then righted himself and paused, remembering the lines he had rehearsed to say and was now prepared to deliver, "I'm going to go now. Going to move on. Going to find my true faith."

And with these words he started towards the door of Clarke's small office.

But before he could take two steps, Clarke shot out of his chair and moved between Goodcut and the door, several feet behind him.

"Wa-a-a-ait a minute, there Captain," Clarke protested, putting his hands up and tilting his head to one side but avoiding Mordechai's eyes.

"You can't just up and leave like that. You know, cut and run. Split the scene. You're already AWOL, any way you look at it, and I'm afraid that the Army's not going to sit for that. No sirree, Bob. Not for one second." His voice was growing higher in pitch as the seconds swept past on his wall clock.

Mordechai paused for a moment. He understood Clarke's dilemma. He had seen scores of newbies trying to pinch out an iota of courage when facing their first real confrontation. Clarke had never seen combat, but he was digging around in the same place where the grunts dug for their courage – only the grunts dug miles deeper.

Goodcut flattened his lips and nodded at Clarke's weakness and he placed his left hand on Clarke's right shoulder, adding in a detached voice, miles away, "I'll be alright. This is something I need to do. You don't need to worry."

Clarke frantically flipped through his options, trying to come up with a line or two that would dissuade Goodcut, but he drew one blank after another. He had no means to control the situation that was slipping out of his hands – and happening now.

"So," added Goodcut, "If you'll just kindly let me pass, I'll be on my –"

But before he could finish, Clarke brushed off Goodcut's hand and closed the exit space between Mordechai and the office door. In a desperate and dangerous move, he squared himself in Goodcut's face, extended both his arms out and pressed his palms against Mordechai's chest. Goodcut's path to freedom was cut off and the smile left his face. It was a move that Clarke would regret.

Mordechai was fresh from war and he instantly felt the ancient heat rise from the pit of his stomach, eclipsing any chance for further rational and dispassionate talk with *this fool*. Gone was his natural sense of patience. Gone was his charity and love of peace, and hatred for violence. And in its place – and in an instant – appeared a transformed, cornered creature bent on survival. His switch was flipped.

His head slowly lifted to meet Clarke's face and in one motion, he brought back his right leg while he removed his glasses and tucked them in his shirt pocket. Clarke saw the signals, but his hands, now trembling, remained on Goodcut's chest.

And they felt the vibrations as Goodcut spoke, "If you don't remove your hands from me and get the fuck out of my way, I'm going to beat you so badly your mother won't recognize you. You get me?"

Clarke swallowed hard. He lingered. But as the second hand crawled from 11 to 12, his counterfeit will evaporated. He dropped his hands from Mordechai's shirt and hung his head to the side. He was left limp and marooned on a stage where a moment before he was the champion of law and order – of all that was right and just.

He half pivoted his body out of Goodcut's path who passed in front of him without looking back. The best Clarke could come up with was to put his hands on his hips, shake his head from side-to-side, while squeezing a note of disdain from his untested mouth. He blurted out in a failed command voice, "Well, it's your neck, Padre."

At the doorway, Goodcut turned and stared at Clarke for several seconds. Clarke swallowed again and cast his eyes back down to the waxed, brown tile floor.

Goodcut was feeling a great release from his words with Clarke and said, "Yes, it's my neck alright." And hoping Clarke's eyes would meet his – they did not – he added, "Not your problem, my friend."

There was no turning back – for either of them.

Clarke lifted his head to see Mordechai walk slowly down the hallway, step to the left and then climb up the stairs to the Embassy ground floor and to the exit on Wireless Road. The sun was hitting Goodcut full in the face as he ascended the stairs. With his hands still trembling, Clarke fixed his eyes on the transfiguration of this man, and he felt a nervous jolt of admiration for someone with that kind of guts. He recalled that his uncle once told him that there is nothing more ferocious and frightening than a coward shoved into a corner. *Was this priest such a man?*

He reached behind with his right arm to grab the Coke and quench his cotton mouth, but he hit the bottle. It tumbled over and spilled out onto his desk, soaking the copy of the farm report he had received from his father the week before, and the bottom few pages of a July 1970 Playboy he had stashed away under a stack of Daily Situation Reports.

He trotted to the basement washroom and pulled several paper towels from the wall dispenser and returned to his desk to mop up the mess – and to dab the beaded sweat from his forehead. His encounter with Goodcut had rattled him. He salvaged what was left of his doughnut and stuck it between his teeth, and with shaking hands he ran a fresh "Report for the Record" form into his typewriter.

He gave a few pulls on the mechanical return lever and then stared up at the clock, its second hand still sweeping. *Nah*, he dismissed his encounter with Goodcut. *This dude is a bona fide nut job. The Special Investigation guys will nab him, but quick. It's only a matter of time. Yeah, a bona fide nut job*, his thoughts repeated.

It was 3:25 in the afternoon when Mordechai emerged from the Embassy and made his way north on Wireless Road to his digs at the Grove Hotel. His links with his past – and with Western thought – had come uncoupled, and the elation he felt while turning in his ID card and dog tags dissolved under the fierce Bangkok sun. He knew that something good was in store but was surprised by the hollowness that welled up from his gut and clenched him by his throat as he walked along. It was the uncertainty that sprang from his spiritual rebirth that gnawed at him – the uncertainty of making the first strides into a new faith.

· · · · ·

The greasy restaurant, next to the hotel's pool, made passable club sandwiches and had ice-cold beer in large bottles. And several times a day someone would drop a coin in the jukebox slot and Staff Sergeant Barry Sadler's tune, "The Ballad of the Green Berets" would blast everyone in the place.

If you were unfortunate enough to be caught inside the restaurant when this happened, the boys from the 26th SF

Company from up-country, near Lop Buri, would pressure you to *get your ass off the red bar stool* and stand with respect. Military or civilian, they didn't care. The fellows could make it unpleasant if you didn't humor them. Nothing physical or violent would go down, just a seriously drunk person in your face, giving you patriotic dribble in a loud and irritating voice.

They started to get on Mordechai's case that evening when he went downstairs to the restaurant for a bucket of ice and the tiresome tune was blaring away. But even the SF boys gave Goodcut his space that night. They recognized the war-worn look in his eyes, and the priest returned to his room with his ice bucket full.

The hotel scenes reminded him that his decision to leave the Army was both providential and righteous. He needed to escape from the mind-numbing madness it exuded. He craved order, but the spiritual variety, and not the kind that the Army smothered him with – he could not find his soul at the bottom of that olive-drab dog pile.

Closing his eyes that evening, he thought back to his confrontational meeting with Clarke at the Embassy. That lava was still fresh, rolling and churning, deep under a cooled surface. And he soon felt the warm breath of St. Paul on his ear, whispering, *I do not understand what I do. For what I want to do, I do not do. But what I hate, I do. For I have the desire to do what is good, but I cannot carry it out.* Mordechai lifted his hands in prayer to offer thanks to God for stirring these words to life.

Understanding what his next steps must be, he murmured, "Old Saul of Tarsus was right. It's time to do what I must do. Time to make my move." *Christ give me strength.*

And he repeated this plea in a mantra as he dozed off to sleep, collapsing in a pose that made him look like he was swimming the sidestroke.

PART III: HUNT

CHAPTER 10

Cole rose early and washed up. He usually avoided the mirror in the mornings, but today he stopped by and had a quick look at the man staring back at him. He had the unsettling notion that the pursuit of this priest was going to be a hunt of a different kind. The relish he felt only the day before gave way to a twisted knot in the pit of his stomach. *Who was this guy, anyway? Why the fuss by Hargraves? Maybe the Old Man had got the hard-on after he read the letter from that damn Mexican cop in T or C.*

His mind turned to the arid Southwest and he could see Pepe, stodgy and leather-faced, sitting down at his desk to write the letter – and he could see Abilene with her matted hair and ventilator tubes, lying on green hospital sheets. *Yeah, this priest is mine alright, and he is going to catch hell for running away... for being in cahoots with that decrepit old priest in T or C... and for royally fucking up my R&R.*

But the knot in his stomach kicked into high gear. He started thinking that it might have been the handful of those nasty bar nuts he ate last night at the OC, in between the drinks that Charley had been pouring. *I bet that stupid gook spilled them nuts on the backroom floor, and then just scooped 'em up back into the jar. Fuck, who knows.* It was a knot that was not going to go away soon.

His mind turned to the conversation he had with Digman last night, when *that asshole snuck up* on him in his hootch – an act that *nearly got his sorry ass killed* had the Glenlivet not taken the edge off Cole's nerves. The thought of Digman retreating into the night after dropping off that envelope was irritating. *What a clown. Such fucking drama.* It reminded him of an old black-and-white movie he once saw as a kid on his neighbor's TV, where someone dropped off an unwanted baby at the convent door, rang the bell, and then slipped off into the night.

The booze at the Officers Club, the mocking laughter of a runaway priest, and the run-in with that moron Digman all gave him a major gut-punch. *Yeah, that must be it… Shit, here it comes again…*

He bent over and grabbed the dial on the black-faced Master combination lock on his upright, street locker. To the right, twice to 25, back left to 36, and then right to 47. So easy. All he had to do was to remember 25 and the number of his quarterback jersey in high school, 11, and he was in: 25 plus 11, plus 11. He liked that symmetry.

Cole popped the lock and swung the two metal doors wide open. He dressed in his travel khakis which hung neatly, at the ready. On the left side was his Class A uniform and below these, his fatigues. The rest of his kit was stuffed in a duffle bag – the same bag he got during basic training at Ft. Ord, 7 years ago. Cole didn't like getting too comfortable in any one place and that meant keeping most of his practical stuff in that stained and scarred old bag.

On the bottom, right shelf of the locker was a wooden tray that held some junk left over from the last guy who had this bunk: two green field-note pads, a half-dozen 2B soft-lead pencils, three spent .50-cal casings, some paper clips, a couple of Bic pens, and a box of Trojan rubbers. "Ribbed for Her Pleasure" was the claim. *Yeah, right. Like I need that.*

On the side of the tray, next to the rubbers, was a plastic string of pink Pepto Bismol tablets. He quickly popped open six of these chewable numbers and stuck them in his mouth. He wadded up the other tablets in the string and stuffed them down into his pants pocket. Cole tossed the box of rubbers into an overnight bag – a gear bag that one of the Huey crew chiefs had given him – along with some socks and skivvies.

Pepto Bismo and Rubbers, he thought. *"Bangkok Belly" and whores. Sure bet.* Having the Pepto Bismo on hand was a good thing. Having the rubbers was always a good thing. He was going to Bangkok, after all, and it had been a couple of months since he and Peacock were tearing it up, down in Saigon.

He grabbed his gear bag and jammed in three days of clothing, his pit stick, Dial soap, toothbrush and a half-empty carton of Camels. He took the magazine out of his .45 and ejected the chambered round which he placed back in the clip. Cole wrapped the clip and the weapon in a white t-shirt which he laid at the bottom of the bag. All the essentials were there. 1st Lt. Coltrane was ready for whatever might come his way *during the hunt for this fuckin' priest. Check.*

Cole secured his locker and was headed out the door when he noticed Digman's brown envelope on the nightstand table. He opened the top drawer and started to toss it in when he caught sight of the red, leather prayer book his grandmother had given him. She would have asked him to take it along for good luck. For good hunting. She might have even looked up a prayer for hunting, if there was such a thing. And he wondered if hunting had its own patron saint. *Probably did. Hell, the Catholic Church has saints for every swinging dick. Probably the fucking dog catcher has one, so why not a saint for a real-deal hunter, like me.*

Cole had no use for Catholic sentiments nor saints. Those notions were all left behind in the deserts of New Mexico. But since his locker was already secured, he opened the prayer book and stuck Digman's letter inside it and tossed both into his gear bag. Digman's scribbled name on the envelope pressed up against the lines in the prayer book which read, "Saint Michael the Archangel, defend us in battle; be our defense against the wickedness and snares of the devil…"

●　　●　　●　　●　　●

Coltrane was going to be late at AirOps, and the C-130 flight to Bangkok would not wait up for him as it might for Army brass – or some hot chiquita from the Nursing Corps. Too much dawdling in his room. He hotfooted it out of the barracks and was moving fast along the gravel path that paralleled the road to the AirOps terminal and his flight. *Not fast enough. Got to get a move on…*

He double-checked his pocket and found his orders where he had stashed them last night: three typewritten pages signed by Hargraves, folded in four. He also found his Camels and quickly reached for the pack and popped one into his mouth while pulling out his Zippo – a silver prize he won from another lieutenant in a game of five-card stud, the last time he was up in Na Trang. The guy was in the Chemical Corps and the inscription on the lighter read on one side: "To Lt. Bill, the Rain Maker." On the other side it read: "Up your ass, with bugs and gas!" and under that, "The Army Chemical Corps – Get Some!" Cole drew in deep on the square. He would have to catch a ride if he was going to make it to the check-in counter on time.

He hailed the first jeep that was headed in that direction. And sometime between lighting the cigarette and taking his second drag, he picked up a rock in the sole of his right shoe. *That damn thing* would give an annoying click to his step and would not bound away from his shoe until later that day, when he stepped onto the sidewalk in front of the US Embassy on Wireless Road in Bangkok.

The jeep pulled up and stopped, and Cole saw that it was driven by an Hispanic "Speedy 4" from air transport. "Where to, L.T.?" asked the driver.

"Can you drop me at AirOps? I need to get there pronto. Catch a C-1 for BKK." Before the driver could answer, Cole threw his bag in the back and jumped in after it.

"Sure, no problem, sir. Headed that way now."

"Cool. Appreciate it."

The driver regarded Coltrane in the rearview mirror. He was staring at the three rows of ribbons under his Combat Infantry Badge. He recognized the Purple Heart, the Silver and Bronze stars, but could not make out the others – one of which was the Distinguished Service Cross.

"Shit, L.T., you got yourself some fruit salad there, homes."

Cole smiled but otherwise ignored the compliment as the jeep gained speed. The passenger up front turned to look at Cole. It was the warrant officer pilot he met in the bar last night, the WO3 fellow from West Texas who was going on about the PsyOps guys and their music up-country. "Hey, Lieutenant. Good to see you again. You bugged out early last night."

Cole missed the connection at first, then recalled the warrant officer and his number two. "Yeah, thanks," said Cole. "I had to hit the hay early. Big day ahead, today." He took another puff and then asked, "Where's your second officer – the Wobbly 1?"

The Texan turned back to stare ahead of the jeep – as if looking for street addresses in a place which had none. He inclined his head to the left and said over his shoulder, in a flat tone, "He got himself killed last night. He went downtown to one of them strip clubs after he left the OC. Was in there for about 10 minutes when some VC cunt rolled two grenades under the bar stools. I'm on the way to the morgue now. I want to see what's left. I owe him that."

Cole thought, *Fucking hell!* but did not speak. He just flicked the last of his Camel onto the gravel as the jeep skidded to a halt in front of the AirOps hanger. He hopped out, thanked the driver, and stood looking at the WO3. Cole said nothing. He only shook his head.

"I know. I know," said the big Texan in a trailing voice as his jeep pulled away.

•   •   •   •   •

Cole strapped himself into the red, nylon seat webbing on the C-130 as the crew chief walked down the two long rows of seats on either side of the fuselage, making his final inspection and collecting personal baggage. He added Cole's gear bag to the heap that was piled onto an aluminum pallet at the aft of the aircraft.

Cole kept a sharp eye on his bag, mindful of his .45 he had stuck in the bottom, somewhere between his skivvies and two extra pair of socks. He was not supposed to travel to Thailand armed, but he frankly didn't give a damn about those rules. He was on a mission, and he needed the leverage if it came to that.

Shit! thought Cole, now remembering, *No windows on this crate.* Coltrane hated flying in planes without windows. His senses were tripped-up without a horizon. For a hunter, wholly reliant on his senses, the C-130 was always unnerving. The only view out was through the porthole on the crew chief's door in the front of the cargo bay, and he wasn't about to shift his seat forward. That would not be cool. Besides, the plane was packed with GIs headed for Bangkok and not easy to move between the pallets of cargo and the feet of the troops seated along the sides.

Most of the GIs were going for two weeks of R&R, and only a few would actually recall their entire leave. The others would recall only a blurred series of days, waking up in some unknown hotel bed, with or without company. Life was looking good.

The crew chief raised the aft loading ramp as the four massive turboprops started up, one after the next. Lockheed didn't worry about sound baffling when they designed these monsters, so the crew chief passed out foam earplugs to help deal with the brain-splitting noise. It was stifling hot and the AC from the overhead ducts wasn't helping.

The seats were made of a framework of angular, aluminum tubing that held the nylon webbing in place, and the cross-piece under Cole had caught him right in the crack of his butt. So he shifted aft about a foot, causing him to rub up against the belly of a fat buck sergeant with his left elbow. *Crap... but better than havin' that tube stuck in the crack of my ass...*

Cole was sweating like a bandit, and he craned his neck to see the last slit of daylight linger before the aft cargo door closed completely. The big plane lurched forward with deafening noise as the wheel chocks were removed and the propellers dug deep into the humid Vietnamese air.

He could never have known that this particular bird – with the same air crew – was the very same escape pod that had spirited Mordechai away from Vietnam, just three weeks earlier. And the fleeing Fr. Goodcut was sitting in the very same place now occupied by the fat and disgruntled, three-striped buck sergeant.

CHAPTER 11

Cole was relieved when the C-130 finally hit the deck in Don Muang Airport and parked. It was a short flight, but the only inputs to his brain had been the loud, incessant growl from the turboprops and the violent banging around in the cumulus-rich, turbulent air over Southeast Asia. The two-hour flight seemed like 100 and he hated every minute. When the rear cargo door opened, it was like the waking eyelid of some giant beast who had squeezed it shut in Vietnam. *Man, I've just flown here in the belly of a dragon. That's some shit.*

. . . . .

Bangkok. The heat and the sweat were exactly the same as this morning in Vietnam, but gone were the funky smells of war. He sucked it in deep.

It was 8am when he jumped into a green and yellow taxi and joined the throngs in the crushing morning traffic, inbound to downtown Bangkok. The driver was a dark and wrinkled old-timer who plied the route from the Airport in the north to downtown in the south. The old buzzard was a modern-day Charon, only working in reverse: ferrying nearly dead GIs away from Hell and bringing them to the land of the living – and with a little luck, a night or two in heaven.

Cole caught sight of the back of the old man's head. It was shaped like a flattened triangle. His hair had a military-style taper at the sides but it was long and thick at the top, combed over in a neat, front-to-back part. His ears stuck out like jug handles on both sides. Just below his sharp, left cheekbone there was some kind of large mole with a single hair about five inches long that sprung out from *the nasty thing*, and wavered around in the air coming out from the dashboard's AC, just barely blowing. Cole could feel the droplets of sweat run from his armpits, down the inside of his shirt and pool at his beltline.

On the taxi's dashboard were nine statues of the Buddha in various sizes, poses and colors, all glued in place at their base. Cole figured them for good luck pieces. He was right. On the roof lining of the cab were mysterious white dots and markings in symmetrical patterns and designs, interspersed with numbers. They looked like they were made by someone with their finger, painting the patterns with a kind of white paste. *More good luck signs?* Right again.

On the old man's neck, and protruding for about three inches above his collar, Cole saw a dark blue tattoo with a similar, but not identical, design to the white patterns on the roof lining. Around his neck the man wore a thick, silver-colored chain which had numerous small Buddha figurines attached, many encased in clear plastic and spaced out about two inches apart. From what Cole could see, he must have had 20 or more of these images on his chain. *That damn thing must weigh a ton.*

"Where you go, GI?" the driver asked, scrutinizing Cole in the rearview mirror. But before Cole could answer, the old man introduced himself.

"My name Somsak. Me 72 year old." Cole was surprised by the brief bursts of English and balked when the driver asked for his name.

"*Cheu-arai, khrap?*" The old man asked.

Cole wasn't much in the mood for conversation as he was still getting his land-legs back under him after the flight, and the knot in his gut – from Charley's nasty peanuts or whatever it was – was still cramping his stomach.

"Huh? Sorry, amigo, I don't speak Thai."

The old man laughed and then asked him again, "*Cheu-arai?* What is you name?"

"Uh… Cole. My name is Cole." He usually wouldn't let his name slip like that, but he occasionally did when meeting complete strangers, people he knew he would never see again.

The old man repeated, "Cone. You name Cone."

"Yeah. Yeah. Close enough." Cole had been thinking about how this could have been his R&R trip into the city, plunking down in some nice hotel, having some drinks by the pool. Some great food. Maybe a nightclub or two. He had an address that Peacock gave him for a club with some nice ladies.

But he got down to business and went to his pidgin English lexicon. "Me go US Embassy, old-timer."

Nodding, and catching another look at Cole in the mirror, the driver tried a lucrative diversion, "OK Cone. But why go Embassy? Want to see beautiful temple? I know many beautiful place. I can show you –"

Cole cut him off, "Maybe some other time. Business in Embassy today, my man. Need to go there first." *Let's just get the fuck goin'.*

"OK… OK, we go," the driver said, and he took a third glance in the mirror. But he was not sneaking a look at Cole's rows of medals. He was not impressed with military men. He felt sorry for them, but not impressed. Instead, he was sizing up Cole's eyes as they scanned through the window, taking in the sights of Bangkok and the masses of people moving around in every which direction, walking, hustling, selling goods on the streets, and opening stores that had been shuttered for the evening. Worker bees zipped through traffic on smoking, two-stroke motorcycles, and school kids rode to school in beat-up, blue and white busses, belching out clouds of black smoke. The old man liked Cole's curiosity. It somehow seemed honest and innocent to him.

"You have *dek-dek*, Cone?"

Cole looked at the driver's face in the mirror but did not reply.

"*Dek-dek*. Kid. You have kid?"

"No, I no have kids. No *dek-dek*."

The old man smiled from ear-to-ear. And the hair on his facial mole seemed to stop fluttering for just a second. The driver wasn't much interested in Cole's family, or if he had one. He was merely delighted that Cole now spoke a couple of syllables in Thai: *dek-dek*. The singsong of these words was easy for just about anyone to remember. It was a very good sign for the old man.

"Yes, *dek-dek*," he repeated. "Me have five *dek-dek*. Two boy. Three girl."

Cole had drifted back to the vision of the ladies' club and was annoyed with the old-timer for rousting him from that fantasy with small talk. At the same time he was oddly grateful to the driver for the chatty diversions. It would take him longer to ride in the back seat of the taxi for the 19 miles to the US Embassy on Wireless Road, than the 460-mile flight from Thon Son Nhut – strapped into the sticky webbing of the C-130. But time had slipped by quickly, and the maddening snail's pace traffic of Bangkok in 1971 did not seem so murderous.

They turned left from Ploenchit and onto Wireless Road, drew close to the Embassy gates and stopped. Cole paid him the taxi fare and placed an extra, red 100 baht note – about $4.80 – on top of the thin pile of lesser green and brown bills. The old man was delighted and put his palms together with his fingertips just under his nose in a gesture the Thais call a *wai*, and said, "*Khob khun*, Cone. Thank you."

Cole returned the act and the old man's grin widened. The driver put the taxi in gear and leaned out the window as Cole stepped up on the Embassy's sidewalk. The old man said with a smile, "Remember, Cone. In Thailand, thing not what look like every time."

Cole paused, disentangling the old man's last sentence and watched as the green and yellow taxi zoomed off in a puff of smoke and was swallowed up in the rush-hour traffic on Wireless Road. He stepped across the sidewalk and turned toward the Embassy front gate. Taking his first step, a small gray rock popped loose from his right shoe and skipped along the sidewalk before it hit the base of a steel lamp pole, making a bright ringing sound.

· · · · ·

Cole knocked on Clarke's office door but didn't wait for an answer. He twisted the knob and stepped inside. He had spotted Clarke from behind his venetian blinds so Cole knew he was in. 2nd Lt. Clarke looked like he was eating a piece of chocolate cake and was just sitting down in his chair to enjoy this treat when Cole entered his office.

Clarke made an attempt to wipe the crumbs from his face with his left hand, as he extended his right to Cole who was making his way to sit down. Clarke spotted Cole's rank, nameplate, and gear bag in that order. And it clicked.

"Welcome to Bangkok, Lt. Coltrane."

"Yeah, thanks," said Cole, settling down a couple of inches into the brown Naugahyde chair that Clarke had managed to scrounge from the Embassy supply room. Cole slid down further so his head could rest against the back of the seat. Taking a quick look around Clarke's office, he cut right to business.

Cole asked, "So, what d'ya got on this AWOL priest?"

Clarke stared at Cole for a second, thinking that they were going to have a quick session of small talk before they got into the priest's story. But he had heard about Coltrane's reputation from the phone conversations he had with Hargraves' office, and the 2IC there, Major Jennings, had warned Clarke not to waste this guy's time. He said, "Coltrane doesn't suffer bullshit very well." *Looks like they were right.*

"Right. The Priest." Clarke had the file on Captain Mordechai Goodcut ready on his desk. He had thought about keeping it in his metal filing cabinet so he could act like he was fishing it out when Coltrane arrived. It would give the impression that he had a lot of cases and was a very busy guy. But he didn't think that the theatrics would be worth it. Coltrane was not in his food chain, so why bother. It was a smart choice.

Clarke reached for the file, stretched up from his seat and over a pile of newspapers, and handed it to Cole who made no attempt to exert himself. He opened it and thumbed through the contents quickly. Hargraves had given him a file with five pages back at Ton Son Nhut; the file that Clarke had just handed him had seven. Cole looked for the two additional pages and found them straight away. One was a photocopy of the flight manifest which listed all the passengers on the flight to Bangkok; the other page was a copy of Goodcut's leave pass. These bits were nothing to go on, but that was usually the case. The hunt was just getting started and, in any event, he prided himself on starting a hunt with very few clues. The taste of the capture was always much more gratifying that way.

Cole ignored Clarke who was blurting out unsolicited information about the priest, and Clarke soon sensed that his usefulness in the case was coming to an end, squashing his secret desire to join the hunt. That was not going to happen.

He waited for Cole to finish skimming through the information in Captain Goodcut's file, and eyeballed his visitor as he was busy with the flight manifest. Clarke saw the long scar that ran down Cole's left cheekbone to the corner of his lip, a souvenir from a sucker punch by a pool cue in a Saigon bar that split his face open. He snuck a peek at Cole's decorations, and the tattoo on his left forearm: "Lover, Fighter, Wild Bull Rider," the letters circling an immodest saguaro cactus whose singular arm was formed into a shape of a huge penis, complete with two smaller lobes below the thorny member, presumably its balls. *Jesus peezus, this guy's got a lot of ribbons...* Cole looked up and tossed the file onto the top of his closed bag.

"I'll take this with me." Coltrane reached into his shirt pocket and pulled out a Camel and offered one to Clarke who hesitated at first, then stood up and pulled one out from Cole's outstretched pack. Cole lit them both up. Clarke did not smoke, but he would not let that be known if he could keep the smoke down. He had taken a shine to Cole and wanted to send the signal that "We're in this together."

Cole had seen this kind of admiration and envy before, and he played along, prompting Clarke to let loose a rehearsed statement about recommended accommodations and places to eat close to the Embassy. But again, Cole wasn't interested. He was going to grab this priest and get back to Vietnam in three days so he needed to get a move on.

Cole took two quick drags on the cigarette and then stood to shake Clarke's hand and, giving him a sharp look in the eye, he added, "Thanks, be seeing ya."

Clarke started to offer the usual salutation, "If you need anything –" but Cole cut him off. "No, I'll be fine. I just need to go and do what I have to do."

The remark caught Clarke off guard as he recalled Mordechai saying pretty much the same thing as he turned to leave Clarke's office, just a couple of weeks earlier. "Right..." Clarke started to say something else, but he was stuck in that memory. He rubbed the back of his head and stared at the brown tile floor before snapping out of it. "Oh, I forgot to tell you. The Thais are insisting that you must have a partner when you go looking for this priest."

Cole stopped in his tracks. He was halfway to the office door. "Come again?"

"Yeah, you will need to have a Thai Police partner. To help with the investigation. To translate. To sort out the logistics – to get you in-and-out of places you could not go by yourself."

"No fucking way, my friend. That's not gonna happen. I'm a solo act – I move fast, and I move by myself. That's how I operate."

"Sorry, Coltrane, but them's the rules. The Thais will not let you go gallivanting around the countryside, tipping over tables and burning down barns just to find this guy. You're gonna have to take 'em along. Like it or not."

"Look, I don't need anybody getting in my way. Under my feet. If I need some help with anything, I'll get a hold of the Embassy... I'll get a hold of you. But I'm not taking anybody with me."

"You can say what you want, but if they catch you acting independently after you've been told, they will PNG your ass and send you back to 'Nam without your priest. I ain't making this up. Serious shit, man."

Cole stood there for few seconds, taking another long drag on his cigarette.

He diverted, "Got a name of a decent hotel? Something cheap. No bugs. I need to get settled in before I start my work."

Clarke eyeballed him, thinking he was making headway with Cole. He wasn't. And he was about to reintroduce the troublesome reminder, *Remember, don't get started without your Thai shadow,* but the words didn't come out.

"Look," he finally said. "The Thais have already got someone lined up for you. They knew you were coming in, and our Ambassador – the big boy upstairs – is evidently good friends with the family of some hot-shot police investigator, and he's asked the Thai Police to select this person as your partner. He's made the request, personally. You really can't say no."

Cole looked at Clarke, wondering why he had name-dropped the Ambassador. *Probably some psychology bullshit this guy's trying to pull. But it ain't workin'.* So he asked again with a poker face, "Hotel?"

"Try the Rex on Sukhumvit. Most of the junior officers stay there. Not bad. Cheap. Decent food. Just tell the taxi to take you there. They all know where it is."

And Clarke added, "Stay in contact. Let us know what's happenin'. I'll tell the Thai Police that you're here. They'll be in touch with you at the hotel."

Fat fucking chance of that happening, thought Cole. "Yeah, right. Thanks for your time."

Cole grabbed his bag and started walking down the basement hallway. Clarke stood behind his desk shaking his head. But he secretly wanted to be like Cole. He envied the man and admired his swagger.

He took his first real puff on the smoke Cole had given him and tried to blow a smoke ring, but he only barked out four deep coughs and then sucked in air as quick as he could.

Fuck me! This damn thing tastes nasty! Clarke marched down to the john, tossed the Camel into the commode and gave it a quick flush. *Crazy bastard.*

* * * * *

Before heading for lunch, Clarke called the Thai Police at nearby Lumpini Station, the station where Major Siriwongdee worked. He let her know Coltrane was in town and that he was staying at the Rex. They should meet.

CHAPTER 12

Lumpini Police Station faces the largest urban park in Bangkok and derives its name from the Lumpini region in Nepal where Gautama Buddha was born. In 1971, that was 2,514 years ago. 543 years before the Christ. It was the Thai version of New York's Central Park, only set in the middle of a sultry concrete metropolis, reclaimed from a jungle in Southeast Asia.

Like most of the Bangkok Police stations built in the 1950s, it was a two-story concrete structure, painted black-and-white – as if the law itself were so easily defined. It was otherwise an unremarkable building in the heart of the city, a building whose architectural style had come and gone, its corrugated tile rooftop now green with moss and radio antennas which poked through the roof like aluminum stalagmites.

The small offices along the main corridor downstairs featured rows of metal filing cabinets, crammed with alphabetized reports created on black-and-red-ribboned mechanical typewriters. Tabletops were stacked with chipped and well-worn Motorola radios, crackling and snug in their chargers; clipboards with out-of-date notices hung in orderly rows along walls, and dusty ceiling fans spun over the desks of secretaries in tight brown skirts; pyrethrin smoke from green mosquito coils wafted about, and stray mangey dogs meandered around outside the building when not sleeping in the station's parking lot.

．　　．　　．　　．　　．

On the auspicious, east-facing walls of the senior offices upstairs, there were shelves which held collections of Buddhist images from various temples throughout the country. Each temple – particularly the large and famous temples – had their own style of statuary. The Commandant's office had the "top five" statues prominently displayed. This collection served as a sign, well-recognized by important visitors to his office, that he was in-the-know about the predominant and popular Buddhist iconography of the day.

His garishly painted office at the top of the cement stairs had shelves full of black binders containing highly detailed and unread reports produced by the novices and aspirants downstairs. The neat rows were interspersed with sets of brass plaques, colorful ribbons, and large trophies for civic awards – and for "best in league" football matches with rival police stations. The *muay Thai* boxing stadium was just three blocks away on Rama IV Avenue and, although the commandant was an avid fan and gambler, none of the trophies in his office had anything to do with boxing.

His office overlooked a small garden with two mature mango trees and a large, fox-tail palm with orchids growing around its long trunk. The garden was tended to by three, enlisted patrolmen who wore white, crew t-shirts with red collars and the insignia of the Royal Thai Police on their left breasts, over their hearts.

His uniform was impeccable, always crisply starched, and his patent-leather, ankle-high boots were kept in a constant state of mirror-like shine by the garden crew when not busy tending to his orchids. He imagined himself to be a "macho man," but to most of his subordinates he was a grubby little fellow with greasy hair combed back into a duck's butt, and a scruffy Charles Bronson mustache that he tugged at when nervous. He tried to convey his fanciful virile image with an exaggerated gait and swagger – a forced strut made more comical by his short, bowed legs. But nobody dared to laugh out loud.

• • • • •

The lockup at the Lumpini Station was downstairs at the end of the main hallway lined with twenty wooden doors, ten aside, painted with a dark-brown lacquer finish. Each door opened into small offices set aside for the more junior officers. The hallway was grimy with handprints and scuff marks, shoulder height, all the way from the booking desk in the front to the lockup in the back. It looked as if a major flood had left its dirty, high-water mark along the walls.

The station had two holding cells, one for Thais and another for *farangs*, foreigners. And the bars on the cells had uncountable coats of black-enamel paint which were, in spots, worn down to the bare metal beneath by prisoners grasping the rods while straining their necks to take in the daily commotion at the booking desk at the front of the building.

Most of the *farangs* who were tossed into the lockup were GIs who got in trouble at the nearby Patpong bar district – GIs who thought they could skip the local bribes. Usually, a few bucks would be enough to cheer up an incensed bar owner, clean up the broken glass and a busted chair or two, and keep the police cuffs off their wrists. But if the damages were substantial, and the cash was not flowing, the cops were called in. All the bar owners knew the score and were not quick to make the call. After all, they could earn an unwanted reputation for being too hard on the free-wheeling GIs. And that was bad for business.

• • • • •

Among the few unforgivable crimes that the Thais could not abide, offensive acts against Buddhist images were near the top of the list. And it was not only the loathsome defacement of these images, but also the illegal sale and export of rare and historical pieces, many from the Angkor period and the "Golden Age of Thai Buddhism." The Thais had seen the foreign movies and the magazines which featured Buddha statues in the homes of wealthy collectors, where they were used as hat racks or irreverently placed on the floor near someone's front door, amongst vile objects such as shoes and dripping umbrellas. Unscrupulous art dealers and smugglers had no compunction about removing these priceless statues from their ancient places of repose and bringing them to the black market in Bangkok.

To most Thais, such despicable acts betrayed one of the three main pillars that defined their country and culture: King, language, and Buddhism, and they were certain that there must be a scorching place in *narok,* Hell, for such persons. Foreigners knew the risks in trafficking antiquities, but the potential rewards often overpowered any sense of propriety, well-understood by even the youngest Thai schoolboy. And the two Belgians brought into the station that day had found it out the hard way.

Major Panthip Siriwongdee was sitting at her desk, three doors down from the Commandant's office when she got the call from the booking desk downstairs about the Belgians. She was halfway through her bowl of rice and vermicelli noodle soup her mother had made for her the night before.

Major Panthip, known as "Pip" to her peers and superior officers – those below her in rank wouldn't dare to address her so informally – was a beautiful woman, perhaps the most attractive the Commandant had seen in the many police stations he had worked in over the years. But she was not beautiful in the classical sense of the petite and pretty qualities that many Thai women her age projected.

She was, rather, a handsome woman with high cheek bones and large, wide-set eyes framed by thick eyebrows that ran in half-moons across her broad face. Her mouth and chin were reminiscent of the female Angkor statues one could see up-country, in Sukhothai. She had thick, full lips, parting downwards in round lines that would circle her perfect chin, jutting out from her flawless face. She was graced with a small mole just below, and to the right of the dimple on her left cheek; it was a dimple she only showed in smiles at home with her mother.

Her solitary window looked out onto the Commandant's small garden, and she could often catch sight of him sitting at his desk when the wind caught and lifted the branches of the mango tree shading his window. He would sit there in his executive-style chair with his feet on the desk, reading the *Thai Rath* newspaper and taking in the boxing matches, his horoscope, and the ads for full-body massages in the back few pages. In that order.

Today, he tossed the newspaper on his desk and came to his window, peering in the direction of Pip's office, and his presence caused her to stand up from her desk and move to the filing cabinet and away from his line-of-sight. He was an insecure and suspicious man, and he viewed her social standing and advanced level of education as a serious threat. Worse still, she was a successful woman in a man's world – an extremely competent and well-spoken woman – not to mention that she was easy on the eyes of everyone who met her.

It was risky for him to have such an accomplished subordinate at work, one who was both intuitive and knowledgeable and whose position was obtained by merit and not by brown-nosing or looking the other way when the situation demanded it. For the Commandant, it would have been far better to have a mediocre understudy than this steadily rising meteor.

Major Siriwongdee was, without doubt, well-situated within the Thai society and greatly outclassed the Commandant. Were it not for his rank, she would have been deferred to by all the others in the Station, an inescapable fact that rankled him. But Pip had no aspirations for his job, nor could she ever imagine wasting away her time at work, looking through the newspaper or strutting down the hallways with her hands clasped behind her back, absorbing the salutes and *wai*'s of the junior police staff.

•   •   •   •   •

Pip hung up the phone with the booking desk, picked up a newspaper from a stack on the wooden bench outside of the Commandant's office, and headed down the steps to the rear of the building, towards the lockup. She was sitting on a folding chair in the hallway in front of the holding cell for foreigners when the booking-desk sergeant brought the two Belgians back. She didn't glance up from her Thai newspaper as the jailer pushed them inside and locked the cell door.

"You stay here now," said the jailer in English. "Me come back with food. *Neung toom.*" Pointing at his watch, "se-*ven*, se-*ven*." The jailer had a lot in common with many of the cops on the beat, and this was especially true for the older cops in the station. Most had outgrown their uniforms issued long ago and the buttons down the front of their brown shirts were straining to hold back years of sedentary, station life and eating tons of *pa-tong-ko*, the Thai equivalent of fat-fried doughnuts with healthy doses of sweet, condensed milk syrup, poured from a tin can.

The two Belgians, one in his mid-fifties and the other about twenty-five, shuffled away from the cell door and sat down on the cement bench, next to a squat-plate toilet. They were taking in their new surroundings in silence, wondering how they were going to get sprung from their current fix. Not the kind of thing their embassy would rush to get involved with.

Pip was aware of the stakeout that had nabbed them – in fact, she had orchestrated the take down – and was glad to learn that the two Belgians were now in the tank. She had one of her undercover cops work with an antique dealer on nearby Silom Road, and her man had been trailing these two ever since they tried to get the store owner to broker the sale of two black-market Buddhist statues from the northeast part of the country. The Belgians had offered to pay $500 each for two stone busts which dated from the Angkor period, stolen from a temple near the Thai provincial town of Surin.

The dealer set up the buy and had arranged for the undercover cop to be in the store when the deal closed and the money changed hands. Turning in these guys to the cops was a pleasure for this semi-legitimate antique dealer whose primary trade was in old furniture, paintings, and other antique household items. The truth was, he probably had his own price where the cops would not be invited to the party, but it certainly wasn't $1,000 for these two exquisite busts.

The older of the two Belgians, the one with huge bags under his eyes, caught sight of Pip who was looking at page two of the paper, and he figured that French was a safe bet to speak to the younger fellow. He knew that very few Thai police could string together even a few words in English, and the chance of them speaking French was next to zero. He was dead wrong.

"*Merde!*" The older man said, and continuing in French he complained, "How the hell were we supposed to know that fucking guy was going to rat us out. The bastard!"

Looking at the younger man, a crewcut hustler from Brussels, he said, "We could have turned those statues into some big money back in Brussels, or in Paris. Probably a cool $5000. How could we be so stupid? Shit!"

"Yeah, well, *you're* the stupid fucker," said the younger one, again in French. "It was your idea in the first place to come over here and get involved in buying this stuff. It's got to be easier to smuggle dope out of this damn country than to sneak out with a couple of statues. You dumb shit!"

"Listen, you ungrateful little turd, I've taught you everything, everything I know about this business, and even ditched my brother to pull you in on this deal."

They both glanced at Pip who had just turned to page three, apparently deaf to the miserable complaints of the two Belgians.

"Some deal. You said lifting these statues out of here was like taking candy from a baby. That the Thai cops were too busy looking for mules and smack dealers. That they'd have no chance to catch us. What did you say? 'Bullet-proof,' right? Fuck. On top of that, you said that even if they caught us, all we had to do was to bribe the right cop or government guy and we could buy our way out." He paused, reaching for the cigarettes that were taken away from him at the booking desk. Finding none, he asked with scorn, "Any more bright ideas?"

"Listen, I've got about $2,500 cash in the room-safe back at our hotel, along with our passports. I know a guy I can call. He can get the money and dash over here. We just need to find the right pigeon so we can feather their nest."

With this, Pip rose from her chair and turned to face the two Belgians. She spoke in perfect and unbroken French, "I'm afraid your pigeons have all flown away – and now your chickens have come home to roost." Smiling at her skill in making the impromptu use of mixed metaphors, she went on, "You won't be going anywhere, anytime soon, and we're going to your hotel now and collect your passports – and the cash."

The two Belgians' mouths popped open and hung there, slack-jawed. They were dumbfounded. "You, you...," began the older one, pointing at her with the index finger on his right hand.

Pip turned on her heels and winked at the younger one over her shoulder and added in English, "And thanks for the contribution to the King's charity for rural orphans. Your $2,500 donation will feed a lot of children."

After a long pause and when his mouth started working again, the older one said in a soft, stunned voice, "son-of-a-bitch."

She started to head back down the hallway and up to her office on the second floor but stopped and returned to the two men. The younger one was now grasping the worn bars and staring through the gap at her in disbelief.

She told them in French, "Let me give you something to consider, something to think about while you are waiting here, and while you spend some time in our prisons." And she added for emphasis, "Oh yes, your next stop will most likely be in one of our nice prisons."

At the very thought of this, the younger one shuddered. The older one blanched and half-turned away.

"You, sir," speaking to the older one. "Here is something for you. We have a saying in Thailand. It goes like this, '*plaa mor taai proh baak.*' It means that the perch fish dies because of its mouth. If we are indiscrete and use our mouths unwisely, the fisherman will catch us easily. So, you should be careful when you speak and what you say, or you will find yourself in trouble. Hooked. Caught. Do you understand?"

He didn't reply. He could only turn his back fully away. From this new position he could see through the bars to the very top of the fox-tail palm in the station's courtyard garden.

Turning to the younger man, the Major said, "And as for you... a monkey who is born in the trees will spend his whole life in the trees, swinging from vine-to-vine and foraging for fruit high up in the canopy. But sometimes, through his own errors and mistakes, he falls and hits the ground to the hoots and hollers of his friends. But it is not a bad thing to fall from a tree if a monkey learns what his mistake was – and does not repeat it. Then it is worth the fall and the embarrassment. Do you understand? We say, '*ling tok dton maai.*' A monkey falls from the tree. This is our expression."

The younger man craned his neck to see Police Maj. Panthip walk down the hallway leading to the stairs and up to her office. The sound of her heels on the cement floor made a rhythmical, clacking sound which could be heard above the normal racket of the police station, and this was somehow calming to the young man – but that sound irritated the hell out of the older thief.

·   ·   ·   ·   ·

When Pip returned to her desk and finished her noodles, she got the phone call from Clarke at the US Embassy. She was expecting his call. The Commandant had invited her into his office yesterday afternoon and informed her that she was going to be assigned to work on a priority project with the US Embassy. She was to accompany a US Army lieutenant coming from Vietnam to arrest a runaway soldier, an officer, evidently a captain.

The Commandant seemed confident and pleased with himself when he gave Pip her orders, but it was her nature to resist encroachment on her freedoms – the freedom to organize and plan her own work – and she launched several objections why she could not accept this assignment. And she ended it with the protest, "I'm sorry, sir, but as you know, I am currently bogged down with several cases involving the illegal movement of cultural artifacts, and the theft of some very famous images from up-country. We believe these are transiting Bangkok, en route to foreign markets –"

He wasn't listening. He knew she was difficult to read and was skilled at the art of masking her true feelings – and that she crafted her words with great deliberation and skill. Worse still, the Commandant knew *she was adept at winning arguments by using complicated words.* She could easily outfox him if he wasn't careful. He was growing nervous and circumspect.

Pip was well into her counter argument, "… and we must ensure that this type of activity is cut off at the source, that it is -"

But the Commandant was insistent and he interrupted, "Look. Of all the officers here, only you have the qualities of personality, language skills, and perseverance that are required for this assignment. And besides, the American Embassy has made a personal request for assistance from our Headquarters, and since we are closer to the Embassy than any of the other Police Districts, we have been chosen."

He had no qualms about pretending that her selection was his personal idea, so he added, "And I, in turn, have chosen you. It is a great honor. You should be grateful for this opportunity – not to mention that our laws require us to accompany foreign investigators while they are on sovereign, Thai soil."

Charles Bronson was only too happy when the Commanding General at Police HQ called and asked him to "volunteer" Major Siriwongdee, per the US Embassy's request. It was a chance to sideline the elusive and uppity Major for the time this investigation would take. And besides, he was not making any progress with his furtive glances at her through his window, or by peeping in on her during his armless walks down the second-floor hallway. Here was a woman that held her own. She was rock solid, and that fact twisted his underwear.

"But, sir," Pip countered, "I really -"

That was it. Sensing that she was gaining the upper hand with her objections against this assignment, he decided to pull rank and awkwardly ended the discussion by rising from his chair and dismissing her by flicking out the fingers of his right hand. "This guy, Mr. Clarke or Lieutenant Clarke… I don't know… will call you from the US Embassy, once this investigator guy arrives from Vietnam. Dismissed."

•   •   •   •   •

When Clarke called the next day and told Pip that Coltrane had arrived, he gave her only a few of the case details he was able to put together from Mordechai's file. He also shared a preview about Coltrane, gathered from the brief phone conversation he had with Hargraves' office back in Ton Son Nhut, Vietnam. Clarke told her that Coltrane "…was kind of like a bounty hunter – some kind of a cowboy from New Mexico…" from what he understood.

Pip conjured up a picture of what that could mean. It was probably an apt description, but not a good one. She detested men with swagger.

Clarke mentioned that this investigator was about five years older than her, but he was only a 1st Lieutenant. He heard the objections in Pip's voice, and perhaps shoring her up as the superior officer might allay some of that resistance. It didn't work. She had already developed an unsavory picture of some self-assured, *cocky butthole* that she needed to accompany around Thailand. She was an unwilling partner for this interloper. But she finally asked in resignation, "For how long?"

Pip had a decided bias against Americans. Although she was born and raised there and went to the best US universities for her BA and Masters, she was fed up with American culture and the opulence and self-absorption that it represented. It was the antithesis of the beauty and grace she knew her Thai culture embodied. And a heartbreaking romantic relationship at the end of her high school days was the cherry on top of a bitter, inedible cake.

She had even fantasized about taking her US passport down to the Chaophraya River, burning the pages, and then scattering the ashes of a dead and forgotten life into the waters that flowed out to the Gulf of Siam. *Who knows, maybe a speck or two of those protesting ashes would eventually wash up on the beach of Southern California.* She was angry for being saddled with this burdensome assignment and made mental notes to get it over as quickly as possible.

"I don't really know," replied Clarke. "I guess a week or so. You'll need to take that up with Lt. Coltrane when you make contact with him. He seems pretty determined to wrap this up quickly, but I know he doesn't have a lot to go on, save that this runaway he's chasing is a Catholic priest and Army Captain. See, you outrank them both!"

"Besides," continued Clarke, "my guess is that you're exactly the right person for this job." And she was, without question. In addition to her language and practical skills, she was a trained marksman in long guns and pistols and had taken several certificate courses in hand-to-hand combat at the police training academy. More important, she had extensive knowledge and connections within the Buddhist community throughout the country due to her department's work in antiquities protection. But Clarke had no way of knowing that. He was merely trying to butter her up, and that was getting under her skin.

Clarke could hear her on the other side of the line, draw in a deep breath, trying to let it out very slowly so as not to let her irritation show. "OK, OK. Fine, fine." She had heard enough.

"So, when and where do I meet this cowboy? This so-called bounty hunter? And what info do you have on the priest? Send me what you have."

CHAPTER 13

The sun appeared in the east-morning sky of Bangkok, after it had first baked fishermen in the South China Sea, the paddies and Highlands of Vietnam, and then the sprawling campus of Angkor Wat in Cambodia. It finally rose like a scalding hole in the Thai sky, egg-yolk yellow, radioactive, and burning everything and everyone in its daily east-west traverse along Sukhumvit Road.

But by this time, Pip was already up for more than an hour. She had been to the market to buy rice-and-pork porridge for her mother, taking the dilapidated local bus that ran up-and-down the red laterite road that terminated at *Talaat Udomsuk*, the Udomsuk market on Sukhumvit Road.

Her home was a large wooden, two-story traditional house in a neighborhood that the Siam Commercial Bank had developed five years earlier in an attempt to "settle" the suburbs of Bangkok, providing upscale housing for those higher up in the social order of things. Her father knew members on the management board of the bank and was able to secure the property and house for a fraction of its market value. Pip was not exactly born with a silver spoon, but close.

• • • • •

From the bus stop to her home, it was a five-minute walk and Pip enjoyed the daily routine: the morning shower, dressing in her police uniform, the trip to the market on the bus, the chatter of the street vendors selling their goods, the trip back down the dirt road, and the contrast of that red road with the blue and white sky. These were the colors of her flag.

But most of all, she liked the smell of the charcoal stoves that were being lit and getting ready to warm the day's meals in the kitchens of small homes hidden in the thick green vegetation. You could always smell the stoves and hear the clank of thin metal lids on cooking pots before you could see the houses themselves. So much like Thailand itself, you were made aware of something by senses other than sight. And the nose, time and again, ruled those five senses. The country was a place full of hidden objects, sometime never seen with the eyes or touched by the hands at all.

Pip rounded the corner of the side street leading to the bus stop and entered the cluster of gated homes. She always brought home sweet desserts for the security guards manning the front gate of her *moobahn*, her village. The guards were, after all, in the same business as she was: watching and protecting Thai treasures. Pip looked after national treasures; the security guards looked after her personal treasures – her mother and her home.

But the similarities quickly ended there. Most of the guards were ex-Army enlisted men who had taken these low-paying jobs to make ends meet. And they lived in small, nearby shacks with corrugated tin roofs. Their wives were now up making rice and the day's meals in thin-lid cooking pots, warmed over charcoal stoves.

She drew near to her home with the warm plastic bag of rice porridge bouncing against her thigh, and the houseboy, a retired army sergeant who had worked for and adored her father, rushed to the front of the house and opened the sliding metal gate. He had a damp washrag draped over his shoulder and a trail of water dripped behind him, back to the wash bucket next to the light blue Toyota he had been washing.

"*Sawatdee khrap, Khun* Pip, Good morning, Miss Pip," he said as he raised his hands to *wai* her in greeting.

"*Sawatdee kha, Leung* Chean, Good morning, Uncle Chean," Pip replied, using familial terms for naming people that accorded great importance and respect to one's age.

"I've just come from the market." Which was obvious and understood by *Leung* Chean since Pip did this every morning. Still, she would start their brief morning exchange this way, with an explanation about where she had been to set the stage for what she was to say next. "I've brought these *sang-ka-ya* desserts for you. Your favorite: pumpkin with sweet, burnt onions on top."

It would have otherwise been rude to simply hand the desserts to him. That would have sounded, without the polite words, something like, "Here! Take it!" And this way of talking would never do. Pip, as with most well-educated Thais, understood the deference accorded to her status, wealth and position, but she never fell in with the privileges and abuses such status offered. She was far too culturally adept to come across with a superior mien, even though the social distance would have allowed her to say such a thing – as many others in her position would do.

Her boss at work was probably barking orders for his house servants at the very same time Pip ascended the stairs in her home, carrying a tray with the porridge, a glass of orange juice she had fetched from the fridge in the kitchen, and five pieces of peeled rambutan her mother loved to eat. She knew better than to ask *Leung* Chean if her mother was up yet. It would not be his place to know so, or to say anything about that.

She knocked on the door of her mother's room. "*Maa ja?* Mother dear, are you up?" She knew full well her mother would have been up long ago, once she heard Pip opening the metal gate that morning. She would have gone to the window and followed Pip up the side street to the bus stop. Only then would she fully rise, shower and start planning her daily activities with Pip's Aunt Tui who lived in a separate apartment on the compound.

While Pip was away at the market, *Leung* Chean would bring the daily newspaper up to her mother's room and leave it outside on the teakwood table which stood against the wall, opposite her door. On the wall above the table there was a black-and-white photo of her husband in full military regalia, and just below that impressive picture, there was a small wooden shelf that held his urn. *Leung* Chean had performed the daily newspaper delivery for years and it was an unbroken routine that was performed simply out of respect for her father's spirit.

Pip's mother did not read the newspaper. In Thailand, most women did not. This task was a man's job – to stay up on the news, the price of rice, the effects of the nearby war in Vietnam and neighboring Cambodia, the boxing match scores, the latest lottery numbers, and items of interest in the real estate section – perhaps sneaking a quick peek at the pictures in the personal ads.

Pip kept only a few of her father's bones in the urn. The rest of his ashes were scattered according to his wishes in the Bang Pakong River which flows next to the famous temple at *Wat Sothon* in the city of Chachoengsao. He loved that temple and its statuary because it was where he once experienced a miracle cure for heart dysrhythmia while lying there, prostrate, praying to the highly revered *Luang Por* statue in the main sanctuary. Pip was with him when it happened and recalled the tears of happiness and relief running down his wrinkled, brown face. His final wish was that his ashes be placed in the river there, as an offering of respect for the temple that gave him back his life, his wife and his Pip, their only child.

She thought of her father every day and would often find herself gazing over at his picture on her desk at work. It was a picture of her graduation from Yale where she had earned her Master of Fine Arts in Asian Folklore. It was her favorite picture. Those were good times.

But his hand was firm then. Her father had insisted that she learn the Thai language and Thai culture along with her studies in English and French and, by the time she graduated from high school, she was fluent in the languages of three countries and knew their respective cultures and histories in intimate detail.

It was no surprise to anyone that, after her graduation, she made the solemn pledge to serve her country in the Royal Thai Police, her father insisting that she devote her career in a branch that saw less exposure to physical violence. He knew that real police work was a very dirty and dangerous business. *"No telling who the bad guys were,"* he would say. It could be a gangster contractor trying to bribe his way into a lucrative contract deal, or it could be the guy in the next office – or three offices down. *Who knew?*

Her father wanted to keep her away from dangerous-crimes enforcement, and instead urged her to join the police task force in charge of protecting antiquities from destruction and unlawful export. At first, she resisted her father's wishes, but later yielded to his urgings and to the family tradition that would rule her life: to become a public servant who would preserve and hold as treasures, all things "Thai." In her heart, she knew this was her duty above all else. It was for her King. Her father was right.

•　　•　　•　　•　　•

Her mother's housegirl, a young Burmese girl named *Noi*, opened the door and greeted Pip with a bow and a *wai*. Pip smiled and handed the tray over to her.

"Mom, I have to go to a meeting today, and I may be late getting home."

"Pip dear, what was that?"

"I said I have to go to a meeting this morning – to meet an American officer who is in Thailand on official business. And I've been asked to meet him. Well, Commandant Supot has directed me to go. It is important, and I need to represent the government."

With these last words, her mother came to the door and met Pip's eyes. "Well, it is good that they finally recognize your talents and that you are called upon to represent the government. I'm sure your father would have been very proud to know this."

Her mother glanced through the open door and behind Pip to a picture of her husband on the wall, above the teakwood table with the stack of unread newspapers. Pip looked up from her shoes and followed her mother's glance to her father's urn and picture, and she smiled.

"Yes, I am sure Dad would have approved."

Realizing the time was going fast, she added, "I'll need to take the bus and a cab. The place of the meeting is on Sukhumvit Road."

She was not about to tell her mother she was meeting this American at a hotel. "So, I will leave my car here and I'll ask *Leung* Chean to come up and see what you'd like for lunch. He can go to the market and get something for you."

"*Mai, noo*, No, dear. That won't be necessary. Aunt Tui and I are going to go to the Army Officers Wives' Club today. There is a function to raise some money for orphans in the Northeast." Pip's thoughts ran to the two Belgian "donors" in the lockup at the Lumpini Police Station and a small smile came to her face.

"It is too bad you cannot come," her mother said. "I'm sure my friends would love to see you."

"Yes, mom… well, maybe some other day. But I'd better get moving along now. I would not want to be late for my meeting – it is set for 10am. And the traffic on Sukhumvit, going into the city today will be bad if I don't hurry along."

"OK dear, well *dern taang plort phai,* travel safely," her mother said, while smiling at her beautiful and successful daughter, all dressed up in her police uniform. *Wasn't she marvelous!*

And with that her mother turned back to the room and her perfume table and applied two doses from three different, imported bottles while she looked at the selection of dresses *Noi* had laid out on the bed.

Pip added over her shoulder and as she left the doorway, "Mom, please don't forget to eat your porridge before it gets cold – you need to eat something before you take your pills."

"*Ja, ja.* OK dear, I will."

Pip brought her hands together in a *wai* while bowing a few degrees at the waist. "Be safe, mommy."

Her mother had since turned her attention away from the array of perfumes to the row of pill bottles. Her favorite doctor at Samitivej Hospital was an old and honored woman neurologist who had kept her on a regimen of pills for vertigo and blood pressure issues for years. Pip was concerned her mother bordered on being a hypochondriac, if not a full-blown case already. But she indulged her since the pills actually seemed to help – at least they were a psychological boost, filling in the void that followed the death of her husband.

Pip came downstairs and passed by the kitchen where she saw Aunt Tui peering into the refrigerator. It was her regular habit, before greeting anyone in the house, to run to the fridge to see what was inside. She would stand there, captivated, staring for minutes as if something miraculous was about to happen. Perhaps the roasted duck leftovers from the night before would reanimate themselves and announce an ice-cold prophesy. This habit of Aunt Tui irked Pip to no end.

"Good Morning, Aunt Tui," said Pip as she passed behind the kitchen table, lifting her hands to *wai* her aunt, before moving towards the kitchen door and out to the driveway where *Leung* Chean was finishing up the morning's car wash.

"Oh, good morning, Pip." Said Tui, not returning the *wai*, which was appropriate social protocol. One rarely *wai'*ed a person younger or of a lower station, and it was normal for Tui not to do so since that reinforced her position within the family's hierarchy as Pip's mother's sister. And she was the only surviving sister – the other sister and two of her three brothers were killed during the Japanese occupation of Thailand during the Second World War, just 30 years earlier.

"Hope you and mom have fun today at the Club," said Pip. Tui eyed her for any note of sarcasm in Pip's comments. Pip had often expressed concern to her mother that Aunt Tui was riding on the family's good nature and wealth and rarely reached for her own wallet when it came to paying for excursions. And no doubt the trip to the Club today was going to be an all-day, expense-paid vacation for her aunt.

Her aunt's conduct rankled Pip, but she was now a master at disguise when she needed to be – although her aunt was much better at the game and could detect even a minute amount of sarcasm if it were to leak out. But today, Pip got a pass. She was preoccupied with what was going to happen next that morning, with the slog through the rush-hour traffic, and the meeting with *this American cowboy*.

"Goodbye, *Leung* Chean" she shouted as she opened the metal gate in the front of her house and headed up the small side street towards the bus stop.

"Goodbye, *Khun* Pip, *khrap*," replied *Leung* Chean. "*Choke dee, khrap!* Good luck!" She was rare, and the house staff loved her.

Yes, I'm going to need some good luck today, thought Pip.

•   •   •   •   •

Pip waited until the bus made a full stop at the Udomsuk street market before she stepped down and out. She had seen too many eager riders hop off before the bus came to a complete stop, only to trip and fall face-first in the mud of the market street drains. And a face-plant in those festering puddles would probably decrease your life span by a good five years.

She gave her preparations for the morning's meeting a quick review. The taxi from the intersection at Sukhumvit 103 to the Rex Hotel would be a bit more expensive than the bus, but once out of the confines of her neighborhood it would appear more seemly for a police major to take a two-tone taxi rather than a beat-up bus. And she had called the hotel the night before trying to contact Coltrane, but he was not in. Not surprised, she left a message that she would meet him at the hotel's restaurant at 10 sharp. She had also brought along her "James Bond Bag," the Thai expression for a briefcase, although it had little inside related to the runaway priest except for some basic HR docs Clarke had sent over, a few black-and-white photos from the airport, and some run-of-the-mill custom forms.

On the taxi ride to the Rex Hotel, she fended off the probing small talk of the nosey cab driver who pestered her for personal details as if that were part of the ride program – part of his "entertainment package" for the two-hour-long grind through Bangkok's notorious traffic. But at least she was now inbound to the "*City of Angels, on the Banks of the Chaophraya River*," she mused over that elegant preamble for the ceremonial name for *Krung Thep*, Bangkok – the twenty-one-word name all Thai school children learn by heart.

Pip was trying to draw a picture in her mind of this American lieutenant and his mission. She had received scant details from Clarke at the Embassy and her curiosity was growing, along with a feeling of aggravation caused by this diversion from her normal duties. She did not have a lot of experience with men, and even less experience with American men. The ones she knew at high school in Washington DC, and at college in New Jersey and New Haven, were uncultured and shallow. They were too easy to read and lacked the genuine mystery and strength she needed for a deep relationship.

Her social life as a police major in Thailand limited her to even narrower circles, and pickings within those circles were worse than those in the States. Still, there was something odd and curious about the idea of a cowboy from New Mexico, a possible war hero, and perhaps someone as dedicated to a cause as she was.

But she quickly buried those thoughts under her cap as she popped open the cab's rear door and slid across the plastic seat cover. She came around the driver's side and paid him exactly the negotiated price, 30 baht, about $1.44. No more, and no less. *No tip for this perverted old prune who's been eyeballing me in the mirror for the past two hours.* He had even adjusted the rearview mirror about five minutes into the trip to get a better view of her skirt.

"Here you go, old-timer," she said as she dropped the one brown and one green note into his wrinkled paw. "Next time, pay more attention to the road. We could have arrived quicker if you spent less time staring at my legs and more time negotiating the traffic."

The old man simply grinned, showing his three beetle-nut stained teeth protruding from his lower jaw. His head looked like the figure from the "prehistoric man" display case she had once seen on a school field trip to the New York Museum of Natural History. Nothing he could say would have saved him from her glare. He was caught red-handed and would probably be imagining her fetching face as he drifted off to sleep that night, under his mosquito net in the *Klong Toey* slum.

Pip was definitely a striking figure, and as she walked in front of the cab and entered the hotel restaurant – the meeting place set up by Clarke – she caught the attention of the few American officers who were sober enough to be up at 10am. The concierge greeted her formally, knowing better than to publicly ogle a police major.

*Wai'*ing her, the concierge said, "*Sawatdee khrap*, Good Morning. May I help you?"

She smiled but did not return the *wai*, and said, "*Sawatdee kha*, I'm here to meet with an American Army Lieutenant named Coltrane. We have an appointment at 10."

The concierge looked at the wall clock that hung behind the bar, off to the left. It was 10am sharp.

"One moment, please. I'll try to find him. Would you please like to have a seat?" He was still in his formal mode of address. In his job, he could slide up-and-down the spectrum of smooth talk and respect, depending on the status of the person with whom he was speaking, and whether they had any tip money they were tired of carrying around. The junior American officers at the Rex often handed him a scattering of notes because they couldn't be bothered sorting out the unfamiliar "funny money." If he was very lucky, there would be a red note or two, worth about five dollars each in those wads of cash.

This police major had no tip money for him, but here was a person who deserved respect – *no telling what she is really doing here. No telling with whom she has connections.* He didn't dare offend her and therefore kept the brief exchange cordial and light. No wisecracks or off-color jokes. He directed her to the best table by the window. It was bright and away from the bar.

"May I bring you a menu?"

"No thanks, I'm here for a meeting. I might order a coffee, but later."

The concierge smiled and bowed slightly and then scurried off behind the bar and spoke into the ear of the bargirl, who then stared in Pip's direction before correcting herself with a respectful nod of her head.

Pip placed her briefcase on the table and opened it. She had about a dozen black-and-white photos of crime scenes from vandalized temples in the Northeast. She was shuffling through these when the bargirl brought an orange-and-mango juice drink to the table.

"*Khun Nai*, ma'am, this is a complimentary drink for you." She *wai*'ed and left the glass slowly on the table without making the slightest noise.

Pip looked up and said, "*Khob jai mahk, nong*, thank you, young lady." She watched the bargirl as she went back to the bar, carrying the tray in her right hand, tucked under her armpit.

Pip tasted the fruit juice. So sweet. Always the same at hotels which did not invest in preparing their own fresh drinks. *Par for the course,* as her father used to say.

She stared out the restaurant window at the traffic jam which had slowed the taxis, buses and the few private sedans to a halt in the quicksand morass of Sukhumvit Road. Pip was glad that she didn't take her own car to the hotel – her little Baby Blue that *Leung* Chean was home babysitting today.

She glanced at her watch. By this time, her mother and Aunt Tui would have left for the Officers Wives' Club get-together. *I wonder if they're stuck in this traffic.* Her brows knitted when she thought of her mother sitting in her friend's Mercedes Benz, stuck solid in this traffic. But she relaxed into a smile when she pictured her aunt in the same predicament, probably nagging at her friend's driver during the entire trip. Poor man. She lifted the glass for another small sip of the orange juice when she saw the concierge approaching her table.

"I'm sorry, I've asked the other tables here for this Mr. Coltrane, but it seems he has not come to the restaurant yet."

Pip knitted her brows again. It was 10:20.

•   •   •   •   •

She had enough of waiting. It was close to 11 and this American guy was a no-show. So much for Clarke. So much for her Commandant back at Lumpini Police Station. She headed for the hotel driveway and was about to call for a cab and go back to her office when she caught sight of the front desk in the lobby. Her police training – and her natural doggedness – kicked in. She walked inside.

"Do you have an American Lieutenant, named Coltrane, staying here?" she asked the chubby shift manager who had just come out of the elevator and was headed for his station.

The portly man did not skip a beat as he went behind the front desk and took a look at his ledger book. He was very young and looked completely out of place. He had apparently inherited the uniform of his predecessor, obviously a much taller fellow since the jacket, frayed at the collar, hung over his shoulders like an overcoat; his hands were barely visible, just his fingers protruding at the cuffs. He looked more like the butcher's son she knew from the market. This plump little fellow was definitely not managerial material. He was too broad-faced and happy, like the fat Chinese Buddha who liked to have his stomach rubbed.

But the young man was good natured and took Pip's question without blinking. "Yes, we have a Lieutenant Coltrane staying here. Checked in yesterday," he confirmed, looking up from the neat, red and black pencil entries on the ledger. "He's in room 357."

An auspicious number, thought Pip – since numbers with all odd digits are favored by the Thais, compared with the even and symmetrical 2, 4, 6, 8. And it didn't escape her that it was also the caliber of a Smith & Wesson pistol she had once seen in a gun magazine. It was her fantasy weapon of choice. They both glanced up at the pigeon-hole key box on the wall behind the front desk. The key for room 357 was not there.

"I think he took it when he went out last night. Yes, I remember this guy – at least I think it was him. He was kind of tall and had a *doot,* mean, look in his eyes. Like he was angry about... something. I think he was saying something like 'no good whisky.' I don't remember exactly. But anyway, he took the key. Not normal."

He turned away from the key box on the wall and faced Pip again, smiling, which allowed for a longer period of direct eye contact with the police major. She did not return his smile.

He went on, a little more nervous, "This guy looked quite drunk – if this is the same fellow. He and two other Americans were drinking in the restaurant's bar and two of them left together about 9 last night – about the time I came on duty."

"I see," said Pip. And then she thought, *Well, what's the chance he's in his room? That he simply came back and went up to his room without this pudgy fellow seeing him. He's probably upstairs. Simple as that.* She prompted the shift manager, "Let's go upstairs and see if he's there."

He paused for an instant, trying to read Pip's face, and his eyebrows shot up involuntarily. She was serious.

"OK, sure. Uh… We can go and see."

"*Dee mahk,* very good then," said Pip.

And with that they both walked across the lobby to the hotel lifts. Only one of two elevators was working in the seven-story building that morning. The Otis Elevator Company had cordoned off an area in front of the second lift, and two men in blue overalls had propped open the doors and were peering up into the darkness, shouting to a third man somewhere up in the shaft.

"We'll take this one," the manager said as the doors of the first elevator rumbled open.

They arrived on the 3rd floor and Pip followed the young man, watching him for any missteps and odd talk. But the happy fellow led her straight to the front of room 357.

He started to knock but Pip signaled him not to, and said in a hushed voice, "*Mai pen rai, kha,* no problem, I can take it from here." She stared at him for the extra second it took for her meaning to become clear.

He opened his mouth slightly as if to say, "Oh, OK." But no sound came out. He bowed slightly towards Pip and then hurried back to the elevator and to the teakwood front desk on the reassuring, smooth marble floor below.

Pip stared at the door for a long time, steeling herself for what was about to happen. She liked adventure alright, *but this was a major and inconvenient pain in the butt.* Then she made her move with three sharp knocks. Nothing. She repeated, knocking even louder the second time.

"What?! What the hell?! Go away!" came the slow and labored voice from inside the room. "Go away!"

CHAPTER 14

She knocked again. And then again. The door swung open and inside the room an empty Singha beer bottle went spinning across the tile floor until it hit, neck first, against the wooden floorboard near the balcony window. Cole followed the bottle's trajectory. Pip didn't take her eyes off the American who now stood in front of her, holding a floor mat from the bathroom across his waist with his left hand, still clutching the doorknob with his right.

"Look! I hung the 'do-not-disturb' sign out already! No Service! No –" he turned his head away from the now-motionless bottle to look at the "hotel maid" standing in front of him. The Singha dead soldier was one of many from last night.

He had been out on the prowl for some Highland mash, but only found the Singha and two pints of rotgut Mekong Whisky – and the young girl whose head now popped out, upside down, from the sheets at the foot of the bed. She began a groaning noise like she made last night, only this time in earnest, and stumbled naked out of bed, fleeing to the bathroom and slamming shut the wooden louvered door behind her.

Cole straightened himself as the apparition in front of him came into focus. *Why the hell was this woman wearing a uniform? Looks like a cop, for fuck's sake.*

Pip stood in the doorway looking at the zoo inside and at the sorry excuse for an officer standing in front of her, floor mat for a towel, covering most of his front, but not without noticing that he had to grasp himself with the mat to keep it from falling off and exposing his mood. Still, Pip stood there. Quiet, with her hands at her side. Her briefcase at her right foot.

"My name is Major Panthip Siriwongdee. I have been assigned to work with you while you are in Thailand. We had an appointment. We were supposed to meet in the restaurant downstairs about an hour ago. You have kept me waiting. Did you forget?"

Cole's brains had been removed from his skull sometime last night and placed in a canopic jar – the one used to hold that gray matter during mummification. This surgery must have occurred sometime after he had returned home with the 18-year-old hooker, and before he placed the empty Singha beer bottle by the door as a trip alarm. On the coffee table by the sofa were five tall, empty bottles of beer, an ashtray crammed with about 20 butts, many with red lipstick, a half-eaten plate of fried cashew nuts, and two ripped-open packs of ribbed Trojans. Pip took all this in from the front door. She didn't flinch.

Meanwhile, Cole kept searching for his brains. He was sure they were here, somewhere. He finally found what he thought were a few pieces, and he stuffed them back in by poking a finger into his ear, situating the brain parts in their normal resting place. Cole rubbed his eyes and yawned wide like a disinterested baboon. He walked to the coffee table leaving the door open and Pip standing there. Finding a cigarette that wasn't soaked through by the Whisky Sour kicked over during the wee-hour's sexual antics, he lit it with his Zippo. Facing away from the door, his ass was hanging out the backside of the floor mat.

Pip sucked in a full breath that flowed out slowly, and she started to repeat her intro. But Cole cut her words out. His brains were talking to him again.

His first thought came to him like a message in the 8-Ball game he played as a child, where you ask a question, shake the plastic 8-Ball, and an answer then floats into view in the ball's window. The message that floated to the window of his 8-Ball now was that the guy at the embassy… *Clarke, yeah, his name was Clarke…* had said some police guy was going to meet him at the hotel this morning… *and something like 10 o'clock* was the next message that floated into view. He returned to the door. He took a long drag on the Camel and had another look at the visitor standing in his doorway.

"Shit!" He said out loud, now remembering he was supposed to meet his police counterpart at 10am – at the hotel restaurant.

His aggressive, alcohol-boosted flex diminished a bit, as did his mood. He pulled the floor mat more squarely even as if it were an actual towel. He peered over the shoulder of the person in his doorway, both to the left and right, looking for this police guy.

"I beg your pardon," said Pip. "You're late for our meeting," she repeated.

Cole's eyes narrowed. "'Our meeting?' Not sure what you mean by '*our* meeting'." He took another drag and blew the exhaust down and away from Pip. "Are you with this… uh… police major guy? Where is he, anyways?"

Pip took a half step towards Cole, as if the closer distance would help him see her more clearly.

Cole retreated the same half-measure, backing away to keep her in focus.

"Look, *I am* the police major assigned to work with you. There's nobody else. No '*guy*.' Just me. Why don't you get a bigger bath towel and then come downstairs? I'll wait another half-hour for you, and after that I'll go back to my office and file my report, saying that 'I couldn't find you because you failed to make the appointment.' I imagine that will make Clarke – and your embassy – extremely happy."

With this she bent sideways at the waist and picked up her briefcase, turned towards the elevator and marched away.

Cole was dumfounded. *Get fucked-up the first night in Bangkok. Screwed 20 ways by that teenage whore – who's now in the bathroom barfing up her guts. Next, I'm told off by some smart-ass police broad...* He propped his hand against the door frame and stared at the gaudy, pink tile floor, taking another deep drag on his smoke. He was putting the tiger back in the cage. He knew what had to come next.

OK... Got to get my shit together. Get it together, dude. You're here on a hunt. He sucked in another draw on the cigarette. *OK. Right. I'm here for the hunt,* his thoughts repeated. He pulled in a final long breath without the smoke, shook his head and said, "Fuck me, yes!"

He popped his head out of the door frame and looked to his right, just in time to see Pip standing inside the elevator with her back against its mirrored wall, holding her briefcase with both hands in front of her, as if she were covering up her female attributes. She saw Cole's head pop out, then dart back into the room once they made eye contact. She heard his door slam shut before the elevator doors rumbled to. It was 11:17. She would wait until 12 and then leave.

Cole dropped the floor mat and went to the bathroom door in his room. "Hey, little darlin'." He tried the door. It was locked. "I need to take a shower now."

He tried the door again and heard the cylinder in the knob pop open. The girl had gotten up from her knees at the head of the bowl and was wiping her mouth with a white towel hanging on the wooden rack. It was stained with her lipstick on one edge, and with her black mascara on the other.

"Hey, you OK? You no smile." Cole made a goofy face at her, drawing up the corners of his mouth with his index fingers.

But the girl was nervous and agitated, having seen the policewoman standing in the doorway and speaking English.

"Me no want trouble. I go. I go," she repeated. And she slid her splendid naked body past his and made it to the pile of clothes at the far end of the bed. Cole turned on the shower knob and started to hop in, but he had second thoughts.

He came back into the room and sat on the bed and watched this girl as she got dressed. *She's beautiful. So simple.* Just four pieces: panties, jeans, bra and t-shirt. She took the brush from her purse and gave her hair a few pulls.

Cole glanced at his wallet, half poking its head out from the back of his pants, like a prairie dog. He walked over to it, pulled it from the rear pocket and reached for three, red 100 baht notes.

"Here. You call room service. Order you some breakfast. Take it easy. Don't worry about that police. Nothing to do with you."

She cocked her head to listen for the authority in his voice. It was there, and she paused for a few seconds and put down her brush, glancing at the money he held out in his hand. But the fear of dealing with the police rushed over her again and she grabbed her purse on the sofa and headed for the door.

"Woah there! *Jai yen yen.* Cool down." He tried the one phrase he heard over-and-over in the Patpong bars last night. It was like a code word for, "be cool." A phrase all foreigners knew within their first few hours in Thailand. "No worry about that policewoman. I her boss, OK? She work for me."

The young girl paused again, but only for a heartbeat. She moved quickly for the door but Cole cut her off. "OK, OK then." He reached deeper in his wallet and handed her five red bills on top of the three for the breakfast that was not going to happen. She misunderstood and took only the five. She looked at him up-and-down and smiled. "You come back my bar, OK GI?"

"Sure," Cole winked. He had no idea where he was last night, less still where she came from or how he got back to the hotel. The chances of finding this beauty again could only be made at the bottom of an empty Mekong Whisky bottle.

"Here you are, little darlin'," handing her the other three bills, too. "Take care."

"You come see me again?" she implored. Her big eyes trained to do that magic.

"Well, sure," Cole managed. "The next time I'm in town. Sure thing. You run along now, you hear," thinking the New Mexico cowboy flavor would put a good ending to their story – and he was pleased that he sounded like a star in a Hollywood Western.

She slipped on her sandals, and pivoted on her toes, smiled at Cole and then went out. Cole locked the door behind her and went to the ashtray to find his smoldering Camel. He took the last swig from a near-empty Singha bottle and then headed for the shower.

This police broad will need to wait her turn. And he hopped in the shower to wash off the smokes, the beer, and the lipstick.

●　　●　　●　　●　　●

It was 12 straight-up-and-down when Cole, dressed in a red JC Pennys t-shirt, blue Levi's and Dan Post shit-kickers, passed through the lobby entrance and into the restaurant, Camel in hand. He was sporting Ray-Ban aviator sunglasses to hold his two, still-throbbing eyeballs in place. He passed in front of the fish tank next to the cash register and caught sight of Pip just as she was going out the front door, held open by the ingratiating concierge who was wearing a huge, ear-to-ear shit-eating grin.

"Hey!" he shouted across the bar to the front door. "Hold up." He took a deep drag on the smoke and sauntered over to the front door in a measured gait. Pip turned to look at him but did not move back nor acknowledge his grin as he stuck out his hand to shake hers. She was in no mood to respond to *his pathetic gesture.*

"Look, sorry I missed this meeting. I thought it was for the afternoon." He was lying, and she knew it.

She gave a half turn back towards the street, but Cole blurted out, "OK, OK, well at least come back inside so we can have that chat you came here for."

Pip said nothing but looked at the concierge whose mouth had come slightly unhinged. But he picked up her signal and directed them to a booth by the window. Cole was familiar with the street view seats and he slid right in. The concierge and the Major exchanged knowing looks, and then Pip sat down.

Cole reached for the ashtray on the table and glanced out the window just in time to see his "little darlin'" climb in the back of a taxi with some *fat, bald-headed Chinese guy.*

Pip had also taken in the scene and finally said, "You know... you Americans come here and the first thing you do is get drunk and go about spoiling our women. If it weren't for you Americans, we would not have such a huge problem with prostitution in Thailand. You and your kind make enormous problems here."

Cole was yet to learn that Pip was a law enforcement officer dedicated to protecting the treasures of Thailand, both inanimate and living. And he stared back at her, mulling over her last words while taking another long drag on his smoke. *Of all the lousy luck, I draw this ball-bustin' bitch to get shackled with.*

The waiter passed by the table with a tray of food in his hands, and Cole stuck out his arm to intercept him. "Hey. Can we get some menus here?"

Pip thought, building her hit list, *Right... a real-deal, rude and crude American. Such an ass. And his volume control isn't working. And that southwestern drawl thing is so damn annoying!* All her cultured upbringing and Ivy education – in the same country which produced this man – were offended by his very presence. She thought, *I bet that little rathole town in New Mexico – at the end of the earth – must be delighted by this redneck, but I am already growing sick of him.*

"What are you having, Major? It is Major, isn't it?" Cole eyeballed her rank insignia but couldn't quite make out the symbology, so he dropped it.

She caught him in the act of assessment and cut him short, "Look, *Lieutenant,*" emphasizing his rank, "Let's get down to business. I've been assigned to work with you – to assist you while you're here on an investigation in my country. Frankly, I don't like this assignment and I have much better things to do. I'm only here because my Commandant insisted that I do this... because evidently the case you're on –"

Damn! This girl can speak English good! I wonder where she picked that up? Got a bit of an accent, but we can work on that. Maybe I can give her a few tips, here-and-there.

"– is a high priority. High enough that your embassy is involved."

Cole was admiring her silken hair and the flash in her eyes. He drew another drag on the Camel.

She caught him in the act. "Are you listening to what I'm saying?"

Cole leaned across the table. "OK, since we're leveling with each other here..." Cole reached for the ashtray and stubbed out his smoke. The opportunity for small talk had come and gone with the floor mat upstairs.

"You see, Major, I'm a solo act. And I don't like the idea of being tied down, slowed down, by anybody. Not by the Army, not by you. No one. Get me?"

She got it alright, but it didn't matter. She knew he would have to unload his protestations, but there was no way around the rules, "You have no choice, Lieutenant. It's either you work with me, or if not me, someone else. But you will not be working solo, like some kind of Lone Ranger in Thailand."

Her reference to his favorite TV show as a kid threw him for a second. *How the hell did she know about that?* He reached for another smoke.

"You see, Lieutenant –"

"Please, call me Cole. My name's Cole. Short for Coltrane." He was not about to explain "Frank X." to her, and why he only went by his last name. He lit the camel. Her continued emphasis on his rank was grating him.

Pip continued, "OK, Lieutenant Coltrane. I'm Major Siriwongdee. And like I was saying, you cannot operate in this country without an escort. And besides, how many words do you know in Thai? *Sawatdee*, hello, *mai pen rai*, never mind, or... oh wait, let me guess, *jai yen yen*, right?"

With the last, mocking phrase of this impromptu language quiz, Cole thought about his escapades last night and his "little darlin'." *Say! Maybe that's who taught me that phrase...* The thought gave him a quick grin and he glanced at the hotel driveway, but the young beauty was long gone. Probably teaching that Chinese guy the same words right now. He looked back at Pip. She had stopped the lecture but was reading his face.

He didn't want to give her the pleasure of scoring a win. His poker face was perfect, but he knew she had the better hand. *Damn it, she's right! Not gonna be able to shake her.* He took a sip on the Singha.

Cole returned to face the music. "OK, OK, so here's the deal, Major Siri..." he drew out her name, hoping she would fill in the rest. She didn't. And he couldn't remember. He settled on addressing her by rank, by plain-old "major."

"So, Major, here's the deal. I'm here to capture and return for justice an AWOL Army chaplain, a Catholic priest and a captain who's come over here and decided to stay in Thailand. I'm here to track him down and bring him back. Simple as that."

Pip moved back to business with a snap of her fingers. "Yes," she said, reaching for her briefcase and placing it on the table. "Captain Mordechai Goodcut. He's with the 25th Infantry in your operations in Vietnam. He arrived in Thailand on 27 April, 1971 at the Military Air Terminal at Don Muang Airport." She popped open the case.

The waiter returned with two menus. Pip smiled and said, "*Khob khun kha*, thank you, but the Major," speaking of herself in the third person, "will just have coffee, with cream, no sugar." She looked at Cole, "You?"

"ahh… Let me have a small Singha. No glass. Just bring me the bottle."

More crude swagger. Such an idiot.

"Having 'some hair of the dog' as we say back home." He winked at the Major.

"Yes, I know of your expression. But here, to use a saying about a dog and a person is not always polite. Usually, it is a very rude thing to say. Just so you know."

The quick lesson escaped Cole. "So, yeah, this priest –"

"I will help you as I can, but even we have limits," she interrupted.

She watched the waiter disappear with the order, and Cole watched her. She turned back to Cole. "Are you carrying a firearm of any type, Lieutenant Cole? Do you have a pistol, for example?"

"Nope. Nothing." He was lying. But she wasn't sure and decided to leave it for the moment. *I'll find out if you do have one, and if you do, I'll fix you good for lying to me.*

The drinks arrived. Pip reached for the cream the waiter had set down. Cole cocked his left arm over the back of the booth, grabbed the short bottle in his right hand and tipped its head towards Pip in a drinker's salutation. Pip stared at first, then managed a quick nod.

She reached into her briefcase and pulled out the pictures she had of Mordechai. Major Siriwongdee had photos that were taken at the Bangkok airport, and these were sharper and more up-to-date than the stock Army ID photo in the file that

Hargraves had tossed across his desk just two days ago. She handed the photos to Cole.

What she didn't share with Cole was the fact that Clarke had sent her a copy of his file on the priest, the confidential content removed. What she received was basically a couple pages of Mordechai's HR bio – content that Cole also saw but happily skipped over.

Pip had read it with professional interest: Father Mordechai Goodcut, DOB 7 September 1944, Detroit, Michigan, parish priest at Our Lady of Grace, Master of Divinity, Notre Dame 1966, Ordained 14 June 1967, Jewish father (Lemuel Goodcut), Roman Catholic mother (Sarah Whitfield). Next of kin: none. *Boring personal details. No story... nothing juicy here.* She found no clues why this man would abandon his culture and faith and cling on to hers. Still, she didn't want Cole to know she had done the research.

And Pip would have no idea that Mordechai's juicy bits were indeed relevant to their hunt for this holy man. He had distinguished himself in philosophy and religious studies, and he had spent hours in the Notre Dame library and squirreled away in his dorm room with piles of books on Hinduism, Taoism, and Buddhism. He wanted to soak up those religions from the other side of the world and reconcile these with his own faith and with his abiding love for the magisterium of the Roman Catholic Church.

His spiritual director, Monsignor Albireo, gave him plenty of latitude, knowing that there were many instantiations of God on earth. And it was the Monsignor's suggestion that Goodcut investigate the writings of Trappist Monk, Thomas Merton, and meditate on how Merton's interest in Buddhism and its relationship with Catholicism, paralleled Mordechai's own fascination with the intersection of these two faiths. The die was cast for Mordechai's transition, well before Vietnam.

"Let me keep these," Cole said as he picked up the photos for a closer look. "So, this is what the bastard looks like."

Pip raised an eyebrow at the word. It seemed harsh to use for a priest, runaway or not. "Yes, this was taken when he arrived in Bangkok."

"Not much to go on. But that's OK." Cole stared at the picture of his prey. He was looking for the telltale signs of fear that always appeared. But he wasn't seeing it. *Probably a poor picture. I'll see it alright, that look in his eyes when we get up close and nab him.*

Pip ignored Cole's insulting language and finally put the most important question between the coffee cup and the beer bottle: "What is your plan?"

Cole knew the question was coming. It had occupied his thoughts for the last 48 hours – except for the sensual foray into Patpong last night.

Clarke had clued him in on Goodcut's Buddhist designs, and Cole had come up with a plan to snare Mordechai, based on his habits and routine. *I'll catch him in the act – at a temple. The only question is: which one?* En route from the airport yesterday, Cole had counted 8 temples along the road. *Jesus H... There must be thousands of temples in this damn country! Got to get this filtered down quick.*

He stared at Pip across the table, took another drag on the smoke and a quick swig. *I'm not gonna show her any of these cards. No, not just yet. Need to get a better feel for this broad... for the situation here. Bad enough she's tagging along. All she needs to know now is that I'm calling the shots.*

Cole was sure that the focus on temples, plus the information he hoped to gain from the priest's last known residence in Bangkok, would give him his first solid bearing for the hunt. He knew the Thais would have captured those details on Mordechai's arrival card, so he asked Major Panthip, "OK, what do his incoming docs say, the docs from the Airport?"

Pip was a step ahead. She had already called the military unit at the airport handling these records, and they gave her Mordechai's declared residence in Bangkok.

She said, "He stated on his arrival docs that he'd be staying at the Grove Hotel. I know where that is. Not far from here. A good place to start."

"Fine," said Cole. "I'll run over there now and then meet you back at your police station this afternoon. How does 4pm sound? We can go over the whole plan then."

Pip studied Cole to see if he was going to give her the slip. Again, she could not read him and that bothered her. She prided herself in being able to sniff out a liar, but with Cole, she hadn't quite got a grip. *Was he planning an escape?* She resigned herself to the fact that he could do that anytime. She didn't have any reins to lay on him. He was free to head out on his own and break the law – and to suffer the consequences. *Mai pen rai,* no problem.

"OK, Lieutenant Cole," putting his rank out there again and keeping her distance. "As you wish. But please make it sharp at 4pm. OK? We need to plan for the next steps and to catch your fugitive. I've got important work to get back to… and I want to leave my office at a reasonable time tonight."

Cole took three long swallows and set the empty bottle on the table with the weight of his forearm. "Good. That's what I want to hear." He tipped the empty to Pip who had just taken her second sip of coffee. "To the hunt," he said.

Pip looked at him over the brim of her cup, and for the first time she brought the edges of her mouth up in a slight smile.

· · · · ·

Cole surveyed the driveway in the front of the hotel as Pip climbed in the back seat of the taxi. She turned at the waist to see him waiving at her with one singular, falling motion of his right arm as if discarding everything she had said so far. She couldn't tell if he was smiling or not, but she imagined that he was. Pip did not return the wave and she was not smiling. She shut the cab door and told the driver to take her to Lumpini Station.

Cole watched the taxi pull out and head into town, the Sukhumvit traffic now thawed out and moving slowly. *Maybe I should have given her one of these "wai things."* He brought his hands together with his palms chest high. *Or a salute, she is a major after all. Yeah, right, as if that's gonna happen.*

He laughed as he pivoted and went into the lobby to fetch his room key. He needed to go upstairs to use the toilet – and to tuck his Army-issue .45 under his shirt before heading to the Grove Hotel and beginning the hunt. Cole thought about his new "partner."

Well, at least she's a woman, and not some hairy old dude. "How bad can that be?" Not the kind of question you should ask out loud in Thailand.

CHAPTER 15

By the time Cole arrived at the Grove Hotel it was mid-afternoon and he was in the mood for a club sandwich. Save for the bar snacks the night before, he had eaten nothing since he left Vietnam.

But business came first, and he made a beeline for the desk clerk in the lobby where he gave a stab at the register. He asked his routine questions, and later probed the hotel staff who might have had any contact with the fugitive priest. Just like he imagined during the taxi ride to the hotel that afternoon, the trail was cold. Not even the smallest clue, especially any bearing where Mordechai was headed next. He had simply disappeared. Vanished. *Of course he did… This guy's not stupid.*

None of the hotel staff mentioned anything about Goodcut other than he was quiet, and he was *"mai kee-mao*, he's not a drunkard," as they gestured with tipped-back heads and a couple of swigs on imaginary bottles. Cole got the embarrassed smiles from the young hotel maids, but nobody was offering any helpful sign. No scent was laid down. Not by the maids, the pool guys, nor the taxi-stand bums – not even the staff in the hotel's greasy-spoon restaurant. Sure, they all recognized his picture, and some knew a bit more, like his favorite evening glass of tea, but nobody knew where this mysterious man went next.

Coltrane had the gift to know when someone was bullshitting him, but he didn't get that vibe from the simple folks at the hotel. They had no thoughts about this former guest and no wish to help Cole, even if they did know some tidbit about Mordechai. Such was the interest of the hotel staff into Coltrane's arrival on the scene at the Grove, up a narrow alley and a long city block from one of Bangkok's biggest arteries. The alley, the hotel, the questions were all dead ends for him, and Cole was hungry. The club sandwich and beer could wait no longer.

•   •   •   •   •

Cole finished the last bite of his meal, and swabbed at the few dabs of mustard from the plate with the edge of a serrated pickle-wedge that the cook had tossed in next to the fries, when he caught sight of three saffron-robed monks heading up the alley towards the hotel. They walked barefooted as was the custom, and they walked along in single file, purposeful, not speaking with each other or exchanging glances with the Thais who were scurrying around with their afternoon chores, in-and-out of jam-packed stores that lined the alleyway that led to the hotel's entrance.

He tried to imagine what kind of man would want to live like that – to dress up in a robe and walk around barefooted, thinking about... who knows what. "They're thinking about their belly buttons," Peacock used to say when he spotted them with their begging bowls, milling around the morning streets of Da Nang. *Same stubborn bunch of knuckleheads who light themselves on fire in Hue*, thought Cole. *Not my kind of drama. The simple bastards.*

Cole continued to watch the trio as they drew closer up the street. And as they passed in front of the hotel's restaurant, single file, he could see that the first and the last in their slow procession were foreigners. Even though their shaved heads, faces, and eyebrows gave them similar, soft features – *the spittin' image of Mr. Clean, but no earring* – the first and last were clearly not Thai. *Now this is a curious thing. Never seen a foreign monk up close. Foreigner – Thai – foreigner, a kind of sandwich. A reverse Oreo cookie: white on the outside, brown in the middle.*

He remembered his Black friends back in 'Nam and the ribbing they would give Eli Pickett, a Cornell-educated black farmer from upstate New York, who enlisted in the Army to "do his part." Such patriotic notions were so lame and white-on-the-inside to the drafted brothers, that they all called him "My Oreo" whenever they would meet and do the ritualistic dap.

But as Cole watched the monks, his thoughts turned to Mordechai and how the priest had lost his compass and wound up with *this kind of a do-nothin' outfit. Bunch of beggars. And My Boy Mordechai's right in the middle of all that crap.*

A smile curled up on his lips as he wiped the remaining piece of sandwich from his face. The lead monk opened the single glass door on the hotel's lobby entrance, and they all slipped inside. Cole knew next-to-nothing about monks, but this small, odd procession piqued his interests. He switched on his radar and waited.

• • • • •

The monks filed out from the hotel lobby, this time with the Thai-looking fellow at the lead. Cole flipped a crisp 100 baht note on the countertop next to his plate and from his red-leather barstool seat. He made it to the alleyway door of the restaurant, just in advance of the monks' procession that was headed back towards the *baak-soi*, the mouth of the alley and the snarling traffic on Phetchaburi Road.

"Excuse me! Sorry!" he said, planting himself firmly in their path and raising his right hand like a traffic cop. "Excuse me," he said again. And they halted.

The second and third monks, the foreigners, smiled and slowly came abreast on either side of the Thai monk, who wound up in the middle. He stood frowning, arms folded with his hands cupping his elbows, scratching at the dry skin on those bony nubs. The foreign monks loomed over him. The tallest shifted his weight as Cole began to speak.

"Look. Sorry to bother you," said Cole, knowing enough of protocol to bow slightly at the waist. He should have offered them a *wai*, but he had yet to learn the proper social manners when addressing Buddhist monks. But it didn't matter. Such manners simply were not important to them. These monks, like all Thai monks, were not harboring expectations. They had rejected self-esteem and usually accepted the routine tokens of respect offered by the laity with just brief, courteous smiles. Sometimes not. But this awkward bowing gesture by Cole, caused even the Thai monk to smile.

Cole sized up the shoulder-to-shoulder trio in *"orange"* robes, arms now at their sides. The booze from the night before was still percolating through his gourd, and he imagined for an instant they might break into a bluegrass song with three-part harmony at any moment. Maybe pull out a banjo from the bags they were carrying. *Man, this Mekong Whiskey is a killer*. He shook the thought from his head.

"Can we help you?" the foreign monk on the right spoke first. Cole turned his gaze from the Thai monk in the middle, to the shorter foreign monk. *This fellow sounds like he's from Europe or somewhere.*

But before Cole could answer, the second foreign monk, on the left asked, "Are you an American?"

Paydirt, an American! "Yeah," answered Cole, now eyeballing the taller, foreign monk to his left – the other white half of the Oreo. "And what state are you from?"

"British Columbia," he answered. And with that, the two foreign monks smiled broadly, but stopped short of laughing out loud. They re-shifted their weight, breaking ranks slightly. The Thai monk was smiling too, but not exactly sure why this was so funny to his foreign brethren.

"OK, got me there." *Smart-ass Canadians. Always getting off on that.*

"And you?" Cole looked at the shorter foreign monk, "Where are you from."

"I'm from Denmark, originally, but have lived here for over five years now."

Cole's eyebrows shot up, *Where the hell is Denmark, anyways?* His mental map of Europe looked much like the surface of a pizza with an "everything-on-it" topping, a multicolored hodgepodge of places and countries. But it did not matter. *Won't need this guy's opinion. And as for the Thai one,* he shifted his gaze back to the monk in the middle. *Nah, nothing there either,* not knowing that "the Thai one" was, in fact, the abbot at the *Wat Bowonniwet* temple, and it was he who had first struck up the warm friendship with Mordechai during his many visits there.

Turning back to the Canadian, Cole asked, "What brings you to this place, to this, ah... hotel?" He wanted to say "shit-hole dump," but checked himself before that popped out. He guessed it might not be the best words to use with *these holy folks.*

The Canadian spoke up. "We came to return a gift. This watch."

He reached into the satchel he was carrying over his shoulder and pulled out a silver Omega timepiece, lifted it up by its elastic band for Cole to see, but did not offer it for him to hold.

"It belonged to a man who was staying here. He gave it to me, well, to the temple, as a gift. He told us he was not going to need it anymore and perhaps we could sell it and donate the money to the temple, or for the alms box, or for the dead who cannot afford their own coffins."

Cole was following, but he fixed on the last part. *For the dead? What coffins?* The monk went on, "Its *plaek,* odd, that we should run into another American, here at this hotel, because the man who gave it to us was also an American. He came to Thailand from Vietnam." Cole's radar lit up with flashing green lights.

"Yes, he came from Vietnam," the shorter foreign monk said. "He used to be in the Army but now he was going to leave and stay in Thailand."

"He had a kind heart." The Thai monk finally spoke up, and Cole turned to him in surprise, not knowing that the Thai was following the conversation.

"Yes," repeated the Thai monk. "He generous man and give watch to *Luang Pee* Brian," gesturing to the tall Canadian monk on his right. "But gift too valuable. We think he need it for travel, for journey. He say he no need it, but I think he do. So, we come here. Find him. Give him."

Cole eyed the Thai monk, surprised by the settling and honest quality of his voice. A closer look at the man revealed something else he had not expected to see: three deep furrows around his neck like concentric rings, and very long, extended earlobes, almost twice the normal length. It was distracting.

The Thai monk went on, "Many times he come to visit at temple. He come for two weeks. He ask many questions. He come with us in morning for *bintabaat*. For –"

He looked at the Danish monk for a translation and that monk didn't miss the beat, "For alms gathering. We receive food from the faithful in the morning when we walk the city streets. In Thai, it's called *bintabaat*." With this explanation, they all hummed in affirmation.

But Cole focused on the kernel the Thai monk had mentioned. "Travels?" asked Cole.

The three monks did not speak. The shorter one looked at his bare feet and at the trail of ants making their way to a half-eaten, discarded mango that was tossed up against the cinder-block wall, next to where they were all standing.

"May I see the watch again?" asked Cole. Without hesitation – and without consultation amongst themselves – the taller monk once again fetched the watch from his satchel and handed it to Cole.

Cole studied the watch and its segmented, elastic-and-metal watchband which he pulled at three times as if evaluating a watch he might someday buy at Sears back home. He looked at the crystal, scratched and yellowed, and at the second hand sweeping beneath the small glass dome. The time was 4:44, he glanced at his watch, 4:42, *A couple of minutes fast*, thought Cole. *Just like this guy. Two steps ahead of me. But not for long.*

He flipped over the case and read on the back, "To Fr. Mordechai Goodcut, Our Lady of Grace Parish, Detroit, 1968." *Bingo!*

"Nice watch," he said coolly as he handed it back to the Canadian monk using his left hand, inadvertently violating the protocol which calls for the use of two hands when handing objects to monks.

He worked up his best poker face so as not to betray the blood-warm, gut feeling welling up inside him. He had just found the deer's signs, the droppings in the sagebrush. And by handling the Omega he immediately grew closer to his prey and his capture – closer to the kill. He was feeling the unmistakable and familiar taste for blood and he had just taken his first sip. "Yeah, nice watch," he repeated.

The taller monk put it back in the satchel. But the small monk from Denmark now knitted his brows, for in the instant of Coltrane's recognition of the watch's inscription, he caught the unguarded dilation in the eyes of this unkind and mysterious foreign man, and he was taken aback.

"You know, you're right," Cole said, looking at the Canadian monk. "It is odd, since I actually know this man. He's a friend of mine from Vietnam. I heard he was in town and thought it would be great to see him, and that's what brought me here. But

I'm sure they told you in the lobby that he's already checked out." He cocked his head to read their faces – to check his trap line for clues.

Cole thought better about asking to keep the watch on the pretext that he could give it to Mordechai when they met up. It would have been a good talisman for the hunt, like the wild boar's tusk hung around the hunter's neck, shoring up courage and ensuring a good hunt. But he knew he would tip his hand if he were to ask, not knowing that two of them already had sensed danger.

From Cole's perspective, all was going well so far – but he didn't like the look of the smaller foreign monk who was now giving him furtive glances, alternating between him and the ants marching to-and-fro from the mango on the pavement. *This runt is on to me.*

"So, did my friend give you any idea what hotel he may have moved to, here in Bangkok?" Cole was fishing again. He believed that Mordechai would have already left the city, but he had no clear idea where his trail led. Throwing in "Bangkok" was a ruse.

The smaller monk had left the conversation and the ongoing lie being spun by Coltrane and was focused solely on the ants and the mango. He was making a mental map of their trail so he would not step on them when they finally parted company with this suspicious American whose words did not ring true. The Thai monk was refolding his robe in preparation for their departure. For these two monks, leaving the presence of this strange man in the alley could not come soon enough.

They pivoted to leave and reformed their short column, but before they started walking, the Canadian monk turned to Cole and said, "He may have gone to the Northeast, to the Laotian border. There is a temple up there. A place where I was ordained. I once told him about it, and your friend seemed very interested. I even marked the village on his map for him. It is a village called 'Bung Wai.' Near the Thai city of Ubon in the Northeast. It is on the River Mun. About 80 kilos to the west of the Mekong and the border with Laos."

"Sorry, what was that name again? The city was –"

"Ubon. Bung Wai village. In the Northeast of the country. Many foreign monks. They will know him, if he's there." And with that they began walking, all three with their heads down, careful to avoid small, sentient creatures with their steps.

Gold. Pure gold. Bung Wai, near Ubon. Bung Wai, near Ubon. He burned the words into his brain. *This tip is the best break I'm gonna get from these jokers.* He put his cordial face back on.

"Well, it was nice to meet you gentlemen. Nice to chat." He, of course, meant none of that. But he no longer had use for them or further niceties, and so he managed a shallow bow as the three passed in front of him, headed for the *baak-soi* and back to their temple. It was time for afternoon prayers, and they needed to move with haste.

They parted company with Coltrane, and the thought the tallest monk held was, *it is good to reunite friends.* The other two monks had disquieting thoughts they were trying to dispel. They said nothing. None of them returned Cole's awkward gesture of respect, nor was it the custom for them to do so.

Mekong River… Bung Wai village… near Ubon… across from Laos. OK. OK, he sucked in a breath and in doing so caught the smell of the rotting mango, the object of attention for the Danish monk.

But Cole was stoked. *OK, padre. We're on to you now… Will be seein' you soon. Pay you a little visit.*

•   •   •   •   •

Cole chased down the discovery offered by the monks with two, tall glasses of cold Singha beer which he enjoyed by the hotel's pool, savoring the view from the deck where three blond backpackers had stripped off into their bikinis and were now cavorting around in the shallow end. He did not care if the show was for him or not. He met their eyes only two or three times. On other days, that would have led to a conquest. But not today.

Cole was fixated on the chase and on what Mordechai's village temple must look like. Dust, chickens, jungle, snakes. He imagined Mordechai, sitting under a tree by the river in an orange robe, *doing fuck all*, while the guys in his unit back in 'Nam were getting their guts splattered into the bushes and trees.

The anger from this picture levitated Coltrane from his bamboo chair, and he walked out past the pool deck to the taxi stand, ignoring the fact that one of the girls had let loose her top and dove under the water, resurfacing like a naked mermaid on the steps a few feet in front of him. All he saw was the green and yellow taxi. *Time to see what's-her-name and get going.*

CHAPTER 16

It was getting dark and the wooden, window shutters on the second floor at Lumpini Police Station were clacking shut. Long-faced maids, weary from work and having had their fill of gossip for the day, headed home to their shacks to heat and stir the evening pots of rice. Their husbands and families cared little of what they did at work and would not ask, and the maids would be too tired to talk about it.

•   •   •   •   •

Pip locked her office door and headed down the two flights of cement stairs to the ground floor and to the parking lot next to the station. She rummaged around in her purse for the keys to Baby Blue, but then remembered that she left her car at home for the day. She would need to take a bus from Lumpini to Sukhumvit Road, and then transfer to the smaller bus at the *baak-soi* of Soi Udomsuk, some 8km away. At that time of the day, it would take her at least two, maybe three hours to get home. She blew the exasperation out through her lips.

She stepped around the corner from the parking lot, just as a green and yellow taxi rolled to a stop at the front of the station, and Cole hopped out. He walked towards the booking room downstairs, hands in his pockets whistling a Merle Haggard tune. The very sight of him, late and with that sloppy, unshaven look, made her bristle.

Cole caught sight of her and, pulling his right hand from his pocket, gave her a wave. That exchange did not go unnoticed by the junior officers gathered at the booking desk and waiting for their evening briefing. Pip ignored their sheepish stares.

Cole cleared his throat, but before he could say anything, she fired, "Do you know what time it is? We were supposed to meet here at 4pm. It's almost 6:30 now."

She took a half step forward with her left foot, tilted her head back slightly to the right, and tucked her hands under her armpits, her purse hung from the crook of her right arm.

"Well, I –"

"This is the third time you've made me wait today."

"Uh, twice?" He said, holding up two fingers in the peace sign while forcing a smile.

"Twice at the hotel and again now. I do not like to be kept waiting. Not by you or anyone else."

She realized that she was probably speaking too loudly and, instinctively, glanced up at the windows of the Station's Commandant. He was there, watching, but her glance caused him to retreat back inside like a naughty schoolboy. He pulled the wooden shutters to. Pip clinched her eyes.

"But–" Cole tried again.

"Look, if we're going to get this job done, you've got to be more professional about your work." She paused, dropping her hands from their place of refuge.

"I can help you. I'm good at what I do – maybe the best. You should know that I was hand-picked to do this job and I intend to do my duty. But I will not let you misunderstand me and who I am – and waste my time."

Cole stopped smiling. *What a cocky bitch.* He didn't like being dressed down by anyone, worse still in public. Apart from the officers at the front of the station who were within earshot, there were off-duty cops, maids and other personnel who were passing by, headed for the busses at the street corner. They would not have understood the lyrics, but they would certainly get the melody – and those shrill notes grated his teeth. He didn't like it one bit. *Who does this broad think she's dealing with? She'd better cool her jets before this "partner" bullshit goes south.*

"OK, look, Major, I was busy getting some leads on our prize and it took longer than I expected." Cole paused to study her reaction, but there was none. She only transferred her weight from one foot to the other.

He shifted gears and tried the straight-and-narrow, "Right, I have this plan, and –"

Before he could finish, Pip swung her right arm up from the elbow, palm out, in his face. She swiveled her head to the right and glanced upwards, towards the Commandant's now-shuttered window. She let her fingers drop into her right palm and said, almost whispering, "Let's go inside, up to my office."

This sudden insistence on secrecy caught Cole off guard. It was unexpected – and yet somehow intimate. His pained brows relaxed and a sly smile crept back on his face. *OK. Maybe this is turning a corner,* he thought.

Pip walked back towards the building and he followed her as she passed the gaggle of junior officers downstairs, near the main staircase. Their back-and-forth banter and glances in Pip's direction were squelched off.

They reached the mezzanine level of the staircase and ran into the Commandant who passed by them on his way down and out to his car, and his chauffeured ride home. Pip lifted her arms, placed her palms together and *wai'*ed him as he passed by, "*Sawatdee, kha.* Good night, sir."

He glanced at Pip and then at the American, and then again at Pip before saying, "*Khrap*," basically a one-syllable grunt to acknowledge her salutation, based on the formality required within the office pecking order.

But it said everything. *So, here is this foreign lieutenant who I don't need to acknowledge. Worse, he's in the company of the woman who turns me on.*

He unconsciously eyed her ribbons and the way her shirt clung to her chest.

He glanced again at Cole for a second, stiffened his spine and adjusted his hat, not missing a step as he descended. *I wonder if she likes this guy? Shit, who cares... She's a pain in the ass... And anyway, I'm going home and have a few tugs on the Black Label.*

•   •   •   •   •

They entered Pip's office, and she stood looking down the hallway for a few seconds before closing the door behind her and flipping the lights back on. Cole scanned her diplomas on the wall, and the ribbons and trophies in the bookcase below the window, all with baffling Thai inscriptions. Glancing at a large, gold-colored trophy with engraved, cursive Thai lettering he thought, *I bet this one is for "busting balls." Probably first place.*

"Please come in and sit down," she said, gesturing to a seat in front of her desk and making sure that hospitality was extended before she sat down, resting her forearms on the leather desk mat, hands clasped and fingers interwoven.

Cole pulled one of the two straight-backed chairs from the front of Pip's desk, spun it 180 degrees, flung his right leg over the seat and lowered himself down. He sat with folded arms and elbows resting at the top of the seatback, head tilted to the right. Pip watched the drama with the chair, unimpressed.

"New Mexico?" She asked.

"Yep. That's right. And what about you? Bangkok?" Cole had missed her point about sitting on the chair as if he was mounting a horse and thought she was now in the mood for small talk. Pip ignored his question.

He tried another track. "OK, so what's with the secrecy?"

She paused for two breaths and said, "Look, you Americans have the expression that 'the walls have ears' and we believe pretty much the same thing. We Thais are very superstitious, and believe that if you speak about your wishes or plans carelessly out in the open air, you can –" she paused again while staring up at the ceiling, rubbing the tips of her index fingers with her thumbs to help conjure up the word "– you can jinx yourself. We must be humble and quiet. And careful to avoid any invitations for trouble. Do you understand?"

She studied Cole for a sign of his comprehension but saw only that he was getting worked up by *her stupid, superstitious crapola*. He expected to hear some plan from her that required secrecy and stealth, but all he heard was... *wishes, plans, open air, humble, quiet... crazy*. He stopped trying to follow what she was saying, and the sly smile returned to his face.

"Did you say you were from Bangkok?" He tried probing her again.

"I didn't say," she replied. Nor was Pip about to tell him that she was born in Washington DC, that she spent most of her childhood in the United States, that she was completely fluent in three languages, that she knew and spoke English better than he did, that she went to great schools in the States – places he may have heard of only if they had a national football team.

And she had never been to New Mexico, nor did she ever want to go. Her father had taken the family on a summer vacation to the Grand Canyon and Monument Valley in Arizona, to Ouray and Silverton in Southwest Colorado, and to the stunning, red sandstone parks of eastern Utah.

They circumvented New Mexico because her father had said that there was nothing to see, just cowboys and "miles-and-miles of miles-and-miles." And besides, they set off the first atom bomb in the middle of that God-forsaken state. If the US Government had that much disdain for New Mexico – enough to test nuclear bombs in its deserts – then there was no reason for the Deputy Military Attaché of the Thai Embassy to take his family there. No thanks. *And now here sits this American cowboy from that miserable place.*

Cole gave her a two-second once-over. He dropped his interest in asking any more questions and got to the point, "OK. Look, let's just talk about what we gotta do next."

"Sure. OK, sure," she answered. But before she yielded the high ground, she leaned back in her chair and proceeded to give him a subtle taste of Thai wisdom.

She said, "You would not know this, but we have an expression in Thailand that goes like this: *'see sor hai khwai fang.'* It literally means, 'one plays the fiddle for the buffalo.' Can you guess it's meaning?"

"Huh? What was that?" He was not paying attention to what she was saying and only caught the words "fiddle" and "buffalo."

"It's an expression we use when one tries to explain something to another person who could never understand nor appreciate what was being said." She paused and looked at Cole's expression, but he was glancing around the room looking for relief.

"It means that, just as the buffalo is not interested nor does he appreciate nice music, the dull-witted person cannot understand, nor appreciate, something valuable being told to them. It wastes everyone's time. Do you get me?"

Cole got it alright. And it pissed him off. He wanted to tilt his head to the left and slap the side of his noggin to force out the last words she said, just like he did to unplug his ear in the shower that morning. *More cocky bullshit.*

"Look, Major, I've got no time for these wonderful little sayings and stories. Let's just get to it."

With that, he unsaddled himself from the chair, turned his back to Pip, and stepped towards the large map of Southeast

Asia that was hanging on the wall opposite her desk. It was a brown and green, USGS survey map, 1:250,000, dated 1961.

Cole stood there, scrutinizing the layout and consuming the symbols, finding the word "Mekong," and making an arc across the map with his right index finger. He traced the river as it flowed past Vientiane, pass the confluence with the River Mun, into Laos, south to Cambodia and finally splaying itself out in the rich delta of South Vietnam.

He slowly spoke the three syllables, "Mor-de-chai" as if the name itself was written on the map.

Cole was trying to recall what the tall Canadian monk had told him earlier today, and he scoured the great Northeast bulge of Thailand – the bulge that resembles an elephant's head. His scarred index finger stopped moving across the surface of the map where he zeroed in on the word "Ubon."

OK, this is it, he thought. *Ubon Rat-cha-tha-ni* he mouthed the syllables silently.

And there, one fat finger's width southwest of Ubon, in the smallest of letters reserved for villages and hamlets were the words, "Bung Wai." *There!* he thought. *That's where we'll find him.* Keeping his finger on Ubon, he half-turned to the Major, "This place is where we'll find that bastard," he announced.

Pip had heard the priest described by Coltrane with those same words earlier that day. She was no longer shocked by the disrespect Cole had for the clergy. *After all, these were his words, his negative karma, not mine.*

"And just how do you know *that*, Lieutenant?"

"Let's just call it a professional hunch," he said, giving her a wink. Cole had no intention of telling her about his encounter with the monks at the hotel today. He wouldn't tell her anything he didn't have to. *Good to keep you guessing, sister. Less meddling in my business.* This was his rodeo and he was in charge.

"Look. I'll explain it later. Trust me." It was an insincere offering and Pip knew it.

"So, what *did* you find out at the hotel today? Any good information on the Priest? How did you come to your 'professional hunch', as you say?" She pressed him.

Cole was poker-faced, saying nothing. He just continued to stare at the map. He was already there at that temple up-country. He saw Mordechai, the river, the big tree, the orange robe. *The bastard!*

"What did they tell you?" She persisted, now standing up behind her desk with her arms folded across her chest. "Did you talk to the manager? Did you –?"

Shit, woman! Give it a rest! He tossed out a bone of appeasement as a ploy *to keep her trap shut.* "Yeah, they said he checked out last week. Last Wednesday," he said as flat as possible to deflect her tiresome questions.

But the hint of a possible target on the map intrigued Pip, and she moved from behind her desk and walked closer to the map, next to where he stood. She gave him a sideways glance and bent forwards, towards the map. Pip could tell that he was on the scent. She saw it in his face, and she recognized the pace and body mannerisms of the hunter. She had, at times, felt the same thrill of the hunt. It aroused her in inexplicable and unashamed ways.

But this American is tight-lipped. He obviously knows something. And this is another deceitful side of his nee-sai, *his core being. He's not telling me the whole story.*

And not knowing Cole's thoughts angered her. To Pip, his reticence was just another way of saying that he didn't trust her, that she was only a Thai, and only a woman – and from Cole's perspective, she would have been right. He thought all those things, and more.

She was also uncomfortable with his lone-wolf routine, but realized for the sake of the hunt she would need to slowly release her grip from around his throat – a grip she had been imagining since he came to the door of his hotel room that morning. Her greatest wish was to get this job done quickly and get back to her real work, to the things that mattered most to her.

She recentered herself and scanned the Thai words, next to the English letters. Cole pressed hard on the map with his finger, as if the pressure would pin Mordechai in place.

"OK, so you think he's in Ubon," she said as she folded her arms again, pursed her lips and nodded.

She did the arithmetic, "If he arrived in Thailand on the 27th of last month – and spent two weeks here at that hotel – then he's just left Bangkok last week. He's only got a week's jump on us."

Cole's ears turned to her when he heard the American jargon.

She added, "We can leave in the morning, by train. Our rail system has a daily to Ubon that leaves from Hua Lamphong, the main train station in Bangkok." She reached for a pen and a small index card from a neat stack on her desk, wrote the time of departure, 05:45, and the station name in both English and Thai, and handed it to him.

"So, you are a walking train schedule? How in the hell do you –," asked a surprised Cole.

"I have family in Ubon Ratchathani… you can call it Ubon if you'd like. They have a small guest house there, nearby the place where the River Mun flows into the Mekong. After I moved back to Thailand for good, I've gone there every year during *Songkran*, our Water Festival. I've been on that train too many times to count."

She smiled and gave a short, falling hum from the back of her throat. "That region is beautiful and the forests, rivers… the ancient history…" She stared at the union of the two rivers on the map for a second too long before she caught herself drifting, letting slip parts of her story she did not want to divulge.

"Look, you need to get ready and it's been a long day," she said, reaching for her police-uniform hat that she had tossed onto her desk. "Let's call it quits for the day."

"Yeah, fine by me, Major. Let's call it quits. We can talk plans on the train."

"OK. Sure. We'll have plenty of time to do so. The train takes about eight hours to get there."

Shit! thought Cole. *Eight hours on a slow train with this broad…* He felt his neck muscles tighten and his eyebrows tipped down in a frown. But he sucked in a quick breath and let it come out slowly, metered, and resigned. *OK. OK. I can hack this. No big deal.*

She turned to adjust her hat in the mirror behind her office door, and Cole stole a quick look at her butt. Pip did not miss his look but said nothing as she flipped off the light switch.

Cole smiled and thought, *Let's get her out of the city and see if we can't take some starch out of that skirt.* She tipped her head towards him and asked in a brusk yet slightly coy voice, "Something funny, Lieutenant?"

"No ma'am, nothing funny here."

●　　●　　●　　●　　●

Leung Chean opened the gate for Pip even before she arrived at the front of her home. He had been standing there for some time, waiting for her and swatting at the mosquitos which were biting his ankles below his *pha-khao-ma*, sarong. *Leung* Chean was relieved and happy when he finally saw her in the distance, getting off the small bus at the dusty stop.

He nodded deeply to her and followed this with a *wai* when she entered her house compound, "*Khrap. Khrap,*" he said with a broad grin, meaning, *yes, welcome home, Pip, it's good that you're home and I am happy for this.*

Pip acknowledged his nod with a smile and said only "*Kha. Khob khun mahk, Leung kha.* Yes, thank you very much, my uncle."

She saw her Baby Blue, washed and polished, out of the corner of her eye as she ascended the steps to the bedrooms upstairs.

Pip opened the door to her mother's room and heard the soft, gentle snoring of an old lady, and she smiled. It was a melodious hum that would always remind her of this home and its warmth. She went out, closed her mother's door behind her and stood for an instant with her back to the door, letting loose a long sigh as she looked up at her father's picture on the opposite wall – and the pile of newspapers on the table below it.

She *wai'*ed his picture above the urn, and then drew in another deep draft of the night air. Something strong was stirring in her. Something powerful was luring her closer to this intense American. It felt at once unwanted and unnerving, and yet somehow wonderful. Mysterious.

●　　●　　●　　●　　●

Cole made it back to his hotel room straight as an arrow that night. He knew better than to try and find that beautiful 18-year-old at the bottom of a Mekong bottle. He had tasted the hunt's first blood at the hotel earlier in the day, and it would be serious business from here on out.

Besides, he *couldn't take another shrill lecture from that Thai Police broad* if he were late for the train. He ordered up a club sandwich from the hotel's restaurant and chased it down with a Coke. The 04:15 wake-up call would come too damn early.

CHAPTER 17

A street vendor stood behind his stainless-steel cart, straining thick Thai coffee through a long white cotton tube into clear drinking glasses. That bitter aroma mixed with the exhaust fumes from cross-town busses as they disgorged their passengers into the parking lot at Bangkok's Hua Lamphong Train Station. The red busses poured out their contents at the station like ripe and battle-scarred salmon, spewing out roe at their spawning ground.

Lucky this was a Wednesday as there were not many people going out of the city. Travel on the weekend, and you would get crushed by the throngs in their exodus to ancestral homes in places large and small that marked every cardinal direction from Bangkok. The exhaust didn't bother Pip who savored the coffee, adding a large dollop of condensed milk that she stirred into her glass.

Her next stop was for *pa-tong-ko* doughnuts, a craving she secretly shared with her colleagues at the Lumpini Police Station. It was a treat she always enjoyed on train rides, and this routine would not be spoiled on account of a tardy American lieutenant – she resisted the professional urge to start looking for him.

• • • • •

She held her coffee and *pa-tong-ko* in her left hand and her overnight bag in her right. She walked past the platform-signalman from the Thai Rail Service, a man perhaps 50 years old who looked like he was pushing 80. He wore baggy khaki pants and a threadbare shirt, decorated with two sweat-stained service medals clipped to his left breast pocket. He had folded a handkerchief lengthwise into a small strip of cloth and placed it over his frayed shirt collar. It was held in place with two large paperclips to keep it from slipping off, down the back of his shirt. It looked like he had worn that same shirt for decades, and he probably had.

The signalman stood near the rear of the train with green and red flags held in opposite hands, indicating that the train was within a few minutes of departure. The Thais, always aware of the situation around them without needing to be told, read his appearance on the platform with precision and those lingering in the station moved quickly to climb onboard. Cole was nowhere to be seen.

The engine whistle blew three loud blasts and the signalman lifted the green flag in his right hand to a high, overhead pose and the train lurched forward.

Pip had already decided that she would board the train, pick a good seat on the south side, and see if the American would show up. Since the train was moving from west to east, her strategy was to avoid the sun blasting in the windows on the north side this time of year. Many people, without guidebooks to tell them so, also knew this fact.

She would let the American catch up with her. *He's tried to come off as the "Great White Hunter." Let's see if he can do even a simple thing... like catching this slow train.* If he was going to be a no-show, she planned to get off at the first stop outside the city limits and then travel back to Bangkok on the next inbound train.

She glanced at her watch. It was 05:46. This morning's train would not reach that first stop for several more minutes, so she had plenty of time to finish her coffee and *pa-tong-ko* before heading back. *Good plan*, she thought.

But no sooner had she comforted herself with "Plan B" and had two sips of coffee and a bite of her doughnut, than the now-familiar, New Mexican timbre boomed out from behind her.

"Good morning there, Major."

Cole swung his gear bag into the overhead rack, above the heads of the two elderly Thais who were sharing the aisle side of the face-to-face bench seats. He plopped down in the window seat, facing Pip who was having another sip of coffee and staring at a fruit plantation with rows of banana trees, spread out in long lines at right angles to the track.

Cole tugged at his shirt collar with both hands, lifting the sleeves to get some air flowing. He had dark, wet circles under both his arms and a "V" of neck sweat, soaking the gaudy, blue and yellow shirt he had bought from the street vendors in front of the Rex Hotel last night. He caught Pip glaring at it. "Nice, huh?" he asked.

She took another sip of coffee but didn't respond as the train pulled into her jumping-off point. She sighed, and then glanced at Cole. "Good morning," she said. With this, Cole grinned a toothy smile.

She was wearing her police uniform as Bangkok protocol required her to do when traveling, and Cole saw for the first time her airborne jump wings – along with her neat, single row of ribbons. He thought about complimenting her on earning her badge and say something about the time he earned his jump wings in Ft. Benning, Georgia. But he stopped short. He figured the Thais would have some different system and, besides, she was only a cop and not full-blooded military. So no need to bring that up. And he figured that *she'd probably come back at me with something sharp and smart-ass.* But he was wrong.

"So, Cole," she said – and she used his name without interjecting his rank for the first time. This courtesy caused him to stop gazing at her chest and to meet her eyes. "Since you're going to be here in Thailand for some time –"

"Look, I don't think this is going to be 'some time.' Maybe a couple of days. Just until we get this guy in the bag."

She stole another look out the window. The banana plantation was fading from view and she pursed her lips. "Mmm... maybe," she said, nodding her head doubtfully and lifting her brows high into her forehead as if to say, *Don't be so sure about that.*

"So," she repeated, "since you're going to be in Thailand, you should learn a few things to say in Thai. And since we're on this train for another eight hours or so, this might be a good chance for me to teach you some words and phrases."

And with this he stopped smiling.

"It's easy," she said, scooting herself closer to the edge of her seat and closer to him. "For example, we say in Thai, '*sawatdee.*' It's kind of like the Hawaiian word 'aloha.' One word for 'hello' and 'goodbye.' And if a woman is speaking, we say, '*sawatdee, kha.*' If a man is speaking, we say, '*sawatdee khrap.*' Got it? Hear the difference?"

Cole glared at her, saying nothing.

"You try it." And she then repeated the words.

Man, this is stupid.

He hated the idea of joining *this dumbass play.* He had flunked out of Spanish in high school back in T or C where he struggled through a semester to impress the parents of Imelda Murrieta. Cole had no particular talent for remembering words that weren't part of his immediate and pressing world, and "*Hola, que tal?*" and "*Sawatdee*" were *part of that bullshit.*

The only foreign-language words he knew by heart were those favorite GI expressions that all the grunts in Vietnam knew. Important words and phrases like *"dee dee mao!* get the fuck out of here!" Or other *gook expressions* like *"mama-san,"* *"baby-san,"* and *"number fucking ten."* The last was the best. Just start off with "number fucking ten," and then add to that phrase any noun or name you wanted to disparage. "Number fucking ten GI" was by far the most popular. These were the words and phrases that were part of his world. He was in no mood for stupid language games.

But he sighed in an uncomfortable moment of resignation and out it came. "OK. OK. Sud-wuddi-crap," he tried.

Pip chuckled and then corrected him, saying, "No, no, you say *sawatdee, khrap. Sa-wat-dee khrap.* Not 'crap'."

Not taking her laughter in stride, Cole reached for his smokes. Thai 101 was over for that day.

Or so he thought.

CHAPTER 18

Mordechai had already arrived at *Wat Phra Nanachart* temple in Ubon one week before Pip and Cole left Bangkok on the train, headed in his direction and bound for his capture. For Mordechai, it was the first substantial step in his spiritual rebirth. For Cole, nothing could be sweeter than crushing the misadventures of this priest.

And when Fr. Goodcut stepped off the train that Tuesday afternoon, he followed the instructions given to him by *Luang Pee* Brian, Monk Brian, the tall Canadian monk and former fisherman who hailed from a small village on the northern coast of British Columbia. He described the temple near Ubon with great relish during his chats with Mordechai during their moments of mutual reminiscence at *Wat Bowonniwet* in Bangkok.

•   •   •   •   •

Goodcut found his way to the outskirts of Ubon city, walking past rows of two-story wooden shophouses, a square brick Thai Farmers Bank building, and an elementary school whose parade ground was full of blue-and-white-uniformed, squealing kids kicking footballs and playing tag. He walked in the general direction of the mark made by the fisherman monk on his map –

Bung Wai village and *Wat Phra Nanachart* were circled in blue ink.

He crossed the new concrete bridge over the River Mun which flowed south from its headwaters in the Khao Yai Mountains, then eastwards through and past Ubon, before emptying into the vast and muddy giant: the Mekong. *Wat Phra Nanachart*, known for its teaching of the "ways of nature" in Buddhism, was a favorite place for Western devotees, and since it was only five kilometers from the Ubon train station, pilgrim Mordechai wanted to walk and soak up the beauty of the rural Thai countryside en route.

When he was halfway to the temple, a teenage boy flew past on his orange Honda 90, kicking up a plume of red dust. He eyeballed Mordechai as he passed, slowed down and made a U-turn, pulling up alongside of Goodcut who was soaked in sweat.

"Where you go?" asked the boy. He wore an old pair of jungle-fatigue pants and a faded, yellow t-shirt that said in cracked, black letters, "Caterpillar Tractors" under a picture of a monstrous machine – the kind used by the Corps of Engineers to build new air strips in Vietnam. He had found the t-shirt at the temple and loved the picture of the big Cat, and although the image was worn and the shirt tatty, he didn't care. The boy was proud of the shirt and wore it almost every day. It had English writing on the front and that's all that mattered. Those foreign words in unfamiliar letters accorded him big respect with his buddies.

"I go to temple, to Wat. *Wat Phra Nanachart*," said Mordechai.

The boy stared at him as he stood there, next to a scrawny *dton farang*, guava tree, and a pyramid-shaped mileage marker that read "3km," the distance to the city center of Ubon. It had been a long walk, and it was hot as hell. Goodcut wore no hat to block the sun and his sunglasses were doing a poor job of keeping the glare and dust out of his eyes. He pulled them off, wiped them on his shirt tail and, squinting, put the shades back on his face.

The boy scanned Mordechai from bottom to top, from shoes to Ray-Bans. He started with Mordechai's extra-large, white Converse tennis shoes without socks. And when the boy's scan reached his Ray-Bans, he gave the thumbs up. "Number one *wan dah*, glasses," he said, smiling.

"Can you give me ride? I'd like some water. Very thirsty."

The boy was a *luuk-sit*, a monk's helper, who followed the monks when they made their morning alms rounds, and then carried the loads that monks would otherwise need to shoulder. He was on his way to the temple when he made the U-turn.

"Come on," said the boy. "I take you temple. OK."

Goodcut stared at him for a second too long, so the boy repeated himself to spur on the flagging foreigner whose face was now beet red. "OK. You get on."

·   ·   ·   ·   ·

The motorcycle pulled into the temple complex and came to a stop under a magnificent, purple bougainvillea that had taken charge of an entire end of the temple's statuary hall. It had spread its long vines across the roof, its paper flowers falling lightly on the cement walkway to welcome Mordechai as he entered the grounds.

By now, Goodcut was thoroughly familiar with the sights, sounds, and smells of Thai temples, heavy with incense and the aroma of wax from burning candles – scents which could overwhelm the uninitiated foreign visitor.

He removed his shoes when he entered the statuary hall and prostrated himself on his knees before a large Buddha image, a ritual practice he had learned at *Wat Bowonniwet* in Bangkok. He *wai*'ed the image with hands clasped together to his forehead, and then bending to the patterned linoleum floor, he placed his hands on the ground, palms down in front of his face. Goodcut repeated this move three times: once for the Buddha, once for his teachings, and once to honor the ordained clergy.

He then stood and moved towards the statue where he lit a single candle from an oil-lamp flame and placed it on the low altar in front of the statue. He lit three sticks of incense from that candle, raised these between the tips of his fingers to his forehead and then *wai*'ed the Buddha image again. Goodcut placed the sticks in a round, sand-filled receptacle on the altar and *wai*'ed the statue for the third time. He then spoke in a whisper, the ancient Pali-Sanskrit prayer known to all Thais. He repeated the prayer three times:

Na-mo-ta-sa, Pa-ka-wa-toh, A-le-ha-toh, Sam-na, Sam-put-a-sah

Keeping his face towards the statue, he slowly and reverently backed away while bowing his head.

Mordechai exited the hall just as a red Isuzu pickup pulled into the temple grounds, directly in front of him. It was missing its tailgate. In the back were four monks and three younger novices who also dressed in saffron robes, but their right shoulders were bare. They had just come back from blessing a house that was under construction in a nearby village, and they were carrying flowers and small gifts wrapped with banana leaves that the house owner had given to them. In the front of the truck, an old monk rode in the place of honor. And when he started to open his door, the driver got out and ran around to the opposite side of the truck to open it for him.

The driver bowed deeply and accompanied this with a *wai* and many expressions of thanks and gratitude, as best as Mordechai could make out. The old monk called to one of the young novices to come and collect his flowers and place them in the sanctuary, a gesture meant to continue the *boon*, or merit-making, for the house owners.

And as he finished giving the flowers to the boy, the old monk caught sight of Mordechai who was making his way over to offer his greetings and respect to *Luang Por*, venerable father, and revered abbot of *Wat Phra Nanachart.*

Mordechai approached, and *Luang Por* stopped walking and stood transfixed for an instant. He was soon joined alongside by the four other monks who had stepped down from the back of the truck, three of whom appeared to be foreigners. The fact that there were so many foreign monks came as no surprise to Mordechai because this was just as the fisherman monk from Canada had described the temple. Fr. Goodcut now stood before the old abbot who was smiling broadly when Mordechai began to speak.

"*Sawatdee khrap, Luang Por,*" said Mordechai as he raised his hands to *wai* the abbot. Mordechai raised his clasped palms, fingertips up to his forehead, to show the proper level of respect to the esteemed old monk.

"*Ja, ja. Watdee, watdee.* Yes, yes, greetings to you, too." But he paused there and continued to stare at Mordechai. The abbot raised his hand to scratch his chin and asked, "Do I know you? Your face looks very familiar to me – like I know you."

What?! This is a relief! His English is great, thought Mordechai who smiled and wanted to blurt out that he was told about the temple by a friend, a Canadian monk, in Bangkok who said he should come here and meet with *Luang Por.* "My friend's name is *Luang Pee* Brian and he told me to say to you –"

"Yes. Yes. Good. Good," said the old monk, interrupting and not the least interested in Mordechai's details. "You come with me now."

And he gestured for Mordechai to follow him back into the hall. Three of the older monks followed the abbot and Mordechai inside where they sat down, cross-legged in a circle on a raised dais near the entrance. The novices followed in as well but were excluded from this circle; they stood watching nearby and fidgeted in silence. Before anyone spoke again, the *maa-chi*, Buddhist nuns, brought out 5 cups of hot tea, knelt, and placed them before the abbot and his circle, including Mordechai, taking care not to touch the robes of the monks.

Mordechai and the other monks sipped their tea in silence, waiting for the abbot to speak. Mordechai's gaze went from face-to-face, appealing for eye contact and finding none. Only the young *nanes,* novices, stared curiously at this new foreign person.

The monks sat quietly, looking out into the temple grounds and beyond. Mordechai had seen a similar, unfocused stare into the distance in the eyes of young combat troops who had seen too much. But these monks were not war-weary. They were, instead, absorbing the natural beauty surrounding them that called the famous school of meditation at *Wat Phra Nanachart* into being. Only the abbot was not in that far-away place. He was intensely present in the moment. And he was staring at Mordechai.

"Yes, I *have* seen you before," he said with a settled tone, happy that he was at last able to recall the face in front of him.

Mordechai did not know how to respond. He was able to glide away from this assertion the first time the abbot had said something, but he now felt compelled to give him an explanation – a Western accounting.

He wished to say, *"No, that's not possible, because, you see, I have never been here before. Not possible, because..."* But instead, he held his tongue and said nothing.

Luang Por spoke again. "Yes, I have seen you. You came into my dreams. Maybe two weeks before."

Confirming his recollection, he said, "Yes. Yes, I saw you in my dreams. You came to see me, and you walked through the forest to come to this temple. To come see me here. And now here you are!" He beamed with satisfaction at making the connection.

The other monks at the table were instantly drawn to the abbot's words. The senior monks sitting there *wai'*ed their spiritual leader, and one muttered, *Sa-ah-tu,* from the Pali-Sanskrit, under his breath to acknowledge the significance of a dream becoming manifested in the flesh. It was the Buddhist version of Amen.

The old monk had not taken his eyes from Mordechai. But his countenance had changed.

"In my dream you come to see me. But behind you, in the jungle, and prowling through the trees, there is a tiger. And the tiger has a monkey riding on its back. And they are coming after you... and they want to catch you."

Luang Por paused to look at him. "But you come here first." And he smiled broadly, pleased with the accuracy of his dream and then repeated, "Yes, you see. You've come here first, before the tiger." And with that he nodded and laughed with great pleasure.

The other monks followed suit, but quickly returned back to their teacups. They looked at the abbot and then at Mordechai. They had smiled at first, but upon hearing about the tiger and the monkey in *Luang Por's* dream they were now secretly worried for this man.

And even *Luang Por* rested his words and turned his wizened face to Mordechai. *Yes, this man came here first, but what of the tiger?* he thought. *This is a disquieting mystery. But this does not need to be mentioned now,* and *Luang Por* let the thought float away. The other monks caught the abbots unspoken worry and they shifted in their cross-legged positions, and quickly took more small sips from their cups. Mordechai had his first taste of the sweet and delicious tea. He felt he could drink gallons of it.

"Yes, I know why you come here. It is fine. It is good."

In silence, *Luang Por* looked around at the hall and the windows opening to the outside and gestured to Mordechai to see the beautiful sanctuary with its graceful architecture and arched *chofa,* the multicolor gold and glass inlay on the roof and walls, the thick growth of trees interior to the temple walls, at the bicycles traveling up-and-down the dusty village road, and at the pale-green rice fields beyond.

Mordechai thought he could see the top of the mileage marker where he had met the boy on the Honda, just an hour earlier. He followed the old monk's bony hand back inside as he pointed to the beauty and the gleam of the satin, teakwood floor they were sitting on. The primitive and rustic detail of everything Mordechai took in with his senses that afternoon was exquisite.

"Yes, you can be a monk and join us here. That is your question, no?"

Mordechai was not surprised by the old abbot's wisdom and the ability to know things that were not spoken. The reputation of *Luang Por's* gift of divination was well-known by Thai Buddhist. But to experience this personally gave Mordechai an unexpected and invigorating chill – to be in the presence of such a holy figure.

The abbot then outstretched his right arm, palm up, and reached for the front of Mordechai's t-shirt. He gently grasped the amulet of the Virgin Mary which had come out of Mordechai's shirt and rested on his chest.

Mordechai said to the abbot, "*Khorthord khrap,* Excuse me," and placed the amulet in his hands, clasped them together and then *wai'*ed the icon before returning it under his shirt. *Luang Por* smiled. He could tell that Mordechai still loved this object of his original adoration: his Mary, the Blessed Virgin.

And that was fine. That was good. For *Luang Por* had also seen this beautiful lady up in the clouds when he traveled there in his meditations.

• • • • •

Because he had worked with dozens of foreign monks, guiding their spiritual growth and presiding over their ordinations for 30 years, the old abbot had come to learn many personal stories from the West. But he was particularly interested to hear the first-hand account from this holy man, this Christian priest, from the other side of the mountains.

The abbot continued, "I want to know your whole story and you can tell me everything. I know you were in great danger before, and your heart is very heavy. But let's not talk of this today. Not now. You can tell me much later."

Mordechai sat, relieved, yet perplexed about the abbot's dream. What could he have meant by the tiger chasing him, and about the monkey riding on the tiger's back? But he knew better than to talk too much about himself on this day, his first encounter with the abbot and with these monks who would become his brothers.

"Yes, tomorrow, you can begin," said *Luang Por*. "You must first become a *nane*, a novice, and learn the ways, the prayers, the habits, the precepts. It is not easy."

He had finished talking and the other monks at the table took their hurried last sips of tea as the abbot got up to leave. The one closest to him offered the old monk his right arm and helped him up. Mordechai stood as the abbot and two of the senior monks departed. He remained with the third monk – who looked about 31, about his own age – who the abbot had left behind to guide Mordechai on the ways to become a novice. He called to the other *nanes*, all local Thai boys, to welcome Mordechai, and they laughed and rushed to his side and held his hands.

And with that, they left and headed for their cottages. The Thai monk, the young Thai *nanes* and Mordechai.

CHAPTER 19

The Ubon train ran north from Bangkok to the ancient city of Ayutthaya and then eastwards, up and over the Khao Yai Mountains that extended to the Thai southern border with Cambodia. Eventually, the line spilled out into the great expanse of the Thai Northeast: *I-saan*. It was Hicksville. The Thai version of US Appalachia, only flat and dry. It was a region characterized by low-literacy, and peasant rice farmers who were bound to a single growing season per year. It was also a region with deep ethnic connections with Laos and a rustic way of life that was held in low esteem by the snobbish Bangkokians, despite the fact that the farmers of *I-saan* were the ones whose brow sweat fed their southern cousins.

·   ·   ·   ·   ·

The train pulled into the next station, the thirteenth stop on its twenty-three-station tour of small towns that dotted the rail line between Bangkok and Ubon. Cole and Pip had already been on the train for five hours and they had another three to go before arriving in Ubon at 2pm, sharp. It was a 360-mile milk run and Cole was growing more impatient with each passing stop.

The white, cement station sign announced "Buri Ram" in black relief lettering in Thai, with English underneath. Small wooden houses with corrugated, scorched iron roofs, discolored with gray patches and red rust, spread out past the station house – roofs hot enough to fry rice on top of them.

Cole stood in the window of the train car with his feet planted between the facing bench seats and stared at the food vendors. They had been waiting in the shade of a giant jacaranda tree for the train to stop and they now rushed towards its open windows with baskets of boiled eggs, rice and desserts wrapped in banana leaves, black *kraejab* seeds, plastic bags with green and red Fanta swirling in crushed ice, and individual cigarettes with small matchboxes on chipped, white enamel serving trays.

A gaunt old man carried plastic bags of *oo-liang*, a rough Thai coffee, which were hung by rubber bands and yo-yo'ed up-and-down under his gnarled fingers. Cole thought he would have a coffee with a Camel, but when the old man came closer and lifted the plastic bags to the window, Cole could see that the dark, brown liquid was sloshing around with the viscosity of motor oil. *I'll pass on the coffee today, old-timer,* thought Cole. *It looks strong enough to stop the heart of a water buffalo. Nah. I'll try the red Fanta instead…*

He called to the young girl holding several bags of the red juice in her right hand. Cole bent through the window, paid her, and came back with a plastic bag full of the cold, sweet drink. He sat back in his seat and pulled a smoke from his pocket and lit it up. He was watching Pip as she smiled at the vendors who now crowded around their window, sensing a buying spree.

The vendors lifted their trays of food and drinks above their heads to the level of the train's window as if they were making a collective offering to celebrities – not far from the truth. Pip and Cole were from an entirely different universe of wealth and good fortune, completely alien to the poor souls hawking goods to the passing trains at Buri Ram Station. The people on the train were going places, on the move, and doing interesting and important things that their lot in life accorded them.

And the poor always gave deference to those who had better luck in life – better luck in this incarnation. It was simply right and just. Their stoic acceptance of fate, this determination to thrive with dignity in the face of poverty was a virtue rarely understood or tolerated by the Western mind. But this virtue was the source of Pip's love and honor of the poor. The scene struck up the feeling of *songsaan*, of pity. And to the Thais, pity is a much stronger emotion than love itself. Cole saw the warmth in her expression as she looked out the window, and it was perplexing to him.

"Lieuten... er... Cole... can you call that elderly lady over there, the one with the thatched tray and the wrapped bundles of *khaotom mat*, banana and steamed rice – do you see her?"

But he was busy scanning the jostling collection of food offerings, the moving feast outside the window in front of him, trying to score something he could recognize. It was all odd-ball stuff to him and most of it was wrapped in banana leaves, so it was hard to say what they carried.

"Uh, no, I don't... all looks pretty much like the same stuff to me."

Pip rose from her seat to call the old lady herself, but the woman had already scurried off to find other prospects in the cars ahead.

With a small voice Pip said, "Never mind. If you are hungry, we can go to the dining car at the rear of the train. OK?" She stood up and rummaged around in her overnight bag and pulled out a plastic sack which she grabbed by its ears.

She didn't wait for a reply from Cole. She turned to him and said, "I'm hungry. Let's go."

Cole flicked the half-smoked cigarette out of the window and three street kids who had been begging for coins scrambled in a rugby scrum to see who would come up with the prize and finish the smoke.

And as the train pulled away from the station, he took the last quick swigs on the red Fanta and then hung the empty bag and its few, remnant pieces of melting ice on the train window by its rubber band. He started after Pip who was already a half-a-car ahead of him.

"Hey! What about my bag – our bags – in the overhead?"

Pip had reached the door of the next car, turned and smiled at Cole, tapping her right shoulder-board on her police uniform with her left forefinger. The meaning to Cole was clear. But he nonetheless looked around the car and at the few passengers near their now-vacant seats. He didn't catch anyone paying special interest in their move to the dining car – nor to his bag in the overhead – so he decided that all was well.

Besides, Pip had said something to the old couple who were sharing the same bench seats with them, and she had pointed to the luggage overhead. He couldn't make out a word, but the elderly woman had smiled and said, "*Ja. Ja,*" a sweet version of "Yes. Yes" often said by old people. Cole guessed all was OK, but instinctively reached behind him and under his untucked shirt to feel the reassuring metal mass of his .45. He wasn't sorry he lied to Pip about it. *It would have been a big mistake to tell her the truth.*

The dining car was two cars down, the very last car on the rocking train. When Cole entered the diner, he spotted Pip, freshly seated in a booth towards the middle. It was one of the few tables that had a white tablecloth on it. The waiter had just come to the table with a menu and a pitcher of water. He bowed a few degrees towards the table as he poured water into two glasses.

"*Khor khaow plaow, song jaan, kha. Khae nee.* We'd like two plates of white rice, please. Only this." The waiter acknowledged the order with, "*Khrap.* Yes, ma'am."

Cole said, "That '*khrap*' word sure gets a workout in your country." Turning to the waiter, he said, "Bring me an ice-cold beer. Thanks." And trying out his best Thai, he hastily added, "*Crap.*"

Pip, ignoring his attempt to be clever, placed her plastic sack on the table and brought out the contents, wrapped in banana leaves. *Here we go again with the banana leaves,* thought Cole.

She undid the twine holding the packages together and opened them flat on the table: two identical dishes of chicken with cashew nuts. "I think you like cashew nuts, no?" But Cole had scant recollection of the nuts scattered across the coffee table in his room at the Rex Hotel yesterday morning. The aroma of the food caught him off guard. He gave an involuntary swallow which caused Pip to grin.

She said, "I brought one portion for me, and one for you." Cole looked at her and smiled closed-mouth as the waiter arrived with two steaming plates of plain rice which he placed in front of them, serving Pip first. He then placed the silverware and opened a small Singha beer which he poured into a glass in front of Cole. He straightened himself and, satisfied that all was in order, left them with a nod.

Thailand, thought Cole. "*Land of a Thousand Smiles.*" He was trying to recall where he had seen that poster. *OK. Right. At the military arrival hall at Don Muang Airport. On…? Shit that was just two days ago. Seems like two weeks…* Time plays an accordion in Thailand, expanding and shrinking the hours and days, and Cole had fallen victim.

He looked away from the window to see that Pip was calling him to eat. She was paddling her spoon and fork over her plate of rice like an oarsman in a skiff. Cole got the message and dove in. Pip watched him enjoying the food, and he was halfway finished before she started to eat. She was intent on making small talk, on striking up a conversation. Something to gloss over the earlier, failed language session.

"You know, Lieutenant, I mean Cole, the place we are going to has a long, even ancient history. Many stories and folktales have emerged from there – the place we call, *I-saan*, the Northeast."

She looked out the window so she wouldn't be upset by his negative facial expression when she asked her next question. "Would you like to hear one of these stories? Not very long."

"Yeah, sure, OK. All ears, sister." His mouth was open, but his ears were shut. The food was great, hitting the spot, and she could have asked him anything and he would have agreed. A few grains of rice slipped out of his mouth and onto the tablecloth, and he picked these up and stuffed them back in.

Pip was not yet fully in-tune with his sarcastic side, so she began her story. Cole was her hungry and captive audience. "Well," she started, "this story is from an ancient time. It is called 'The Serpents and the Porcupine'."

Cole thought that hearing this boring story was like having a bad TV dinner: OK food. Lousy show. *Just so long as she don't try to ask me any dumb-shit questions when she's done.*

"Before men inhabited Southeast Asia, much of Thailand was covered by a shallow sea, and in that sea lived two giant serpents who had long and beautiful names, as long as their golden tails. The one was named *Pinta Yonak Wati* and the other was *Thana Mun* – but we can say *Pinta* and *Mun* to make it easy for you."

Cole was scooping up the last of his rice, using his spoon and the thumb on his left hand as a backstop. He glanced up at Pip, *Shit… here she goes…*

"Since these were very large serpents, they were hungry all the time. And so, they agreed to share all the food they killed so neither one would be without food. They even shared an elephant that had fallen into the sea and drowned. But one day, Pinta found a drowned porcupine in the water and before bringing it to Mun, he plucked off half of the quills.

He gave it to Mun who ate the part without quills, but Mun was still hungry and realized that the other half – the half with the quills still on – looked much bigger than the portion he had just eaten. He then blamed Pinta for being dishonest, and a huge fight broke out which lasted day-upon-day."

Cole had now finished his portion of the cashew nuts and chicken and reached back across the table for the toothpick jar near the window, and he shook one of the unwilling sticks free from its lodging.

"The other animals, fearful for their own lives because of all the destruction and waves these two giant serpents were causing, appealed to the god Indra to put a stop to the fighting. Indra took pity on them and commanded the two serpents to immediately cease their war."

Cole was working hard on his back molar, trying to free up a cashew that had gotten stuck under a cracked filling, *a patch that a quack Army dentist in Da Nang* had placed there during a rushed job.

"So, Indra commanded Pinta to leave the area and go northwest, and commanded Mun to leave the area and go southeast. And as the serpents left, god Indra dried up the sea.

When Pinta left for the northwest, his body carved out a large channel in the soft, muddy earth. This became the River Ping, which now empties into the Chaophraya River which, in turn, flows out to the Gulf of Siam."

Cole broke the toothpick in half and flicked it out the window. He reached for his smokes and found only one Camel left in the pack, flattened into an oval. He pulled out the cigarette, tossed the empty pack on the table and reached for his Zippo. But before he could light it, the waiter rushed over and did the job with a blue, plastic butane lighter he kept in his apron.

"And when Mun left for the southeast, his large body carved a deep channel in the soft earth. This became the River Mun which flows into the Mekong River and then out to the South China Sea." She paused for a moment to give her finale better effect, "And this is the river that flows past Ubon to this day. You will see this river when we get there this afternoon."

Pip had finished her story with satisfaction and folded her left arm over her right, hands near her chest at the edge of the table. She glanced at Cole who was pulling a piece of tobacco from the tip of his tongue. She smiled, hoping for some pleasant observation. None was forthcoming.

"So," he began, blowing a smoke ring out of the corner of his mouth that drifted towards the open window, vanishing the instant it crossed over the toothpick jar, "was there supposed to be some kind of point to that story? If so, I didn't get it. Like 'don't mess with big snakes', or 'be careful what you eat'."

He cocked an eye in her direction. He was happy to eat the chicken with the cashew nuts but did not see that he had to pay for that with good manners.

She thought, *No, you stupid moron!* but instead said, "That's not the idea of this story. There is no *'point.'* It is merely an ancient story about how these two rivers got their names." She tried to bring it home by offering, "I'm sure the American Indians have similar stories, about how places in, say, New Mexico got their names, no?"

But by this time, a disinterested Cole was checking his watch. It was 12:20. Another hour and forty minutes to go. "I'm gonna go back and catch some shuteye. How much to settle up here?"

"No, it's OK. I can pay. It's not much – just the two plates of rice."

Standing up he reached into his pocket and pulled out two, green 20 baht notes and flipped them on the table, "Here. This should cover the beer."

He took three steps back towards their seats, but stopped and turned around to face Pip and said, tugging on his chin and conjuring up a faded courtesy he once knew, "Oh, yeah. Thanks for the food."

CHAPTER 20

Cole and Pip were enjoying the cashews and chicken at the same time Mordechai was boarding a small passenger ferry at the riverfront dock at Ubon, along with *Luang Por*, three senior monks, and four other *nanes*. All were headed down the Mun River to the village of Khong Chiam, situated on the north side of a spit of land that jutted out into the water and marked the place where the blue Mun flowed into the muddy Mekong. At that place, they were to meet with the abbot of *Wat Suwan* temple, and together they would all travel by foot to the meditation retreat in *Pha Taem* Forest, at the foot of the *Soi Sawan* Waterfall.

•   •   •   •   •

Mordechai was ecstatic. At long last, his reason for being called into the religious life was materializing with each footfall. He was walking in the company of men on a pilgrimage, all wrapped in flowing saffron robes, the perfect colorful counterpoint to the lush, green forest surrounding them.

He caught, at times, glimpses of the Mekong off to their right as the trail under their bare feet rose higher and away from the river valley. The trail passed through trees whose ancestors gave shelter to the prehistoric people of the area – the ancient ones who left cryptic sandstone paintings on the cliffs and rock outcroppings overlooking the valley below.

When they reached an open meadow at the trail's end, the three older monks gathered the five *nanes*, including Mordechai, and instructed them to collect wood for the central fire pit they would light later that evening. The pit would serve as an object of focus for their meditations and a way to reflect on the lack of permanence in the world – how the living, once green wood had died, forming brittle brown firewood which, in turn, would burn and become embers, dying into mere ashes and then smoke. And then nothing. Mordechai was a man who well understood that *there is no permanence to the physical life*. Vietnam had taught him well.

The *nanes* were careful not to collect green wood for the fire tonight, but only those branches and twigs that were long-dead and dried. And they tapped these pieces on the ground sharply to make sure that they had dislodged any living creature which might have found a home within the wood. *The sanctity of sentient creatures...* Every small action by his brethren took on heightened meaning for Mordechai. The physical activities were making spiritual sense. *Much like the Sacraments of the Catholic Church...* He recalled his seminary lesson, *'the outward and sensible signs of inward and spiritual graces...'*

In preparation for their evening meditation and sleep, the entourage formed a circle with their umbrella-shaped tents around the fire pit, the hub for their encampment. The two abbots then drew everyone together to pay respect to the elegant Buddha image that was residing on an altar, built into the side of the mountain that rose up at the far end of the meadow. It had a glittering glass frame that enclosed the niche in which the beautiful golden image sat in the "pose of meditation." Mordechai knew this particular pose of the Buddha corresponded to Thursday – an auspicious omen since they would all pass into Thursday during their meditations that evening.

He knew his spirit was supposed to be calmed and his emotions quelled by the chanted prayers of the two abbots and the senior monks as they stood, paying respect to the image. But Mordechai could not resist the sensations of pleasure and delight – and ultimately an abiding sense of being spiritually satiated. Full. It overpowered him. And as the chanted prayers ended, he noticed *Luang Por* was looking at him, smiling broadly, beckoning him to walk together across the meadow and back to the circle of umbrellas where one solitary monk was lighting a small fire in the center of the pit. The others drew close to *Luang Por* as they walked. Mordechai had never felt such pure and unbounded contentment in his entire life. He was coming home.

●   ●   ●   ●   ●

But tonight would be a trial by silence, an inquiry into the soul for Mordechai and the other truth-seekers who gathered around the fire. They were to reflect upon their calling and to see whether they were in the right place, in the right time, and in the right incarnation. It would not be an easy task, as *Luang Por* had warned them.

The monks chanted ancient prayers well into the night. The sounds of the Pali-Sanskrit words filled Mordechai with immense peace and sacred well-being. And as the prayers ended, and the last of the twigs and logs were reduced to red embers in the fire pit, the two abbots came to visit Mordechai under his umbrella.

"*Nane* Mordechai," *Luang Por* called to him. The old monk called him by his given name. "How do you feel? Are you fine and good?"

Mordechai, came out from his umbrella tent and greeted both abbots with a deep *wai*, smiled and said, "Yes, reverend fathers. I am fine – and good." And both abbots were greatly pleased.

Luang Por felt a special connection to Mordechai that even he did not fully understand. He only knew that he was familiar with Mordechai's old soul. It was known to him. Mordechai possessed something very special within his *nee-sai*, his core nature. He exuded an aura that was at once powerful, and yet benevolent. And the Abbot loved him for it.

But he was also worried for this *nane,* for *Luang Por* knew something dark and ominous was on the prowl, and it was moving in their direction. He spoke to Mordechai, "I dreamed about the tiger and monkey again last night – they are growing closer." He studied Mordechai's face who was also puzzled. Such an encounter had been the furthest thought from Mordechai's mind that night.

The two abbots left for their umbrella tents, and Mordechai sat next to the last embers of the fire and tried to calm his mind. He wanted to become a monk above all other things and was committed to take his vows. And he was mindful of the requirement that a Buddhist monk must control his thoughts to achieve an inner peace.

But that night in the forest would be his "dark night of the soul." His trial. He recalled the abbot's warning about forest meditations, "*Although the forest may look peaceful, and it is true that it is beautiful, it is also a very active place for many spirits in the night. Be on guard.*" And for Mordechai, the night began with sheer terror.

During the first hours after prayers, he heard the distant bellows and saw with his mind's eye, scenes of wickedness and evil afoot in the world. He felt their encampment was being assaulted, as if a cadre of demons were diverted from their vile acts of subversion around the world and redirected to attack their small circle of prayerful monks in the middle of that dark forest.

And, at length, Mordechai heard the sounds of the tiger crushing the nearby undergrowth, pursuing him, and he glimpsed the chattering monkey riding on its back. His eyes flashed open and he could see their fleeting images retreating into the shadows that marked the treeline – outside the large circle of cotton string that *Luang Por* had strung around their encampment before dusk.

This perimeter string was a spiritual wall, made holy and fortified by the blessings and incantations of the two abbots. And the monks' circle of umbrella tents rested safely within this venerated ring of holy string. All were protected from true spiritual harm. But that night, the forest sounds evoked a range of feelings for all the *nanes,* from the sublime to absolute dread – even some of the senior monks were troubled by their encounters.

The abbots, on the other hand, had grown inured and immune to these distractions through decades of active practice. However, even they admitted there might be a sound, a vibration out there, somewhere, that would cause them to tremble with fear. They insisted, out of humility, that they were mere mortal men.

But the other monks knew the abbots in a different way. They knew them to be exceptional beings with steadfast strength of heart and wisdom, each possessing unique spiritual attributes. Their miraculous gifts, such as time travel, the ability to levitate to great heights, and the reading of *win-yaan* – souls from previous incarnations – were powerful and profound, and to their ardent followers, the abbots were holy men. And indeed they were.

Falling into slumber that night, Mordechai remembered the Abbot's warnings about a wandering mind as he navigated flashbacks invoked by the sounds and cries of his time spent at night, in the jungles of Vietnam – flashbacks to the mayhem that was afoot there, just over the mountains to the east from where he sat in a meditative pose – as the earth turned beneath him and night passed into Thursday morning.

CHAPTER 21

Cole was the first to jump off the train. After eight hours on that crawling beast, he bolted for the exit door. He had enough of planning, and enough of Pip's sermonizing and folk stories. He had heard tales about serpents and rivers and, while he was trying to sleep during the home stretch to Ubon, there was yet another story about a lucky forest woodsman.

That assault on his stubborn ears was enough to last him a lifetime. Missing the point, he recalled Pip's earlier attempt at schooling him. *She's right. Only a stupid buffalo would listen to that fiddle-playing bullshit.*

He was chomping at the bit. *Where is that damn woman, anyway?*

•   •   •   •   •

Pip finally appeared in the doorway of the train car. She was helping the old woman who had been sitting with them, down the steps of the train and onto the platform. She handed the woman the small cloth bag she was carrying for her, and both the old woman and her husband *wai*'ed Pip, who curtsied and returned the *wai*. "*Kha,*" she said.

Cole stood on the platform, hands on his hips, and watched this *tearjerker* unfold in front of him. *OK. OK, let's get going! dee dee mao! Or whatever the hell they say in this country.*

"Very touching," he said to Pip.

Ignoring the sarcasm, she said, "Yes, they're coming back to Ubon from Bangkok. They are both day-laborers on a construction site on Phetchaburi Road. A new hotel, or something like that and –"

"Let's get going, it's late and I'd like to wrap this up. OK?"

"– they've come up here to attend the funeral rites for their daughter who had ended her life when she found out that her husband was killed in Vietnam." She turned to look Cole in the eyes. "Killed in Vietnam while working for *your* Army. For *your* war."

Pip fussed with the collar of her uniform and faced away from Cole. "She was the youngest of their five children and they are completely distraught."

Cole paused but didn't drop the beat. "Sorry to hear that." He wasn't, and Pip knew.

She couldn't resist turning to look at the old woman and her husband as she and Cole walked past them, out of the station and onto the street. She had secretly slipped three, red 100 baht notes into the old woman's bag, but could now only offer them a parting smile.

On the station side of the street they found a bright red, *saam-lor*, a three-wheeled motorized version of a pedicab. But unlike its pedaled cousins, this monster was outfitted with a full-sized engine from a junked pickup truck, hand-welded into a beefed-up iron frame. The unit was complete with a four-speed gearbox and it could fly much faster than was ever safe. As long as it stayed on the straight-and-narrow, there was not much danger – unless barreling along at 70 mph on a dirt road in a homemade rickshaw with a 180-horsepower engine was not considered dangerous.

Pip gave the instructions to the driver, a stocky and dark Laotian fellow who had on a Marlon Brando motorcycle cap from the 50s. It was pulled down tight over his head and pushed out the tops of his ears. He wore a pair of Ray-Ban look-alikes, yellow tinted, and he admired the real McCoy's that Cole was sporting. He gripped his glasses with his right hand and pointed to Cole's with his left, giving the thumbs up in approval.

Cole nodded and slid into the seat next to Pip, their bags tossed onto the wooden floorboard at their feet. He noticed the tin cut-out design that was tacked onto the back of this rig. It was in the shape of a Buck Rogers rocket. Tin cut-out stars completed the picture of the universe.

Pip shouted over the roar of the unmuffled engine, "*Rao ja pai Wat thee moobahn Bung Wai.* We're going to the temple at Bung Wai village. *Ruujak mai, kha?* Do you know it?"

"*Khrap, ruujak.* Yes, I know it," Marlon Brando replied. "*Khao riak Wat Phra Nanachart.* They call it *Wat Phra Nanachart.*"

All set, thought Cole. He heard the words "Bung Wai" and some kind of "Wat" name that he didn't catch. It didn't matter. He knew he was getting close.

• • • • •

No sharp and fast curves on the road to *Wat Phra Nanachart*, but the many quick left and right zigzags – avoiding giant potholes on the dirt road – pressed Cole into Pip, and then Pip into Cole. He could feel her arm and thigh rub up against his, and they were warm and soft. After the fourth jolting movement, she made no attempt to avoid his contact. They zipped along in the red rocket, in silence.

Pip paid the driver and Cole sat their two bags on the road, under the arched gateway to the temple. He did not want to drive directly inside the Wat because the noise from the *saam-lor's* free-flowing exhaust pipe was deafening. No need to heedlessly alert anyone that they had arrived on the scene. Cole reasoned that Mordechai was still unaware of their intentions, but his hunter instincts kicked in. No need for his prey to catch a whiff of the hunt, panic and run for the hills – like an elk spooked by a hunter's failed, first shot.

The *saam-lor* left in a cloud of dust and noise, and Cole rummaged around in his bag. He found his handcuffs in their leather holster. And when Pip bent over to pick up her bag, he checked the back of his shirt at the beltline for that comforting metal bulge.

They turned and walked under the gateway of the temple and into the *Wat's* compound. Lining the road for the first 300 feet to the main sanctuary, were alternating yellow "candle trees" and blue jacaranda in full bloom. The picture was stunning. And Pip was delighted to see that the trees formed an immense garland of blue and yellow flowers that ringed the road to the sanctuary. *A fitting offering to the main Buddha image residing here.*

She stopped, placed her bag on the ground, faced the sanctuary and lifted her hands in a *wai*. Cole watched her, her graceful moves, and the innocence of her response to being there, and he was caught off guard, annoyed with himself for being moved by what he saw in her. He shrugged it off.

When they arrived at the entrance to the main statuary hall, Pip stopped a group of three monks who were traversing the old wooden building and were on their way out of the large door. She asked whether she could see the abbot. If they were to grab Mordechai today, she needed to inform the abbot of their plan and the reason for Mordechai's arrest, and then seek his approval for this intrusion.

Cole was busy scanning the prospects in front of him for his errant priest. With shaved heads, faces and eyebrows, it was hard to see distinguishing features apart from tall, short, fat, thin, brown, white. If Cole had known more about their faith, he would have understood that this anonymity was precisely the idea. The loss of self – a distancing from the world and one's recognition within that world – was a necessary precursor to serious monastic life. But such abstractions were not part of the world in which Cole lived. He had narrowed his scan to tall, thin, and white.

He saw Pip pull a photograph from a file she had tucked into her bag and show it to the monks. It was Mordechai, arriving at the Don Muang Airport three weeks earlier. "*Hen khun nee mai, kha*? Have you seen this man?"

And they all nodded with smiles of affirmation. *Evidently, Mordechai has made a big hit here*, thought Pip.

Cole came rushing over. "So what did they say?"

"Well, there's good news – and not-so-good news. Yes, it is true he was here, and has become a novice monk here last week, as a matter of fact. But they said he's left this morning to the village of Khong Chiam with the abbot here, and a group of other monks and *nanes*. They are going to see the abbot at the temple in Khong Chiam and then go for a meditation retreat in the forest nearby. Seems they will be gone for a day. So, we can go there tomorrow and catch him when he returns from the forest. That may be –"

"Shit!" Cole blurted out. "We've come all this fucking way and –"

"Listen lieutenant! You've got to watch your language here. You can use your toilet mouth all you'd like with your buddies back in the Army, or wherever, but you can't use that language here. This is a holy place. You wouldn't speak like that in Church, would you?"

He did not say anything more, only offering a slight nod in her direction. But his steam kept leaking out. The needle was well into the red zone. *Can't believe we just missed that bastard! Fuck me sideways!*

Ignoring the small group of monks present, Cole marched outside. He reached for a fresh pack of Camels and the zippo from his pants pocket, lit one up and drew in a big drag which he exhaled with anger. *Son of a bitch!*

The three monks filed outside and walked past him, down the blue and yellow garland lane. Pip made her way to the large Buddha image at the north end of the hall, knelt, embraced the floor three times with her *wai's*, and then stood and offered a brief prayer for clarity and calmness.

Cole flicked the half-smoked butt onto the ground and watched her as she came back outside. "OK," she said. "We can go to my relatives' place for tonight. Tomorrow we can continue on by river to Khong Chiam. We'll find Mordechai then."

Cole said nothing but just picked up his bag, and then hers, and they walked together towards the side road to find a ride back to Ubon. And they didn't need to wait long. By the time they reached the main road that led into town, and traveled north another 200 feet, an orange Honda 90 zoomed past. The driver glanced at the two as he flew by and then circled back, coasting to a stop in front of them.

Sporting a yellow t-shirt with a giant Caterpillar tractor, and a newly acquired pair of genuine Ray-Bans, he asked, "*Pai nai?* Where are you going?"

Pip explained they needed to get back to the city. And maybe he could go send a *saam-lor* out from the train station to pick them up. "*Dai mai, kha?* Can you do this for us?"

Nodding, but without saying a word, he sped off.

"It's getting dark," said Pip. Cole was still sulking and said nothing. "Let's wait here. That boy will send someone to fetch us. And don't take it so hard, we will do what we came here to do, tomorrow. One night is not going to make a difference."

But Cole was not listening to anything she had to offer. It was a waste of a day for him.

• • • • •

The two stood in silence under a broad mango tree which was rife with sprouting flower buds. It was sticky hot and they were not moving any more than was absolutely necessary, only to shift their stance from foot-to-foot.

In a long five minutes, they heard the roaring sounds of the three-wheeled, red Toyota devil bearing down on them. They would be at Pip's family's guest house in no time.

CHAPTER 22

The sun had fallen into the jungle to the west of Ubon when Pip and Cole roared up to the front of her aunt's guest house in the bright red *saam-lor*. The place was situated directly on the River Mun, just downstream from the new concrete bridge on Highway 24 – the main highway that passed over the river and headed south to the Cambodian border, before turning to the west and on to the Thai city of Korat.

Aunt Nida, or *Naa* Nid as Pip still called her, was her father's youngest sister. She had gone to Ubon with her husband, Uncle Suwit, who had given up a lucrative medical practice in Bangkok in favor of working in the countryside. Midway through his career – and by fate – he heard the King offer an inspiring speech about dedication to public service. Those stirring words had put his heart on fire about working for the poor in *I-saan*, and Uncle Suwit abandoned his practice in Bangkok and moved, lock-stock-and-barrel, to Ubon where he established a regional hospital some 20 years ago.

Naa Nid was obliged to leave her well-heeled life in Bangkok, but she remained ever resilient and upbeat. She was old school. A diehard. And she eventually found work in a local exporting firm that transported goods in-and-out of neighboring Laos. *Nah* Nid and Uncle Suwit prepared for their retirement by renting, then purchasing, the modest 10 room guest house on the river.

And both were extremely happy to know Pip was coming to visit.

* * * * *

"Pip, *ja!*" cried her aunt as she rushed out of the lobby and held her niece tightly – close to her heart. The elderly lady couldn't remember the last time she had seen her niece, even though it had only been a few months earlier, during the *Songkran* water festival.

The old woman blurted out, "It has been too long since I saw you last! Look at you now!" It had seemed like years to her and she didn't want to let go of Pip – and Pip, indulging her respected aunt, did not wish to correct her fading memory.

She stood back from Pip and held her at arm's length, admiring her and her sharp uniform. "Oh, your father would have been so proud." And Pip recalled her mother's same words just yesterday morning.

Speaking in Thai, Pip smiled and said, "Hello Auntie! I'm so happy to see you! Yes, it has been a while. And yet you still look like *yaa-oorn*, young grass." And they embraced again and laughed out loud.

"Oh, Auntie, please let me introduce a work colleague of mine. This is Lieutenant Coltrane, from the US Army." Aunt Nid turned to look at Cole. He had been standing there in silence, holding both bags the whole time since the *saam-lor* tore off.

The first look she gave Cole betrayed her displeasure. Old people often make that slip. Nearing the end of their run, they unconsciously drop the instincts to hold up their masks, and their true feelings are often on full display. Those first seconds with Cole were not happy. But she recovered quickly, not wanting to interfere with whatever business her favorite niece had with this man.

"Hello," she said in English. "Nice to meet you." She stood there by Pip's side, both of them looking at Cole.

Protocol called for him to *wai* her and give her a short greeting, but Cole had no clue about proper social behavior in Thailand. Instead, he only came up with, "Thanks, me too." And he fished around in his shirt pocket for his Camels and lit one up in haste. *This old broad comes from the same cut of cloth as her niece. Stiff, and the look she gave me was a killer. The old prune. I feel like the spare prick at the wedding.* Indeed he was.

In Aunt Nid's mind, here was an American GI, fresh from the war – the war that was reigning bombs down on neighboring Laos and killing large numbers of people – and many of those innocent folks were her friends who were just minding their own business, riding their bicycles, or walking up-and-down the highways, blown to pieces in the next instant by a plane they could not hear nor see.

Naa Nid knew the stories of the people affected by the American campaign in Laos, a backcourt drama to the main event in Vietnam, its neighbor to the east. Her eyes narrowed as she rescanned Cole with these fresh thoughts that had floated into her mind.

However, Thai *ma-ra-yaat*, manners, prevailed. "Won't you come in, Lieutenant?" and she motioned for the houseboy to come and pick up the bags. But Cole was not releasing the grip on his bag. The houseboy looked at Pip for some intervention, but she said nothing.

She asked instead, "So where is Uncle Suwit? I haven't seen him."

"Oh, he's fine. But he's taken the truck and his grandson, Lek's son, to Khon Kaen city to buy some art supplies he can't get here. He'll be back tomorrow. Since he's retired, he spends most of his time painting pictures from the boat dock there, in front of our restaurant. He's not interested in doing much of anything else. He no longer sees patients. And he used to go up-

and-down the river in his motorboat, but he's no longer interested in doing that, either. Lek uses the boat now. I think your uncle believes he's the Thai van Gogh. But... well... well, he enjoys himself."

As with all successful couples, there was no guarantee that their own children would enjoy the same measure of success that their parents did. The saying goes, "You can pick your friends, but not your relatives." So it was with Aunt Nid and Uncle Suwit. They had two children, a boy and a girl. The girl, the younger child and Pip's cousin, had gone to live in Bangkok after she married into a wealthy family that sold construction machinery for highways. The boy, Lek, stayed in Ubon and was now on his third wife. The other two had fled due to his "problem" and his violent behavior when drunk – and the third was likely to be a repeat performance.

"Come on up to your room," said *Naa* Nid. And with that she led them to the first, and only, floor above the lobby, restaurant and boat dock downstairs. She stopped at the top of the stairs and fussed with the key for the first room on the left – the first of 10 side-by-side rooms which opened onto a wooden walkway with a floral wrought-iron railing, directly above the restaurant. With no rooms to the right of the walkway, there was a clear view of the river below.

A small brass sign on the door said, "Room 101," which sounded much better in Uncle Suwit's estimation than "Room 1." Along the way, both Cole and Pip counted six renditions of the "River Mun" that her uncle had painted and placed on the wood veneer walls in canvases without frames.

"I hope you don't mind," Aunt Nid said, looking over Pip's shoulder to see if Cole could hear. He was taking in the view of the river from the walkway railing in front of their room. "But we're full up now due to a government delegation which has just arrived from Bangkok. They're here to inspect the local hospital, so your uncle was nervous and invited them to stay here. They are checking out tomorrow and I can give you separate rooms then. But hope you don't mind, just for now."

She opened the room and Cole turned from the view of the river and followed them inside. He saw it had a raised platform, mid-room, with a single bed on it behind a room divider which split the room into two parts. In the part of the room closer to the door was a long sofa.

"Uh...," Cole started. "That's OK. I can find somewhere else to spend the night. Maybe in the lobby or –"

"No that's crazy," interrupted Pip. "The mosquitos would eat you alive. And besides this room is OK just for the one night, its nicely split down the middle for privacy." Eyeing the bed Pip added, "And you can take the sofa."

Cole was too tired to argue, and Pip seemed OK with it – and her aunt was too far along in years to consider any potential impropriety, or to think that such sleeping arrangements for two professional officers were the least bit odd. It was settled.

"So," Cole began. "Is the restaurant open? I'd really like to get something to eat – and drink."

CHAPTER 23

Cole's day was at an end, and so was he. *What kind of a shit-hole bar is this?* He scanned the modest liquor cabinet behind the restaurant's bar, and the only quality booze he found were two bottles of liqueurs that some foreign tourists had left behind. But there was not a drop of decent whisky in the place.

He didn't care if they had Glenlivet. Just anything imported would save him from drinking that *Mekong rotgut*, a whisky perfect for getting the great-unwashed masses drunk. Cole knew Mekong kicks you squarely in the head the next day – a built-in penitence device for those who didn't stop at the third or fourth glass.

•　　•　　•　　•　　•

Pip stepped away from the table to talk with her uncle Suwit by telephone, and she left Cole in the company of her younger cousin, Lek, and two of his river-rat friends whom Aunt Nid detested. The refined old lady had turned in over an hour ago, right after the dessert was served, a coconut milk and banana dish she knew Pip loved. The two local girls in the kitchen had cleared the table and brought out a fresh quart of Mekong Whisky and another bucket of ice. They placed both items on the table then retreated to the veranda overlooking the boat dock, remaining out of sight but within earshot.

"So," Lek was continuing on about the good Thai-American relations, "you see, we help America in Vietnam. And we like Americans." He grinned and looked at his friends who were grinning too, even though they were not exactly sure what he was saying.

Cole thought, *These two guys look like they just ate a couple of bowls of shit.* Because he was the son of the owners, Lek was flexing and his friends were admiring his skills in a language that they could not comprehend. They caught an English word every now and then, like they were watching boxcars flying down a train track, catching only the general drift, force and direction of the conversation. But no matter, all four of them were getting to a low boil, following Lek's insistence to keep the shots flowing.

"Great. Great," started Cole. "Since we're such good buddies and all, what say we take your boat down to Khong Chiam village tomorrow morning? You can skipper us down there. I can pay you. Good money. No problem."

Lek looked at his friends and said in Thai, "This guy's gonna go with my cousin to Khong Chiam tomorrow and I'm gonna take them down there. I can pluck his ass clean of feathers and stuff them in my pockets – make some good money!"

They all erupted in laughter and Cole figured Lek was giving them some sarcastic bullshit, but he let it slide. He was drunk, but not drunk enough to make it into an issue. "Sure, sounds good. Let's make it 6am. OK?"

Lek laughed and said, "Are you a monk or something?! Six in morning too damn early. Eight OK. Sun up over mountain at eight. Can see trees in river then."

Cole's ears picked up on Lek's last words. "Trees in river? You mean snags?" asked Cole.

"OK," replied Lek.

Now, that's a stupid answer, thought Cole who was already sore when he found out earlier the lousy restaurant didn't have any decent whisky, and Lek's laziness and evasive answer just annoyed him more. *But fuck it!*

Cole offered up his glass and gave the ice a swirl as Lek poured in another round, and the conversation shifted to local news and American football. Lek had once seen a foreign movie downtown that featured American sports, and he was fascinated by football and the violence of the game. He was big enough to play defensive end, and Cole told him so. And Lek was doing a decent job of being a good drinking buddy, until he stumbled onto the taboo topic of religion.

"Look," said Cole, now three sheets in the wind. "I'm OK with being here, and with your country... and its great we get along and all of that. But I don't have much time for religion of any kind these days. Not mine, not these guys –" pointing to the river rats, "– and not yours. No offense, but it's all pie-in-the-sky, mumbo-jumbo bullshit to me."

Lek stopped smiling and stared at Cole. He sat his glass down quietly on the table. He understood that English perfectly. And he didn't like what he heard. And the two river rats also stopped smiling, on cue.

"So, what's going on here, guys?" Pip had returned to the table and sat down into the thick silence. She reached for her now-warm glass of beer, the same glass she had been nursing all night. She smiled at her cousin and then at Cole. "So... what *is* going on?"

"Nothing. Nothing," said Cole. He stared at Lek for a few long seconds, long enough for Lek to do something froggy if he wanted to leap out there. But he didn't, just like Cole figured. He knew this guy was not up for a fight tonight. He smiled at Lek and held his glass up for a toast. Lek studied him for two blinks and then lifted his glass and laughed out loud. The rats piped in and saluted with their glasses.

And a loud chorus of "*Chai yoor*! salute!" rang out from the Thai side of the table as everyone killed their drinks. Only Cole and Lek had the slightest clue as to what was going on.

"OK. OK. We go now," said Lek as he pushed back from the table. "See you in morning. Baht OK, dollar OK," he added with a wink.

The three Thais rose from the table and headed for their Nissan truck. Lek turned to *wai* his older cousin, "*Sawatdee khrap*," he said. She smiled and waved to him as the drunken crew ambled off.

One of Lek's friends struck up the first few bars of an *I-saan* love song about a beautiful Thai woman who falls for a foreigner. They all joined in and laughed as they sang. Pip stood looking at them as the truck disappeared and, shaking her head, came back to the table where Cole was still seated.

"You know, Cole, we Thais love our *sasanaa*, our religion. It is one of the three things that makes us 'Thai.' The King, our language, and our *sasanaa*. My advice to you is not to comment on any of these three topics while you are here. It can be misunderstood."

She watched him for a sign he was listening to her, but then added quickly, "I'm going to go check on my Auntie. I'll be back in a few minutes."

But Cole was still brooding after those three morons had left, and he poured another two neat shots before Pip would come back to the table again. Given enough time and enough ethanol, solitary drunks usually seize on hot-button topics on any given night, and so it was with Cole. He had his fill of both and Religion and Death. And without fail, the place he always wound up when drunken images of these topics sloshed around in his head, was a hospital bed on the other side of the earth and his sister lying there in a coma. He could not possibly have been any farther from her, physically and spiritually, than he was that night – and the booze was talking as Pip sat back down.

He asked her, "Do you ever wonder what happens when people go into a coma? Do you know what they are thinking… or if they're thinking at all?"

Pip wondered where this was coming from. She pressed her ears to hear his sounds. *Was he imagining a fight with Lek, or…?*

"Is it the same place you go when you die, only you're still breathing? So, if it is a good place, you're OK. But if it's an awful place…" He took another swig of the Mekong.

He paused, and his head bobbed. He lifted up his face and without hesitation said, "You don't know this, but I got a kid sister."

The Mekong whisky had burst his dam and he let it flow, "And she was raped and knocked into a coma by some animal back home. I'm gonna kill the bastard that did that."

Pip could not believe her ears and she inched closer to where Cole was sitting, hunched-back, and staring at the boat dock and the river beyond.

He turned to face her, "You hear me, I'm gonna kill the bastard that did that!"

Pip was shocked. Rendered speechless. Not only by the revelation, but because this rock-hard American lieutenant was saying these things out loud – and to her.

He let his story spill out, sharing his secrets with a woman he barely knew, about the dreadful things that happened to his sister. He even said her name, "Abilene."

Pip had no way of knowing about Cole's sister and his underlying anger for what happened to her – and she wasn't sure whether or not his sister was still alive. *It seems not.*

After a long and awkward silence she offered, "Well, I don't know what happens when we die… But in Thailand, we believe our souls will be born again. In your Christian *sasanaa*, you believe you go to heaven or hell. I think you can –"

"You believe! We believe! Your sama-sam-sa… or whatever you call it… shit!" Cole cut her off at the quick, glaring at her over the rim of his empty glass. He was looking for a sparring partner and Pip had unwittingly obliged.

"I don't believe any of that goddamn rubbish. 'Back again.' 'Heaven or hell.' None of that matters to me." He stood up fast and his chair fell backwards, banging on the floor. The kitchen girls came around from the veranda, but Pip waved them away.

"None of that matters to my kid sister. She could use a little bit of that help now, but she ain't getting it from anybody upstairs. And why not? She deserves it more than anyone. More than you. More than me. But she ain't getting any. *Nada*."

He took his glass and walked to the riverside railing of the restaurant and looked out at the water.

Pip watched him from the table, and then slowly walked over and stood beside him. She was unsure of Abilene's fate but risked offering some few words of kindness.

She thought it might bring some comfort to him – but Cole was a world away, walking through the badlands of New Mexico. He was not listening to any of her words. He just fixed his eyes into the dark water of the River Mun.

She paused and stared out into the river with him before softly beginning her story.

"A woman once went to the Buddha, grief-stricken because her infant son had died. She begged him to resurrect her child. He told her that he would do so if she could find just one household which had not been touched by death. Willing to try anything, she went from house-to-house over the entire countryside, but could not find one home where death had not touched the people's lives. So she returned to the Buddha and admitted that it was an impossible task. 'Every household knows death,' she reported. And with this understanding, she accepted the death of her own child as a natural part of life. Death touches us all."

She turned to face Cole and placed her hand on his forearm and repeated, "You cannot find the house which has not experienced death. Every house –"

But with her touch, and the word "death" in his ear, and the picture of Abilene in his mind's eye, he snapped at her. "Look here, Pip!" it was the first time he had used her name. "Nobody's gonna die *here*, and nobody's gonna die *there*!" Pip withdrew her hand.

She tried to peer into the picture that was tormenting him, but she couldn't see the same image he had conjured up, that of a battered and scrawny kid lying in an ICU bed at the Las Cruces Hospital.

"Listen and listen good. I don't want to hear another one of your stupid fucking stories about *anything*. I'm sick and tired of all this preaching... all these stories... all this hocus-pocus bullshit." He squared his feet to look her directly in the eyes.

"And your little fairy tales are for simple-minded idiots – like you! Shit! Like your snake digging up this river," gesturing to the Mun before him with the bottom-end of his whisky glass. "Does this look like a fucking snake made this goddamn river?!"

The simplicity and wisdom of these stories which had percolated down through centuries of Thai culture was of no use to him that night – or on any night. He was a man whose few stories were scraped off a hard-fought life – not the kind of stories that would be welcomed by those who had not lived them. And certainly not by those in Pip's polite social circles.

"And what the hell do you think you know about me, anyway? You know shit. You know nothing!" And with a gnawing grief for Abilene welling up in his gut, he reared back and threw his glass as far as he could into the Mun.

Pip stood and stared at Cole, wondering what kind of demon must be clutching him, and a wave of pity swept over her. She displaced any anger from his insults to herself and to her culture, and she was suddenly and intensely sorry for this man. It was a dangerous place for her feelings. *Songsaan*, pity. Saddened by the force of his immense pain, she feared she was going to melt into the River Mun.

Before she could stop her words, she let her worries for this man loose, "Well, I know something about you that you don't know yourself. You're not as tough as you act – you're hiding something. You're a hunter, alright, Cole. But it's not just the hunt, this hunt for Mordechai – or the hunt for all the other men you've tracked down. Your real prey is deep within *you*. And you need to name and then kill this poisonous thing inside of you. You ache for the release that this kill will give you... You crave it. And you know it yourself, but you can't bring yourself to face it."

Without another word, she turned and went to the stairs leading up to their room, dreading the idea that she had agreed to put up with this fierce American character, even for one night. For the first time, she felt afraid to be there. But it was not his drunken demeanor that she feared. What Pip feared most was the insidious draw of his story. It was chipping away at her will to resist, and she was more worried about that attraction than the dangerous man himself.

"You don't know nothin' about me," Cole mumbled through his whiskey breath. And he repeated these last words, eyeballing her as she reached the top of the stairs. "Yeah, go ahead and slink off to your room." *Such a royal pain in the ass.*

He returned his gaze to the slow-moving current of the river with complete indifference.

After a few minutes had passed and the picture of Abilene faded, dissolved by the booze that was coursing through his brain, he turned to leave. But as he did so, he caught out of the corner of his eye, a stirring in the water near where his glass had landed.

A phosphorescent swirl in the water glowed with white and blue, and brilliant pink lights, and he saw a huge, lustrous serpentine shape rise from the swirling waters where it lifted up and bent into an inverted "U", and then descend in a long graceful arc, finishing with a bright golden tip which shimmered as the figure disappeared, deep beneath the water.

Cole looked on in astonishment. He spun to see if Pip was there, or the kitchen girls. But he was alone, and alone with his thoughts, unable to speak in words that which could not be expressed. What he had just seen – or thought that he saw – was a universe away from his headstrong and callous world.

"No way!" he cried aloud. "That didn't happen!" *I'm drunk alright, but this takes the fuckin' cake!*

He moved towards the stairs to his room, but froze and looked back again at the water, now just the slow-moving, somber, dark current. It lapped up against the small motorboat that was moored there. He shook his head and, trying to remove all images of the evening, shrugged his shoulders and staggered off towards the steps. But the picture of the motorboat came back into his head and he waved at it without looking. *See you in the morning.*

●　　●　　●　　●　　●

He paused outside their room and pressed his forehead against the smooth, teakwood door. *Man, I've made a mess of things tonight. Too much booze. No brakes. Shouldn't have told Pip about Abilene.* He sucked in a long breath and pushed open the door. It was unlocked.

He found her sitting on the only chair in the room. It was on the platform next to her bed. She had just come out of the shower and her head and body were wrapped in towels. Pip sat motionless in the straight-back chair, staring at Cole as he entered the room. She looked like the seated Egyptian goddess he had once seen in a book from his high school history class. He glanced at the sofa where the housegirls had laid out a pillow and a blanket for him. He looked at Pip and then at his bed, and then at her again. She was stunning.

But he was dead drunk. And he knew it. He walked slowly to where she was sitting, and she removed the towel from her hair. He bent down and tried to kiss her on the forehead. She did not fully resist, but only said softly, in a whisper, "You're drunk. Get away from me."

Her hair smelled wonderful, and he took in a second breath. She rose smoothly from the chair and looked at him with her piercing brown eyes. He bent to kiss her on the mouth, but she turned her head. She reached up to place her hands on his chest as if she wanted to push him away.

Cole grabbed her on the shoulders and whispered, "No more talk of death. Nobody's gonna die. Not here. Not there. Nobody."

With these words, she turned her head back to him and lifted up an anxious face, her eyebrows forming a question. But before she could ask what he meant, he kissed her. Soft and light. A goodnight kiss. And so it was. Good Night.

CHAPTER 24

The evil rooster strutted around the dirt parking lot in front of the guest house, the very same villain that had ran for its life when the red *saam-lor* rocket tore into the place yesterday evening. He had just given his fifth, encore performance of the wake-up call when Cole woke and unwound himself from his bedsheets, now mummification linens soaked in his own sweat.

The air conditioner, one of the few in the guest house, had died a death sometime during the evening and the only overhead fan in the room was spinning and creaking over Pip's bed. Without the means to circulate the thick, sultry air in Cole's half of the room that night, he had sweated buckets. Worse, last night's Mekong Whisky was alternating between a jackhammer and a concrete-boring drill at the back of his skull. *Fucking Mekong!* He flung the sheet across the room and it came to rest against the floorboard, with the top half of it stuck against the wood veneer wall.

He swung his legs off the sofa and onto the floor, sitting there bent at the waist and holding his head in his hands, both elbows pinned to his knees. Cole sat motionless for a minute before pivoting his head towards of Pip's bed. He recalled the pause at the teakwood door last night, and the picture of her sitting in the straight-back chair, her body as straight as the chair itself, and the smell of her hair – and the kiss. He grimaced. *Ahh... shit!*

Cole remembered the fortunate decision to hold down any urge to move towards her bed. *Not just yet*, he remembered thinking. *'Sides, she's a royal pain in the ass, alright. Good lookin' but a pain in the ass. And I wasn't that drunk.* But he was. And the dive onto the sofa last night was a blessing for all. Lights out. *Thank God for that call,* he prided himself.

From his position on the sofa he could not see her bed, but he did see her uniform blouse and skirt, neatly placed on misshapen aluminum hangers and hung on the wardrobe closet by her bed, under the recently deceased air conditioner. He called out, "Pip!" and then "Major!" But the only sounds he could make out were the whirring and complaining of the ceiling fan over her bed, and the low vibrations of the nearby boat traffic, plying up-and-down the River Mun.

Cole got up and walked towards her bed. It was neatly made and had the appearance she didn't sleep in it last night. The only convincing signs to the contrary were the wet towel from her morning's shower, hung lengthwise over the straight-back chair, and her overnight bag which was situated at a sharp right-angle to the sheet, tucked in under the broad-striped guest house blanket. The bag was open and Cole could see that the contents were neatly arranged inside. Her makeup box was the last item on top of all else in the bag. But Pip was not to be seen. *Where the hell is that broad? Dammit… Time to get going.*

He lumbered off the platform by her bed, back to his sofa. He found his shirt from yesterday, inspected it for *food on the front and B.O. in the pits,* and tossed it on the bed. Cole rummaged around in his gear bag and found a fresh shirt – the identical pattern from the blue one he wore yesterday, only in green. The vendor at the Rex Hotel had given him the second shirt for half-price of the first. He still paid three-times too much, but both he and the vendor were happy. No victims on Sukhumvit Road that night.

Cole reached inside his pillowcase and withdrew the .45 and its short, leather holster and tucked it into the back of his pants – the pants he used as PJs last night – and he pulled his green shirt down over it. He went for a pee and squeezed an inch-long patch of Pip's toothpaste onto his right index finger and gave his teeth and tongue a quick, field-expedient brush job. He turned on the sink water, peered at his stubbled face in the bathroom mirror, dabbed some water on the sides of his head and his close-cut hair, and cupped both hands in the running water, rubbing them in his eyes. *A few drops of water for the eye boogers and I'm off.*

· · · · ·

Pip had finished her bowl of pork congee and was sipping a glass of milky tea, talking with her Aunt Nid and her aunt's older brother when Cole walked up to their table. She caught sight of him as he bounded down the stairs and headed in their direction, but she didn't want to take her eyes away from her aunt who was in the middle of reciting one of her favorite memories which had floated up from the past.

He glanced at his Casio and then in the direction of the guest house's motorboat, still tied to the dock. *It's 10 past 8. I overslept. Dammit!* And no sign of Lek.

"Where is this guy, your cousin? He was 'sposed to be here at eight." He quickly dismissed the thought that Lek had come earlier, didn't see anyone, and then split. *That guy was shit-faced drunk last night. Now, either he's blown us off 'cause he's a lazy S.O.B. – or he's still too drunk to move. But he's not gonna miss a chance to make a few easy bucks. It don't add up.*

"Well, good morning to you, too," said Pip, her salutation tinged with sarcasm. "*Sawatdee, kha,*" she added.

Cole grumbled a reluctant "good morning" in their direction. He couldn't remember *that sawatdee crap* Pip had taught him the day before on the train, and even if he could have, he would not try that again. And besides, Pip spoke perfect English *so why bother with this cute shit.*

He scanned the others at the table. He didn't like Pip's aunt, *that old broad*, and she clearly didn't like him. *And never mind the old guy with the pipe* who sat sipping his coffee, staring at the river.

Pip expanded her greeting, "Did you sleep well?" Cole didn't reply. His head was still throbbing from the Mekong and he didn't want to complain about losing a gallon of sweat in that hot box of a room. He just gave her a half smile.

Aunt Nid got up to leave and, as soon as she rose, the kitchen girls ran to attend the table and brought some fresh toast and strawberry jam, a delicacy in Ubon, and placed these in front of Cole who refused to sit down.

He looked at Pip and said, "Uh. OK. Thanks." But she acted as if she had nothing to do with the orchestration of the toast and coffee.

She noticed they were both wearing the same color civilian shirts. Not identical, but a very similar shade of green. She wore a green T with small yellow letters over the left breast pocket that said in both Thai and English, "Long live the King," with the royal symbol for the King on the pocket. She looked at his *god-awful green shirt with that stupid, winsome tropical pattern* and shook her head.

Cole caught her inspecting eye, prompting Pip to volunteer, "Green is my good luck color," although she thought she should go back to the room and get her red-and-yellow jersey her mom gave her last year as a birthday present – any other color but this green would do. She did not want to send any unspoken signals that she was in-league with Cole and his unholy mission, and that they were on the same team. Because, in her heart, she wasn't.

It was her duty to follow orders. But she never imagined that she would have to arrest a priest, of all people. To her,

Mordechai was just following his own conscience, and that was a commendable thing. Getting involved with a plot to capture a holy man who was called to exercise his faith must surely be *baap*, sinful. *Not good.* "No, not good," she repeated under her breath.

But she didn't want Cole to catch on to her displeasure with the mission – and her distaste for his ridiculous shirt. *Such an objection would lead nowhere.* She took another sip of coffee and sucked in a quick breath.

"So, no uniform today?" he asked, interrupting her penitent thoughts. "What's the deal with that? I thought you had to stay all wrapped up in a uniform."

"No, not necessary. Out in the provinces we're allowed, and even advised, to wear undercover clothes. It helps to disentangle us from the local authorities and others who could be confused to see uniformed officers from Bangkok – especially senior officers like me – moving around in their province."

The emphasis on "senior officers" was a dig at Cole but, as was his habit by now, he was only half-listening to her. She added, "The less visibility, the less questions, the less problems." To Cole, that sounded like police department dribble, but he let it slide.

Cole, still standing, took a swig of the coffee and a bite of the toast. The coffee was dark and bitter and the toast, without jam, was burnt at the edges. By chance, just the way he liked it.

She added, "You get it, right? And besides, you are also in civilian clothes, and together we won't attract attention or suspicion that –"

"OK, great," he interrupted again. "If that works for you. OK for me." He took two more swigs of coffee, washing down the rest of the toast, and said, "So where the hell is your cousin? This Lek guy?" Cole glanced at his watch. It was 8:15. "He should have been here already."

"Yes, it is strange." Pip looked towards the dock. "He should be here by now. Let's give him another 15 minutes and then we find some other –"

But Cole was not in the mood to be patient. "Let's go!" He put his coffee cup on the table and nodded at the kitchen girls who covered their mouths to hide their laughter and embarrassment of being acknowledged by this mysterious foreigner.

Cole was halfway to the boat before Pip rose from her chair. She looked at the entrance to the restaurant and to the guest house lobby, but Aunt Nid was nowhere to be seen. She walked nervously towards the boat where Cole was already in the back, fiddling with the engine cover on the outboard. Pip called to the kitchen girls to come quickly to the boat.

She told them in Thai, "*Noo*, dear, please tell Aunt Nid that we're leaving now and taking Uncle Suwit's boat. We'll be back this evening. Tell her, '*yaa huang, na!*' don't worry!"

The suddenness of Cole's move to the boat had caught her by surprise and, had she a few more minutes to collect herself, she might have run upstairs and had another look in her overnight bag for... *who knows what?* She just needed to look into it for reassurance. Pip checked her over-shoulder purse for the essentials: mirror, lipstick, perfume, and a thin first-class envelope with two pictures of Mordechai. *OK. Got it.* She also grabbed the two small packets of dessert her aunt had given her at the breakfast table. "*They were for her – and* not *for the American,*" her aunt insisted.

Pip jumped into the boat as Cole was checking the fuel levels. It was a shallow-draft skiff about 20 feet long in Cole's estimation, with a flat-bottom that made muddy riverbanks accessible. She was painted white as salt with the gunwale railings in bright orange lacquer, and blue Thai lettering on the bow: the "*Choke Dee*," the "Good Luck."

It was steered amidship by a home-made, wire-and-pully apparatus that maneuvered twin rudders, each placed on the transom on either side of the 25hp, Russian-built outboard motor, fixed in place. The steering wheel was lifted from a junked pickup – the "Toyota" imprint on the defunct horn ring had long since peeled off from years of hard use under the broiling tropical sun.

Cole made a quick study of the mechanical steering linkage to the rudders and the throttle control located next to the small captain's chair. It was all foreign to him, but he knew enough about piloting flat-bottom bass boats along the sandy stretches of the Rio Grande back home, and this one had the same basic stuff: made of wood, propeller in the rear, a means to steer and a lever to work the gas. *Check.*

Pip had settled in at the bow and was facing backwards, looking at Cole as he hovered over the engine, searching for the choke control and the rip cord to get the engine started. He worked the mechanical throttle controls to prime some fuel into the engine, pulled on a nob that may have said "choke" in Russian, coiled the starter rope around the exposed, round flywheel cone, and gave it a rip. Nothing. He gave it a bit more gas, another tug on the nob, and another rip. Again, nothing.

"Are you sure you know what you're doing?" asked Pip, watching the antics at the back of the boat. "Maybe we should wait until Lek –"

Cole had given it another crank and this time the old Russian motor sputtered into life, belching out a blue-black cloud twice the size of the small boat, a feat aided by his invocation of the magical words: "You fucking piece of shit!"

The small skiff immediately began to move forward since there was no clutch to stop the propeller from spinning. When the motor was going, so was the boat. Cole shouted and signaled to the shorter of the two kitchen girls who were both standing on the dock, that she should throw off the dock line which she held fast in her hands. She dutifully tossed the line into the water and Cole steered the craft away from the dock, slowly moving towards mid-current on the Mun. It was not a fast river-cruiser but had enough horsepower to push them along a bit faster than the current moving downstream towards Khong Chiam.

"OK. Let's go!" shouted Cole. He was primed and ready to get moving. Pip looked on as he moved from the transom to the captain's chair where he gave it some gas, increasing the RPMs, along with the engine's loud objections. But the extra strain only delivered a small boost in their speed across the water. *Russian piece of shit!*

Pip could see the kitchen girls standing on the dock, the shorter one *wai'*ing her; the other, taller girl was waiving "good luck" with both of her lanky arms crossing back-and-forth over her head, recreating a scene she had once seen in a Thai "B" movie at the local, downtown cinema.

Pip glanced up from the girls at dockside and finally caught sight of Aunt Nid, standing on the balcony in front of the room she shared with Coltrane last night. Aunt Nid was motionless, and perhaps did not see Pip *wai* her or lift her hands to wave to her aunt. She just stood there and stared at them.

And the small boat made its way to mid-channel on the Mun, motoring towards Khong Chiam where its blue waters would meet the broad, chocolate Mekong, 80 kilos to the east as the crow flies – and more than four hours on Uncle Suwit's skiff.

● ● ● ● ●

The River Mun winds down from its headwaters in the Dongruk Mountains in the southwest of *I-saan* and, along its way to the Mekong in the east, it collects the offerings of smaller streams and rivers that drain the high plateau of Northeast Thailand. The cartographers' maps of these regional tributaries resemble spreading patterns of watery veins, drawn over taut, dry skin.

And Cole's eyes were fixed on this ancient waterway as he wrestled with the boat's wheel, navigating the many sharp, fast turns and the wide, slow bends of the riverbed.

Pip sat at the bow, observing the shoreline of the river which rose high into cliffs above the fast turns, and then broadened to shallow mud flats where the river's turns were soft and relaxed. All along, the river expanded and contracted in width and depth as it meandered, without interruption, to the Mekong. She admired the fishing shacks that dotted the shoreline and the networks of *phong phaang*, fish traps, that fishermen had staked out in strategic spots in the river to channel and trap fish into their woven, reed-and-wicker weirs.

At every small, weed-patch village along the banks she saw remnants of old fishing nets hung up on bamboo poles, next to ramshackle thatched homes, and children running and playing in muddy flats, many of whom had stopped their play when they heard the discordant sound of the Russian outboard sputtering by them. They ran to the water's edge from the shallow banks and from the cliffs above to wave and shout in the local Lao dialect, "*Pai-sai-der*? Where are you going?" Pip would smile and wave back at them, to the full delight of the barefoot kids.

Cole scanned the banks for submerged trees and other river debris, mindful of Lek's comments the night before. *That tip was the only useful thing that S.O.B. said all night*, thought Cole. Except for the large mats of water hyacinth that flourished in the hinterland streams and canals of the *I-saan* plateau and then floated down the Mun in large green rafts, there were no navigation hazards. No snags to be found that morning. Maybe the unseasonable rain that *Pip was blabbing about* on the train the day before – making small talk when none was welcome – had pushed the water level up. *Who knows. Clear sailing so far. Check.*

Cole looked at his watch. It was 11:13 and they had been on the water for about three hours. He scanned the north shore of the river on their left for any signs of a large village, for an increase in the number of people moving around, for power-line poles, for clusters of houses and rows of shophouses, or any evidence that would tell him that they were drawing near to Khong Chiam village and his prey. But none of the signs were there.

Pip walked aft from the bow where she had been sitting, distancing herself as far as possible from the racket of the outboard. She had been watching Cole, craning his neck back-and-forth across the river as he cut the steering gear with ever-increasing, harsh spins of the wheel.

She thought, *I bet "Mr. Great White Hunter" could use this about now*. And she reached into her back jeans pocket and pulled out a single, yellow piece of paper with wide-spaced blue ruling – the kind school kids would use for their writing lessons. It was folded into fours, and she opened it and spread it out in front of Cole on the small wooden platform that doubled as a chopping board to cut bait. She flicked off some silver remnants of fish scale with her fingers and smoothed the paper flat with the palm of her hand.

A black arrow pointed to the top of the page and it had an "N" scribbled beside it. Cole looked away from the course he had set since the last, sharp bend and glanced at the paper laid out sideways on the rough-hewn board. It was a handmade map she had drawn this morning when she sat at the breakfast table and jotted down the approach into Khong Chiam as described by Aunt Nid's brother, *Leung* Loat – Uncle Suwit's oldest and best friend, riverboat pilot, fellow pipe smoker, and occasional chess adversary.

Cole glanced at the sketch of the Mun, written in black ink as a snaking path that crossed the paper from left to right, mid-page. It little resembled the myriad sharp bends and long turns they had just traversed this morning.

Another wavy line descended straight down from the top right-hand part of the page and intersected the Mun at right angles. The overall picture was that of a "T" tipped over to the right. The second line was labeled "Mekong" and the spot where the two lines met was circled. It read "Khong Chiam & Wat Suwan." And from that place on the yellow page where the two rivers met, the Mekong flowed down and to the right, and off the page. A dotted line cut across the river there, and the word written on the map in English and underlined read, "Danger!"

OK, I get it. He put on his scoffing face but was paying more interest in the map than he wanted to show. He was careful not to study it in long passes, but to take it in with short, sideways glances – as would a singer who pulls in air with very short, but deep, drafts before hitting the next notes.

Pip studied him for a hint of appreciation, but finally broke her vigil and volunteered, "This is a pretty good sketch of the place we're going. And look, here on the side of the river's north bank, to the left –" she said, pointing to two small scribbles in Thai, "– here are a couple of landmarks we should see… to know when we are getting there."

"The first is a giant mango tree. It sits on a cliff that rises from the mud-flat shore, about 60 feet above the river. It's overgrown and interlaced with an orange bougainvillea – and can't be missed unless you are traveling at night."

She thought she sounded funny for saying it that way. "Well, the locals and all the fishermen along this span of the river know it very well. They call it *dton maai sawan*, the bright tree. They say, if the sun hits it from behind just right –"

"Yeah, yeah. Very nice." Cole cut her off. "And what's the second one – the second landmark?" Cole was not interested in the tourist propaganda.

"Well," began Pip, "we should next see a long wooden dock at Khong Chiam that extends into the Mun. It was built by local fishermen and they have cobbled it together over the years.

Leung Loat said you can tie up the boat there and walk on the planks laid out on top of the dock. No problem. From there, it is maybe 200, or 300 yards to the temple. It's near the river's edge."

"OK. OK. Got it," said Cole with an air of disdain.

The familiar juices started to churn and roil around in his stomach. He was getting pumped-up and ready, and quickly thought through his options. *OK. Dock this crate and tie it up. We hotfoot it up to the temple and put Mordechai in the bag. Job done. Worse case, we beach the boat. No drama there. We still get our priest. It's as easy as that.* Plan B was the ace up his sleeve.

But his curiosity got the better of him and he took another look at the map Pip had laid out. "So, what's with this dotted line? What's this?" Cole knew that the border with Laos was close and he had a hunch that's what the dots meant, but he did not want to give credence to this crude sketch. He was interested in precision – like US Geological Survey maps – not these homemade scribblings. But the last good map he saw like that was the one in Pip's office, two nights ago.

The time accordion was playing in his head again. *Was that only two nights ago?*

Pip gave voice to what he had already guessed, "At this very place –" she extended the forefinger of her right hand and pointed to the junction of the two rivers, "– where the Mun and the Mekong meet, this marks the last of the River Mun. From this point, the Mekong flows into Laos. It is the end of the world for us Thai people." She moved her finger to cross the dotted line she had drawn earlier that morning.

She added, "And this area is a Pathet Lao stronghold, loyal to, and supported by North Vietnam. Very dark and dangerous." And her finger ran off with the river, off the lower right-hand corner of the page.

She looked at Cole. "Do you see? This is the place where –"

"Yeah, yeah, I get it." He knew southern Laos was trouble. The place was crawling with NVA logistics, moving weapons, ammunition, and war materiel down the many branches of the Ho Chi Minh Trail.

Cole wiped the sweat from his brow with a single swipe of his palm and squinted into the distance where he could make out a large green and orange, massive object rising on a cliff bank, dead ahead, *about one klick downstream.* It was a brilliant, glowing orange. It looked like it was on fire.

CHAPTER 25

When the sun's rays finally broke over the mountains of Laos to the east on Thursday morning, they were earnestly welcomed by all. The night's ordeal was over.

Mordechai, his fellow *nanes*, and the senior monks finished their morning prayers, packed their umbrella tents, and left their circled encampment around the fire pit. They were led by the two abbots, down the mountain path to the *Soi Sawan* Waterfall. And they made the hour-long journey to the base of the falls in silence, appreciating the sounds of nature that the Abbot had been teaching them.

•　•　•　•　•

Last night they struggled to block the thousand sounds of the dark jungle and seek an abiding, inner peace for their souls. Today, they were instructed to open their eyes and ears again and expose their senses. The abbot had taught them that, "The many voices and sounds of nature can be both soothing and confounding, and it is up to the devotee to create an ascending sense of the soothing, and to diminish the confounding." It was an exercise that needed practice, and the abbot's task was to lead them to this doorway of perception.

Luang Por knew that there was no better place to hear the perfect sounds of nature than through a quiet, reflective walk to the base of the *Soi Suwan* falls. Here, in counterpoint to the soft sounds of the wind coming up from the Mekong River in the valley below, the loud and incessant sound of the water falling onto the rocks below, rushed into their ears.

When they had all drawn up into a small group at the base of the falls, *Luang Por* spoke. In Thai he explained:

"At the top of these falls, countless small drops of water flow along, together, in a stream. In time, they move towards the precipice, unaware of their pending demise. And when they spill over the edge, they change their state of being. They fall as small, individual drops.

And they fall in advance of other individual drops of water also moving towards the same edge. And when these drops, one-by-one, reach the bottom, they reform into a body of water again, flowing along in a new part of the same stream.

It is the same with our lives. Our souls flow along in life with families and friends. And when we fall over the precipice we die, sometimes ahead of, and sometimes behind, our family and friends. We are swept over the edge and die as individuals. As we are born alone, we must also die alone. Nobody can do this for us.

But, like the water, we also form again at the bottom of the falls, and our souls are reborn into a new life. The same soul continues its journey, but with a new body, new family and new friends.

This is what it means when we say in our religion, our *sasanaa, kaan-gert-mai,* reincarnation. We will all be reincarnated."

He turned to look at his disciples. "Do you all understand? This is another lesson on the impermanence of life. We are all moving forward, contrary to our nature to stay in one place. We cannot resist the force that moves us forward through time, and we cannot resist the waterfall. All of us will go over the falls, some day."

He scanned his small group again and his eyes came to rest on Mordechai's countenance. The older monks were looking at the falls from the top to the bottom, at the endless stream rushing over the brink. *And so it was with humanity*, they thought. "*Sa-ah-tu*, Amen," they whispered.

All the *nanes*, except Mordechai, were looking at their feet and some fidgeted with their satchels that were slung over their bare shoulders. They knew they were in the presence of a holy man, but barely caught the gist of what the abbot had just taught them. They knew it had something to do with death, and being reborn, but the rest was fuzzy. The younger ones would understand in due time, but Mordechai could not stop the smile that came to his face. Yet he said nothing, nor did anyone else.

Luang Por looked away from Mordechai to the other abbot, who was also smiling, and then back to Mordechai. Two of the senior monks also beamed with the satisfaction of persons who had just heard an absolute truth.

And with that *Luang Por* turned, and in silence, beckoned the others to follow him. It was still a long way to go to reach *Wat Suwan* in Khong Chiam that evening, and they had many kilometers to travel.

· · · · ·

Mordechai and his fellow *nanes*, senior monks and the two abbots began winding their way down the long mountain trail from the *Soi Sawan* Waterfall, back to Khong Chiam and *Wat Suwan*. Mordechai was brooding over *Luang Por's* premonition of the danger that was in store for him and it troubled him deeply. He walked along in silence. Constrained. It troubled the abbot as well, but the old monk kept his heart still. What loomed in the future for Mordechai was something ominous. Dangerous.

Luang Por was therefore in no hurry to press a quick retreat back to Khong Chiam village and he set an unhurried pace of descent from the high forest, stopping often to teach his small entourage about the place of humankind within nature. He liked to speak about how humans had warped the relationship with the good spirits of nature who had retreated in fear of man's cunning and destructive behavior. "But the spirits of nature will prevail," the old monk would always assure them. It was welcomed solace.

When they had descended from the narrow mountain trail they joined a wider path of brown clay, worn smooth and grassless by the years of pilgrims' feet journeying to the holy shrines along the river, and by local villagers who visited relatives and friends in small fishing camps that dotted the Mekong's banks. The path meandered in-and-out of riverbank trees and thickets of bamboo, sometimes opening onto gaps in the foliage which yielded clear views to the river, only a few feet away. The thick forest canopy above, rustled by the river breezes, often blew open to let in bright shafts of sunlight that lit up the meadows and the forest floor below.

They passed along a shady bend in the path and came across a group of five men who were tending two large female elephants, working to push teakwood logs into the river with their trunks. The men had cut the timber from higher up in the forest, and they used steel chains and the elephants to pull the logs down to the riverside clearing below. Here the trees were trimmed and cut in half. They then pushed the logs into the water's edge where three of the men used long pikes to form two rafts of about 12 logs each.

They would float these rafts down the Mekong into Laos – past the confluence of the River Mun at Khong Chiam – where this illegal activity would be richly rewarded by Laotian traders.

They, in turn, would mill the logs into highly prized lumber which would be then smuggled back into Thailand for export. Eventually, this beautiful and durable hardwood would find its place on the deck of someone's luxury yacht in Seattle, or in a parquet floor in an upscale Tokyo apartment. It didn't matter to these men. The only thing they were interested in was cutting the timber and getting out quickly – before the Thai authorities caught them.

The monks came upon this scene and they stopped to watch, all standing behind the two abbots who now faced the men at work. They stood there, silently observing for several minutes, witnessing the harsh treatment the older female elephant was receiving by her mahout. He was shouting obscenities at her in the local dialect, *"E-saat, mueng kee-giat mahk*! You lazy beast!" and, "*Gliat naa mueng*! I hate your face!"

But when he reared back with his wooden prod to strike the old girl behind her worn, leafy ear again, shouting in Laotian, "I'm gonna hit you harder if you don't –", he caught sight of a bright burst of orange that suddenly lit up the clearing, just when the tops of the riverbank trees swayed and opened to the sun and sky above. He halted his curse mid-stream and stared at the monks and *nanes* who were standing in a rough semicircle at the edge of the forest glade.

The three men maneuvering the logs with pikes and forming the rafts on the river caught the direction of the mahout's stare and froze. But one of them, working on the bank with a long pike in his hands, walked briskly to where the monks were standing. Mordechai was immediately on alert. This man did not look malevolent, *but you could never tell*. The quickness with which Mordechai went back to his war-footing both surprised and disappointed him. He glanced at *Luang Por* who stood stoically as the man approached.

When the suspicious fellow got within a few feet of the monks, the man let his pike fall to the ground and he dropped to his knees, lifting his hands high to his forehead in a *wai* to greet the abbots and to show his deep respect. At the same time, the mahout on the old female gave the command that she should turn to face the monks, which she did. He dismounted and joined the first man, kneeling in front of the holy men.

All the monks were surprised to see that the older female had a small, male calf that was hidden behind her the whole time. It was trying to seek shelter between its mother's busy legs and to catch a few quick drinks of milk from her weathered teats. The second mahout on the smaller female, seeing this gathering forming in the clearing, dismounted, and walked towards them, and he was then joined by the other two men from the raft, having secured their teakwood treasure to the bank with long twine tethers.

Together, they all knelt and supplicated themselves before the abbots. On the forested bank of the Mekong that afternoon, Mordechai saw five rough and sinewy men, criminals by some standards, bending on their knees with hands clasped together at their chests, all offering their respect. The two female elephants and the baby were looking on, over the men's shoulders. The adults were intense. Curious.

The men were caught out and embarrassed and asked *Luang Por* for forgiveness of their rough behavior and words, and they sought his blessing for the animals. For a long while the revered abbot said nothing, he only stared at the men. But his gaze was neither hostile nor benign. He was simply absorbing the drama of the circumstances he had just witnessed and, in the end, felt disposed to grant their request. Mordechai could not work out why *Luang Por* agreed, but he said nothing and kept his thoughts to himself.

But the old abbot was not going to let them off easy. He aimed his words at the mahout of the mother elephant and, in Mordechai's best estimation of what was being said, *Luang Por* admonished the man for the harsh treatment he gave to the large female. The abbot spoke to him in the local Lao dialect, "You see, this elephant here. This one." Touching the mother's trunk. "She works very, very hard. Do you see the tears falling from her eyes, to her trunk, to the ground?"

The Mahout did not reply but looked down with shame at the ground, and at his dirty, calloused hands held at his chest.

"You must not work an animal until it cries. They have no voice to speak, and tell you, 'I am tired and need to rest.' You need to see this yourself. You need to have a heart. You need to have *songsaan*, pity. You work with an elephant for many years, yes? But do you not understand this?"

"*Khrap, Luang Por. Pom khorthord. Pom khorthord mahk.* Yes, reverend father. I see, and I am sorry. I am very sorry."

But *Luang Por* was not finished. "Do not do this again! She works hard for you. Do not make her cry anymore!" Mordechai was astonished to see this man of peace dig into the woodcutter with such displeasure and passion. *But this guy deserved it, and more,* thought Mordechai.

"*Khrap, Luang Por,*" were the man's only words.

Mordechai watched as *Luang Por* took out from his satchel, a small jar of white, holy paste used to draw secret and magical symbols when performing blessings. The old monk looked deeply into the eyes of the mother elephant, and he mumbled a soft prayer in Pali-Sanskrit while the baby peered from around its mother's rear leg. The younger female had placed her trunk over the smallest one's back, as any older sibling would do to allay the fears of a child.

Luang Por stood with his left arm under the elephant's trunk and opened the jar of the white paste. He placed a generous dose on his right forefinger and anointed the matriarch by placing nine white dots as far as he could reach, up towards the elephant's broad forehead. One dot on the top, and underneath that single dot, three more. And underneath those three, five more. It formed a small symmetrical pyramid of nine dots, an auspicious shape and number in Buddhist liturgy.

Luang Por repeated the same blessing on the smaller female elephant. And when he approached the baby, the other *nanes* and monks joined him, arms extended, making calling and cooing sounds. But this sudden attention spooked the youngster who ran off to hide between its mother's rear legs again. When the *nanes*, monks and the abbots saw this, they all laughed out loud. "He surely knows the safest place to be!" the abbots agreed.

The saffron-robed men returned in silence to stand on the pathway, and the five workers stood by with their caps tucked under their arms. *Luang Por* glanced up at the sun. From its position in the sky, he knew they would reach the temple at Khong Chiam in another two hours of walking. They would arrive back within the walls of *Wat Suwan* around *neung toom*, around 7pm, before the evening prayers began – the same time that the sun would move out of the western Thai sky and shine with an orange, afternoon brightness over Lumpini in Nepal, birthplace of Gautama Buddha.

That thought suited the old abbot very much. He glanced at the senior monks, and then to Mordechai and the *nanes* and he told them, "All will now be well. Let's finish our day's journey."

The loggers bowed deeply at the waist and *wai'*ed the monks as they left the clearing. And as the abbot passed, he told the men, "*Yoom, dern plort phai, na ja,*" the endearing version of "be safe along your journey."

"*Khrap, Than duay.* Yes, and to you, too, sir." Said the men in unison.

And with that, the abbots, monks and *nanes* left the clearing, and reentered the forest and the riverfront path to Khong Chiam.

CHAPTER 26

The skiff moved quickly through the narrow cliffs along the river and Cole fought with the steering controls to keep the craft in the middle of the swift channel. When they had cleared the last sharp turn to the right, the river broadened and there, up on a rise above the riverbank, was the majestic old mango tree. Pip stood from where she had been sitting next to the captain's bench and raised her hand to her brow to shield the sun's low angle of attack across the river.

It was the largest mango tree she had ever seen in her life, more than twice the height and volume of the trees she had seen in Bangkok – or anywhere else in her travels throughout Thailand. Around its base was a wild, orange bougainvillea whose many long strands had wound themselves midway up the old giant. Its orange blossoms caught the sun from behind which gave the tree an incandescent glow, like a fire lit around its ancient base. It was magnificent.

Cole's eyes narrowed as he made another hard-right turn to stay in the deeper waters and to avoid the rocks below the cliff upon which the huge tree stood, overseeing the comings-and-goings on the river below as it had done for over a hundred years.

"Cole!" implored Pip. "Look at this! I don't remember seeing such a beautiful –"

"Yeah, sure. Real nice," scoffed Cole, cutting her off. He was busy scouring the river ahead for the second landmark, the place that marked their arrival at Khong Chiam, and he had no time for playing tourist.

·   ·   ·   ·   ·

They had not gone more than two klicks farther downstream when the river curved around a broad bend to the north and there, sticking out into the Mun like a splintered finger, was the ramshackle boat dock from Pip's map – and the village of Khong Chiam. *Now that's a sorry-ass excuse for a dock*, thought Cole. It looked as if a long pile of scrap wood and loose sticks had washed up and stuck to the bank, much like the branches of debris that line the gullies and washes in the deserts of New Mexico after a flash flood. Random and accidental. Not man made.

Drawing closer, Cole could see only one small boat that was tied up there, towards the very end of the dock. In the center were a few, vertical sticks of bamboo which formed a latticework, upon which several torn fishing nets were hung. An old man stood scrutinizing the largest net, picking out leaves and twigs that were tangled in it and tossing the rubbish into the fast-moving current underneath the dock. A few laughing, naked boys took turns jumping into the river near the shore where the water was moving more slowly. Their dogs were barking and chasing them up to the water's edge, but unwilling to jump in.

Cole steered the boat to the down-river side of the dock and powered up the motor to compensate for the current, rather than letting the boat run into the dock from the up-river side where he would have less control. *Good plan.*

But as he came past the dock and pulled a sharp left turn to make his approach, a loud "Bang!" rang out from the transom –

and a single, violent jolt went through the Toyota steering wheel. Pip froze when she heard this sound. She thought the motor had blown up.

But Cole realized the problem immediately. The linkage to the twin rudders at the rear of the boat had snapped in two.

He quickly spun the wheel to the left, and to the right, and back again, but without effect. The steering was gone. No way to control their heading. He increased the RPMs to the maximum, trying to steer with the increase in power and *the old Russian piece of shit* roared into life. A rooster tail of prop-spray erupted from behind the boat, and the sudden impulse caused the bow to surge within 3 feet of the dock.

Cole yelled to Pip who was now standing in the bow and watching the drama happening back at the steering wheel, "Turn around! Grab hold! Grab ahold of the dock!" he shouted.

But she was confounded by the sudden rise in the tension of Cole's commands and by the deafening sound of the old motor. She hesitated, drawing in her arms to her chest and defensively hunching her back before she summoned her wits, straining to reach the shaky crisscrossed pieces of brittle wood at the end of the dock.

But it was too late. Despite the full power Cole applied, the boat drifted away from the dock, faster and faster. And with no means to control its heading, it spun its bow to point downstream, hurried along by the outboard motor at full throttle. Cole cut the power back to idle and he sprang forward to the bow where Pip was in full panic. He grabbed her by the arms and pulled her to the shore-side railing of the boat.

"What are you doing?!" she demanded in fear.

"C'mon, let's jump! We only got 50 yards to swim. Then we're ashore. Forget this fuckin' boat. Let's go!"

"No! No! I can't do this! I, I can't swim!" she pleaded. "I can't swim! Don't leave me here!"

Cole gripped her tightly by the biceps of both arms and gave her a paralyzing stare and a head-jarring shake, "What?! You've got to be shittin' me! We got to go! Now!"

"But I can't do this. I just can't do this!" And she shuddered when she thought about breathing in gallons of blue river water and the way her life would end. And it was happening now. Happening too fast. Their craft was swiftly drifting away, further into the wider channel that marked the point where the Mun spilled into the Mekong.

He looked at Pip and then at the shore, and Cole saw his prize slipping away. His only hope was a quick jump into the Mun and swim back to the Khong Chiam river dock, but that chance was now disappearing by the second. It was as good as gone.

She bent at the waist and sobbed. Useless. Cole cursed, "Dammit!"

He glanced up, across to the north bank of the river where he saw three monks who had been washing their robes in the Mun's waters. They were now running along the bank, shouting and waving at the drifting craft. But the boat was gaining speed on the monks, its bow alternating between the river's course and the riverbank, their bearing now dictated completely by the changes in the river's current.

The monks stopped running. They had reached lands' end. Their waves were not goodbyes. They were shouting to the two drifters to come back, and to do so urgently. Cole sucked in deep. His ribs heaved a giant sigh.

"Son of a bitch!" he said, now resigned to stay onboard.

Cole stood erect at the captain's controls and continued working the throttle back-and-forth, trying to maneuver the boat towards the shore and stop its downstream drift. *Maybe I can run this ol' piece of shit ashore by working the power.* But it was no use. As soon as he applied power, the boat would right itself in the direction of the main current of the river.

But the loss of the boat's steering was not their most pressing problem. Pip was the first to realize this. They had flowed out of the Mun and were now dead-center in the middle of the vast Mekong. From here, the river veers through a steep gorge in the hills on both sides, and then flows to the southeast and deeper into Laos. Further on, it spills over the rapids at the Lao-Cambodian border and into the Cambodian countryside beyond, before finally emptying its contents across the flat delta lands of South Vietnam. Rage, shrapnel, chaos and cordite lie in wait along this course.

•   •   •   •   •

The two were quickly slipping through the Asian version of Dante's Gates. Pip knew they were crossing into Laos, and the helplessness of their plight began to dissolve her aloof confidence. She looked to Cole for some hint of salvation.

But all he could offer as he fought for control of the boat was the cursing he muttered under his breath, "Son of a bitch!"

The Mekong made its first grand turn to the south, where the huge river entered Laos. And they were moving much faster now, the river's tireless and massive current pushing them steadily past the Thai frontier.

Cole's brain replayed his regrets. If only he had jumped back then, he would be at the temple gates now, ready to collect his trophy and to notch his belt with yet another capture. *Having this woman along was a pain in the ass from the get-go*, and this was precisely why he loved to work alone. *No entanglements, no responsibilities to others. Solo.* The mission objective was all he needed to worry about. *And now we're totally screwed.*

He caught sight of Pip, crouching as low as she could near the bow of the skiff. They were now well into Laos and adrift, and completely alone. Both of them knew the grim prospects for a Thai policewoman and an American Army officer in this remote segment of the river, rife with communist guerrillas of every stripe. It was the most remote thing they could have imagined when they sipped their tea and munched on toast in Ubon earlier that morning.

Pip cried out to Cole, "Can't you do anything?! We can't go further into Laos – very dangerous for us here. We need to get –"

"For fuck's sake, woman! Would you just shut up for a minute! Do you think that all your shouting and freakin' out is gonna help?" Cole did not yet realize that her starch was already gone, and he glared at her while wrestling with the throttle and the broken steering linkage.

He ran back to the transom, peered into the muddy water and saw the broken linkage-wire. *Shit. It's busted alright.* Worse still, the line had wrapped around and entangled both rudders. He reached down into the water and tried to free them so he could move each rudder by hand and steer from the back. But they were jammed solid in the neutral position and there was no possibility to direct the boat's course.

They rounded the second bend to the south and Cole saw the river was completely void of traffic – of any signs of human activity. It was the landscape of every no-man's-land. Still. Desolate. It was as if Death had just passed through the place – and would be coming back soon for the unwary. To be safe, Cole cut back the throttle to silence the old Russian motor and let the boat settle into the center of the river's main current.

"Look," he ordered Pip. "Just stay down where you are and don't move. When we come to the next bend to the south, I'm gonna gas it and see if I can't run it aground on some mud flat, away from all them trees and bushes on the shore. This may take a few minutes to get her in position. So, just be quiet and still. OK?"

Her composure was shredded, but she but managed a peek over the railing. She could see the cliffs behind her, and it was all she could see of her Thailand, of her home, her mom, of everything she knew and loved. In an instant they had slipped out of paradise and were now entering a world of hurt and chaos. She felt the muscles in her calves twitching spasmodically.

Cole bent down low and eyed the river ahead. He instinctively checked his watch. It was 12:33pm. The sun was beating down with full force on top of them as they crouched and waited – the two of them in green shirts on a boat as white as salt.

In a few moments, Cole saw his opportunity. The river had made a major pivot towards the south, turning in a broad, slow bend to the right. And as they entered the elbow of the turn, Cole kicked the motor in the guts and set the throttle control to full open. The boat lunged ahead – the din of the old Russian outboard assailed their ears, but it dutifully pushed the small craft closer and closer to the east bank. Another minute and they would get there. *Another minute. Just another fuckin' minute!*

Cole took a quick look back behind them. The Mekong's main current had steadily moved them southwards, farther into Laos and farther from the Thai frontier. *We're probably seven or eight klicks into Laos by now.* But at least they were now making headway towards the riverbank on their left. The plan was working. *Check.*

But their luck was short-lived. They were not going to make it to a soft, mud-flat landing. They were headed directly towards a large patch of bushy undergrowth, enclosed by a grove of tall bamboo which jutted out from the riverbank. And they were seconds from running onto the shore and the old motor was gasping, giving it everything it had. *No choice. Fuck it – here we go!*

"Hold on!" shouted Cole, as the bow of the boat penetrated the bushes and ran up on the shore, sending twigs, pollen and birds flying in every direction. Cole looked around for Pip and then hit the engine kill-switch. Their ears were ringing from the full-throttle blare of the outboard.

He turned to her and said in a low voice, "Stay here." And he jumped off the bow and slid into the shallow water and silt of the shore.

"Gimme the dock line." Pip looked at him, confused. "The dock line," he tried not to raise his voice at her. "The green nylon rope by your feet. Toss it to me." He looked at Pip, but she didn't speak. She only nodded as she threw the rope to him.

Her panicked eyes had softened, knowing that she would not drown that day. But her face still held onto fear because she knew they were on the wrong side of the river, and well into Laos. Somehow, they needed to get back across to the west bank and many kilometers upstream. *But maybe Cole can get this boat fixed soon, now that we are stopped. And the water is shallow.*

Cole stood knee-deep in the water and tied the line taut to the trunk of a *dton po,* bodhi tree, sapling that rose out from amidst the bamboo stalks. The other bushes provided a good deal of camouflage for the boat, but not completely. The ass-end and the big Russian outboard stuck out into the river. He waded back to where Pip was now standing in the boat, crouched over and trembling.

And he saw in an instant that she was shot through. Had it. He held out his hand, palm up, and told her, "Come on now. You're OK. You can jump down now. We're gonna get through this. Just stand here for a moment."

Pip heard. And the calm and reassuring tone in his voice surprised her. She did not know that the hallmark of many of the toughest soldiers was their skill in calming the weak. It was the paradox of warriors that, when confronted with danger, the strongest and the fiercest could tuck away the anxiety of the weakest person and make them feel safe and unafraid – folks they *might not give a shit about* in the day-to-day world. In danger, however, souls bonded quickly.

Without yet inspecting the damage, Cole said with confidence, "I think I can fix this boat and we can be on our way. Don't worry. Here. Come out of the water."

Cole grabbed Pip by the arm and they pushed their way through the stalks and bayonet leaves of bamboo, moving towards a small sandy clearing up on the riverbank, a few feet away. But as they stepped low and cautiously into the clearing, Cole heard the chargers of the AK47s being pulled back.

CHAPTER 27

Cole threw Pip to the sand bank and turned on the ball of his left foot and the heel of his right, and started to reach behind and grab his .45, but it was too late. There were two of them, both raw and putrid, the ends of their rifles alternating between Cole and Pip. They wore lime green camouflage, and the older of the two had on a Chairman Mao cap. They had the distinctive purple and red, checkered scarves wrapped around their necks. *"Fuck me. Khmer Rouge,* thought Cole. *We're royally fucked.*

Pip began to gently rise from the sand, but Cole placed his hand on her shoulder, pressing her down.

The older one shouted in Khmer, "*Chob!* Stop! *Anh bahn ey-lov!* Or I'll shoot your ass!" Pip froze. Her eyes cast down. She sank back on her knees. Cole read the face of the guy closest to him, the older one with the cap, and it told him that *this guy is a seasoned, old son-of-a-bitch. Fuck!*

Pip raised her arms over her head. *Oh my God, we're going to die! Mama!*

The one with the cap shouldered his rifle, grabbed Pip by the arm, jerked her up to her feet and shoved her forwards, towards the center of the clearing. The shorter one then motioned to Cole with his rifle, while barking in short burst of Khmer for him to join her there. Cole, with his hands on his head, did so.

"Lut chong-kong!" he barked, ordering them both with the barrel of his rifle to get down.

Behind these two guerillas Cole could see a battered-up, old Laotian oxcart with three local peasants onboard, trundling off down the jungle path that led back to Highway 13 – a main north-south highway in Laos. The road doubled as a western tributary of the Ho Chi Minh Trail, along which goods moved out of North Vietnam to the south, where they would later fan out into Laos, and to Cambodia. These weapons and ammunition were directed against Americans who were fighting up-and-down the Vietnamese countryside, down-river to where Cole and Pip now knelt in the sandy clearing.

Cole looked at the crates stacked next to the path and he sized up the situation quickly. The Vietnamese – and their local Laotian proxies in the oxcart – had just delivered six crates of AK47 ammo, and two crates of what he thought were RPGs. The Russian marking and lettering were not that familiar to him, but he could work out RPG-7 from the *РПГ-7* stenciled on the crate. The Vietnamese, coming down Highway 13 had dropped the weapons at a small Laotian ville near the oxcart trail.

It was not a big haul of stuff in the grand scheme of things, but *big enough to ruin your fucking day.* Just the kind of party the boys from NKP and Takhli airbases in Thailand would love to bomb the shit out of – the kind of bombing that Aunt Nid was yapping about. *She should have her sorry ass here now... the old bitch.*

The two KR cadre were getting ready to load the crates onto the old riverboat they had sailed up the Mekong from Cambodia when they heard Cole and Pip's motor racing and the *Choke Dee* crashing into the bushes – just upstream from where they had hidden their own boat in a bamboo thicket. It was about 5 feet longer than Cole and Pip's broken boat, and it had a small, covered wheelhouse. And fortune had smiled on them that day as they now had a couple of prisoners to help haul the cache of weapons onto their old rust-bucket.

The one with the cap motioned for Cole and Pip to get up and then, holding his rifle by the stock in his right hand, gestured to Cole to pick up the crates by the rope handles and put them onboard their boat. Cole knew what he was told to do but acted like he didn't understand. He brought his arms down to the level of his shoulders, palms up and shrugged. The old one with the cap, raised his rifle to Cole's head. *"Ey-lov nung!* Now!" he shouted. The barrel of the AK47 did the convincing.

The crates were heavy, especially the crates with the ammo. Each one weighed over 80 kilos and Pip was struggling, her knees wobbly and shaking. Only the fear-induced adrenaline coursing through her body gave her any degree of strength. One-by-one, they carried and dragged the crates to the side of the gray boat where the small one grabbed the rope handles, pulled the crates over the boat's railing, and then yanked them onto the forward deck where he put them in a stack, four wide and two high. *Cock-strong little son-of-a-bitch,* thought Cole.

Cole eyed Pip as the last crate was positioned on the deck, and he then watched the small one as he bounded off his boat and climbed onto the bow of the *Choke Dee.* He scoured Cole and Pip's skiff to find whatever he could pillage while the older one herded them back to the clearing. After grabbing Pip's small purse and the yellow, paper map she had drawn that morning, the small soldier jumped off their boat and walked towards the clearing, studying the map, rotating the paper in every direction, and settling on no one in particular.

Illiteracy was probably the very reason he survived Pol Pot and was chosen to be part of this duo, running guns and ammo out of a southern terminus of the HCM Trail. If he had even an elementary education, he would have known that he was looking at a map, and he would have known the value of his prisoners. But he simply folded the paper along its four folds and put it in his shirt pocket.

The small one then leapt onto his boat and moved to the wheelhouse and fired up the engine, an old diesel by the sound of it. The one with the cap motioned Cole and Pip into the center of the circle and waved at them with his hands, motioning for them to step back a few feet from where he was standing, his back to the river.

Her heart in her throat, Pip tried to grab Cole's hand but he pushed her away. She looked up at him in despair.

The old one charged and raised his rifle – and at the same time, the old diesel gave out a loud backfire in protest, belching out a plume of black smoke from the vertical exhaust pipe, just aft of the wheelhouse. The soldier turned his head to look at his comrade in the boat, and that was just the moment Cole had been waiting for.

With one motion, he reached behind his shirt back, pulled out his .45 and fired one round cleanly into the left eye of the one with the cap. The force of that heavy slug took off the back, top half of his skull, hat and all, and he flew back about seven feet from where he stood.

The other, shorter one raced out of the wheelhouse and grabbed his weapon where he had left it propped up against the crates that had just been loaded. But Cole had enough time to plant his feet, aim carefully with both hands and pull off the second round. It was about 50 feet between Cole and the young KR soldier and the shot missed a clean kill to the chest, but it spun him completely around, his rifle flying off into the river. He was down but not dead.

Cole jumped into the bow of the boat and walked slowly to where the short KR soldier was laying, grabbing the bullet wound in his left shoulder with the cup of his right hand. It was not a fatal wound. And Cole was about the fix that.

He raised the .45 that was hanging in his right hand and pointed it at the young man's face. The soldier said nothing, and he looked away from Cole's fierce gaze, but not out of fear. He may have been thinking about earlier times in his village of Kompong Som, before Brother One came to power and the madness and chaos descended onto Cambodia. Or maybe he was just thinking, *"Fuck it. Do it."*

But Cole never got a chance to finish the job. Pip, who had been invisible in his mind's eye, reappeared and pulled on his trigger arm, yelling at him, "No! Don't do this! Don't do this, Cole!"

The ringing in his ear from the muzzle blast of the first shot could not filter out Pip's imploring shouts. She pulled down on his arm and finally, in desperation, clenched him tightly around his chest with her hands clasped in the armpit of his raised right arm – the arm with the .45 aimed at the boy's face.

They stood for a minute, frozen on the deck of that boat. He, pointing the gun. She, seizing him. At long last he lowered the hammer and let his arm fall by his side.

He had just killed one enemy and had another in his sights. He felt defeated and that was a taste he didn't like. *There's nothing good about not killing this KR motherfucker.* He was sorry that he didn't, but that moment had now passed. Pip owed him. *She owes me big time.* Cole swallowed the familiar salty, metallic taste in his mouth from the killing.

"You!" talking to the KR soldier. "Get the fuck off my new boat! Get off! Go! Go!" Cole grabbed the man by the front of his fatigue jacket and pulled him to the bow of the boat where he flipped him overboard and onto the muddy shore where he landed square on his back with a thud, knocking his wind out.

"Go get me some rope from our boat. Do it now!" he said to Pip. "There's a short piece near the bow. Go get it."

Pip went for the rope while Cole dragged the soldier to the center of the clearing, the place of their thwarted execution.

When Pip returned with the rope, Cole tied the man's feet together and hogtied his hands behind his back. Satisfied that *this fucker* was going to be kept bound-up long after they left, he reached into the man's jungle-fatigue pocket and retrieved the yellow, hand-drawn map, now stained with Khmer Rouge blood.

"This is mine, buster boy. You ignorant fucker." He was about to kick him in the balls for good measure, but instead stepped full force on his crotch and said, "Next time I *will* kill you."

Cole grabbed Pip who had been blasted into an ugly world and had not yet gotten her war legs under her. He helped her onto the rusty KR riverboat and untied its mooring line from the bamboo thicket. He sat Pip down next to the wheelhouse, and then jumped off the bow and pushed hard to unstick the boat from its muddy berth in the silt. When it started to float freely, he shoved the bow away from the bank and hopped back aboard.

He fumbled with the new set of controls and found the throttle, pushed it far forward and headed out into the river, aiming for the center channel to avoid snags and sand bars. They passed by the *Choke Dee* where she was hard aground in the bushes. *Yeah, 'Good Luck' my ass*, thought Cole.

They were both exhausted, but they had many klicks yet to go and their guard was still full up, their eyes sharp as they chugged back up-river – back to the Thai frontier.

When they had traveled about three klicks, they reached the center of the river channel and Cole called to Pip, "Say, uh... Can you please come over here for a second?"

She turned to look at him and felt a warmness come to her face at these kind words. She didn't realize that he was still using his soft approach as a way of talking to someone who had just witnessed major trauma for the first time. She had seen the brains in the cap and had smelled the hot gun oil and the burnt powder from the two rounds. Pip was fractured. But she managed a smile, rose up and stepped to where Cole was standing.

"Look, all I want you to do is hold this steering wheel steady and keep it pointed to the top of the hill over there. Do you see it?"

She grabbed the wheel as one born with a new purpose in life. "OK, OK, that's it. Good job. Good job."

It was a tough call to turn down the RPGs and the AK47 ammunition, but Cole figured his .45 and the rounds he had left would do the job and get them back to Thailand. He walked forward to the cargo deck, grabbed the end of the crates by their rope handles, pulled them to the boat's railings and, one-by-one, let them slip off and sink into the river.

•　　•　　•　　•　　•

It was late afternoon as they passed back through the cliffs that marked the Laos-Thailand border. Their progress had been slow. The old diesel was running flat out and just barely offset the current of the river moving downstream – just a bit faster than a man could walk along the bank.

Making the last great bend to the north in the Mekong, Cole could see ahead, and to his 11 o'clock he saw the village of Khong Chiam and the walls of the temple at *Wat Suwan* that they had drifted past, out of control, only a few hours before. Rather than turn west and enter the River Mun, and try again for the rickety old dock that had eluded their fingertips earlier that afternoon, Cole planned to go up-river on the Mekong for about another klick or two and then beach the boat on the west bank – on Thai soil – and then walk back south to Khong Chiam.

But he miscalculated the strength of the Mun where it entered the Mekong's channel from the west, and the boat was pushed aslant, out of its mid-stream course and close to the

Laotian shore to the east. With the diesel straining, he worked the controls to regain their up-river heading to the north and, finally moving past the Mun's current, he continued the push towards the Thai shore on the west bank.

Cole figured that this unexpected inflow from the Mun would now cause them to land about four to five klicks north of Khong Chiam, but that was alright. Besides, putting in to shore out of sight from any Thai village was a good thing since no one would see the Khmer markings on the boat and sound the alarm. *Good plan.* They would have farther to walk back to Khong Chiam, but the extra few kilos distance was not a problem. *A walk in the park.* At least, for him.

He looked at Pip and saw that she had collapsed into the spot where she had been sitting for the last hour. She had folded her arms on the railings and propped up her face, onto the back of her hands. She was taking in the color of the blue Mun meeting the brown Mekong, and how these two colors had merged into one – and how the brown color of the Mekong dominated this fluvial embrace. She looked at Cole and imagined that he was the brown, forceful Mekong – and she, the blue Mun. Pip thought of his power and quickness and how, in the matter of a few hours, he had saved her life not once, but twice. She nearly drowned. She was almost shot.

The fact he lied to her about the pistol vanished with the first shot, when their would-be executioner was blown backwards, his brains and hat leaving his body as if he had tossed them on a hat-rack. Cole's second shot assured their freedom. She could taste the relief. And in gratitude, she wanted to enfold him with her body and finish kissing him where they had left off last night. The close brush with death she had just experienced, and the sight of all that blood, evoked unexpected yearnings for this man – and she was left quivering. And she quivered until Cole pulled back the diesel's throttle and they glided up on a clear sandy bank on the Mekong. Back in Thailand.

"OK. You ready?" She nodded but didn't speak. "Right, let's go now. We have to get away from this boat." He judged correctly that she still needed to be mollycoddled, so he made his language do the work rather than slapping and shaking her out of her shock. It had worked so far. *Check.*

Cole was first off and he held out his hand for her, and she grabbed his gritty, sweaty palm, the blood of the young KR soldier caked on the back of his right hand. He pulled his shirt up in the front and wiped the sweat from his head. His gun stuck out from the back of his pants. Pip gazed at the instrument of her salvation. She had not mentioned the gun since, nor would she ever.

Pip saw him wipe his sweaty face and she mimicked him. She had a lot to say, or so she thought, but she could not speak. If she could, it would be to confess her freshly discovered attraction to this hard man. But she simply had no strength to form any words with her mouth nor the air to push them out. He reached up under his left armpit where he had tucked away her small purse. "Here. I believe this belongs to you," he said with a slight grin.

And she laughed out loud for the first time in days.

·   ·   ·   ·   ·

They began their walk towards Khong Chiam along the river's edge, and he figured they would arrive at the village just before the sun sat in the west. Pip stumbled several times, but said nothing of her discomfort, and Cole held her under his right arm to keep her steady and moving forward.

About 15 minutes into their walk, they heard a crashing sound from behind them. Something large was moving along the path in their direction. Cole grabbed Pip and eased her quickly over a fallen tree and into a clutch of bushes. He pushed her shoulders down and put his finger to her lips in case she started to speak, out of panic. He reached for his pistol and slowly brought it around in front of him. It would be a clean shot from under the log if he needed to peel one off. Very disorienting to an enemy, to be shot from ground level.

But as he cocked back the hammer on the .45, two huge elephants burst out from the path and into the clearing across from the fallen log. They were walking side-by-side on a path barely wide enough for one, and they looked as if they had something important to say to each other and needed to stay abreast to do so.

Cole looked again and saw two men mounted on top of the elephants, sitting on their shoulders behind their massive ears. And then a baby elephant emerged from the rear. It was running in between the legs of the larger one as she lumbered along. Three men followed the procession, one of whom was carrying a large rack of bananas over his right shoulder, feeding the tasty morsels to the baby.

Pip pulled herself up just high enough over the log to see the parade draw closer. She knew she could not speak up and watched in silence until they were within a few feet of their hiding place. The larger elephant, a female Pip quickly determined, turned her massive head to look in Pip's direction and held their hiding place in its gaze for several moments, her large brown eyes blinking slowly.

Pip could see the patterns of white, anointing dots on the foreheads of both elephants, symmetrical and pyramid-shaped. Cole put his hands on Pip's shoulder and kept her from rising further. They waited in their hiding spot until the elephants and the men had passed, and then gave it another 20 minutes for the path ahead to clear before the two followed that odd entourage south. They were all headed for Khong Chiam.

That was fine. That was good.

CHAPTER 28

They reached the outskirts of Khong Chiam as the sun was setting, and as the village watchman was ringing out three bright notes on the steel, tractor-wheel rim which hung on a jackfruit tree at the market square. The peal made by his metal rod against the steel rim could be heard all across town, and the inhabitants marked the time and began their routines and chores which that hour dictated.

The water blister on the ball of Pip's right foot had burst, so Cole now slung her under his left arm and held her around the ribs, allowing her to favor her right foot and yet move together as one. Evening stove fires were being lit and the smell of these charcoal fires drifted out from the homes that lined the street. He could feel her inhale these aromas deeply.

$$\bullet \quad \bullet \quad \bullet \quad \bullet \quad \bullet$$

They moved along the street which sloped down from the end of the forest path, through the town, and down to the River Mun – and the ramshackle wooden dock at the river's edge. It was the main street, and the only paved street, in a rural Thai village with little electricity and precious few streetlights. Most of the villagers thought that there was no need for these fine things.

Pip dropped her grasp of Cole's broad shoulder and stopped walking. She eyed a small, raised wooden platform on the street corner which was used during the day to sell fruits gathered from the forest, and in the afternoon as a place where old men would congregate with their bicycles and go over the latest news. At this time of the evening it was abandoned. She made her way over and sat down.

"Cole, *dichan tone mai wai*, she said. I can't go on now. We need to find a place to rest. It's getting dark, and here they have no lights at night. Let's find a place to rest," she repeated.

Cole said nothing. The shootings on the riverbank in Laos that afternoon had his blood roiled and coursing about in his veins, and he wanted to go now to the temple and grab his prize. *I can rush down to the temple, kick the doors open and grab Mordechai by the scruff of the neck.* He savored the thought of how much he was going to enjoy the moment of capture and the look in the priest's face. He had rehearsed that scene one hundred times since leaving Tan Son Nhut Air Base. And now his moment was here.

He scanned down the roadway towards the River Mun, about 1000 feet from where they stopped. He was looking for the temple. And as the bright evening sun melted into the jungle canopy to the west, he caught the golden glint of the temple's landmark stupa. It was a lodestar for him.

"There! He's there!" he said out loud without muffling his excitement. His juices were in full flow. "If you want to rest, you can stay here. I'm gonna go down there and grab this guy!"

She stood bolt upright, completely annoyed and exasperated by his childlike glee. "Don't be crazy! We're here. And *he's* right there. And that's good enough for today."

She sucked in a breath, "Besides, the monks don't go out at night, and you can't just go down there and barge into the temple. And even if you try to take him tonight, what do you intend to do with him? Chain him to that banana tree over there? Think about it *you dumb jerk.*"

It was a satisfying outburst, even at Cole's expense, and it helped to reanimate her languid demeanor. "Let's go in the morning... early in the morning. The sun's up, we're rested. You grab him and we go."

He grudgingly knew she was right but lingered on the delicious image of the capture – and he just stood there, unwinding, and staring at the golden stupa.

Cole was not about to give her credit for coming up with a decent plan and wanted to give her a sharp comeback to settle the score. But he saw that she was clearly at the end of her rope. Her face sallow. Her body weak and vulnerable.

"OK. OK," he said at last. "We move out at first light and grab him. I can hire a boat to Ubon and be on the next train to Bangkok. Lock him up there, pending his transport back to 'Nam."

He had quickly worked out a way to rationalize and embellish the plan that was just staked out by Pip. The credit was going to be his, not hers. "Yeah," convincing himself, "that will work."

●　　●　　●　　●　　●

The two had walked another 150 feet down towards the main part of the village when they came to a small, one-story inn. It was barely an inn, but it would do. Each room had a small, rock-hard bed, but only one had a toilet and basic shower. They took it. Pip ordered up some fried rice from the housekeeper after they checked in, and Cole dashed across the street where he bought three large quarts of warm Singha Beer.

The housegirl brought a plastic cannister of ice for the drinks and Cole righted two glasses on the small, round nightstand table by the bed, and put the ice in both glasses and poured the beer. The girl lit two kerosene lamps for the room and handed one to Pip who took it in to the bathroom and closed the door.

Cole kicked off his shoes and rubbed his feet. He sipped the lukewarm suds and waited for the beer to take the desired effect. He didn't need to wait long. The few crumbs of toast from that morning were long gone and the ethanol was ready to do its work. A young housegirl with hair cut short, bobbed for school, arrived with two plates of egg-fried rice which she placed on the low dresser at the foot of the bed. She *wai'*ed Cole, who slipped her a smile and reached into his dirty pants and pulled out a red, 100 baht note and handed it to the girl and waved her out.

The girl nervously mumbled something to him, pointed to the note and frowned in confusion, but Cole just nodded and said, "No problem." She erupted into a smile and backed out of the room. Cole followed her, pushed the button on the doorknob lock and slid the latch to.

Their bathroom had a round concrete cistern full of rainwater collected from the sheet metal roof. It was used to shower, scooping up the water by hand with a blue plastic bowl. A separate, identical bowl, red in color, was used to flush the "bomb site" squat-plate toilet. The Thais were very careful not to mix up the two bowls.

The room's single overhead fan was doing a meager job, but the proximity of the inn to the two rivers made the room cool and tolerable. Or maybe it was just his exhaustion, mixed with the beers that gave a coolness to these otherwise backwards and primitive digs. He had gone through his third quick glass of beer when Pip emerged from the bath.

She used the blue hotel towel to dry her hair, and she then wrapped that towel around her body. Pip closed the bathroom door behind her, turned and looked at Cole who was watching the scene in the dim lamplight. She stood there for a moment, looking at him, and then walked slowly to where he was sitting on the edge of the bed.

She stood in front of Cole. *I should slap your smug face for what you're thinking. And for what I had to endure today.* She hesitated for an instant, but then felt the heat rise from her gut. She raised her right arm back to deliver the smack. Cole caught her signals but did nothing to defend himself. She bit her lower lip. She hoped he would have at least flinched. He didn't budge. She dropped her arm.

All pretenses gone, she was aroused by the power of this man who dealt death to those who would snatch life from her. His world was tough and dangerous, and she could not resist its gravity as it pulled her in. At last, she was with a real man and not just a handsome city boy, masquerading as a man – or just another weak-willed actor in uniform who hovered around her in Bangkok. She dropped her towel.

In one motion, she pushed him onto his back, and then climbed on, reaching between her legs to undo his belt buckle. The rest Cole did quickly. She felt herself blending into his strength and the passionate sex was a tremendous release for them both.

•   •   •   •   •

Cole and Pip had finished their final act for that day, and Mordechai had preceded them in sleep. He was dreaming about his ordination as a monk that was to take place next week, back at *Wat Phra Nanachart* in Ubon. And those thoughts led him to a place of calmness, his spirit resonating with long waves of peace flowing over him.

Luang Por had been standing in the doorway of the *nanes'* *kuti*, the novices' cottage at *Wat Suwan*, and had been watching Mordechai for some time. He offered a small prayer for the safe spiritual journey and the well-being of all hearts, and especially Mordechai's. In the span of a few days, he had come to love

Mordechai as an uncle would love a nephew, and he stood there looking at his sleeping form. His spirit at rest.

This is fine. This is good. And then the old abbot whispered, "Yes, I pray for you, Mordechai. But I fear the evil tiger and the monkey are close. The moon is waxing and I believe you shall soon see them."

1,000 feet away, their fried rice was untouched. The tiger and the monkey lay embraced, sleeping without dreams, gathering their strength for the next day.

PART IV: AWAKENING

CHAPTER 29

Pip was the first to slide out of bed in the morning, leaving Cole teetering on the edge of the mattress, one leg in and one leg out on the floor, outrigger style, in deep sleep and barely moving a limb since the evening's climax. She saw the simple white blouse and the clean and pressed, checkered *pha-toong*, sarong, the housegirl had left last night, folded on the table next to the two cold plates of fried rice. But Pip was in a hurry and time was against messing around with a blouse that might be too large or too small and fussing with the sarong, as tempting as the fresh set of laundered clothes might be.

Instead, she pulled on her soiled jeans, the brown sand from the banks of the Mekong chaffed her calves as she yanked them up. She slipped on her green t-shirt and quietly lifted up the tray with the uneaten food and walked out of the room into the bright day. Pip placed the tray on the rough cement floor outside their room and gently closed the door behind her.

She left these unclaimed offerings on the floor, and a tinge of red embarrassment came to her cheeks. But it was not shameful recollections of the pleasure she felt last night that caused her to blush. It was the thought of wasting food in a place which had such thin children, like the school kids passing in front of her – walking sticks, clad in blue and white. Her mind searched for consolation. *Lord Buddha, I pray for their success and well-being,* she whispered.

Knowing that they would not accept food from a stranger, she hid the untouched plates from the childrens' stare with a tattered hand towel that was hanging on the parched wooden rail in front of their room.

•   •   •   •   •

The sun was just up, rolling over the hills of Laos to the east, scene of her baptism by blood into the Land of the Living the day before. Dogs were stirring from their sleep and monks and *nanes* would soon make their rounds for alms, Mordechai amongst them.

She moved quickly and fast-walked in the direction of the 50-meter communications tower she had spotted the evening before, its red beacon glowing in the dark Thai sky. She knew there would be a government telecoms operator at the base of the tower; it was a model for rural communications she had seen everywhere in the sticks. *I'll wake him up if I have to.*

She had two messages to send: a private note to her aunt in Ubon, and the update she needed to provide her bandy-legged boss back in Lumpini. He would be on the lookout for her report so he could, in turn, brief the US Embassy and the Thai brass and earn his cherished points.

Pip decided when she woke that Cole did not need to know about her business. But she had to move fast as he would soon be rousted from his sleep, once the images of an AWOL Mordechai came into his morning's consciousness.

•   •   •   •   •

DATE: 21/05/71

TO: Commandant Supot Chaisri, Lumpini Police Station, 139 Thanon Witahyu, Lumpini District, Bangkok, 10330

FROM: Major Panthip Siriwongdee

SENDING AUTHORITY: Khong Chiam PTT, Ubon Ratchathani Province

CLASSIFICATION: Confidential/Secret

"Have arrived in Ubon and further to Khong Chiam village with Lt. Coltrane. Expect to make arrest this morning and anticipate return to Bangkok within two days with prisoner. Will advise upon departure. [STOP] Regards."

DATE: 21/05/71

TO: Mrs. Nida Chukchoern, Proprietor, Tam Sabai Guest House, Soi 7/3, Moo 6, Ubon Ratchathani

FROM: Major Panthip Siriwongdee

SENDING AUTHORITY: Khong Chiam PTT, Ubon Ratchathani Province

CLASSIFICATION: Routine

"Greetings Aunt Nid. A change in plans. Expect to return to Ubon late this evening. Will then go to Bangkok the next day. Regret Uncle Suwit's boat was lost in the river. Don't worry. We are both safe. Americans will pay you for boat later. [STOP] Important: Please tell cousin Lek and Uncle Suwit to hire a fast boat this morning and come to Khong Chiam. Not later than this afternoon. We cannot otherwise return as planned.

Thank you. We hope to see you soon. [STOP] With deep respect, Nong Pip."

She handed the scribbled notes to the sleepy-eyed telecoms operator and produced her ID to inject her rank squarely into his mind, diverting him from his usual wake-up routine: sitting on a wooden plank outside the radio room with a bowl of rice porridge, watching the morning shenanigans of his mongrel dog, pet chicken and monkey who played a game of "animal tag" – a daily sideshow which kept him company and amused in an otherwise dead-boring assignment.

"*Khrap, khrap,*" he said, coming to attention behind the counter and stumbling on the stool he had knocked over in the process of snapping to. He added in Thai, "I'll take care of this right away, Major, sir... I mean, madam. Will do this now. Yes. Now..."

"Thank you, Sergeant..." she strained to read his nametag on his government-issued tan shirt, the kind worn by all telecommunications officers in Thailand, "...Sergeant Pichet. I appreciate that very much. Very important messages."

"*Khrap, khrap,*" he repeated as she turned to leave. He admired her silhouette which filled the doorway of the communications shed as she left, but wondered why her clothes, the clothes of a major, were so disheveled and dirty – and so early in the morning.

•   •   •   •   •

Pip stood in front of the door to their room at the inn and reached for the knob, but she dropped her arm. She lowered her head. The plates of cold rice were gone. She felt the full weight of her obligations once again press down on her shoulders. This priest was going to be arrested within the hour. It was her duty to assist, but Pip felt sadly complicit in this regrettable act. And the very hunter of this holy man – the man who had caressed her and made love to her the night before – was just beyond this threshold.

"What am I doing?" she whispered out loud, her reluctance mixing with a fear of spiritual trespassing. She sighed deeply and blew the breath out through her lips, pursed into a tight "O."

She pushed open the door. And there, sitting on the edge of his bed, naked and smiling, was the devil himself – as if he were positioning himself for a repeat performance of last night.

"Morning," said Cole with a broad grin and a wink. "Out for a stroll?"

Caught by surprise, "Good morning," was all she could wring out.

He smiled but did not say anything more.

Pip darted into the bathroom where she shut and faced the door, pressing it hard with the top of her head as if to keep his intensity deflected behind this wooden shield. She waited and counted the heaving motions of her chest... 21, 22, 23... The intervals grew farther apart.

OK, OK, this is stupid, she admitted, and poured some water into the empty toilet to sound as if she had used it. She opened the door and found him slipping on his socks and underwear, and reaching for his grimy pants.

"Ready to go? Let's go get our man!"

He offered not a single word about their moment last night. No kind words. No slippery remarks. It was all taken in stride. Pip was grateful for not having to speak about it, yet also disappointed that he failed to mention anything about his feelings, or about her performance. To say something. Anything. She imagined he might say, *'Last night was great! Let's do it again!'* But those words would not be spoken, and the mere imagining of such kindness would have to do for the moment. He was a man in a hurry.

"Yeah, sure, I guess so," she threw in. She watched as he pulled his still-buttoned, dirty green shirt over his head and reach into the pillowcase nearest him. He dug out his .45 and stuck it in that familiar spot in the back of his pants.

Cole stopped smiling and stood up, shoulders back, and walked quickly to the door. Pip followed slowly on his heels. But before opening the door, he turned to her and said, "I know these guys' story. They go out begging for food in the morning. And since he and his buddies could be anywhere out there, we're going right down to the beehive - this temple down the road - and wait for the bastard. We'll catch him outside as he's goin' back into the gate. Easy pickin's."

Pip could say nothing. She could not garner the courage to speak the words she held in her nettled heart, protesting the pursuit of this holy man. And she knew the momentum was moving quickly and in the wrong direction. *But, at the very least, why not do this discretely and away from the Wat, where so many people would be wending their way at this early time of the morning: the faithful bringing food to the monks as they made their rounds; storekeepers beginning their daily commerce; fishermen walking to the river with their nets, and housewives sweeping the night's dust from their porches and hanging out the morning's wash. It doesn't need to be such a public spectacle.* But she could only repeat, "Yeah, I guess so."

Cole caught on to her silence and her gaze at the floor. "Look. Let's do it this way. It will work. Clean and simple, and then we'll just slip away."

He was thinking about their trip to *Wat Phra Nanachart* two days ago - about having to ask for permission to do their job there and about the hassles of going through that rigmarole again. "No, we're going to do this outside the temple gates. As soon as they come streaming back with their begging bowls, we'll nab him."

Pip just wanted the whole thing to end quickly. *Cole's mind is set. OK. OK. This plan should work, if done discretely*, she thought.

● ● ● ● ●

Cole braced against the tree, straight and still. And Pip sat next to him, squat down with her back against the wall that formed the arched gateway to the temple, her biceps resting on top of her bent knees, exposing her soft mocha forearms. Her palms were up as if she were begging and praying at the same time – two acts which required a contrite heart. And her heart was indeed small and tight.

The spotty shade of the young tamarind tree provided scant relief from the squinting sweat that ran into their eyes, and Cole lifted and rested his left hand against the tree's upper trunk while drawing deeply from a freshly lit Camel. He stared down the dirt path, searching for the bobbing orange entourage of monks returning from their morning alms round. *No. Not yet.* They waited.

But Pip could no longer contain her anxiety, and she felt her mouth opening and speaking before she could disengage the urge. The tension couldn't have been worse for her. She was duty-bound to fulfill her orders, and yet poised to commit an egregious sin against "Thai ways" since his capture was to be made during alms gathering – during an act of piety and respect for things holy.

This entire mission has been troubled by bad karma, she thought, and the payback did not need to wait until the next incarnation to manifest itself. It had already worked its way onto the surface of her present world – the episode with the near-death boat trip and the killing on the riverbank yesterday was enough evidence to convince her of this bad luck.

In her nervousness, and unable to stop herself, she blurted out from a defensive place, "You know, Cole, I was thinking about this arrest – this act of capturing your priest, and an ideal story came to my mind."

She anticipated his contempt for her stories and didn't bother to ask him if he wanted to hear it, nor did she look in his direction. And Cole wasn't the least bit interested. He was already in the kill zone. Focusing. The sounds around him were quickly fading, including any *boring and droning story by Pip*. Her voice blended in and faded away, along with the sounds of birds flitting around in the tamarind tree, the local gossiping murmurs of passing Thais who stared at the duo, and the staccato purr of smoky, two-cycle Hondas, zipping up-and-down the dirt path to the market.

Pip didn't care that he wasn't listening. She would tell the story to calm her own frayed nerves. She began, "Well, I am going to tell you, anyway." And she recalled the short fable from her childhood memories, word-for-word.

"This is a story of the Buddha in a previous incarnation, before he was the Buddha. In this story he takes on an animal form. He is a deer, but not just any deer. He was the prince of his herd. And there was also a ruthless human king who ruled over the forest in which the deer prince and his deer subjects lived. Each day the king and his men went into the forest and killed many deer, so much so that a great fear spread amongst the deer that soon no one would be left. So, the deer agreed that each day one amongst them should be selected and presented to the king for slaughter, harsh as that may sound.

On one particular day, a pregnant doe was to be sent for sacrifice, but the Buddha was so moved with pity for her and her unborn child that he volunteered to die in her place. When he presented himself to the king for sacrifice, the king was so deeply touched by this act of compassion, that he renounced the hunting of deer forever. He said, 'you, who are an animal by nature, have a superior heart than me, a human.'"

She finished her story and then peered up at Cole, but he was still locked into a stare down the road. Frustrated by his indifference, she added a sarcastic conclusion, "And they all lived happily ever after." She had seen all the Disney movies. Cole had seen none.

She slumped at the shoulders, but then righted herself as the anger to his scorn built up. "Did you hear what I said?"

Pip cupped her right hand over her brow to block the sun's glare. "You are the hunter-king in that story, Cole." He didn't budge. His hand was stuck to the tree as if it were nailed there. "It is within your power to let Mordechai go. To just walk away."

He had heard alright – at least the last part, but he wasn't having any of it. He half-turned his shoulders in her direction, but held his eyes fixed down the path ahead. "You like deer stories, do you? Well I got one for you. I like deer, too. I like to hunt them. And I like to *kill* and *eat* them!" he said with great relish.

"You see," he began his story, "I was once up in Reserve – a little town in the heart of the Gila Forest in New Mexico – and my buddy Gus and me were deer hunting." He glanced at Pip who was smoldering at the rude disregard he had given her story. *Such an uncouth asshole!* Her lips were flat and her eyes narrowed.

"So, me and Gus had been sittin' behind a large sage bush, and there were plenty of signs – droppings on the trail that ran to the outwash-plane below us. It was about evening time when we saw a ten-point buck come out from behind a piñon pine. He was too far off for a clean shot, and he just stood there and looked right at us, but he didn't move a step closer.

So, I very quietly took a white t-shirt from my backpack and wrapped it around the end of a long stick of pine – we were downwind, you see – and I slowly raised the stick over our heads and above the sage bush."

Cole sneaked a look at Pip who was drawn into the story against her will. Noting that, he cracked a slight grin and went on. "The trick is to wiggle that flag a little bit. Not a lot, or you'll spook them off. Just a little. You see, antelope, mule deer – and even some elk – will be drawn in by curiosity. They'll approach that wigglin' little white flag just to see what the hell it is.

Sometimes they'll walk right up to you, close enough that you can see the dark black slit in their brown eyes... reach out and feel the roughness of their coats... and then... Bang! You nail 'em!"

Pip's head rocked back with Cole's explosion and her eyes opened wide, imagining the drama and the death – the spurting blood.

"That Winchester 30.06 is a great rifle. Model 1917. My grandfather brought it home from WWI. But he replaced the stock with maple," he added, matter-of-factly.

He returned his shoulders to square with his vision down the path and added, "The ten-pointer went that way." Cole turned away from Pip without reading her reaction. He didn't need to. He knew he had bested her story. Great stories always end with a kill – in that exhilarating moment.

The intensity of his stare down the path could have incinerated the adjacent patches of dry, dead grass.

•　　•　　•　　•　　•

The walled, temple compound of *Wat Suwan* had only a single, arched gate to the outside world, through which the monks traveled out-and-in every day on their way to make their holy rounds within the community. Daily, without fail, they traveled out for *bintabaat*, to collect alms. It was a holy duty.

And just when the sun was making its debut onto the plain of *I-saan* in eastern Thailand that day, before Pip had sent her telegraph messages, and before Cole sat naked on the edge of the bed, *Luang Por* led nine monks, *Nane* Mordechai, two other school-aged *nanes*, and three *luuk-sit*, helpers, away from the temple in a long, single-file column.

When they reached the central market in the middle of the village, they would split into three smaller groups: one going north, along the Mekong's riverbank to the edge of the forest; one south towards the fishing shacks near the River Mun; the last group walking along a main road which ran through the village to the west, and out to the remote huts strewn about there.

Their three pathways were dotted with groups of devotees, often small family gatherings who waited patiently for their handful of monks and *nanes* to arrive. In silence, the faithful would present their offerings of food and flowers, and then receive the chanted blessings of merit from the monks.

And after many such stops along their appointed paths, the monks would return to midtown, reform into their single column and then, on the road that began at the River Mun, walk back uphill on the temple pathway and through the arched gate in the temple wall. This circuitous route was their daily practice over the decades, affording the Buddhist villagers a fitting means to make their offerings without foregoing their endless chores. Antlike in its order and singleness of purpose, alms gathering along these pathways and trails was a custom as old as the faith itself.

•   •   •   •   •

When the long orange line finally came into view, slowly padding its way up the hill, Cole flicked his cigarette butt onto the gravel and stretched out his right foot to crush it, swiveling on the outsole of his shoe.

"Here we go," he said mechanically under his breath and slowly stepped out from the shade of the tamarind tree. Hands at his side, he positioned himself at the edge of the path that led from the road to the arched gateway, and the shady temple grounds within the compound beyond. Pip bobbed her head down between her knees, closed her eyes and slowly uncoiled from her squat. The monks were still 100 feet away as she rose and crept forward to where Cole stood, scanning the single-file line for his prey.

Cole flexed his fists as the column drew near. The pull and the tensions of the past week were reaching a climax on this dusty brown path, and the sinews in his neck were drawing tight, his back teeth set against each other. Here comes his buck. The hunt would soon be over. Pip stood beside him, but slightly behind, as if he were a fence post and she a door pivoting around him, leaning her body out from behind his shoulders to catch a glimpse of the shot being fired.

His begging bowl concealed under his saffron robe, *Luang Por* led the procession, followed by the monks, *nanes* and *luuk-sit* as the column reached the front of the temple gate. All eyes were turned downwards to avoid treading on small, sentient creatures under their bare feet.

And as *Luang Por* turned to lead his group through the gate and into the temple grounds, he caught the long shadows of Cole and Pip which were cast across his path, motionless like stone sentinels. He turned to look at them. He caught in an instant the facial expressions of the two strangers: *a man with smiling, hungry eyes... completely dissonant with his teeth-bearing grin. The other, lurking behind him... a nervous and furtive woman... no eye contact.* He slowed his pace and looked up at them again, and with this second look he stopped walking. The column behind him halted in formation.

He raised his right arm from under his robe and pointed with his boney index finger to the pair not more than 10 feet away and declared in Thai, "*Nee-ngai! Seua lae ling!* Here! The tiger and the monkey!" *Luang Por* said it loud enough that the entire column resurfaced from its walking meditations.

Cole moved in closer, slowly and without talking. Pip followed in his footsteps. But before he could close the remaining space, the nine monks quickly pressed in and around *Luang Por*. They didn't need to hear any words from Cole to discern that this man presented danger. His aggressive character filled the space in front of the temple gate. The *nanes* and *luuk-sit* flowed in behind the monks, Mordechai looming behind them all, peering over the cluster of orange in front of him.

Cole looked straight at Mordechai, but it was not Mordechai he saw. It was just a foreigner with a shaved head, eyebrows and face, almost indistinguishable from the others, save for his white complexion and height. He tried to imagine that face with hair, with jungle fatigues, with captain's bars and chaplain's insignia on his collar. It was Mordechai all right. And Cole's knitted brows relaxed when the ID had been made. *This priest is now going in the bag.*

"Pip, come out here. I need you to explain to this monk –"

But before another word was said, *Luang Por* spoke, "You do not need her if you wish to speak with me. I know who you are, and I know why you came. You mean to do harm to one of us." He stopped to let his words sink in and to catch Cole's reaction. "I cannot allow you to do this."

But Cole had only half heard the old monk and was now trying to move closer to Mordechai.

"Captain Goodcut?" Cole asked, but it was not a question. It was a declaration. He knew this was his man.

Mordechai looked at this strange pair and, at first, he had no idea who these two could be. But Cole's official air and hostile tone – and the way he used his name, "Captain Goodcut," told him everything. Instantly. He was hearing a warrant being read. Mordechai quickly sized up the situation, but he had no instinct to flee. He simply stood there and stared back at Cole who was now trying to part his way through two rows of monks that stood between him and his prisoner.

"Sorry, 'scuse me. Please move aside," as he attempted to move through the front row. The only word the monks would have understood was "please," but they were not budging.

Luang Por saw the imminent danger, and spoke, "*Yaa hai man jahp nane Mordechai! Phaa khow nai wat deow-nee! Reo reo!* Don't let him grab *nane* Mordechai! Take him inside the gate, now!"

And, directed by *Luang Por*'s words, the nine monks instinctively moved to form an orange phalanx, shoulder-to-shoulder, protecting the rear row. The two other *nanes* and the *luuk-sit* understood their orders and grabbed Mordechai by the hands and tugged him the few remaining feet towards the temple gate.

Mordechai turned to see his brethren block Cole's movement towards him. He also had a quick look at Pip who stood in the place where Cole had left her. She was bent forward at the waist, her long arms pressed together, meeting at her palms and pointing at the ground beneath her as if she were *wai'*ing mother earth. Her eyes met his. And then he was in.

Seeing Mordechai escape from the back row through the gate, Cole tried to run around the group and tackle him inside the temple grounds, but Pip moved quickly and interjected herself with her body. She held out both arms, her small hands pressing hard against his chest. "No Cole. You cannot violate the rules of this sanctuary. *Luang Por* has just spoken and he has forbidden this arrest."

Cole reached across his chest and pushed her hands away and took a long step towards the gate, "Better get out of my way, sister!"

But she held fast and thumped his chest with her fists, "Remember, this priest has not broken any of *our* laws – only yours and your stupid Army," she shouted. "If you persist and pursue him within the temple against the wishes of the abbot, you are going to cause a big problem, and not only here."

Cole stood, mid-stride, for a second. The quickness and surety of Pip's movements had caught him off guard. "Look, whose side are you on, anyway? You got a job to do here – so do it!"

But Pip was on righteous footing and spouted the scripture and verse of the law, "In any case, you would never leave Thailand with your prisoner. As a matter of fact, they may arrest *you* for such transgressions. Do not underestimate the anger of an insulted Thai people and the repercussions from violating *Luang Por*'s words. That move would be a serious misstep!"

With two or three monks he would have taken his chances, despite Pip's obnoxious speech-making and her meager physical resistance. But with nine monks to deal with, even a hard-charger like Cole had second thoughts. The monks were, after all, men – and Thai men at that. Men whose loyalty to their faith was strong and steadfast, and one had only to lift a finger against a person of *Luang Por*'s stature and there would be hell to pay.

These jokers are determined. Pain in the neck, all of them, especially the old guy. He threw a hard glance at *Luang Por*.

"Such fucking bullshit!" Anger and frustration spilled out of Cole and onto *Luang Por* and the monks who remained outside the gate, but they only returned his hostile glare and vile words with curious looks, as if they were observing a crazy man. And they were.

Pip implored him, "Cole, please don't make this any worse! Don't say bad things to insult the abbot and the monks here. He speaks English perfectly, and the things you mutter, and the pacing back-and-forth here will not help anything."

She tried to reason, "You need to calm down. You need to speak to the abbot – but not today. Today is ruined. Finished. We'll come back and speak with the abbot later. Tomorrow." She repeated, "Tomorrow."

But Cole was not calming down. And the suggestion by Pip that he do so only infuriated him more.

Luang Por spoke again, "Yes, tiger, listen to your monkey." And at these words, Pip cast her eyes to the ground. *Luang Por* had called her for what she was. A monkey – a weakling monkey riding on a tiger's back, complicit in this unholy deed. At least his chiding pronouncement was in English. If *Luang Por* had said this in Thai, the stares of the other nine monks would have been hard to take.

"*Kha*. Yes. *Kha*," was all she could say, and she curtsied and *wai*ed the old monk and his entourage as they reformed into a single column, turned and walked through the temple gate and into the grounds beyond.

Cole stood there, left hand on the wall of the gate, peering in and watching the procession of monks and *luuk-sit* as they entered the great hall. One-by-one they entered. Not one of them looked back. That was not necessary. *Luang Por* had spoken – and his word was the law inside these plastered, white temple walls.

Cole reached into his pocket for his last smoke and lit it quickly. His boiler was still glowing red, and he sucked in the situation with the first, deep drag. By the time it had burned to a nub, he flicked it into the open gateway of the temple as a parting gesture of disrespect.

Two monks who were sent out from the great hall to meander inside the gate and keep an eye on this aggressive foreign man caught the ungracious act, but said nothing nor looked in Cole's direction. One of the village *luuk-sit*, passing by on his way home, kicked the butt out from the gate with his flip-flops. He gave Cole a quick once-over but avoided his eyes.

In the meantime, a large crowd had gathered. The word had gotten out this morning that this was the pair who had sailed past the *Wat* yesterday and headed down the Mekong. And the gossip started.

So, these are the strangers who sailed off into Laos. I see. But what were they doing there? They must have had some secret business, returning mysteriously. Yes, I heard they swam back, up the river. A handsome foreign man and a beautiful Thai woman. She went to see Pichet at the tower this morning. Then we saw them come from the inn. Are they together? Why did Luang Por speak so strongly, and what exactly did the abbot say to this foreigner? You're right! What is going on? Such chatter about this extraordinary and provocative pair provided the threads from which local legends were woven – and they grew thicker by the hour.

Pip was soaking in the entire disaster. Time to leave.

Outside the gate, one dejected figure in a green tropical shirt shuffled away; the other had a brisk smartness to her step. And they both retreated to the inn. She could not hide her secret joy. She was elated. But Cole thought, *There's got to be a way to get that son-of-a-bitch out of there. Got to be a way. I'm going to get that bastard if it's the last thing I do...*

Exasperated and hollowed out, Cole walked without talking, pushed open the unlocked door of their room at the inn, and crashed on the bed. *Loaded. Aimed. Missed the shot! All this time on the trail, and this guy gets within arm's reach... only to come up empty-fuckin'-handed. Man, that's some bullshit! Fuck this place and their fucking rules!*

The room was stifling hot. Pip clicked on the overhead fan, wired to the wall switch. "Position 4" on the selector was broken, so she dialed it down to "position 3" and walked out the door.

CHAPTER 30

It was 5:30 that evening when Pip wandered back up the street and found both Uncle Suwit and his son, Lek, sitting in the tin-roof noodle shop across the road from the inn. Uncle Suwit was drinking a glass of Thai tea and Lek was gulping down a tall Singha beer, his third by her count of the dead soldiers under the table.

She also noticed that they had brought her overnight bag and Cole's gear bag from Ubon, and these were placed separately on two empty plastic chairs next to their table. *Why in the world...* she wondered, but broke off her thoughts when she made eye contact with her favorite uncle.

· · · · ·

"*Sawatdee, Leung* Suwit, *kha!* Hello Uncle Suwit!" she shouted out with a huge smile, *wai'*ing him.

It was a genuine relief to see him here, a person – like his wife, Aunt Nida – with strong, old-school values. Pip loved him for his kind and pure nature, and she felt a tear well up in the corner of her eye from the joy of seeing him. But that drop soon retreated, drawn back by the gravity of her predicament.

"*Ow!*" exclaimed Uncle Suwit, in Thai. "Pip *ja!* Are you OK? We got your message this morning and Lek and I came here as fast as we could."

Pip turned to look at Lek and he greeted her with a *wai.*

"So, what *is* going on? We were so worried," her uncle asked.

"No. Don't be concerned, dear uncle. We had a little problem with the boat yesterday, that's all. It got away from us after a motor failure." It was easier for her to make up a story about a motor failure than to tell the truth – and she did not really understand the problem with "the steering wheel thing," in any event.

"And I'm very sorry about your boat. The American I'm with said that they would buy you a new one." It was another fib. She glanced at Lek and caught his suspicious eyes.

"A new boat? Really?!" asked her uncle. He had seen the pictures of the sleek, varnished Chris-Craft speedboats with American-made, Evinrude outboard motors and he smiled. "Well, I guess that will be alright – but the important thing is that you're OK. And you *are* OK, right?"

He wavered for a second when he saw how dirty and upended she looked. But it was getting dark, and he could not see well enough to be sure.

"Ah, OK, then," he said. "Well, the boat for you is here, but it's too late to go back to Ubon tonight. We can leave in the morning."

"Yes, well, um... we may need to leave a bit later – like in the afternoon. Will that be OK?"

The old man stood and fumbled around in his pockets for change to pay for the drinks. "Huh? What's that? Oh, OK. Tomorrow afternoon. Sure, OK."

"Here. Here are your things. Your aunt insisted I bring them, even though you were supposed to come back this afternoon." He shrugged his shoulders and added, "I don't get it." He reached up with his right hand and scratched the back of his neck, shooing off a fully engorged tiger mosquito. "She worries a lot about you."

"Yes, I know," Pip said with an embarrassed smile, which soon faded. "And where are you staying tonight?" She gestured across the street, palm up and fingers pointed, "Do you wish to stay at this inn?"

"No, no. Not necessary. I know the village elders here and they are going to put us up for the night. Don't worry, *Ja*. We'll see you tomorrow. Down by the wooden dock."

How could I forget that? she thought.

"OK, see you then." She stood, *wai*ed her uncle, returned her younger cousin's *wai* with a smile, grabbed the two bags off the plastic chairs and walked across the street to the inn.

She left the table and heard her uncle scold Lek, "Hey, go easy on that beer. You can't go there and be a drunken fool in front of my friends..."

·   ·   ·   ·   ·

Pip turned the knob on the room door, picked up the two bags and walked inside. Cole was already up, sitting on the side of the bed. He had a wrinkled sheet of paper in his left hand. It contained text and looked like a telegram from the PTT – it had the appearance that it had been wadded up, and then flattened out again.

In his right hand was an empty glass of beer, half-full of melting ice chips. The tall bottle of Singha beer on the floor was knocked over and the contents had flowed out and across the uneven concrete floor and under the bed. Cole's face was pale and his eyes were bloodshot red. *Was he crying?! What the hell?*

Cole stood, ignoring Pip's presence. Animated by a torrent of memories from the past, he tossed the paper on the floor and walked, glass in hand, in a slow and measured cadence towards the door. He opened it and moved out into the humid Thai evening of Khong Chiam. His only words were, "That melon-headed, stiff-necked son-of-a-bitch..."

He didn't close the door behind him, but it was not an invitation for Pip to join him outside. She went to the door and watched from the jam as he shuffled across the street to the tiny food shack and bar. A dog, disturbed from its rest, howled furiously at the sight of this stranger, as all dogs do when a crazed person passes by. Pip came back inside, closed the door behind her and placed their two bags on the bed.

•   •   •   •   •

On the painted, pea-green cement floor, the paper Cole had held was now blotting up the spilt beer. She walked over and picked it up. It was a telegram, alright.

Sergeant Pichet from Thai Telecoms had received it that afternoon and brought it directly to the hotel in an envelope, but of course he had read the message – read it many times. And he was wide-eyed when he gave it to the hotel's senior housekeeper who was always primed for gossip.

By that afternoon, everyone in Khong Chiam knew who the *farang,* foreigner, and his Thai lady friend were, where they were staying and what they were up to, thanks to Pichet's other skills as a communicator.

Pip read the telegram:

DATE: 21/05/71

TO: Lt. F. Coltrane, c/o Khong Chiam PTT, Ubon Ratchathani Province

FROM: 2nd Lt. Richard Clarke, Military Liaison Officer, US Embassy Bangkok

SENDING AUTHORITY: Pathumwan PTT, Pathumwan, Bangkok

CLASSIFICATION: Confidential

"Lt. Coltrane, relaying following full-text message received this morning from your commander in Vietnam, Lt. Col. Earnest Hargraves. Requires your immediate attention."

Rgds, Clarke, 2nd Lt., USAF, US Embassy, Bangkok.

FROM: Lt. Col. E. Hargraves, 16th MP/Thon Son Nhut, RVN

TO: Lt. F. Coltrane, 16th MP/Thon Son Nhut, RVN / TDY Thailand

ATTN: MACThai/ForceComm – Bangkok, 2nd Lt. Clarke, US Embassy

INFO: N/A

Classification: Secret

Date: 20/05/71

1. Regret to inform Lt. Coltrane of the death of Sergeant E5, Angus Digman.
2. Sergeant Digman was KIA during a patrol on 19 May near Binh Long while on voluntary assignment with LRRP unit of 25th Infantry.
3. Sgt. Digman to be posthumously awarded Bronze Star for bravery demonstrated during engagement with the enemy, night of 19 May.
4. His remains to be repatriated to New Mexico, US. ETA is TBD.
5. Grateful you acknowledge above and provide info on next of kin for shipment.
6. Signed: Lt. Col. Hargraves/ Commander 16th MP – Special Investigations.

She was puzzled. *Was this the Gus in Cole's deer hunting story? I mean… to daze Cole like that… it must be…*

"Damn it!" She tried to dab the beer from the telegram with her shirttail. Where the ink didn't run, it could still be read clearly: *KIA... ETA... TBD... such brief and sterile letters... So cold...* She reached across the bed from where she was bent over, placing the beer-soaked sheet on the bedcover and under the spinning ceiling fan. *This should dry it off completely.*

She stood and righted herself and glanced at the two bags. Hers was zipped up and tidy, but the zipper on Cole's gear bag was almost undone. *Now, this is odd. Not something that guy would leave open.*

Her mind raced to a picture of a drunken Lek, poking his nose where it didn't belong. She nodded and bit the inside of her bottom lip. *That sneaky butthole! He better not have stolen anything from Cole.* She reached across the width of the bed to lift his bag closer to where she stood. But as she did so, her left knee buckled and she flung her arms out behind her to brace herself for the fall, dragging his bag to the edge of the bed and tipping its contents out onto the floor.

"Oh, shit!" She quickly grabbed the clothing – underwear, t-shirts, jeans, a bush hat, his Ray-Ban case, pit stick, and a small book with a red-leather cover, and began putting these things back into the bag. She picked up the book and ran her soft hand over it. Her eyes caught the dirty, gold-embossed letters on the book's cover and she read the title out loud, in a whisper, "*Catholic Prayers.*" Pip was stunned. *What in the world?! No, this can't be! What in the hell is* he *doing with a prayer book? This guy, of all people.*

She quickly scanned the door for a sign that Cole would burst back into the room. Satisfied, she opened the book and read from the inside cover. "To my Precious Grandson, May the prayers in this book protect you and bring you back safely to us. I love you, Grandma Elenora." Pip felt her face heat up. She flushed red. She knew she was in private, forbidden territory. Next to the writing was a small, yellow crochet bookmark in the shape of a cross, and inserted towards the end of the book, a sealed plain manila envelope with Cole's name scribbled in the addressee space.

She held the book by the spine and fanned through the pages. *Prayers.* An involuntary grunt came from deep in her chest and a soft smile came to her face. *He needs these prayers more than he knows. He's got no idea…*

She repositioned the yellow bookmark and the letter, closed the book and placed it back into the bag along with his underwear, pit stick and t-shirts. She zipped it up quickly.

CHAPTER 31

Cole woke before dawn but lay motionless next to Pip. He had been up since he came back from the tin shack across the street last night. The plate of fried noodles and three beers did little to unwind the knot in his stomach.

The news of Gus' death, the run-in with the old monk yesterday, and a gnawing complaint caused by Mordechai's escape made sleep impossible. And the knot had been steadily tightening after he saw *Mordechai's holier-than-thou face* escape into the temple grounds, smiling as he looked back over his shoulder at the debacle at the gate. *No problem, my friend... Will see who laughs last, you jackass.*

When Cole paid for the noodles and beer last night, he caught sight of two Thais as they walked together, down the road towards the river at the bottom of the hill. He swore one of them looked like *that fat fucker Lek*, Pip's cousin, who stood them up at the boat dock two days ago. But he couldn't make a positive ID from the back, and Cole sure as hell was not going to shout out his name.

Yeah. Thanks to this asshole our boat was busted – and then we had that shit-stop in Laos. But what the hell is he doing here now? And who is that other dude with him – the shriveled-up old fart with the long, white hair?

• • • • •

Cole knew the monks would be up early, praying and getting ready to make their rounds and he was going to be there as they streamed out of the gate, just in case Mordechai was bold enough to think he could get away with it a second time. *Old monk or no old monk, I'm bringin' my insurance piece this morning…* and if Mordechai didn't come along peacefully, Cole was resolved to brandish his Colt 1911.

As if she could read his troubling thoughts, Pip turned over on her back, brushed her ribs under her right breast and moaned as if someone was pulling a wooden splinter from her side.

Cole gave her a quick glance, but she was sound asleep. He swung out of bed, peeled off all his clothes and headed for the shower, but as he moved around the bed he noticed Pip's overnight bag sitting on a white, metal folding chair against the far wall – and there was his gear bag on the low dresser. *Now… how in the hell did those get here?*

He looked again at Pip's bag, looked at her, and then back to his bag. And in that brief span he remembered the two guys in the street yesterday evening. *So that was that fat fucker, alright. OK, so what did he steal?*

He quickly unzipped his bag and found everything he remembered stuffing in there, three days ago. *But wait a minute… This shit's upside down.* He found the pit stick, the underwear and the prayer book on top, and all the stuff he had put on top, like his glasses case, a clean shirt and pants, on the bottom.

So, Lek did go through it. That dumb bastard! Although he had scant few items of any value in the bag, Cole could not abide the thought that they had been molested.

He dumped the contents on the bed next to Pip's sleeping form and then replaced them, one-at-a-time as originally packed, taking a mental inventory as he did so. All went well until he reached for his red-leather *Catholic Prayers*.

Cole bent down to pick it up from the bed, but before doing so he went to the bathroom and took a bath towel to cover his naked body before returning. The weekly catechism lessons of the church – and the proddings of faithful Grandmother Elenora – were buried deep, a vestige of respect he could not shake off.

He picked up the prayer book and saw the manila envelope that Digman had given him, jutting out from inside the rear cover. He pulled the letter out and then placed the book into the bag. The oath he had reluctantly swore to Gus came crashing into his head, but at 4am he was in no mood for the antics of the dead melon head.

"You're an asshole for getting yourself killed – you stupid fucker," he said out of love.

He started to toss the envelope free into the bag along with the other contents but stopped and tapped the letter against his left thumb, like he was shaking the last drops from a ketchup bottle. *I'll get to this later today. Gus's a goner – the dumb shit – and this can wait.*

And with that he tossed the letter on top of his bag, peeled off the towel, flung it over his shoulder and sauntered into the small cement bathroom for a quick splash.

Pip thought she heard the sound of water being poured from a height onto the cement floor of the bathroom. She rolled on her side, and noticing Cole wasn't there, made the connection and drifted back to sleep.

•   •   •   •   •

Cole passed by the young tamarind tree that stood near the temple gate of *Wat Suwan*. Yesterday morning it had provided a small bit of shade as he and Pip waited in ambush for the monks to return uphill. It was the site of their botched attempt to snatch Mordechai – *Too close to the gate… won't make that mistake again.*

And as Cole drew nearer the gate, he slowed his pace and then stopped.

His shoulders squared with the archway and he looked into the temple grounds beyond. The sun had yet to appear over the mountains of Laos, but the ambient morning light was increasing all around him. The few, burning bare bulbs on the outside of the temple's buildings were being extinguished by a dutiful *luuk-sit*.

Cole started to move off down the path to scout out a new ambush site, but as he turned to leave, he heard the first faint refrains from an ancient Pali-Sanskrit prayer being offered up in thanks for the morning. It wafted through the air, the sound carried and modulated by the westward breeze which moved across the Mekong River and gently swirled into the temple grounds and out the gate. The melodic sound of the prayer was haunting and exotic, yet also calming – the droning was dangerously hypnotic. He shook the pleasant pull of those sounds from his head. *No time for this bullshit.*

He moved on. One hundred yards to the south the dirt path bent slightly to the east where its left edge was overgrown with tall elephant grass. The place would provide an ideal hunter's blind for him to watch the orange entourage as it came out from the temple, turned left and then headed south along the path – the route fixed by the monk's daily rituals. By the time they reached his ambush site, any wary monk would have lost his jitters about seeing "the dangerous foreigner" at the gate again. Surprise was everything.

Near the clump of elephant grass at the bend in the path, he kicked a golf-ball-sized rock with the toe of his boot. It sailed up and over the grass and hit the trunk of a large banana tree, full of ripe yellowing fruit, and careened off. Cole was happy. He was confident. And he repeated the promise he had been mouthing that morning: *If Goodcut is bold enough to make the rounds today, I'm taking him with me… and no old monk – or a gang of them – is going to say otherwise.*

He instinctively reached behind his shirt and felt the metal bulge of his .45. He laughed at the thought of drawing down on a group of monks. *Now that would be some shit…* But he affirmed his oath out loud to dispel the image, "Hey! It is what it is… I'm the one doing the decidin' here… and today, I'll do what I have to."

He checked the left side of his belt for the round leather holster that held his cuffs, and slowly backed into the grass, careful not to slice the skin on his exposed arms. Cole had that nervy and sharp taste of salt in his mouth he always had when waiting in ambush. He stopped 10 feet in from the path at a point where the grass would just cover him if he were to bow his head slightly – as if standing for the benediction at the end of mass. He did not have long to wait.

He looked up the path towards the temple and saw the bright orange procession leave the gate and turn south. His eyes were as razor-sharp as the grass that enveloped him. The monks grew closer. One-by-one, they grew closer.

But he noticed that the first monk was *not the same old fart* that led yesterday's procession. *Where was that old joker? And who is* this *dude?* Cole would not know that *Luang Por* had remained behind today and the abbot of *Wat Suwan* temple – the very same abbot who joined *Luang Por* in the forest meditations two days earlier – led the group today.

OK, OK, never mind that… Where is that fucker, Mordechai? He looked for any sign of the tall, white *nane*. But as they all passed in front of his ambush site, he saw that Mordechai was not amongst them.

Where the hell is that bastard, anyway? But Cole half-knew the answer. When he rose out of bed this morning, he wondered whether Mordechai was savvy enough about the real world – *lost as he might be with all this spiritual bullshit* – to know how foolish and stupid it would be to expose himself again.

But Mordechai knew that. Both abbots knew it. And the other monks knew it as well. And now Cole knew it, too. Mordechai was holed-up in the sanctuary and was not leaving. Catching him on the outside was not going to happen. Cole stepped slowly out of the blind and looked to the left, watching the departing saffron procession and the back of their bald, bobbing heads as they flowed off the temple pathway and onto the road that led to the market at the center of town.

He reached into his pants for his Zippo and cigarettes and pulled one from the pack, lit it up and took in a long draw. He moved out of his ambush nest and back onto the path, paused and blew a cloud of smoke in the monks' direction. Cole was hoping that the smoke would cover up their irritating image. Blot them out.

He took some consolation in knowing *where* his would-be prisoner was holed up. But the granite-eyed resolve of that *old monk* yesterday was unsettling, and the prospects of getting to Mordechai on the inside of the temple were not looking good. *I mean that guy's got fresh food and water streaming into the place every day. Gravy job. No wonder he don't want to come out – and get his sorry ass busted.*

He took a second drag on the Camel and turned up the path towards the temple gate and the hotel beyond when he heard, "Cole! Cole! What are you doing?!"

It was Pip, shouting to him as she sprinted past the temple gates. She slowed up her run and fast-walked the last few feet. She was in his face and he could feel her hot breath.

She repeated, "What are you doing? And why are you out so early?" Cole ignored the questions.

Pip looked past his left shoulder and saw the small orange thread of walking monks, several hundred yards down the road as they neared the center of the town.

"Oh, OK. OK, I see," she said with sharp confidence, after sizing up Cole's newly hatched mission. "I thought we went over this yesterday. There is no change to that, Cole. You need to understand. Mordechai is protected by *Luang Por* and you will not be able to act against his decision."

"Hey, hold your horses there, sister. You'd better uncork yourself," he shot back, erecting his spine, riled by her early morning criticism.

"First of all, he's not in that bunch. Second of all, if he *was* in that bunch and outside the temple, then all that 'violation' crapola you spouted yesterday don't stand up. I'd be free to grab him and, besides, I'm prepared to do this alone. You got it?"

She got it alright – and she was red-ass sore. Pip already had enough of his rogue cowboy act, but she cut off the temptation to respond. She would not waste any more of her words. She swiftly did an about-face and stormed back up the path, towards the inn.

Cole watched her move away and took several more drags from his smoke. *Man, she's a pistol when she's pissed off...* And a quick devilish grin came to his face. *Not bad. A real pain in the ass, but not bad. At least she's got some guts.*

But as Pip passed in front of the temple gate, she slowed, her huff burning off with each passing step. Cole saw her stop. *What the hell?*

He walked quickly to catch up with her from behind, and in the last few steps he tried to sooth her, "OK. OK, look. So here's the deal. I'm going to –"

But before he could finish, he saw that she was distracted. Not listening to him. She had been talking to a monk who was standing under the archway. Cole looked on as Pip lifted her hands into a *wai* and then dropped her left arm at her side. The rising sun's brilliance flooded through the temple gate and she shaded her eyes with her right hand, as if saluting.

She watched the monk in silence as he moved back across the temple grounds, his saffron robe made radiant, lit from behind by the morning's sharp light.

Cole broke the spell. "So, who was *that* guy? What did he want?"

"First, he is not '*that guy.*' He is a monk at this temple – and a senior monk at that. OK?"

Cole heard, but said nothing in reply. His cigarette had three long tokes left and he hurried the first one, "And?"

"*And*," said Pip, "he said that *Luang Por* had sent him out to meet us, and to invite us into the temple."

"Oh, yeah? Just like that, huh?" The invitation was completely unexpected, and Cole was both surprised and suspicious. He had imagined that the battle lines had been drawn – and he wanted to defeat any cunning, one-upmanship by *Pip and her little Buddhist buddies inside.*

Probing her, he asked, "So, what the heck does this mean?"

"Well, for one thing, it means he knows *where* we are – and he likely knows *why* we are out here again this morning." She paused before going on, "So, he has asked us to come in. You alright with that?"

She squinted her eyes to prevent her aggravation from pouring out. The need to explain everything to him was fast becoming a tedious task.

Cole took the last two drags on his Camel, all in one go. "*Has* he, now?" He blew out the smoke, upwards, and looked at Pip. She twisted up the left side of her lips, biting the inside of her mouth, and nodded twice.

"Well, OK then. Let's go see what the old guy wants." And with that he flicked his cigarette butt onto the path outside the temple grounds, and they entered the gate.

CHAPTER 32

Pip walked beside him with a sense of protection and freedom she lacked outside the gate. In here, Cole was stripped of his control and authority over the physical world around them. In here, she could deflect the self-styled superiority that this rough American projected. The calming spiritual power she drew from within these walls was a counterpoint to his combativeness – a spiritual antipode to his day-to-day grit and grime. This was her Thailand after all, and its fascinating temples were places of solace and refuge in her heart-of-hearts.

And yet her initial relief upon entering these holy grounds was tempered by a recurring sadness she was doing her best to suppress. *Yes, in here lies freedom and truth*, she thought. *But we're not after freedom nor truth. We're here to catch a priest. A holy man.* She glared at Cole. *It's like he owns this man.*

• • • • •

To distance herself from these distressing thoughts, she began to extol the beauty of the temple grounds and the spiritual qualities of *Luang Por*. "You know, Cole, *Luang Por* is not like other men, not like other monks. He is an authentic holy man, known to work miracles. And these few holy men we have are just like your saints in the Catholic Church – but many of ours are still alive and living with us, in our present world."

She turned to look at him again. Cole was not interested in the spiritual qualities of any holy man.

He had a growing, hollow feeling welling up in his gut that he was weakening with each step as they walked deeper into the complex of temple buildings. He entered the grounds thinking he was *"the big fish in a small pond,"* but he was now fighting the notion that the size of this sea was immense, and the fish swimming around in this place were ancient and mysterious. Powerful. And he didn't like it.

Pip went on, *"Luang Por* must be about 88 now, although no one knows for sure. Even he is not exactly sure. Well, he knows he was born on a Thursday, in the month of the Thai New Year, and many years before the turn of the Western 20th century. At least that's what the popular legends say about him."

She paused before continuing, dithering on the idea of giving Cole a deeper view into *Luang Por's* story. To her, these insights were pearls.

True, this foreigner has pig's feet, but in the end her passion for this holy man won out, and she volunteered, "In addition to the many miracles attributed to *Luang Por*, he has many other powers. For example, he has the power to appear in different forms, and sometimes his body is present but his soul is away, traveling to many places – including heaven and hell. And he tells of his journeys when he returns from these excursions. He also has the power to rise to great heights in the sky, and many people have reported seeing him in the clouds surrounding the mountains."

"As a matter of fact, he is so revered in Thailand and Laos that there is already a vibrant trade in protective amulets, bearing his image. His ardent followers throughout the country seek these out and wear them with unshakable confidence. They are talismans for protection. For good luck and success. For wisdom. Healing."

To add a point that she knew would needle Cole, she said, "Oh, and by the way, he is a fantastic storyteller. He can make the most complex topic readily understood by the most common man. That ability shows great wisdom, don't you think, Cole?"

"But perhaps one of his most wondrous qualities," she went on, "was described by a recent biographer, a former monk who knew him well. It is his ability to catch hold of wickedness and evil and pull these spirits from a person's *nee-sai*, their essential being, and transform them into different creatures. He does this when they succumb, not to him, but to the power and beauty of a spiritual awakening. He merely leads them. The accounts I've read are riveting. These stories give me, *khonluk,* goose bumps." She hunched over her shoulders and rubbed both of her forearms together.

She glanced over at Cole, who was now walking with his arms folded across his chest. He was thinking about what kind of adversary *Luang Por* would be, and how he could wrestle Mordechai from a man who has *all this magical ju-ju going for him. He certainly has the locals, and the monks here, hoodwinked. Listen to Pip, she's also bought into this, hook-line-and-sinker.*

"OK, so what else does he do?" he blurted out, as if the previous set of qualities were lacking something.

Pip smiled and added, "Well, he's become a favorite of the Thai Royalty, and they regard him as a holy figure, not only in these parts but in the whole of Thailand. He is honored, even by them."

Cole had heard enough and stopped to light up another smoke. Pip said nothing more and cast her gaze up to the splendid golden *stupa* in front of them. It was the signature edifice of this temple, and its golden surface glowed in the morning sun.

Cole was also taking in their surroundings, but he was only interested in where Mordechai would be hiding, and what plan could he come up with for getting him out of there. He was drawing blanks on both questions.

They stood in the courtyard of the temple, and the monk who had relayed *Luang Por*'s invitation returned to them, asking Pip if they could please wait outside in the courtyard for some moments. He gestured for them to sit and to make themselves comfortable on the cement benches that were placed along the riverside promenade, affording them a shaded view of the Mekong just beyond the eastern wall.

The *luuk-sit* who accompanied the monk brought them two glasses of cool water which he left on the railing near the bench. Pip *wai*ed the monk as he and the *luuk-sit* left.

"OK, what did he say this time?"

"He said that we are to wait here until *Luang Por* is free, and that he will call for us. Not long."

Cole lifted the glass of water to his mouth and caught sight of the orange procession of monks as they entered back into the temple grounds, their morning's round of alms gathering completed. It looked similar to the procession he ran afoul with yesterday, but today Mordechai was not amongst them. He watched them disappear into the great hall.

• • • • •

The monks streamed inside the temple's great hall and carefully removed the offerings from their begging bowls and placed them in a neat mound on a long table near the entrance. Mordechai, and another four novice monks stood at the opposite side of the table as the monks passed by and began sorting the contents in front of them: food dishes, rice, desserts, bottled water, flowers, candles, envelopes with money – and anything else that had been placed into the begging bowls.

Once sorted by kind, the *nanes* and *maa-chi* placed an assortment of food, rice, water, and desserts on large serving trays. These items were set aside to offer the monks when the midday meal was eaten. The *nanes* and *maa-chi* would eat after the monks, followed, in turn, by the poor and needy, orphans, and anyone else who came to the temple and asked for food. Such was the natural order of things within Thai temples. And food was always given, without question.

The money in the envelopes, mostly rumpled, brown 10 baht and green 20 baht notes, about 48 cents and 96 cents, was collected and put into the coffers in the great hall. Mordechai noted how often only a few coins would be given and was reminded of the parable he learned in seminary, about Jesus' praise for the woman who had so little and yet gave what she had. Two small coins. *The same spirit is afoot here*, and he smiled at the universal goodness of true generosity, *a rare virtue, to be sure*.

With this morning task completed, Mordechai turned and walked across the smooth, wooden floor to where *Luang Por* was standing, bidding goodbye to two elderly parishioners who had come early that morning to seek his guidance and spiritual advice.

Mordechai discretely waited until they left. He wanted to confer privately with *Luang Por* about the problems he was causing by his presence. But before Mordechai could lift up his hands to *wai* his venerable, spiritual guide, *Luang Por* clasped him on his shoulders and beamed a disarming smile at him.

"*Mai pen rai, ja, mai pen rai. Phoot gan phrung-nee dee-kwaa.* It is not a problem. Don't worry, let's speak of this tomorrow."

"But *Luang Por* –" Mordechai started.

But the old monk simply smiled at Mordechai and nodded in affirmation of the thought Mordechai brought, but could not utter.

Luang Por had an immediate and intense liking for this curious Catholic priest before Mordechai ever said one word about his past. In truth, Father Goodcut barely mentioned his history – and, apart from personal histories, *Luang Por* had little use for Western résumés. The old abbot had repeatedly taught him to focus only on the present, on the here-and-now.

"Consider the very point where the bow of a boat cuts across the still surface of a lake," *Luang Por* would explain. "That very instant is precisely the present. We need to grab hold of that instant and then expand it. Make the present as wide as the lake itself. This is the present in which we should dwell."

But, as was often the case when dispensing his practical wisdom, *Luang Por* would admit with a smile, "Alas, this is a difficult thing, even for monks, to achieve. We are creatures prone to reminiscing about the past and dreaming of the future."

Luang Por turned to join the senior monks who were sitting, cross-legged, in the first circle to the left of the dais, waiting for their midday meal to be served by loyal parishioners and the *maa-chi*. Mordechai was left to reflect on the words of insight from this holy man as he joined the circle of *nanes* at the far-right end of the dais.

And these small clusters of religious men were already well-formed by the time the giant temple drum boomed out the call to the midday meal. Cole looked at his watch. It was precisely noon, straight up.

●　　●　　●　　●　　●

Luang Por sat eating, and he asked the *luuk-sit* serving his table to go outside and invite the foreigner and the Thai lady to come in. He had not forgotten them. He was seeking an opportune time to accord his hospitality, and to teach the two guests about manners – and about his authority within the temple.

When Cole and Pip entered the hall, they saw five small circles of monks and *nanes*, sitting on the dais of the great hall: *Luang Por* and the most senior monks sat in the first circle on the left, the *nanes* sat in the last circle at the far right, and a gradation of monks, based on seniority, were sitting in the circles in between.

Pip tugged on Cole's shirt, motioning for him to sit on the mats laid out on the hall's wooden floor, away from – and lower by two feet – than the dais upon which all the monks and *nanes* sat eating. The proper vertical hierarchy of space was a tenant of Thai Buddhism observed in every temple: monks up, laity down. The natural order of things.

The pair's notoriety from the day before had escaped no one in the hall, monks, *nanes*, *luuk-sit*, and parishioners alike. *Luang Por* beckoned Pip to approach his circle which she did, careful to bow and then kneel as she approached the dais.

"*Kha, Luang Por,*" she said with her hands held in a *wai* at her chest.

He was busy spooning some curry onto his rice and barely looked over at Pip, but said to her, using the Buddhist form of address in the third person, "*Yoom phuying*, dear lady, Please, you and your friend stay for a meal after we have partaken of ours. We should talk."

He said no more, and he did not need to. Pip *wai*ed him and, bent at the waist so as not to have her body higher than his, went back to where she left Cole, sitting at the back of the hall.

"Well, what did he want?" he asked.

Pip did not answer immediately. She was trying to work out exactly what *Luang Por* wanted to talk about – and why he would extend his hospitality to them after the exploits and language of yesterday. It was odd, but she knew better than to question his wisdom.

She said, "He wants us to stay and eat, and then he wishes to talk with us."

"What?" blurted out Cole. "You got to be kidding me. We didn't come here to eat. We came here to get our man, Goodcut – and then straight back to Bangkok. Got it?"

"No, you don't understand. It is a common practice for the people to eat after the monks, and it is a rare opportunity for us to have an audience with such an esteemed abbot. We don't dare say 'no' to this invitation."

Cole was silent, but his gears were fully engaged. He did the calculations. "So, what did he say we're going to talk about?"

"He didn't say. We just have to do this. That's all I know."

Cole drew a deep breath and then said, "OK, OK. We can do this – if it don't take too long, alright? And besides, when you say we 'eat after the monks,' are you saying we eat scraps, the leftovers? 'Cause *that* ain't happening, sister. No way."

Pip looked at him in disbelief. *How could anyone be so stupid and crass?* "No, not leftovers. *You dimwit!* The *maa-chi* will make sure we have fresh food. This is an honor, so why don't you just accept it as such – and count your blessings that you have gotten this far today, alright?"

"Yeah, yeah. I feel blessed alright," said Cole as he stared at Mordechai's tall figure, sitting at the last circle, farthest away from *Luang Por. Man, just look at him. He's really going to town on that bowl of rice... Better eat up, padre. You're gonna need it.*

And with that, his stomach gurgled so loudly that Pip was startled, and she turned to glare at him, saying with a harsh staccato whisper, "Un-be-liev-able!"

•   •   •   •   •

At the conclusion of the meal, *Luang Por* led the monks in a prayer of thanks and gave blessings of merit to all those who had offered the meal, and he then rose and moved towards the other end of the hall. Cole started to get up but Pip grabbed his arm and said, "No, not now. He will call us when he is ready."

"What's that? We've got to wait *again*? What the –" but before he could finish and the expletive pop out of his mouth, two *maa-chi* appeared next to where Pip and he sat, and with a few words and soft Thai smiles, urged them to come and sit at a long, folding table where food had already been carefully laid out for them.

"*Kha, khob khun kha*, thank you very much," said Pip.

Cole managed a weak smile, but added a quick "thank you" as they both sat down in the stiff plastic chairs. The *maa-chi* laughed at having English spoken to them, and by a genuine American, no less.

• • • • •

The two finished their meal, and the *maa-chi* asked Pip whether they would like to have any *khong-waan*, dessert. But the involuntary summoning of *kraing-jai* came upon her, the deeply rooted and distinctively Thai feeling of not wishing to bother anyone, and she declined the offer, as tempting as that was.

Cole was scouring the table-top for a bottle of toothpicks. There they were. He reached for one so he could pry a cashew nut from their favorite hiding place. He was growing impatient again. "What was that about?"

"No, nothing. She just wanted to know if you wished to have any dessert. That's all. I told her 'Thanks. Not now, but maybe later'."

Cole tilted his head back and raised an eyebrow in Pip's direction. *Nice to see her deceive someone for once – even for such a diddly-squat thing.*

"Yes, we have a feeling when we're a guest in someone's house – as this is *Luang Por*'s house – not to put anyone to trouble. Do you know what I mean? We call it *kraing-jai* and it means 'not wanting to bother someone' – especially your hosts. It has no clear English equivalent, and…" she added quickly, "that says a lot about your lack of civility and fine manners in the US, by the way." The dig was choice and timely.

But Cole was a man who was not concerned with good manners and etiquette. "So, what *do* they have for dessert?" he asked.

Pip shot him a glance that killed his sweet tooth. But he was only playing her and grunted a small chuckle when he got the predictable rise.

Cole righted his chair which he had propped up on its rear legs to afford a better angle to deal with that pesky cashew remnant. And as he did so, the monk that had met them earlier at the gate came to their table and said, "*Luang Por* will see you now. Please follow me."

Pip *waied* the *maa-chi* who were waiting nearby, hands clasped at their sides. They smiled at Pip and said, "*Ja, ja. Choke dee, nah ja.* Good luck to you."

Cole picked up the *choke dee* phrase and was pleased with himself for deciphering, at last, some Thai words without having to ask Pip. She never answered with a single word. Her answers always came packaged *with so many other, unnecessary and boring words – and then there were those goddamn stories.*

They rose from the table in the great hall and walked towards the western entrance. The hall was used by the monks for day-to-day activities such as ritual blessings and the chanting of prayers, and it was located next to the *Boort,* the main sanctuary, with its exquisite roofline and tiled designs. As in every Thai temple, the *Boort* had an east-facing platform so that the temple's most holy objects, the venerated Buddha statues, could face the rising sun each morning. The sanctuary was the heart of the temple complex.

Wat Suwan was no different. But the great hall at the temple also held a number of large, revered statues arranged on a teakwood platform. It was a place dedicated for the supplications and prayers of the many believers who, with their candles and burning incense sticks, passed through the *Wat* on a daily basis. Worshipers would leave their worn and dusty shoes outside in neat rows before entering the hall, its satin teakwood floor polished bright and smooth by the decades of the faithful's bare feet, softly shuffling across its surface.

On a raised platform at the far end of the great hall and near an expansive open window that looked out at the Mekong and the hills of Laos on the opposite bank, sat *Luang Por*. Three elderly monks, including the abbot of *Wat Suwan*, sat at his right side. Sitting in a small group on the floor in front of *Luang Por* were five *nanes*, including Mordechai.

Cole stiffened when he saw the back of Mordechai's *bald, white noggin. There's my boy. So close.* "You're goin' in the bag, my man." Pip shot Cole a mean side-eye.

And as they approached closer, they heard *Luang Por* teaching in English, evidently in answer to a question from Mordechai. The monk who had accompanied Cole and Pip invited them to sit on the floor, several feet behind the *nanes*.

Pip was listening intently to *Luang Por* and was trying to imagine the question that prompted this explanation. Cole was looking for windows and doors, trying to estimate how far they were from the gate. He glared at Mordechai who saw them approach. But *Nane* Mordechai ignored this distraction.

Luang Por finished, "I have to confess, I have also heard this so-called, 'house-on-fire' test. It has often been cited by Western thinkers as a way to understand the different schools of Buddhist thought: that of passive observance, and that of active compassion. It is a false distinction in my opinion, and therefore not much help."

"If you were to ask me what would I do if I saw a house on fire with somebody trapped inside, would I merely observe and say 'well, that is just the way the world is,' or would I rush around to find water to put out the fire. Of course, I would have to choose the second way. I truly do not understand the first way at all. The first way means we have no compassion. We are dead inside and have no love of life. This neglect seems like *baap,* a sin, to me, no? I am confused why some would say the first way is also Buddhism."

And he added with a quick smile, "Or so the Westerners say it is." *Luang Por* then concluded his lesson by summarizing the main and, to him, the obvious point, "You see, *Nane* Mordechai, we monks straddle two worlds. Detachment does not mean a lack of compassion."

Mordechai sat quietly, smiling, absorbing the abbot's wisdom. He said nothing, but nodded his head, hands clasped together at his chest. The other *nanes* looked to Mordechai to pick up his cue, for they did not understand the English, but they knew *Luang Por* had made his point by the dropping tone at the end of his last sentence. They smiled nervously.

"Well," said *Luang Por,* changing the flow and speaking in Thai, "I see we have our two guests here. Let me speak with them now, please, *nah ja.* You can all go back to your studies."

And with that the five *nanes,* including Mordechai, got up to leave. The three senior monks stood fast. They knew what was to follow – and besides, they had also seen Cole "in action" yesterday at the temple gate and were not about to leave *Luang Por* alone with this man.

Luang Por spoke loudly to Mordechai, "*Yoom. Yoom. Nane* Mordechai. I would like for you to stay, please. Come here. Come sit close by."

He motioned for Mordechai to sit on the floor next to the raised platform upon which *Luang Por* sat. It resembled a pulpit in its ornate, enamel red paint and embossed goldwork, but a pulpit intended for sitting and praying, not standing and preaching. And *Luang Por* sat squarely in the middle, legs crossed in a position that only those with decades of practice can achieve. His leg bones were crossed and locked with ease and without discomfort – like the folding legs on an old pair of glasses.

He motioned to both Pip and Cole to draw closer. Pip advanced on her knees without rising; Cole stood and walked to a place next to Pip, his head unbowed. It was a minor transgression, forgiven of a foreigner. *Luang Por* thought nothing of it, but Pip was embarrassed.

Luang Por, turned sideways on his platform and poured himself a cup of strong, black tea. "May I offer you some?"

They both declined, but *Luang Por* knew Pip would refuse from *kraing-jai*, so he motioned to the *maa-chai* who was standing in the back of the hall for her to pour two cups for both Cole and Pip.

"So, let us begin," said *Luang Por*. And he swung his left arm in a circular motion, his robe winding around his arm, and he brought the tea to his mouth and had a sip.

Finally, thought Cole. *I ain't got all day.* But *Luang Por* did, as Cole was soon to find out.

Luang Por sipped his tea slowly and deliberately. He had invited them to the temple not to debate the law or to find out what grievous crime Mordechai may have committed. He did not care about the law – nor any alleged crime from Mordechai's past. That history was not his business. Rather, he went straight to the spiritual heart of the matter – *this* was his business. He was waiting for the propitious moment to speak, and it had arrived.

Luang Por spoke to Cole. "*Yoom,*" using the Pali-Sanskrit form of address, "You must have come here, to Ubon, on the train from Bangkok, right?" It was small talk. But Pip listened closely.

His arms extended to his sides, palms up, Cole glanced over at Pip and then turned back to *Luang Por* and he said, "Now what does this have to do with why we came here? You know very well what I want to see happen here today." He shot a quick look at Mordechai.

Pip scowled at him and whispered harshly, "Stop pushing! Why must you always be so rude?"

"Yes, yes, I know what you *want*, young man. But what you want is not what you *need*." He took another sip of tea.

He had no actual interest in knowing Cole's name – or Pip's name for that matter. Names were just tags assigned by parents, and these tags rarely aligned well with one's *nee-sai*, one's true nature. And for *Luang Por*, one's true nature was the essence of the human persona. A name was a nice thing to have. To receive letters in the mail and to be called by family members. But for the old abbot, Cole's name didn't matter. He saw before him a man whose *nee-sai* was complex, angry, and unforgiving. This wouldn't do.

However, he knew that polite conversations in the secular world often required the use of names, so he asked Cole, "What did your parents call you?"

Cole heard, but paused, thinking about outsmarting the old man and wondering why he was asking for his name. He gave *Luang Por* a long look. *OK, what the heck.*

"The name is Cole. They called me Cole."

"Cone," the abbot repeated, nodding his head. "Cone. Ok –"

"No, it's Cole. Not 'Cone.' Cole."

"Ok, I see. OK Cone, I have something to say to you." He glanced in Pip's direction, but did not ask her name, but stared at her for the longest time, smiling, but not speaking.

Pip grew uncomfortable, and re-crossed her legs, making sure that her feet were pointed in the opposite direction to where *Luang Por* and the other monks were sitting. To have inadvertently shown the soles of her feet would have been extremely rude.

At long last he returned to Cole. "So," he began, "*Yoom,* Cone. Back to the train." He took another sip of tea. "Can you tell me which of the train cars arrived first in Ubon station? The engine, or the caboose?"

Cole looked up at *Luang* Por and shrugged his shoulders. He wanted to say, "*Now, that's a stupid question,*" but a mere shrug was less damaging than blurting that out. He also felt Pip's pinch on the flesh of his left calf, warning him not to say the obvious and insulting thing.

But even Cole now understood that the old monk was going somewhere with this line of questioning and resolved to keep it cool and play along – he was there to collect his prize, *so let's humor the old guy.*

"You see, Cone, everyone knows the engine must come first. It is kind of a stupid question, is it not?" With this, *Luang Por* turned to look at the other abbot and grinned, then back to Cole and Pip who were giving each other uncomfortable glances.

But *Luang Por* stopped smiling, and his face softened. It was his teaching face. He spoke as if he were relaying, not his own thoughts, but thoughts that were merely passing through him, from another world.

He said, "You need to think about what comes first – and what happens next. The sequence of our development in life. Your brain comes first. But that is not enough. Even an animal has a brain, no? Insects also have brains. But insects and animals lack the ability to move to the next level of being. They lack compassion and pity. This is the second car on the train. Do you follow me so far?"

Hell no, thought Cole, *I'm not following one word of this 'train car' and 'animal' and "bugs' bullshit... and you'd better get to the point quick, old-timer...*

"And beyond compassion and pity there is finally – at the very last level of being – forgiveness. This is the last car in the train. The jewel that surpasses all others. The best and purest of our human virtues."

Luang Por had arrived at the crux of his lesson for Cole, and he elaborated, "When you forgive and let your anger flow away, you will be transformed as a human being. Just as the lowly caterpillar transforms itself into a beautiful flying creature. This is the sequence of development for the human being: from brain, to heart, to transcendence. Knowing. Compassion. Forgiveness. Three levels. Three cars on the train. It is the way we are meant to be. True and pure goodness arises when we arrive at forgiveness."

"And this, *yoom poochai*, my son, is what you *need* in your life. Forgiveness."

Luang Por drank in a deep look at his unwilling and stubborn student, and the old monk paused to weigh his next words carefully. He was making healing plans for his newest charge.

"*Yoom* Cone, I think you secretly want to forgive, but you don't know how. And forgiveness is the true thing you are hunting. But your angry mind is binding your ability to change. To transform. You are stuck, enforcing human-made rules that really mean nothing for the spirit."

Luang Por looked to Mordechai and then back to Cole. "Does this forgiveness abide in you, Cone? I think not. Now, you cannot forgive. But I can help you."

Pip sat on the floor, her feet pointing behind her, her head was bowed. Her jittery hands were pressed together in a permanent *wai*, which she held at her chest – the proper way to receive the profound teachings from this holy man.

She could feel the sweat beading on her forehead with each word of *Luang Por*'s lesson to Cole, for his words were so close to her own suspicions of Cole's secret needs. She was embarrassed by this coincidence. Her face blushed red.

At last Cole said, in a nervous attempt to divert the spotlight, "Seems like a pretty short train."

And *Luang Por* roared with laughter at these words, which he repeated, in Thai, to the other abbot who also laughed out loud – but he did so more to keep cadence with *Luang Por*'s rhythm than on the understanding of Cole's quip.

"Yes," said *Luang Por*, "a short train. It is true. But our lives are short, too. No?"

Grudgingly, a small grain of respect for the old monk was growing in Cole's estimation. *This old guy did it yesterday and he's doing it again today.* Cole gave him credit for his grit and unconsciously nodded. But he was sitting cross-legged, and his legs were beginning to cramp. He grimaced when he shifted his position.

The old monk said, "It is OK, please extend out your legs. Do not torture yourself." However, Pip was not having that, so she spoke up for the first time since sitting down before *Luang Por*.

She said in Thai, "Reverend father, it would be better if the foreigner could sit in a chair. It would be more proper." She added quickly, "If you agree."

With this *Luang Por* looked at the *maa-chi* who was standing at the back of the hall and he raised his right hand with his index finger pointed up. A white plastic chair was brought for Cole who rose from the floor and offered a self-conscious, "Thanks."

He pulled the plastic chair up close to his butt, like a hermit crab, and moved forward to a place on the flower-patterned linoleum floor alongside Pip. Even a hermit crab knows where to put its shell down. Not closer. Not farther.

Luang Por returned to Cole. "You are a hunter, Cone. And it is good to have a very strong mind. A hunter's mind. But it is not sufficient. You need change. Change so you can purge your anger."

The old abbot looked at Cole who was wondering *when is this tired old man going to get to the point about Mordechai – and stop this double-talk "change" crapola?*

And yet Cole was struck by a pin-point truth that the abbot had poked his finger into. It was an old wound, but it was there, a world away in New Mexico. And although it was a lifetime ago, his abusive past was pricked by that boney finger – by his mother's preferred love of rodeo stars over him. Something was stirring and he didn't like the feeling. He wanted to *crush out that insight from this old man… crush it like a cigarette butt.*

"So, can we get to the point?" he finally spouted out, stunning Pip who sat quietly, floating inward on the words that *Luang Por* had just pronounced. It was a slap to her face. Her mouth opened and she drew in an audible gasp.

Luang Por just smiled at this outburst, and he turned to the abbot of *Wat Suwan*, a shorter man and former student of his. *Luang Por* spoke softly in Thai to him, "This tiger has more than just an animal heart. There is much more here."

He drew in a long breath which he held while considering the remedy, and then said, "Let's see if we can change his stripes. These stripes are not his. Someone has painted them – perhaps someone put them on his back with a lash. In my vision, I've seen his stripes wiped off by tears. He is a strong challenge, but he is ultimately a human being. And he will succumb. His anger will be transformed into something wonderful."

He returned his gaze to Cole. Pip was still trying to piece together the few words of Thai she had just heard.

"OK, Cone, I will make you a proposition about the earthly thing you are seeking. But there is no negotiating. Either you agree to do as I ask, or we can finish our tea now, and you may go along your way back to Bangkok. The choice is up to you." With this he looked at Pip for the third time.

Cole did the quick calculus. *Whatever the old guy wants, agree to it. When the time comes, I'm taking Mordechai, no matter what.* He threw in his bet and said, "Look, OK, as long as this guy –

pointing to Mordechai – figures into this proposition, I'm all ears."

Luang Por again sipped at his tea. "Here is what you must agree to: you must stay with us for one full day, here at this temple and if you do so, and if you perform the ceremony I have planned for you – and do not back out – and if your heart is still hardened to take Mordechai, he will then leave peacefully with you. Do you agree?"

Mordechai caught the glint in the abbot's eyes, and he felt buoyed up and smiled, and nodded to signify his faith in *Luang Por*'s wisdom.

Cole picked up on that communication. *So, what kind of crazy ceremony do they have in mind that would make Goodcut break out in a shit-eating grin like that?*

But Cole was not about to be outdone by this deserter priest. He looked up at the abbot and said, "OK."

He was expecting a hardcore wager. A bet with high stakes. *This don't seem too bad. Whatever they have cooked up, they can bring it on. I've seen tons worse than whatever these "holy men" can stitch together. What? Like walking on coals or something? Yeah right.* He turned to Pip and gave her a quick, self-assuring smile.

"I know of your anger – I have dreamed of you as this angry tiger," Said *Luang Por*. "Even the monkey sees you this way." *Luang Por* looked directly at Pip. "Yes. It is in her heart to change you, too."

With this pronouncement, the red returned to Pip's cheeks. She thought they would burst from the blood rushing there. But *Luang Por* did not dwell.

"You see, Cone, to be fair, I have already seen the outcome of this wager. But if you wish to proceed, that is up to –"

Cole didn't hear the rest. He was sure that the old monk was *laying down some psychology bullshit* on him. "Sure you have," said Cole with a wink to the abbot. "Sure you have."

The abbot turned to the other monks gathered there and said quietly in Thai, "Please prepare the Sadao-khroh ceremony." He looked once again at Pip and said to the *luuk-sit* who was sitting nearby, *"Tong chai khae long-sop an neung, sumrap phuchai thaonan,* We'll only use one coffin. For the man."

Not understanding a word the old abbot had spoken, Cole turned to give Pip another hot-shot, confident look.

But the red was fading from her cheeks. She heard *Luang Por* clearly – and her face now blanched white.

CHAPTER 33

They all rose as a group and walked to the far end of the great hall, past the statues of the Buddha images in the center, past the giant drum that had called the monks to the midday meal, and past the *maa-chi* who were finishing up with the dishes.

Cole turned to Pip as they were walking and said, "Funny, I didn't take your ol' monk buddy for a gambling man."

"He's not," she said, giving him a sidelong look. "Betting on a sure thing is not really gambling, is it?" Pip returned her gaze to the wooden floor, contemplating the ceremony that was about to take place. "He's trying to teach you a lesson, Cole. And you know you will lose, no?"

"Look, I'm going outside and have a smoke. I'll catch up with you." He nodded in the direction they were all headed.

"OK, sure," was all that she said, the walk bringing the color back to her cheeks.

• • • • •

Cole took slow drags on his cigarette, planning tomorrow's activities and how they were going to get back to Ubon with Mordechai. With the sighting of Lek in town last night, maybe there was a chance they could catch a ride back to Ubon with him. He had no idea about Pip's behind-the-scenes work to get that transport organized. He had no idea about a lot of things concerning Pip – especially her worry for what was about to happen.

Cole crushed out the cigarette and returned inside to the far end of the hall. He found Pip sitting on the floor at the foot of a long dais, upon which nine monks sat, cross-legged in a long row with their backs to the wall, facing those gathered before them. *Luang Por* sat at the head of the nine, to the far left.

From the angle as he approached, Cole also saw what looked like a large, rectangular white box on the floor in front of the dais. And as he came closer, he saw immediately that this was no ordinary box. It was a coffin.

And it was meant for him.

"Hey! What the hell is this?" he asked. But no one offered him a word.

Luang Por told Pip to light a single candle and two incense sticks, and to pay respect to the golden Buddha statue on a small stand to the left of the dais, near to where *Luang Por* sat.

Cole looked at Pip and asked, "Hey! Did you hear me? What's with the coffin? Is this some kind of fuckin' joke?"

She turned from the altar where she had just lit the candle and incense, bowing three times and paying respect to the Buddha image. She walked over and stood next to him and placed her right hand gently on his forearm.

"No Cole. This is no joke. This is a very serious ceremony; it for the purification of one's past wicked deeds and vile thoughts. And *Luang Por* has ordered this for you."

Cole ignored her unwanted explanation.

But she caught his wide eyes, surveying the coffin. "Yes, well the coffin... think of it like dying, being dead, and then reborn. It –"

"Oh no, no, no... I didn't agree to *this*!" said Cole, shaking his head and taking two steps back.

He turned to *Luang Por* on the dais and tried to get his attention by waving his arms over his head, but all the monks were bowing their heads in unison to the wooden floor, paying their respects to Buddha.

Luang Por would not speak to him now because the old abbot was centering himself for the long prayers which were to come. There was no stopping.

Pip was joined by a *luuk-sit* from the temple who handed her a small bouquet of three unopened lotus flowers. He took Cole by the crook of the elbow and guided him back towards the coffin, urging him to stand in the middle of the long white box.

But Cole balked at making the first step.

"No. No way! I'm not doing this. This is damn stupid..." These were the best words he could marshal to cloak his annoyance and embarrassment – and to crush the life from the small, kernel of dread that was clenching at his gut.

Cole had dropped anchor.

Pip read his agitation and caught, at quick intervals, the fear he was trying to hide. "OK, Cole, you can have it your way. You always do," said Pip, trying to goad him.

She pictured the ceremony being derailed, and soon. She pushed harder, "Only this time, 'having it your way' means that Mordechai will never come with you. Not now, not ever – unless you wish to wait outside the gate for years, with your stupid gun and handcuffs and all of that. I'm sure that they will not miss you back in Vietnam."

But her sardonic words weren't having the intended effect. He fired an angry look in her direction, pointing a mean finger.

"You! You're the one that got me mixed up with all these goddamn lunatics. Coffin, incense, monks! All of this..." He gestured around to the dais, the monks, the coffin, the statues, incense, candles.

He spotted a large roll of white string held by the *luuk-sit* standing next to him, and Cole watched with curiosity and annoyance as the man held on to one end of the string, and then passed the roll to *Luang Por*.

"And what's with the string? What the hell are these guys up to?" For a hunter and warrior, Cole's bravado was flickering. He was entering uncharted territory and he didn't like it one bit.

The old abbot, unwound the roll of string and passed it on to each of the other eight monks, one-by-one, all the way down to the last monk on the dais. All nine now had the string firmly clasped in their hands.

The *luuk-sit* again motioned for Cole to get in the coffin and to sit. Cole shot a hot second round at Pip. "I'll get you for this. For roping me into this stunt!"

He glared up at *Luang Por* and tried to shoot him the evil-eye, but the old monk was already settling into his place of prayer – a place at an immeasurable distance from the dais upon which he sat.

Cole drew in a sigh that could be felt by all there, even by the *maa-chi* who had finished their chores and were sitting silently at the back of the hall. He spun through the options and ground his molars. "Damn her, anyway!"

And his final thought which flowed out with resignation was, *I'm in it to win – and no fuckin' way I'm gonna let this wrinkled-up old monk, or any of these other clowns, beat me. No weakness in front of this mob.*

He stepped over the side boards of the coffin and stood inside. *This is the most dumbass thing I have done in my entire life. But screw it... Let's do this.*

"*Nang, khrap, nang... nang,* Please sit down, sir, sit down." The *luuk-sit* gently pushed Cole's shoulders down with both hands, encouraging him to sit, and then again, slowly but with steady pressure, pushed him back to the prone position inside the coffin.

The *luuk-sit* then took the free end of the ball of string he had passed to *Luang Por* and wrapped it three times around the top of Cole's head. This simple, white cotton string formed the spiritual conduit between Cole and the monks, tethering him to this side of the spiritual divide – the side of the living.

Pip approached the coffin, bent down and handed Cole the lotus flowers. "You're supposed to hold these across your chest, with both hands."

But Cole was not in the mood. He shook his head, snatched the flowers from Pip and tossed them out, over the side.

• • • • •

The monks reached behind them and retrieved their ornate, wicker prayer-fans which they placed in front of their faces. And led by *Luang Por*, they began chanting ancient Pali-Sanskrit prayers in sonorous, lulling tones.

Cole shouted to Pip from the coffin as she walked away, "Hey! How long's this gonna last... and what's with the damn droning sounds?!"

She turned, and said, "They are praying for you, Cole. For your soul. For the transformation of your hard heart and the healing you need – for all the things that have wounded you. This is the purpose of the *Sadao-khroh* ceremony."

He thought he spotted a tear on her cheek but wasn't sure because she turned away quickly. It was hot, and inside the box it was stifling. *What the hell is she crying about?*

Pip returned to sit on the floor, in front of Mordechai who sat next to the dais. But she did not exchange looks with him. She assumed a position for receiving prayer, with her legs tucked back behind her and her palms pressed at her chest, *wai*'ing the chanting monks.

Cole gazed up. The ceiling at that end of the great hall was painted white, and he could see nothing else above him except for this monotonous tone which blended, without a seam, with the white color of the coffin's interior walls. The still heat and the loud, incessant droning of the monks' prayers were weighing heavy on him and, after the first 30 minutes, he began to doze.

His mind floated up and drifted away, the penetrating prayers in the ancient language transforming him. At length, he recalled the admonition of his parish priest as he anointed his forehead with the sign of the cross on Ash Wednesdays when he was young, "Remember that you are dust, and to dust you shall return..."

Francis Xavier Coltrane slowly sauntered into the deepest dream he ever had, into landscapes he knew, yet did not know. He stumbled across a cairn of desert flagstone rocks on the round gravel banks of the Rio Grande, but the water smelled like the muddy Mekong – not the pure, sand-filtered streams that flowed down from high up in the Sangre de Christo Mountains of Colorado. And he saw his sister Abilene, with Pepe at her bedside holding a blank detective's notepad on which he had doodled symmetrical shapes of triangles and circles with white paste. A translucent scorpion scuttled across the hospital floor. He saw his ex-wife, Imelda, sitting naked, her waist-length, long black hair flowed down her back, her shoulders and hips rounded, perfect and symmetrical, like an amber viola. But when she turned to him, he saw that it was Pip. She said, "I have something you need to see," and she faced him, slid down her pants, and ripped open her shirt – a green uniform, Chinese military-style with single, red stars for buttons which flew off in every direction. Her mango-shaped breasts pointed up to the heavens and when he gazed up to where they led his eyes, he saw a soldier's body floating down softly from the forest canopy above, without gravity, spinning slowly like a propeller seed from a boxelder maple. But he was not in the highlands of New Mexico. It was an LZ – in Vietnam. His nostrils stung with the overpowering stench of burnt powder, and violent shell concussions blew all the leaves from the nearby trees, as if they were dandelion spores. And when the soldier's body came to rest at his feet, he saw that it was Gus who opened his eyes and said, "I'm sorry, Cole." His vacant eyes then retreated, sucked back up into his enormous skull. And there, raising himself up amidst the swirling, purple and yellow smoke, and the razor-sharp, blown-down, elephant grass of the LZ, was Mordechai – the risen St. Mordechai, resplendent and pure in a white flowing robe and bearing the marks of the stigmata on his palms. Cole spoke to him with a proclamation, *Mordechai, it's you. I'm coming to get you! Mordechai, I'm coming to get you!* he repeated. The words swam around and around in his head, increasing in speed like a centrifuge, but he couldn't get them to his lips. They flowed down into his throat but were stuck there. He couldn't spit them out. He couldn't breathe. *I... I... can't breathe. I can't breathe! My heart's stopped!*

"Let me out!" he shouted as he tore himself through the veil of his dream and sprang out of the coffin.

He bolted for the door of the great hall. *Crazy bastards! Mordechai or not, I've had enough of this shit!*

He was moving fast, but only for that first, fearful burst of adrenalin. He collapsed within a few feet of the massive teakwood portal.

Pip ran to him and grabbed him around his shoulders. His arms were flaying about, but only loosely, weakly, and she held him tight. "It's OK. It's OK." She repeated to him. "It's over now, there's nothing to fear. It's OK."

And as he slumped, Pip lowered herself on her knees and held him by the shoulders, pulling his head tight to her chest. He was drenched in sweat and mumbled something to her – but the words were odd. Not the sounds of English.

Cole sunk from her embrace and lay flat on the hall floor, his legs jutted out straight, towards the monks who were finishing their prayers. But nobody cared which way they pointed.

Luang Por ended the prayers with a long, falling tone as he uttered the last of the ancient words, "*...sah-mah-pahn-tay-y-y-y...*"

With their prayers concluded, the monks bowed and *wai*'ed the Buddha image on their right, and without comments or noise that would have perturbed the holy vibrations which still lingered in the hall, they departed.

None of them looked in Cole's direction. They had all been there themselves. They knew that many vile and soiled artifacts had been washed away from his soul. The monks knew of the journey he had been on. Over the falls. And, save for the last few minutes of his dream, Cole had traveled to many wondrous places – places with miraculous healing powers he would never remember.

From her kneeling position comforting Cole, Pip *wai*'ed the procession of monks as they left the hall and made their way to their *kuti*, cottages, for tea and evening prayers.

She helped Cole to his feet. "Look, let's go outside – get some fresh air. Find something to eat. You need to eat. And we need to talk about tonight."

•　　•　　•　　•　　•

After a few steps into the evening air, Cole stopped. He took his arm off Pip's shoulder, arched his back and bent left and right a few times to limber up. He shot a glance towards the gate and reached into his pants pockets to fish out his Zippo and smokes. Cole pulled one out with his teeth after flicking the bottom of the pack with his forefinger. The smell of the Rosignol fuel in the Zippo was familiar and welcome and displaced the thick perfumed incense he had inhaled during the last hour.

The events of the evening thawed out and were flowing through his gourd. He took in a deep drag. He was coming to. Getting his bearings. But all was not well.

He dipped his head to the side and looked askance at Pip, lifting both his eyebrows. Nodding. *She looks pretty damn satisfied, don't she? Happy with herself. Getting off on this.*

What followed was Cole's response to being duped. Being played. He saw the red curtain drop before his eyes and he let loose.

"That magic trick in there was the most fucked-up nightmare I've ever had. That shit damn near suffocated me! Just what the hell did you rope me into, you crazy woman?!"

Pip had been watching his cigarette routine in silence. Smiling. Her arms across her chest. She was glad to see him back on his feet. But she was completely unprepared for this eruption and, stunned by this blast, her head rocked back.

But she gathered herself, and started out cool, "Well, Cole, you were the one who agreed to the abbot's wager, and you must have known that it was going to cost you something. I mean it was not going to be f–"

"Not going to be what?! Not going to be 'fun'? Yeah, that shit was some fucking *fun* alright!"

"No, it was not going to be a free ride," she came back. "Not without consequences. You knew–"

"I knew shit," he shot back. "What I *do* know is that you tricked me. You–"

"Tricked you? What... what the hell are you talking about?!" she demanded. The brakes were off. Her body squared off with his. "And why are you yelling at *me*?" She was baffled and shaken by the thrust and volume of his anger. But she was unwilling to hear those insulting words from him.

He wasn't finished. After two more deep drags on his cigarette, Cole said, "Yeah, you and that smart-ass old monk must have cooked up the whole thing. I saw you talking to him just before they brought out that goddamn box? What the hell was that all about?"

To Cole, she got the drop on him and being hoodwinked was too much for this lover, fighter, and wild bull rider. He was not budging from his spot until she admitted that *the damn ceremony and the bet with that old monk were all her ideas* – ideas she had cooked up to thwart his mission.

"I know you've been dragging your feet – ever since we met at that lousy hotel in Bangkok. You, on your damn high horse, always digging under my skin... always against my plans and hassling me – from day one. And all those stupid stories."

And he mocked her, "'Oh, poor little priest. Let him go, Cole. He's the deer Buddha, Cole'."

He took another drag. "And there was the miserable mess you made at the ambush, running interference for that bastard. 'Temple rules' and all that bullshit. And now this mind-fucking coffin stunt!"

Holding up a half-inch space between his thumb and forefinger of his left hand, and poking it in front of her face, he said, "You're this close to crossing that thin red line, woman!"

And he upped the ante. "In fact, I think it's been in your screwed-up little brain to sabotage this whole damn mission."

The fingers on his right hand slid down his cigarette, now clenched between his teeth, and the cheery-end stuck between his fore and middle fingers. The flesh sizzled and he yelled, "Son of a bitch!" and flung the cigarette into the dark temple grounds.

But Pip was not having this drama. "*You're* the crazy one! Crazy *and* paranoid, you ignorant jerk!" She gave it to him with both barrels.

"Yes, it's true I never wanted to get mixed up with you and your stupid 'mission', Mr. James Bond, but my duty always outweighs my personal... my personal..."

Her mind jumped to the small truth in Cole's last words – she truly wanted to see the priest escape. She scrambled to tighten her thoughts, stammering around for the missing words to patch her unfinished sentence, but found none.

Cole saw the flicker of uncertainty in her eyes and knew then he had gotten the best of her. But he couldn't spit out the bitter taste of betrayal. "I just don't understand," he said. "You've lied to me all along."

"Lied? No, Cole, I never lied." She was back in it. "But you would never know that. Your problem is that you *live* a big lie. You don't know what the *truth* is – the only truth you know are the stupid damn Army rules that you follow, like a slave!"

Ignoring her last salvo, Cole said, "Yeah, you're such a deceitful little liar."

But it was almost an afterthought. He was spent. The ordeal in the coffin, and now this gut-deep brawl with Pip. "Yes, well, No. No, I don't understand," was all he could give. And he was finished. Spleen vented.

But Pip was getting in her last digs. "Well, you understand everything else. Your cocky swagger forbids you to open your mind to so many things you don't know about. And you *don't* know very many damn things. You're a fool!"

Feeling vindicated and weary of the need to explain herself, she headed for the gate and to the inn. Cole lit another smoke and watched as her silhouette passed out of the gate and made the right turn up the road.

He had peaked. Shot the wad. He could only add a few feeble words aimed at the temple gate, "…and how could I have been so stupid to let you bamboozle me into doin' that shit tonight."

And yet he was puzzled. He was convinced he had been *tricked and misled by this woman. She played me for a fool. And, yeah, that pisses me off alright.* But he was, despite those gut punches, moved by her fragility. By her weakness.

He felt embarrassed when a rush of warmth came over his chest – when he thought of her anger. Her passion. And he remembered the sweet night after Laos. *What the hell is going on here? Am I falling for this girl?*

He arched his back again and lifted his arms over his head and then dropped them at his side. He swung his head from left to right. Unwinding. *Nah, that's just fucked-up, any way you cut it.*

Cole drew in a full breath and exhaled slowly, whistling a low note, before taking another deep drag on his cigarette. *OK. OK. Time to eat. I can sort Pip out later...*

We're done, though. That shit's over.

CHAPTER 34

Rice or noodles. Noodles or rice. "Look, I don't give a damn. Just bring me what they got cooked already and be sure it's not too spicy – and it gets here pronto," Cole told Pip. His stomach had overpowered his sense of indignation at Pip's deceit.

The cussing she gave him in the temple courtyard was still ringing in his ears, but he was used to suppressing his feelings when practical matters pressed up against his world, and her insults had finally rolled off his back. Yet he was still tender in places and in no mood for small talk, and Pip knew better than to give him any.

But she finally broke the chill and said, "You do know, right, that after we eat we have to go back to the temple. That's part of the deal you made with *Luang Por.*"

He grunted when she brought this up, trying to ignore her as if the vacuum created by an absence of words would translate into a greater physical distance between them.

Pip discounted his silent treatment, walked to the door and gave the waiting housegirl their order. She told her, "*Noo, tong tam reo reo, na ja,* please try to do this quickly now, dear."

Cole waited for the dinner-ordering drama to be over. "Well, I don't recall signing any contract. And they got their money's worth out of me today with that fuckin' stunt in the coffin."

Pip knew better than to argue with him. "OK. Have it your way. You stay here and when you go there tomorrow to get Mordechai, *Luang Por* is just going to stare at your face. OK?"

He dug around in his gear bag and pulled out the remaining clean pair of jeans he had, a striped pair of JC Pennys boxers and a new pair of socks.

Pip read those signs and understood. *He'd go back to the temple tonight, alright. But no need to push or talk about it. He'd find his own way of caving in to Luang Por's demands.*

And Cole knew he had no choice if he wanted Mordechai. He had come too far now to let the deal slip away. *A night at the temple. Fuck it! No big deal.*

·　·　·　·　·

He stood up by the bed and peeled off down to his skivvies. He glanced over at Pip and wrapped the threadbare towel around himself before he plucked off his underwear and flung them into the corner. For the second time that day, he hid his nakedness. Once "before the Lord," and now *in front of this female ball-grinder – or whoever she is.*

Cole gave a quick look at Pip who was sitting in the white metal chair that had been holding her overnight bag. She was waiting her turn in the shower. He moved towards the bathroom when the familiar, unwelcomed warmth spread across his chest as her frailty and vulnerability came back to him. She had the same deer-eyed look on that riverbank in Laos and, once again, the urge to shield this woman from danger and harm welled up inside of him. *Damn it, but she's so soft. And her smell…* His mind turned to their passionate sex, just the other night. *Man, that was the best. Maybe ever.* But he didn't dare look again in her direction and he tried to cut out that image.

"OK, going for the shower. If the food comes before I get out, go ahead and get started." It was the only kind thing he could offer.

Pip looked up from her chair and cocked her head towards the door as Cole crossed her line-of-sight. She did not follow him. She thought she heard a gentle knocking on the room door.

Pip heard Cole slide the bathroom latch to, and the knocking came again. Louder. She went to the door and let in the girl holding the tray with two plates of rice and a bowl of lukewarm chicken soup. No cashews this night, but the kitchen tried to come as close as they could to fulfilling Pip's order.

The housegirl sat the tray at the foot of the bed, and trotted out of the room, giggling, before Pip could fish around in her purse for the money to pay her. *OK, she can put it on the tab.*

Cole was out in a quick five minutes and walked over and stood looking down at the food, an index finger poking the face towel into his ear canal. "I told you to go ahead."

But Pip said nothing to him. She no longer felt the heat from his tantrum delivered at the temple earlier that evening. But she wanted to snuff out any remaining ember of anger that he might still be keeping lit.

She stood and undid all of her clothes, undid her bra and slipped off her panties – and she came and stood naked in front of Cole. She said to him, "See me for what I am, Cole. Naked. Pure. I am not deceitful." She said only that, and then walked to the bathroom door and stopped.

Cole turned to see her delicate and alluring body as she opened the door. She was drop-dead beautiful. Feeling his stare, she pivoted and walked back two steps towards him, and then stood there looking at him and the ridiculous cartoon characters on his bath towel. For the first time since he had been with her, he felt overpowered. *My God, she is sweet.*

He tossed the face towel on the floor and dropped his hands by his side. She gave him a hint of a smile, and as he started to move towards her, she softly shook her head, walked into the bathroom, closed the door and slid the latch to.

Cole nodded in appreciation of her splendid theatrics, pushing out his bottom lip in approval. *Nice job. Had me going. I already said that we're done. And we are.*

•　　•　　•　　•　　•

He slid on his skivvies and jeans and was pulling on his first sock when he saw the manila envelope that had tipped onto the bed while he was digging around in his gear bag. He let the second sock fall on the floor. *Alright, Gus old boy. Let's see what you've left me.*

He knew Gus owned an Indian Head penny collection his grandfather had passed on to him. And there was that disassembled 1960 FL Duo-Glide Harley he got at a swap meet for $55, the summer after high school. Gus told him of his dream about putting the bike together, painting it candy-apple red, and cruising up to Cheyenne on I-25 as Cole's loyal sidekick. Tonto.

Cole was confounded by his own nervousness as he tried to slip the letter out of the envelope without tearing it apart. It wasn't coming out easily. What did plop out onto the bed was one of Gus' dog tags. *What the hell?* He propped up the pillow at the head of the bed and threw his legs up on the mattress. He unfolded the letter and read:

> 16 May 1971
>
> Cole, I wrote this letter in a hurry tonight cause I know you're leaving for Tailand tomorrow. So hope you can read it when the time comes. It's important. Like I told you I don't think I'm gonna make it home. I'm pretty sure of that. And I don't deserve to go back.

You've always been a big brother to me. Always have looked up to you. Even when we was kids I always knew you were looking out for me. And now in Nam you're doing the same thing. But you were always tougher than me. Everybody respects that. You never talk much about being in the bush but I know that you were in the deep shit man. Danger stuff! I never talked about it either but that was cause I was never there. Never been in any danger. Never killed nobody. Once a REMF always a REMF right? Well I'm tired of that shit so I'm gonna change all that and make you proud. You'll see. And I'm gonna do something now so you can respect me to. I'm gonna show you.

The other thing I have to say is important to. You can't tell nobody Cole. You know that old priest from Our Ladys back in T or C right? Well after you came back from Nam the last time he and I got into it.

Cole swung his legs back onto the floor, sat up straight on the edge of the bed, and kept reading.

Well he lied and told me some bad things Cole. He told me some very bad things. Said I done it. That he'd have to tell the police. I was in that confession booth at church and all I told him was that I thought I saw Abilene there on the sidewalk with blood on the side of her head. But I don't remember walking up that street and I don't remember leaving either. I just don't know what happened. And I was having bad dreams about that. Real bad dreams and I thought this priest could help me. But he said he was sure I must have hurt Abilene. Said he was gonna tell the police. Well I waited outside for him to come out and I shoved my pistol in his ribs as he was getting in the churchs old green Chevy and I took him down to the river and pushed him in and jumped in after. He shouted for help cause he can't swim but I wasn't having him spread lies about what I done. He bobbed up and down a couple of times and then I held him under until he stopped thrashing around. But I don't need to hear him anymore. I did away with that old priest McGowan cause he said I hurt Abilene Cole. But I swear that I don't remember nothing about hurting Abilene. That old priest was a crazy son of a bitch.

You can have my indian head penny...

Like the telegram the night before, Cole dropped the letter onto the concrete floor. He didn't need to read more. He, like Detective Luis Contreras back in Truth or Consequences, knew that the chance of two violent crimes in that small town being unrelated was zero.

The connection was clear. Sharp as a razor. Gus had confessed to killing the priest. Connecting the dots to Abilene was easy.

"You fucking bastard!" he shouted. It's a good thing you are dead, or I'd kill you myself! I'd kill you a thousand times!" The years of loving him as a brother vaporized in an instant.

He stood up and grabbed Pip's white folding chair and bashed it into the wall until the seat, hinges, legs, and rivets went flying into a hundred pieces.

Pip flung open the bathroom door and yelled at him, "Cole! Cole! What the hell is going on here?!"

She saw the smashed chair and spotted the torn manila envelope on the bed. Very slowly she came over to Cole who was now standing, back to the wall looking at the floor. His fists were clenched in a death grip around Gus' dead neck.

"I trusted that fucker with my life! My baby sister! Gus... you lowlife, motherfucking traitor!"

Pip was stunned but she came to him quickly and held him as tight as she could. His tensed muscles were hard as bricks, and yet he did not push her away. She kissed his chest, again and again.

The night-shift housegirl had rushed to their door with her boyfriend who carried at his side a three-foot cane. Pip cracked the door and hid behind it since she was still naked. The two outside stood, straining to gawk into the room through the crack, the tall boyfriend behind the gangly girl.

From their position they could not see the broken chair and before the housegirl could speak, Pip cut her off. "*Mai pen rai, ja.* Never mind. All is OK now." The girl opened her mouth to speak but Pip swiftly shut and locked the door.

Cole sat, slumped down on the bed. He had peaked fast and emptied as quickly. He picked up the letter and read the last few lines:

> You can have my indian head penny collection. Got to be worth something. And I guess I'm croaked if you're reading this. Don't hate me Cole. Take my dog tag and toss it in the Rio Grande when you get back. Gus

"Right, Bronze Star, you fuckin' coward... 'Show me'... Show me what, you worthless fucking piece of shit!"

Pip knew better than to add any sounds to the room. She quietly slipped on her clothes and sat at the other side of the bed, facing the window.

Not knowing what to do, she reached over with her left hand and lifted the plate of chicken and rice, poked at it with her spoon and took one bite. The explosion in the room put her off food and any acts of civility.

Cole's mind was somewhere else right now, but she knew he would come back to that room and when he did, she vowed to grab him. She also knew he would have to go back to the temple tonight so he could collect his prize tomorrow. *No matter what, I'll see to that. He deserves this,* she finally admitted.

But Cole was several thousand miles away. He was picturing the alley shortcut where all this went down, and at that time of year the cottonwoods would have been turning yellow. He saw Abilene on her way home from school. *That fucking Judas walking her home... and probably trying something funny. Perverted bastard!* He tried, unsuccessfully, to piece it all together as if it were *his* crime scene, now knowing who the perp was. But it was just too close to home. Too fresh.

Why couldn't that stupid fucking Mexican cop, Pepe, put it together? Cole had no appetite to tell Pepe. *That asshole can figure it out for himself.*

And Detective Luis Contreras was soon able to do just that. His steadfast Sunday prayers at Our Lady's in Truth or Consequences – and the prayers of hundreds of others who knew Abilene and about her condition – were about to pay off.

CHAPTER 35

The moon lit their path as they walked through the single, yellow circle of light that marked the last streetlight in that part of Khong Chiam village. The reluctance by Cole to make the trip back to the temple that night was wearing off and, as soon as the temple walls loomed in front of him, the competitive drive to complete his wager with *Luang Por* began to reanimate his character.

•   •   •   •   •

The animus held by Pip for this assignment was outweighed by the steady and arousing pull of Cole's gravity. But it was a conflicting tug. She had once wanted him to fail and let Mordechai be the man he was born to be, but she also wanted Cole to succeed. She knew that the priest's capture would feed Cole's worldly needs, heal his wounds – especially his anguish over his sister and contents of the explosive letter in that manila envelope.

And the moral quandary she faced with Mordechai and Cole was compounded by a growing dislike for Gus, a man she had never met. *Yes, this must be the Gus from the deer hunting story. His "best friend."* And recalling Cole's painful, drunken confession that night at Aunt Nid's guesthouse, she now understood *that*

this was the monster who had raped and bludgeoned Cole's kid sister.
He's dead, but that didn't spare him from Cole's wrath and fury. No
wonder – his crime was too horrific for words. Too horrific to bear.

This tension had taken a physical and mental toll on Pip,
straining her Buddhist capacity for compassionate thinking. She
found her thoughts trapped in an empty, dead-end alley – a dark
place where her faith did not dare venture. She had never been
there before, and thought, *Yes, me too. I'm glad this guy is dead.*

But such a *baap*, sinful, thought crashed against her nature,
like a rogue wave against a stone seawall, and she felt immediate
and immense shame for allowing such a judgment to enter her
mind. She glanced up at Cole, hoping that he could read her
thoughts and free her from any duty to join him in his hatred for
Gus. But that was fantasy. Cole was not providing any
absolutions that evening.

He walked along quietly, resolved to *go through with that old*
monk's bet. He would get Mordechai back to Ubon, back to
Bangkok, and back to Vietnam.

And then he could retreat back into the bush and live the life
he knew best.

· · · · ·

When they were within sight of the temple gate, there was
frenzied rustling in the dry grass next to the trail and a small,
dark figure shot out in front of them. It scurried halfway across
their path and then stopped, turning its head to look at them
while standing on three legs; its right foreleg tucked underneath
its chest, like a pointer on the hunt. Cole instinctively reached
behind his back, but it was bare. Nothing there. He thought he
would not need his metallic insurance piece tonight, and the
lucky creature escaped a certain death.

Pip caught sight of Cole's quick maneuver and shouted. "No,
stop! It's a mongoose!"

Then, realizing that he was unarmed, she unwound herself saying, "Uh... OK... I'm glad you didn't bring that damn gun. Do you know that having a mongoose cross your path is very good luck?"

She glanced at Cole, but he was staring into the bushes to see what else might come rushing out. *Another one of these damn things – or maybe a big-ass snake.* He remembered the mongoose and cobra matches he saw in Vietnam. *Only a dumb shit or a newbie would ever bet on the snake.*

They moved on, Pip walking ahead of Cole. She knew the unnerving stories about Thai temples at night and did not want to tarry on these grounds. The temple, and its holy objects, often provided an irresistible attractant to powerful entities and spirits, creating a spiritual vortex of mischief, or worse, if one is not strong. They were not places to be wandering around after dark.

She was anxious to see *Luang Por*, for the security his presence provided – and to find out what else he had in store for them that evening. Cole was anxious too, but it had nothing to do with spirits, and everything to do with nabbing Mordechai.

They entered the temple grounds and caught sight of the dark purple outline of the sanctuary, its graceful, curved roof and ornate fascia glittered in the moonlight, reflecting off the golden trim and the countless blue, red, yellow and green mosaic tiles. The Mekong provided a massive, silver-black stretch of water in the background. It was stunning. Pip's fears faded fast and she paused, looking back at Cole and seeking his validation of the beauty before them. She caught his eye as he came up to her. He only nodded once but it was enough for her.

They neared the great hall and the site of that afternoon's coffin ceremony, and a solitary figure in a saffron robe rose from the steps and came to them. He had been waiting for them. It was Mordechai.

Pip smiled but did not *wai* him as he drew near. Her downward glance when Mordechai approached was enough for good manners. She was embarrassed to view him as a prisoner and felt sure that her anxiety was reappearing in her face. *Better to keep my eyes on the ground and wait for him to speak.*

Cole stopped dead in his tracks. Here was the last person he had expected to see this night. "Well, well… if it isn't Father Goodcut himself… Mr. Monk," he said. And here he was.

It was the first one-on-one with his nemesis and Cole looked him dead in the eye, scouring for that few flickering seconds of terror his prisoners revealed when he made his busts. But he found none of that. *Yeah, he looks pretty cocksure right now. Protected by that old codger monk, and all of that. But your sorry ass is mine tomorrow, amigo.*

Still, he couldn't resist poking Mordechai with a stick, "What the fuck were you thinking about, Goodcut. Running away like that? You knew we'd come after you, right?"

He didn't need Pip's sharp tug on his arm to keep him at bay. He knew there would be time for those questions on the boat tomorrow with Mordechai in cuffs, and the following day on the train, and next week in Vietnam. *Yeah. Your ass is mine alright, padre.*

Mordechai ignored Cole's jabs. He spoke plainly in a flat, yet cordial tone, as if all three of them were complete strangers who had just met on a street corner somewhere – one clergyman and two lay souls, as if there was no animosity coming from Cole, and no questions of wonder coming from Pip.

He simply said, "Follow me, please. We have made accommodations for you both. You will see *Luang Por* in the morning."

With this he turned and led them to a row of small *kuti*, cottages, in the back of the compound between the great hall and the sanctuary, and the eastern temple wall which ran along the riverbank. The Mekong that flowed past there was now sending cool breezes over the wall as if to apologize for the day's blistering heat. The full moon overhead orchestrated the rapprochement.

Mordechai stopped at the first cottage, which had a small candle illuminating the interior. He said to Pip, "This is the area for the *maa-chi*, and you can stay here for tonight." Mordechai, pulled aside the thin curtain at the doorway so Pip could see inside as she stepped in. The contents were sparse: a simple grass mat, a small pillow, a glass of water and a mosquito net that was hung in suspension above the mat.

Before she could say anything about her accommodations, Mordechai let the curtain fall.

He motioned for Cole to follow him, past the cottages for the *maa-chi* and deeper into the temple complex. Cole passed in front of Pip's cottage window, and he looked inside. She was staring back at him and started to raise her hands, wanting to say something about the evening, but she could only sigh and watch Cole pass by into the night.

He walked behind Mordechai and imagined, *Man it would be dead easy to knock this jackass out, toss him over my shoulders and head out the gate. But he's a big fucker, tall… lanky… That wouldn't be no problem. But then what, genius? How are you going to get him up to Ubon? That old monk would have everyone out beating the bushes for both of us by daybreak…*

Maybe the drama of the day finally wore him out, but Cole's brain kicked into neutral, *Better cool it, dude. You're the hunter… He's the prey… Get him on your terms. Walk out the door with him tomorrow. Just a few more hours of this shit and that deal is done. Check.*

"OK, we are here." Mordechai came to a stop in front of another *kuti*, one of many that were stretched out in a long row by the east temple wall. "You can stay here tonight. And *Luang Por* will see you in the morning," he repeated.

And without any more words, *without any hint that this dude's monk gig would soon be over*, Mordechai disappeared into the darkness and found his way back to the *nanes'* cottages.

• • • • •

Pip went to sleep that night thinking about Cole. He had grown large in her heart, and she was now genuinely worried about him. Despite his tough exterior and bark, she had seen enough to prove that the feelings she had about him back in Ubon were correct. He was hiding something good deep inside, and his rough exterior was just a performance of who he thought he was – a product of his life's hard-scrabble lessons. This man desperately needed life-saving relief from this soul-twisting contradiction.

She knew him to be an extraordinary warrior – a protector of the weak – and not the hunter-killer he imagined himself to be. *He needs to know that the faithful protector is the most courageous kind of man. It is perfect courage. And it is a great virtue. His macho act is just that: an act. And this act is strangling his true and good nature.*

His kind and comforting words to her when he witnessed her weaknesses, and his own weak moments when he would look to her, unguarded, told her what she needed to know. *If he collects his prize tomorrow, I will be happy for him. Mordechai will have to accept that too, for* Luang Por *has spoken. I pray for Mordechai's soul. And this Gus fellow, may the Lord Buddha forgive my sinful thoughts that I was glad about his death. I am not glad. And I pray for his lost soul as well. Most of all, I pray for Cole's small sister, the sweet spot in his hardened heart. May she be fully recovered.*

And with those last tender thoughts, she closed her eyes and dreamed of summer picnics with her father and mother in western Maryland. The thick summer air of the mountains near the West Virginia border smelled of rain-soaked clay and mats of green leaves on creek banks. She felt a great release from all the strain and effort her life had taken over the years. It was a freedom she had not felt in decades. It was delicious.

•　　•　　•　　•　　•

This has to be one of the most fucked-up days of my life, thought Cole as he sat on his mat and pulled down the mosquito net from its fasteners on the wooden walls of his cottage. The placed smelled of thick incense, and there was a night-blooming jasmine outside the window that poured its fragrant scent into the mix. The strong perfumed air was not pleasant for him.

The world he had worked so hard to create had been shaken to the point of collapse today. It had been upended and turned on its head, and he was no longer so sure-footed. He glanced at the wall and imagined his prey, Mordechai, sleeping just a few feet from his cottage.

Goodcut had escaped arrest yesterday and *he was now sheltered by a tough old monk who's made some dumb-shit wager about letting me grab him tomorrow. And dozing off in that coffin – I must have been crazy. All that jiggery-pokery for nothing. "Prayin' for my soul and for the health of those I love," yeah right. And if I don't get Mordechai tomorrow, there will be hell to pay, old monk or not. And then this woman… What the hell does she know about anything. Shit, that's just fuckin' nuts! How could I be so stupid to fall for her?*

Still smoldering, but with sleep drawing close he thought, *I can't forgive them. Mordechai for breaking the rules, the code. For dishonor. Pip for deceiving me and getting me to screw her – and then that coffin stunt. And, oh yeah, there's Gus. My "best friend" who raped and knocked my kid sister into a coma, and then killed that priest – a rap they were trying to pin on me! I will never forgive that son-of-a-bitch, no matter what. That evil bastard. I'm glad he's dead. The dumb fucker – being dead's too good for him.*

And his last words that night as he lay down formed a promise, "No. None of these losers. Never forgive them."

He slipped off to sleep with that oath crushing down tightly on him, and it smothered even the faintest chance of dreams. His powder was wet.

•   •   •   •   •

But an hour later, as the earth turned and the giant moon passed directly over the Mekong and shone its brightest, he suddenly woke. He heard a voice calling his name.

"Francis." Softly.

"Francis." Clearly.

"Francis Xavier." It was a woman's voice.

CHAPTER 36

Cole felt the tug on his foot, steady and measured. But there was no sensation of a hand, no fingers and no heat from the touch. Just the pull, now increasing in strength – and then the voice again, "Francis."

It was a woman's voice and was speaking to him as if it were affirming his name, calling him to rise. The voice moved closer to him, and then hovered above him. He propped himself up on his elbows and strained his eyes upwards to peer through the sheen of the mosquito net, but he could see nothing. Just the bare ceiling of the cottage and the flickering reflection from the blades of a small floor-fan, spinning away at the foot of his grass mat.

"What the hell is –" And the voice now came from inside his net, close to his face and saying in a whisper, "Francis Xavier, come."

He sat bolt upright. *Alright! That's enough of this freaky shit.* He twisted around at the waist and flipped over his sweaty pillow, looking for the cool dryness on the opposite side. He lowered himself down and closed his eyes, but as he did so, the door on his *Kuti* opened wide.

"Pip, is that you?" he asked. "Quit screwing around! I'm beat."

He sat up, and then swung his legs around, lifted the net over his head and slid out. He asked again, "Pip?"

But it quickly came to him that nobody there knew his full name. Pip might have seen "Frank Coltrane" on official communiques before they met, but she never called him that, let alone "Francis Xavier." No one in Thailand knew him by that closely guarded name.

He took two steps towards the door and reached out to shut it when the voice came again, "Francis Xavier, come. Come and see."

For the first time he heard clearly that it was not just the simple voice of one woman, but a composite voice with the blended tones of many women, speaking as one. "Francis, come and see. Come and see."

Each word was formed by a modulated and harmonious chorus, folding in with the words before and after. It was the voice of his mother when he was a small child, his grandmother, his ex-wife Imelda, the girls of New Mexico and Vietnam, his kid sister Abilene, and Pip. It was all of them – and many more. He could rightly have added the voice of Adam's Eve, for she was there too.

And as he reached out to touch the door latch of the *kuti*, he saw a brilliant reflection on the front wall of the *Boort* near his room, and it spread from the mosaic tile roof, down the complete riverside wall of the building. It was lit up with iridescent pink and blue lights that whirled around in a circular pattern, interspersed with blazing flashes of white-hot light, as if stars where being born and expelled from the wall itself.

Cole heard the voice call again, "Come, come and see." And he stepped out into the night and turned around to see what could possibly be causing such a beautiful array of lights on the east-facing wall of the *Boort*. Something was shining on it from the river. Something was moving with dazzling colors in a fluid, circular motion and it was creating these exquisite patterns.

He walked along the path near the front of the monks' *kuti* in silence, surprised that he was the only one who had stirred to see such an amazing spectacle. *But where were these lights coming from? Where was* – and then he saw the source, at the end of the brick promenade that terminated at a small and ornate boat landing, jutting out 30 feet into the Mekong.

He took a few steps in that direction. He had not willed himself to move but his feet were moving, nonetheless. It was involuntary. Spontaneous.

Underneath his feet, the cracks between the red brick tiles of the riverside promenade were lit from behind, beneath the ground's surface, in hues of fluorescent yellow and green. The landing itself was glowing and pulsating in a soft cadence of color, keeping time with his slow steps towards the railing at the river's edge.

He walked with his hands hanging at his sides, fingers out and palms parallel with the vibrant bricks below him. *I can hit the deck if I have to*, he defended. And yet, there were no triggers of fear in his mind.

The feeling he had was unnerving, yet extraordinary. Something extremely good was about to happen. Something wonderful.

And as he drew closer to the end of the promenade and the landing that jutted out into the river, he saw it – and he immediately remembered the night in Ubon.

There! 100 feet in front of the boat landing, swimming rapidly in large clockwise circles, was the brilliantly bejeweled river creature of Thai legend: the fierce-faced *Phaya Naak*, a giant and sinewy serpent that swims in the border waters between this world and the next. Its luminous skin and serpentine motion turned the muddy waters of the Mekong into a white and turquoise-blue, phosphorescent foam. Its pink and deep-blue glittering body emitted a radiance that shone out through its skin, through its very being, lighting up the waters, the landing, the nearby monks' *kuti*, and the east face of the sanctuary wall. It was mesmerizing.

Cole checked himself. *What the hell... Is this a dream? What...* Such discernment seemed small and artificial – it didn't matter now. He was a man who flourished within the hard world of war, thriving there based on the keen acuity of his senses. He trusted them.

But now he was propelled into a landscape he did not ask to go, and he had to believe his eyes and reject any thought they were lying, and that he was dreaming – because he knew he was not. He could not reject this netherworld offered by his senses. His vision was as real as the breaths he pulled in and expelled out of his heaving lungs. Cole felt as though he had just sprinted for miles. His heart was pounding on his chest's door. It wanted out! It wanted to see for itself the amazing story the body's eyes were telling it.

The creature began to swim in smaller circles with ever-increasing speed, and the voice beckoned to him again, "Francis Xavier, come and see." Cole inched closer to the railing. And he stood there, transfixed.

In the center of the circle where the *Phaya Naak* swam, the waters withdrew. Deeper and deeper, the *Phaya Naak* circled, again and again, faster and faster until the waters were pulled away from the center, exposing a round golden sandbar dome. It rose up, lifting gradually from where it had been resting beneath the surface and crested there, remaining fixed above the water line, its circumference outlined in a shimmering ring of bright, golden light.

Cole turned to look behind him at the *Wat* and the splendid buildings of the temple complex, and at the vivid lights reflected there just moments before. But the buildings were now gone. He turned back to the river and looked across to the eastern bank, towards the mountains of Laos which had been lit by the full moon. And they were also gone.

And he looked at his feet and saw that the landing under him had grown smaller, reduced to a pad of only a few bricks at the railing's edge, now detached from its moorings on the west bank of the river. The world around him was no more. No structure. No form. No sound and no scent.

Tonight, the Mekong was as quiet as space. Nothing existed before him nor behind him but the water, clear and blue, and the astonishing jeweled spectrum of vibrant lights circling the round, golden dome. The scene was struck and set ablaze by an enormous incandescent moon, fierce and radiant in the darkness. All else was gone.

And Cole felt a gentle, cool breeze flow onto him from above. The great moon had stirred the winds awake from their midnight doldrums and he lifted up his face to behold its lustrous power.

He shielded his eyes from the intense glare, and over his outstretched hand – and over the tips of his fingers – he saw that the moon itself was not the solid, sensible sphere he had known his whole life. It was, instead, a white-hot hole in the arched canopy of the firmament, through which poured a single, round ray of searing white light from the heavenly domain beyond. Cole saw the immaculate light from heaven pour through the hole from above and flood the golden dome in front of him with such intensity that he could barely withstand its eye-piercing brightness.

He strained to look upwards, and he saw from the corners of his eyes, two human figures walking on the surface of the water towards the golden mound. They looked somehow familiar, and he tried to make out who they were. The features of their faces were obscured by an unending blaze of fire which emanated from their bodies and peaked above their heads in halos of luminous yellow flames.

Cole could see that they were both Buddhist monks, and they moved carefully and deliberately to climb and stand atop the golden sandbar dome. And as they neared the top, they turned to face each other and the holy flames about their faces flickered slightly. Cole caught in an instant that these entities were *Luang Por* and the abbot of *Wat Suwan.*

Cole tried to wave, but his arms could not rise from his side. He tried to shout their names, but he could not speak. He could make no contact with them, and they did not look at him.

The taller monk produced a pillow of golden silk from under his robe and they both took hold of the ends of it, placed it on the apex of the mound and kneeled, deep in the gentle slope of the golden sandbar, their heads bowed.

And then Cole saw movement from above. Through the white hole in the starless sky, a figure descended without sound – a figure wrapped in elegant flowing robes of blue and white, its face dazzling and resplendent as the sun itself. Gently, the figure descended, steadily downwards. The soundless wind blew strongly in his face, and yet he could hear the fabric of her robes flutter as she alighted softly, delicately, on the golden pillow. Her face was too brilliant to look upon, and only when the radiance waned could he see her glorious and exalted countenance. She stood on the golden pillow, glowing white arms at her side. Cole had seen her image, high in the statuary of Our Lady's Church.

It was Her. The Blessed Virgin. Holy Mary.

His mouth agape, he found himself kneeling, not able to move his body or mouth, or blink his eyes, and he panicked as his skeleton and his muscles froze in place. In his mind, he tried to utter the first words of the Rosary, "Hail Mary, full of grace..." but the words vanished. His language collapsed, and even his thoughts slowed down and stopped. His forward and back sense of time disappeared. He was paralyzed in the moment – in this precise, timeless moment.

She lifted her arms to offer him the sign of peace, it was an invitation for an embrace with the Mother of God. It was a pure and absolving grace, and it flowed over Cole when she began to speak to him the few perfect words he needed to hear. And with this flood of unrestrained love, he felt the first tears streaming down his face.

"Francis, my child. You are troubled."

"And I have come to bring a gift for you to accept."

"It is what you need most. It is the righteous gift of forgiveness. And by God's infinite grace and His loving mercy, I give this to you now. Accept this from the God who loves you, Francis."

With these words, the old Cole died. He was no longer there. No cynical shell of toughness remained. His former self was washed away by a majesty no hardened soul on earth could resist. Darkness fled, and a life bounded by hatred and revenge was swept into the river by her mere presence. It was a moment of life-changing ecstasy, and he now sobbed tears without stopping. They were tears of bliss, of a homecoming. Of spiritual unity. He had surrendered.

"Francis, you must forgive all others for their transgressions, as your Father in Heaven has forgiven you."

"And do not be afraid. The gift is with you now."

Our Lady then looked down to her left and right, and then lifted her hands over the heads of the monks in a blessing and said, "There are many faces acceptable to my son. Many faces of Christ on earth." With their robes blowing in the wind from above, the monks holding the pillow bowed their heads deeply.

She looked again upon Cole and said, "Your sister is waking as you hear my words. The silent prayers in your heart, and in the hearts of all the people who love her, have been heard. Her journey will strengthen as your forgiveness grows. It is upon your faith that her full healing will come to pass."

She then lifted her face towards the heavens and, in an instant, ascended back through the round portal in the sky, pulling the light from her magnificent aura back with her.

Cole saw the monks bend and place the golden pillow in the river where it swirled in the current made by the *Phaya Naak*. The miraculous creature dove once, surfaced and opened its mouth, consuming the pillow in one swallow – its long body swimming out and away from the circle and into the depths of the Mekong out to the east, its blue, pink and white swirling lights, gradually disappearing.

Cole's frozen form watched the *Phaya Naak* as it swam away to a point on the opposite bank of the Mekong, below the hills of Laos which had emerged from behind the evening's veil. The two abbots stood on the golden dome and watched in reverence and quiet joy as it swam away. They then turned and bowed to each other – and walked softly on the water, returning to *Wat Suwan*. They had their hands clasped in a *wai* at their chests, having just received the beatific blessing.

Reaching the landing, they elevated themselves onto the brick pathway and passed by Cole's immobile and kneeling form, his head bowed in awe and contemplation of what had just occurred. They smiled warmly at him before disappearing into the *Wat* and their day ahead. *So rare and so wonderful.*

CHAPTER 37

It was early morning in Las Cruces, New Mexico, when Cole sat, transfigured on the ornate Mekong boat dock. In fact, it was precisely 6:14am on Thursday morning.

The shift change for the night-day nurses at the Doña Ana County Hospital had just taken place, and Nurse Susan Atkinson was coming on duty. As protocol required, she accepted the handover of duties, including a bed-by-bed check of the patients in the long-term, ICU unit. That procedure normally did not take very long since there were rarely more than two or three patients in that ward at any given time.

Their star, long-term patient was Abilene Coltrane. She had been with them for over ten months. And many of the nurses had daughters about her age, with similar, soon-to-be-women baby faces. Daughters who wanted to be cheerleaders. Daughters who belonged to the 4H, went to rodeos, and loved John and Paul – but not George or Ringo. The nurses all adored her and many privately, and publicly, prayed for her.

Her chart was as thick as an Albuquerque phone directory. And pasted on the back of the clipboard which hung at the foot of her bed was a half-page, type-written sticker with the instructions that her condition was, "a matter of legal interest to the county court – and should there be any change in her status, the hospital was to immediately notify Detective Luis Contreras,

Sheriff's Office, Truth or Consequences." But all the nurses knew the drill. So did the doctors and everyone else on that floor.

And when Nurse Atkinson came on duty that morning, accompanied by the outgoing night-shift nurse, they were both surprised to see Abilene lying on her side, I.V. tubes and ventilator wires pulled taut.

"I just checked on her 30 minutes ago, and she was lying flat. Who could have moved her?" The night nurse's eyes darted to the ICU desk, not more than 30 feet away through the tall glass wall. But all the other nurses were also out, making their own handover rounds. Only the night janitor was behind the desk, bent down, replacing a plastic trashcan liner.

Atkinson and the night nurse looked at each other and they both knew.

"Abilene. Abi! This is Susan, Abi. Can you hear me?" asked Atkinson. She turned to the night nurse and said, "Get Dr. O'Conner and tell him to come here now! Tell him to step on it! I think she may be coming to."

Susan bent closer to the bed and squeezed Abilene's hand and gasped when she saw Abi swallow and turn her head a few degrees away from her pillow. She was struggling against the ventilator, trying to speak.

Nurse Atkinson removed the head strap and lifted the mouthpiece slowly out of Abilene's mouth. If need be, she could replace it in a second. It was risky, but it might be minutes before the ICU doctor could be located and she had no time to lose.

She sat the ventilator piece down at Abilene's side, the monitor now flagging red lights, indicating the lack of back-pressure and an incorrect air flow. But that didn't matter. Abilene was breathing on her own and a quick check with the stethoscope indicated that her breathing was normal, as were her heart sounds – and gone was the chronic whistling in her lungs caused by months of sustained use on the ventilator.

But she was not moving, and not otherwise responding. Susan again squeezed her hand. Nothing. She squeezed once more. Again, no squeezing response – but she felt the tension in

Abilene's arm muscles increasing, her palm shaking as she slowly, but with purpose, pulled Susan closer to her. Susan closed the gap between their faces and she saw Abilene's dry lips part and then move to mouth words. But the words were not coming. No wind was pushed out.

But at last she summoned a small breeze from deep inside her and she said, faintly but clearly, "Tell Cole. Tell, Cole."

"Yes, dear. Susan here. Nurse Susan. Tell Cole what, honey?" encouraging Abilene to finish her words.

And Abilene squeezed her hand, gently but with purpose, "Tell Cole, Gus did this."

And with that Nurse Atkinson raised from her position bent over Abilene's bed, just in time to see Dr. O'Conner and the night nurse racing down the hallway, past the ICU glass-wall partition.

"Don't you worry about a thing, now dear. Don't use any more strength. Not just yet." And she bent back down, stroked Abilene's hair away from her forehead and placed a long, soft kiss on her cheek. "Welcome back, Sweetheart."

Dr. O'Conner rounded the corner and came to the bedside. "Is it true the patient's coming around?" He took his flashlight and, without moving Abilene's position, checked the pupil reaction in her right eye and brought his stethoscope from around his neck and did his doctor duties.

Abilene hadn't budged or made any movements since whispering to Susan. O'Conner looked confused.

"So, what's going on here, Susan?"

She smiled at Abilene and said, "Well if you ask me, I'd say it's nothing short of a miracle."

She then turned to face the doctor and said with a sober face, "Come with me outside, please. You need to make a phone call."

CHAPTER 38

The sun crawled its way over the hilltops of Laos to the east, and Cole's rigid body began to thaw and loosen. He could at last stir himself. He rotated his neck muscles in small round circles and stood up, staring into the sky that was turning out its daytime, azure routine. No moon. No stars. Only the bright burning sun.

To the east, he could see the far riverbank of Laos, and behind him the temple buildings of *Wat Suwan*. In the front of the boat landing, a small brown, round sandbar divided the water that flowed placidly around it. No monks. No river creature. No vision of Mary.

He scanned his surroundings and took in the world around him: the sounds of the temple coming to life at dawn, the smells of the village drifting over the temple walls, the sight of small fishing boats putting out on the river, and the touch of the red paving stones under his bare feet. He stretched out his arms, palms up, fingers pointing to the horizon, and he felt the ethereal weight of the air in his hands. All felt normal and reassuring. He was back. *Check.*

But Cole was also filled with the overwhelming sense that he now belonged in a changed world. It was new and he felt untested, but it was not unpleasant. It was not the feeling of relief he would get in the morning after he woke from a fitful dream and to know that it was not real. Because this was no dream. And it was not fitful. It was an encounter with an ineffable beauty – and Cole knew that he had been remade from the experience.

But the pouring out of pure grace had shocked him. Nothing in his roughneck world could have prepared him for this. This unconditional grace. Undeserved. He was a mortally wounded man. Dead. Now reborn. He was healed and made fully whole. His old world had collapsed somewhere out there on the boat landing last night. His hard exoskeleton had molted off and floated down the Mekong – floating down-river with a tributary of his tears.

And there was no going back.

His hands rose to a prayerful position at his chest, and he made a hesitant and rusty sign of the cross as he recalled, with a sad longing, the return of Our Lady into the heavens. He was overcome with an intense attachment and loyalty to her that he could not explain – and an unusual affection for the two old monks who were there as well. They were helping him. All along, they had been helping him.

He left the landing and staggered around in the fresh skin of a newborn creature, shaky and uncertain. And he reached the promenade that led back to the cottages just in time to hear the end of the morning's prayers being chanted in the timeless language. He recalled, just yesterday, the same prayers being said as he stood outside the gate, looking in. Yesterday the prayers were merely odd and exotic, maybe even musical, but now the ancient and mysterious words echoed and resonated in his heart. He stopped and turned towards the great hall from where the prayers were emanating across the temple grounds. Melodious. Wonderful. They were the most beautiful sounds he had heard in years.

•   •   •   •   •

Luuk-sit swept the temple walkways and villagers strolled in through the gate to make their offerings to the images that graced the sanctuary in the *Wat*. For today was *wan phra*, Buddha

Day, at the temple. It was a special day of celebration. Today, the *Boort*, sanctuary home to the most holy objects, would open its doors for parishioners to come in and pay their respects. Like so many of the activities on the religious calendar of Thai Buddhism, *wan phra* was a date determined by the cycle of the moon, a reverential and natural way of organizing holy days shared with Christendom on the other side of the earth.

Cole ambled on to his *kuti*. He was completely exhausted from last night's spiritual encounter and needed to rest. But as he turned on the pathway towards his bed, he saw the two abbots leading the daily procession of monks out of the great hall and towards the gate. They were going out for *bintabaat*. All the monks in the *Wat*, *nanes*, including Mordechai, and *luuk-sit* were in the procession – Mordechai's figure, towards the rear of the line, loomed tall.

Cole looked away and then back to Mordechai. It was Mordechai alright. He could plainly see him. There was no mistake.

And while Cole was aware in his memory why he came to this temple, and what plans he had for capturing this man, he felt no wish whatsoever to perturb this thing of beauty, this honoring of things holy, and the humility with which the givers and recipients interact. He watched them pass out of the gate with their empty bowls and made no attempt to move in that direction. It was the farthest thing from his mind.

Watching the last *luuk-sit* turn and head south along the path outside the temple, Cole was suddenly struck by a strong sense of melancholy. It was a remorseful look back at his adult life. He was feeling the unrequited love of the working man: blindly loving your job, something false and uncaring, and never being loved back. Unrecoverable, misspent years, redeemed only by the hope to make the best of what time was left – and to get it right.

Cole drew in a deep sigh. He was hit hard by this unexpected sense of loneliness, something he had not known before. It was the cleaving act of separation from his past, now dead. A look over the shoulder. A whiff of the last vestige of his former self... *dying into ashes and smoke. And then nothing.*

"Yes. Hope," he said under his breath as he tried to pick up his pace on the way back to the *kuti* where he began last night, now a lifetime ago. *Flip the pillow. Close my eyes. Get some rest.*

And as he neared the door of his *kuti*, he looked across a small garden towards the sleeping cottages of the *maa-chi*. He stopped walking. Again, he felt the surge of warmth spread across his chest, and he finally spoke the word that he secretly held on his lips, ever since the afternoon on that muddy beach in Laos.

He said her name, "Pip."

An old *maa-chi* was sweeping the fallen, red and purple bougainvillea flowers from the walkway as Cole drew near the door of Pip's cottage. The *maa-chi* saw him but did not look up. The old woman knew, and it was a good thing. She turned her back and swept in the other direction with her long broom of bound twigs.

Cole came to Pip's door and peeked past the curtain. She was still sleeping, but he entered and stood looking at her, tucked in a fetal position under her net. Cole took off his shirt and threw it on the chair by the open window. He lifted the net and slid onto the mat smoothly, embracing her from behind and cupping her body with his. He draped his right arm over her thin waist and kissed her on her neck. She did not stir. He felt her warm body, soft against his. Welcoming. The trace of the previous day's perfume was still on her neck. He kissed her again and was soon fast asleep.

He would recall later that he had dreamed the two of them were riding down a red-dirt path in the piñon-pine highlands of New Mexico; she was on a strawberry roan mare, he on an appaloosa gelding. They were trying to catch up with Abilene who had just galloped past them, shouting, and waving her red hat high over her head. Pip was laughing uncontrollably. He never felt happier.

PART V: RELEASE

CHAPTER 39

Cole woke to the sounds of Pip moving about in the room. She had just returned from her morning shower and put her clothes on. She folded up the mosquito net and tossed it over the ropes that hung it in place, bent down over Cole while stroking the strands of her loose, long black hair with a fork fashioned with her fingertips.

Pip sat down at his side and turned at her waist, leaned forward and kissed him on the forehead. It was an apology for yesterday evening, but he pulled her to his face, kissed her on the mouth, and smiled.

"Good morning, young lady," said Cole, opening his eyes and drinking in the beauty before him.

Surprised by his move, she whispered, "Good morning," but she pulled back from his face and tried out a frown, "I'm not sure that I understand. What time did you come here, and… are you still angry with me? I thought…"

Cole put his fingertip to her lips and said, "You really don't have to understand. It's for *me* to understand. And I do."

He paused for a moment, smiled at her and said, "OK, let's get going. Let's head back today."

"Uh… 'head back'… what are you talking about? You do remember that you need to see *Luang Por* this morning? Right? You know, your bet with him about Mordechai, and –"

"I mean, I think it is time to leave this place. Just get going. Split back to Bangkok. You know, we need to –"

The old *maa-chi* who had been sweeping the leaves and flowers from the walk came to the door of the cottage, knocked and said, "*Khun kha, Luang Por khor phop gan deow-nee, na ja. Chern, kha.* Hello, Miss, *Luang Por* would like to meet you two now. Please come with me."

"Ok *nah kha, ja,*" Pip told her. "Sure, we'll be right there." She turned to Cole and said, "See. I told you so."

·   ·   ·   ·   ·

They entered the great hall and saw *Luang Por* sitting in his pulpit, encircled by the entire clergy of the wat, except for several *maa-chi* who were scurrying about with the *bintabaat* offerings and making ready for the midday meal which would be served at noon.

Luang Por beckoned both Pip and Cole to come closer to where he was sitting, sipping on his favorite tea. Pip bent at the waist and walked to a place just in front of the venerable old monk. Cole followed in behind her and, for the last few feet, bowed as he drew near.

Pip turned to watch Cole as he sat down and was surprised to see his respectful posture, and the fact that he insisted on sitting on the ground although a plastic chair was offered. Seeing this, the two abbots exchanged glances. For Pip, this odd behavior was completely out-of-character. Her curiosity was piqued – but she could not resist a smile.

Luang Por asked them both, "*Yoom,* how did you sleep last night?" He looked first at Cole, a hint of a smile breaking out on his wrinkled, leathered face, his eyes twinkling. He then turned to Pip, "*Fan dee, mai khrap, yoom phuying*? And you, did you sleep well last night?"

Pip replied, "*Kha, krob khun kha, Luang Por.* Yes, thank you, *Luang Por.*"

Cole said nothing. He didn't have to. Both of the abbots were there at Cole's transformation on the boat dock last night, and the question was just to be polite.

Luang Por wasted no time and began, "You see, Cone, there is a reality that exists that is unseen and unknowable by most of us who dwell on this side of the divide – the divide that separates us from the spirit world beyond. And although people do not see that other reality, it does not mean it does not exist. It just means that our senses are not attuned to see it. We are not meant to dwell permanently in that reality as human beings.

But when we are invited to go – and when we obey and visit there – we will see many marvelous things that we cannot immediately understand. Do you follow me?" He paused to look at Cole, and then at Pip who had no idea about the secret episode that Cole shared with the two abbots last night.

Cole only nodded and muttered a very quiet, "Khrap, yes sir..." under his breath. And with these courteous and conciliatory words uttered by Cole, Pip was stunned.

Luang Por continued on, "And what we see in that reality contains an absolute truth. It is pure and uncorrupted. And if we are given a gift or a message while in that world – as you received last night – we will be forever changed by the sublime power of that message." *Luang Por* paused to study Cole.

"You see, our very being is changed when we come face-to-face with our creator, a creator who has decided to intervene and change our path – to change the very core of who we are. We cannot now find some other path that suits our selfish ways. And no one can resist this power." Palm-patting his chest, and then pointing his boney finger at Pip and then Cole, "Not me, not her, not you."

He drew in Cole's entire being with his eyes and said, "And now, Cone, you are also forever changed."

Pip looked on, completely baffled by the sermon that *Luang Por* was giving to Cole – and by Cole's demeanor, nodding and accepting the words that came from *Luang Por*'s mouth. *What in the…?! This is not the Cole I know!*

But she stopped her questioning mind, mid-thought, and yielded to the wisdom being bestowed on all souls gathered in the great hall that morning. She regained control. Buddhist. Mindful.

And she whispered again and again, after each sentence *Luang Por* spoke, the ancient words, "*Sa-ah-tu, Amen.*"

"Yes, *Luang Por*, I see," said Cole.

"And the gift you received from the Holy Mother is the gift of *forgiveness*. She has willed this for you, and it is now yours to keep, and to manifest in your being. Forgiveness is the most difficult Christian virtue to obtain, is it not? And you were given this gift by the grace of the Mother of your God, herself. How fortunate are you, Cone!"

Luang Por glanced at Mordechai who mouthed the word "Amen" and raised his hands in a *wai* to the heavens. He didn't yet fully comprehend the story that was unfolding, but he knew he was witnessing a miracle. And, through the grace and intercession of Holy Mary, it was apparently happening to the man who had been hunting him.

"Praise be to God," Mordechai blurted out loud, for he could no longer contain his emotions. No one present strayed an eye towards him nor noticed the loud affirmation in a language they did not understand – the joy he expressed was unmistakable. Bright and clear.

Luang Por went on, "You are still a warrior, Cone, I see that strength in your character. But it must be lived out in another way. A way that suits your true *nee-sai* – your true self as a human being."

"You are a guardian and a protector, Cone. A protector and comforter of weak persons. And *forgiveness* is the key strength for that kind of warrior. Do you understand me?" asked the abbot.

"I mean that you need to forgive people for their weakness, in order for you to protect them," he emphasized. He paused and looked at Pip. She raised the *wai* she held at her chest to her forehead.

"Yes, sir, I understand," said Cole, looking at the back of his hands and his scarred fingers.

"And do you truly forgive, Cone? Can you forgive now? Forgive those who have caused harm to you, and to seek forgiveness for the grief you have caused others? Can you do this, Cone?" he repeated.

Cole halted at first. He could not yet give full voice to the new creature that was born inside him.

But then the words started to drift up from his heart. Words he thought he would never say. Words that just yesterday were for weaklings and losers to speak, for men who were not battle-tested and lacked courage. Words to be spoken by men who had never suffered and sacrificed – never paid the price with blood. But then, the radiant image of the Crucified Christ in Our Lady's Church back home, and the words of a long-forgotten homily burst into his mind. The disembodied voice of Father McGowan spoke to him, "Christ suffered and paid the price with his blood." *Yes,* Cole thought. *The price. It's been paid.*

Cole was immediately ashamed of his hesitation. He got up from his sitting posture, knelt and placed his prayerful hands to his chest and spoke about the huge rock pressing down against his heart – and he burst forth with a flood of words, forgiving all those who had harmed him, and asking forgiveness from all those he had caused to suffer from his hatred and persecution.

He asked for forgiveness from his grandmother for his rebelliousness – because she was tough and pushed the Bible on him after his mother ran away with the rodeo. Cole forgave his mother for her neglect. He paused and dug deeper, asking forgiveness from his ex-wife for not loving her fully, and from Pip for his anger at her timidity and weakness. He now knew her shyness was not deceitful. He looked at Pip who was shaking her head and trying to stave off the love she felt welling up in her heart for this man.

And he asked for forgiveness from all those he had pursued and captured and put in prison, for *there was no dishonor to God by breaking those man-made rules – such stupid rules.*

Mordechai watched intently. He was finding it hard to breathe. He was gripped by the riveting honesty and humility of Cole's confession. But he was no longer hearing Cole's voice, but the open, confessing heart of the Apostle Paul. He heard St. Paul speak the words – and Mordechai shuddered:

> *Even though I was once a blasphemer and a persecutor and a violent man, I was shown mercy because I acted in ignorance and unbelief. The grace of our Lord was poured out on me abundantly, along with the faith and love that are in Christ Jesus… who came into the world to save sinners – of whom I am the worst.*

Mordechai was witnessing a miracle of transformation and he was moved to tears. *Oh yes, this is a miracle alright.* And he crossed himself under his saffron robe.

Luang Por astutely picked up on the connection between Cole's words and Mordechai's stirrings, and he brought his main question to Cole, "*Yoom* Cone, do you remember our wager?"

He paused to look at Cole, but the old monk already knew the answer. Still, Cole needed to say so. Publicly. So, he asked him again, in a slightly different way, "Cone, do you want Mordechai to go with you today?"

Cole was kneeling. Unanimated. And he searched his mind for the words to answer the old monk's pressing question. The memories of the long days of preparation for the hunt and all the complications in tracking down Goodcut were there, but the purpose – the mindless drive to bring in Mordechai at all costs – had lifted off and vanished.

He drew in a quick breath, followed by a long exhale of the words he was now ready to say, "No. No, he is meant to stay here." The answer came immediately and without the need for additional thought. Cole's will to capture and return the priest, Father Mordechai Goodcut, his would-be prey, had evaporated.

Cole looked up at Luang Por, sitting in his ornate pulpit. He was glad to have lost the wager to the old monk. Pip sat aghast at what she just heard.

Luang Por beamed with satisfaction. It was a confirmation of the prophesy he had foreseen in his dreams – a verification that the cosmic clockwork he knew so well was working just fine. *The outpouring of forgiveness will always change one's spiritual karma. It is such a beautiful, rare, and powerful boon,* merit, thought the old monk. All the clergy and laity gathered there, many lacking the understanding of the English words, nonetheless knew that something good and marvelous was occurring before them.

Looking at the Abbot of *Wat Suwan, Luang Por* said in Thai, "His mind and heart can now see each other. His Holy Mother saw to that with her gift. We are all most fortunate for this blessing. Sa-*ah-to*, Amen."

Pip did not understand completely but she, like Mordechai, knew that something wonderful was at work in Cole's heart and it had transformed him – overnight.

She looked at the man she could no longer resist and thought, *Cole needs this peace. To turn away from war and hatred... death and fear. He must surely hate these things as much as Mordechai.*

She looked past Cole to where Mordechai sat, transfixed, and she tried to disentangle the different natures of these two men. *The priest is driven by forces from deep within. And Cole is... well...*

a surface-dweller. A cowboy from New Mexico, no less. And she smiled at this last thought and lifted her head to look at him.

Her smile lingered as she offered in silent prayer, *He's been delivered from the things that have been tormenting him. He is now unburdened.* And giving praise where she felt it due, she offered, *Lord Buddha, thank you for this miracle.*

But Pip had one restless thought that she kept sending away, only to have it return again. Again and again. She finally spoke up, "I'm sorry, *Luang Por.* I have something to ask of Cole. May I ask it now?"

The old abbot looked at her and read her troubled heart. "Of course, *yoom.* Cone is sitting right here. Ask him."

And *Luang Por* listened attentively since he understood the signs of Pip's urgency. He was unaware of the story about Cole's sister but knew Cole had many more wounds than his confession this morning had divulged.

"Cole," she turned to look at him. "Cole, do you forgive your friend, Gus? Can you forgive him? I know he had something terrible to do with Abilene. I could figure that part out." She paused. "But do you forgive him for what he did?"

Cole knew the question would have to come. But the look he gave her was not sent in anger. He recalled the thoughts he went to bed with, just last night, and his oath to never forgive Gus for what he had done to Abilene. He swallowed hard and stared down at the spirals and knots in the teakwood floor of the great hall.

Cole recalled... *my "best buddy" Gus... his brutal attack on Abilene... his murder of Father McGowan....* He knew the crimes committed by Gus, and he knew the recourse under the law, but the letter of the law was not the question here. It was the spirit. It was the trust of a best friend – and the deep, personal stake in Gus' life-story – made putrid and spoiled by the revenge that had been festering in Cole's heart.

He drew in a long breath, his ribs ready to explode, and he dove in deep to retrieve the answer to Pip's question. But as deep as he could go, he couldn't find that hatred anywhere. It was gone. Disappeared. The stone was rolled back. Only the cave-like, empty tomb that once held it in check remained. And he knew then that his hatred had been drawn out from that tomb and washed away into the river last night, along with the binding cloths and the burial spices. Along with his tears. It was a forgiveness of the most majestic kind. Our Lady's gift.

"Thanks be to God," he murmured under his breath.

Cole rose to the surface quickly and said to Pip – and to all who were there, hanging on his words, "Yes, I forgive him, too." And he bowed his head and wept, unable to contain the weight of the releasing emotion.

Pip reached over and embraced Cole, and kissed him on his cheek, in front of all the monks, *nanes*, *luuk-sit* and *maa-chi* who had gathered and made themselves still for this occasion. She did not care if the affection was offensive. No one was offended – least of all, *Luang Por*.

"*Owa-laa. Jop.* Well, that's the end of this." *Luang Por* stood and all the others sitting on the dais next to his pulpit heard him say as he lifted his *wai* to the heavens, "*Sa-ah-tu*, Amen. *Dern plort phai, took took khun.* Go safely in peace, everyone."

All gathered there looked on with immense satisfaction for they had just witnessed a true and beautiful thing – so rare and so wonderful.

CHAPTER 40

Cole sat and watched the river. A large mat of water hyacinth ferrying several coconut husks and a torn, bicycle innertube with several pink patches floated by, about 10 feet from his riverbank perch – a flimsy bamboo bench that local fisherman had cobbled together over the years. This seat had to do since the dilapidated boat dock on the River Mun had no proper place to sit, and at least these few sticks kept his large frame from squatting directly on the muddy bank. Besides, he was tired of standing.

Last night, in the crummy little tin-roof noodle shop opposite the hotel, Pip had asked Lek and Uncle Suwit to go down to the dock mid-morning today and wait for them. Cole had been there for over an hour, but he wasn't much perturbed by their tardiness. *Lek and old Uncle Suwit ought to be here any minute. But where the heck is Pip?*

•   •   •   •   •

Lek and his father had tied their boat to the dock on the Mun for the past two days, waiting out Cole and Pip's story. Today, they would finally get a chance to go back home. Just as well. Lek had run out of beer money and his father was in no mood to spot him any more cash to support his habit.

They all could have met at the boat landing at *Wat Suwan* since it was a proper cement dock and easier to board the boat there. But Cole did not want to go back to that holy place, as if seeing the site of his transformation in broad daylight would somehow dilute the power of that experience. He wanted to keep that picture tight and pure. Pristine.

This world's flipped upside down. Damn straight. He inhaled the raw smell of the riverbank while looking out to the end of the dock and the makeshift wood scaffolding that had eluded their desperate grasps, the day they drifted off to Laos.

He craned his neck to scan across the Mun to the point where it met the Mekong in the east. The muddy Mekong, its massive current incessantly moving southward and finally flowing out through the Mekong Delta in Vietnam – home of the 25th Infantry. Mordechai's old outfit. *And now this guy's going back to Ubon this week and become a monk – and we're leaving him here to do just that. Well, I'll be dipped in shit.*

He shook his head in disbelief, gave a quick sarcastic chuckle and then spat the irony out with a piece of tobacco that was stuck to the tip of his tongue.

Pip had told him this morning when they woke that Mordechai would be coming down to the river with *Luang Por* to bid them goodbye, and that two other monks wanted to catch a ride on the boat that Uncle Suwit had rented. He stood and looked up the road to see if he could spot her. *So where was Mordechai and Luang Por, and where was Pip?*

Cole started to reconsider the plan to wait and say, "goodbye, good luck and all of that stuff." He secretly hoped that when Pip showed up, and Lek and Uncle Suwit arrived on the scene, they could just neatly and quietly shove off and make their way back to Ubon without the farewell whoopla. But he knew better than to bring that option up with Pip. She was now over-the-moon happy, and he did not want to spoil her mood.

Cole sat back down on the bamboo bench, and as he bent over the gold chain around his neck with the single brass Buddhist amulet of *Luang Por Boo Wan* – a saint from Chiang Mai – fell out of his T-shirt and dangled against his chest. It was Pip's father's amulet, and it was a treasure she took everywhere. Last night she gave it to Cole, and he held it now in both hands and lifted it to his face. "*Sa-jah-tuk*" he said, trying to remember the pronunciation of the Thai "amen," as he placed the amulet back inside his shirt. He no longer felt the need to laugh at himself with the flair of self-depreciation that always hid his awkward public moments.

The drifting hyacinth debris-mat hit a snag on the river's shallow bottom and a few, small silver fish swam to the surface to investigate. Cole flicked his cigarette butt in the direction of the mat and the fish scattered. From up the road he heard Lek's voice booming out, and when he turned to look, he saw Lek and Uncle Suwit walking down in his direction. And further up the road, he could see the fluttering saffron robes of *Luang Por*, two other monks and *nane* Mordechai as they walked along. Pip followed closely, just slightly behind.

•   •   •   •   •

Luang Por was busy giving instruction to the two monks who were going back to *Wat Phra Nanachart* in Ubon with the boat. He wanted to be sure that preparations for Mordechai's ordination to become a monk were done properly and that the *maa-chi*, the backbone of the temple, would have all organized and ready for them when they returned in three days' time. *Luang Por* had conferred with the Abbot of *Wat Suwan* and they both agreed – after consulting the astrological indicators and numerological signs associated with Mordechai's birthday – that next Thursday, 27 May, at 9:27am would be an auspicious day and time for his ordination. It was fine, and it was good.

Lek and Uncle Suwit were carrying fuel cans along the wooden dock and loading them into the boat, making ready for the five-hour, up-stream trip back to Ubon. They fired up the diesel engine and a great belch of smoke shot out of the exhaust. *"Dee, dee mahk,* Good, very good," said Uncle Suwit, pleased that the old girl would start up after the two-day break.

Lek undid the mooring line and they motored away from the dock, coming around to the upstream side, and headed for the muddy beach where Pip, Cole, *Luang Por*, Mordechai and the two monks were standing. Lek ran the bow onto the soft mud flat, just far enough to allow their passengers to hop onboard without the boat drifting off with the current.

While everyone else was busy with the preparations, Cole stole the moment to ask Pip, holding her shoulders with both his hands, "Did you get the telegram sent to Clarke? Did it go out?"

She tipped her head to the side and smiled, mocking him that she would forget such an important thing. "Of course." But she stared back at him for a second too long and Cole pulled her close and kissed her softly. He cracked a cunning smile to match hers and said, "Lemme see it."

"Ok, Mr. Thorough Guy – here you go," said Pip as she raised her right hand and gave him a snappy and exaggerated salute, poking fun at the vestige of Army starch that still lingered in his character. She reached into her shirt pocket and pulled out her copy.

Date: 24/05/71

TO: 2nd Lt. Richard Clarke, Military Liaison Officer, US Embassy Bangkok, Thanon Witahyu. Lumpini District, Bangkok, 10330

FROM: Lt. Frank Coltrane, 16th MP/Thon Son Nhut, RVN / TDY Ubon Ratchathani, Thailand

SENDING AUTHORITY: Khong Chiam PTT, Ubon Ratchathani Province

CLASSIFICATION: Confidential/Secret

Further to earlier communique from Maj Panthip Siriwongdee, dated 21/05/71, wish to advise that suspect US Army Captain Mordechai Goodcut not, repeat not, found at this location. [STOP] His current whereabouts unknown. No credible evidence discovered directing further attempt for arrest. [STOP] Standing down search effort. Suggest this file be reclassified as "missing person." [STOP] ETA, Bangkok, is Friday, 28 May via local train. [STOP]

On second issue, the disposition of remains of Sgt E5 Angus Digman: Please be advised that Sgt E5 Digman has no known next of kin. Recommendation to Lt. Col. Hargraves, 16th MP/Thon Son Nhut, RVN is to ship remains to Fr. Felipe Azul, Our Lady of Perpetual Help Catholic Church, Truth or Consequences, New Mexico. [STOP] Regards.

Cole smiled and reached for his Camels. He had actually planned to have a victory cigar when he got back to Bangkok, and a drag now would taste pretty good. But since there were *no stogies within 100 miles*, he settled on having a Camel and patted down all his shirt and pants pockets before remembering that he just smoked his last – and Pip had stuck the rest of his cigarettes in her overnight bag. *No problem. I'll get one later.*

"Ok, we should get going now," Cole shouted to get everyone's attention. Both *Luang Por* and Mordechai looked up and then slowly walked over to where he and Pip were standing.

Luang Por gave them his blessing, "*Yoom Cone, laew kor yoom phuying, dern plort phai, nah ja. Chaluern pon*, Cone, you and this lady travel safely on your journey. Blessings and may your wishes come true."

"Thank you, *Luang Por*," said Cole, suddenly serious. Pip *wai*'ed the old abbot and said, simply, "*Kha*, yes, thank you."

Mordechai called Pip and Cole over with a waving hand gesture, and reached into his shoulder satchel and said, speaking to Pip, "Here. This is for you. Please wear this all the time." And he handed his medallion of the Virgin Mary to Cole, adding self-consciously, "I have to give this to a man first, as I cannot use my hand to give it directly to a woman's hand… because I am a *nane*."

Cole looked as puzzled by the rules as by the surprise of this gift. He nodded and then handed the medallion over to Pip, who received it with both hands and said to Mordechai, "*Khob khun, kha*," and curtsied when she did so. She lifted her hands and *wai*ed the medallion in front of her face, and then placed it in her top shirt pocket. She would wear it later that evening.

Last night, as he sat in the room at the inn, under the overhead fan doing its best on "position 3," Cole had practiced how he was going to say goodbye to Mordechai – or whether he would say anything at all. And now, he reached into his gear bag and took out the prayer book his grandmother had given him. He rubbed it in his rough hands, smoothing out the leather cover, and conjured up a short prayer said in his heart. Pip had watched him go through the rehearsal last night but didn't realize until just now – standing on the muddy beach of the River Mun – that Cole was actually going to give Mordechai his priceless possession.

Cole removed the yellow, crochet cross bookmark and stuck it in his front shirt pocket, and he handed the book to Mordechai. "Here," he said. "You should have this."

Cole added, with a quick smile, "Remember where you came from, Padre. You're only half-Buddhist."

Mordechai laughed at first. Then paused and said, "Well, yes. But Cole, I know what this is, and I know almost all the prayers in here by heart. I thank you for the gift, but it is too valuable a thing for a monk to own. Please forgive me if I refuse – and besides, I think this should be given to your children."

Mordechai glanced at Pip who was blushing red, and he realized that he had overstepped with his words, but Cole broke in, "That's OK. Don't worry. We get it."

Pip *waied* Mordechai and *Luang Por* who were standing next to each other. They smiled and turned to leave, but Mordechai turned back to face Cole and the smile left his face. He said, "Yes, I know that the Virgin Mary has spoken to you. I have no idea what she has in store for you after this, but I would let her finish the conversation and see what happens."

Cole nodded.

Mordechai was not finished, "And yesterday, in the temple, *Luang Por* said that you had received a gift – a gift of forgiveness from the Holy Mother. Are you clear about that message?"

"Why is that, Padre? Do you think I'll change my mind and come back and put you in cuffs some fine day?" he said with a wry smile. Cole answered his own question. "Nah, I don't think so."

He looked at Pip and she drew up a warm smile. "I have other things to think about now. More important things than hunting a holy man."

•   •   •   •   •

Cole, Pip, Uncle Suwit and the two passenger monks boarded the boat and stood as close as possible to the transom, providing just enough weight in the aft that, when Lek threw the prop into reverse, the boat moved easily off the mudbank shore.

Lek headed the boat out into the main channel of the Mun and Cole called Pip over, telling her that Lek should take a short diversion and steer her out towards the confluence of the two rivers. "I've got something to do before we head back to Ubon."

Lek was not too happy about this spontaneous change of plans since the small detour would cut into his evening drinking hours when he got back home. But Uncle Suwit and Pip saw to it, and he obliged.

When they had reached the mid-river point on the Mekong, the meeting point of those two great rivers, Cole walked back to the rear of the boat and stood there, looking south across the massive, moving body of water.

He reached into his pants pocket and pulled out the single dog tag with the stamped details: *Digman, Angus, 562-86-4409, Roman Catholic, O-*. Cole rubbed it between his thumb and forefinger, pulled in a deep breath and then flung it into the water like he was dealing the last card in a game of poker. *Not the Rio Grande, but close enough. From either place, you'll wind up in the ocean. Someday.*

He took in another, deep breath and said, "Yes. And I forgive you, too... you jackass."

Cole reached behind his back and in one move, brought out his .45, holster and all, and without the slightest hesitation, tossed it over the side. "Won't be needin' this anytime soon."

Pip stared into the confluence of the blue and muddy waters, smiled and pulled him in to her with both arms.

ABOUT THE AUTHOR

Michael Fletcher has worked in international humanitarian relief programs for 35 years, primarily with United Nations Peacekeeping and the United Nations World Food Programme. He served in Cambodia, Rwanda, Uganda, Bosnia-Herzegovina, East Timor, Israel, and Darfur-Sudan. He's lived and worked in Thailand and Cambodia, and throughout Southeast Asia since 1971. Fletcher served in the United States Army for seven years, including three years with Psychological Operations in support of the Cambodian government during the War in Vietnam. He holds a BA (Arizona State University), an MBA (Syracuse University), an MAR (Yale University), and a Doctor of Letters in Creative Writing (Drew University).

NOTE FROM THE AUTHOR

Word-of-mouth is crucial for any author to succeed. If you enjoyed *To Hunt a Holy Man*, please leave a review online—anywhere you are able. Even if it's just a sentence or two. It would make all the difference and would be very much appreciated.

Thanks!
Michael Fletcher

We hope you enjoyed reading this title from:

BLACK ROSE
writing™

www.blackrosewriting.com

Subscribe to our mailing list – *The Rosevine* – and receive **FREE** books, daily deals, and stay current with news about upcoming releases and our hottest authors.
Scan the QR code below to sign up.

Already a subscriber? Please accept a sincere thank you for being a fan of Black Rose Writing authors.

View other Black Rose Writing titles at
www.blackrosewriting.com/books and use promo code
PRINT to receive a **20% discount** when purchasing.

Printed in the USA
CPSIA information can be obtained
at www.ICGtesting.com
JSHW021200111023
49714JS00001B/23